The
Saturday
Girls

ELIZABETH
WOODCRAFT

ZAFFRE

First published in Great Britain in 2018 by
ZAFFRE PUBLISHING
80–81 Wimpole St, London W1G 9RE
www.zaffrebooks.co.uk

'The Valley of Golden Plunder' on pages 143–145
is used with thanks to Roy Kelly

This is a work of fiction. Names, places, events and
incidents are either the products of the author's
imagination or used fictitiously. Any resemblance to
actual persons, living or dead, or actual
events is purely coincidental.

A CIP catalogue record for this book is available from the British Library.

ISBN: 978–1–78576–442–4

also available as an ebook

1 3 5 7 9 10 8 6 4 2

Typeset by IDSUK (Data Connection) Ltd
Printed and bound in Great Britain by Clays Ltd, Elcograf S.p.A.

Zaffre Publishing is an imprint of Bonnier Zaffre,
a Bonnier Publishing company
www.bonnierzaffre.co.uk
www.bonnierpublishing.co.uk

The
Saturday
Girls

Elizabeth Woodcraft was born and grew up in Chelmsford. She became a mod at thirteen, and worked in the local Milk Bar. She then took her suede coat to Birmingham University, after which she taught in Leicester and Tours in France. Moving to London, she worked for Women's Aid, an organisation which supports women who suffer domestic violence. Her experiences there led her to become a barrister.

Elizabeth Woodcraft's other published work includes *A Sense of Occasion – the Chelmsford Stories*, and two crime novels, featuring barrister Frankie Richmond – *Good Bad Woman* and *Babyface*. *Good Bad Woman* was shortlisted for the CWA John Creasey Award for Best First Crime Novel, and in the US won the Lambda Literary Award.

She lives in London with her partner.

Contact her on www.elizabethwoodcraft.com
Follow her on Twitter @lizwoodcraft

In memory of my parents,
H Alfred Woodcraft (1912–81) and Peggy Perry
(1924–96)

CHAPTER 1

The Corn Exchange

THE CORN EXCHANGE WAS NEVER full at half past eight on a Saturday night. It wouldn't fill up till the group started playing. Tonight the group was Geno Washington and the Ram Jam Band. But now it was still just records. We paid our money and then the men at the door stamped our hands and, as always, the ultraviolet light made the mark blue and our skin eerily white.

As we stepped into the empty, cavernous hall, the vinyl hissed and the first notes of 'Green Onions' rolled round the room. The single chords of the electric organ, low and smooth, touched the pit of my stomach. It was an anthem to mod superiority. Mods had all the good music, the latest music, the cool music.

Sandra and I walked across the dusty floorboards in step, in time to the music, past the out-of-town mod boys. They came from Mile End, Ilford, Colchester. Their sludge-green parkas were loose over their leather coats, their thin knitted ties slightly askew. They had come to listen to the music seriously, to actually watch Geno Washington. One or two of them were already dancing, passing the time, tiptoeing forward and back in their suede Hush Puppies, shrugging their shoulders.

The really interesting people weren't here yet. The Chelmsford boys would creep in about ten o'clock through the window of the men's toilets.

'Hello girls,' Brenda said as we reached the top of the queue for the cloakroom. Brenda knew us because, for the rest of the week, she worked in the mods' coffee bar, the Orpheus. She hauled our precious coats – Sandra's leather, mine suede – over the trestle table and gave us each a raffle ticket: the prize would be to get our coats back intact. I looked anxiously at Sandra. I'd only had mine a week. 'Go on,' she said. 'No one's going to nick it. Not with those sleeves.'

We still moved to the beat, now the rhythmic drums of 'Going to a Go-Go', as we walked through into the ladies' toilets, a room of sinks and mirrors. I ran my eyes over the other mod girls jostling for a space. Some were regulars in the Orpheus; others were from villages on the edge of town, Ingatestone, Hatfield Peverel, Marks Tey, the stops on the railway line. Like Sandra and me, they wore twin-sets, and straight skirts two inches below the knee, plain, pinstriped, fan-pleated, and the same shoes, flat moccasins, low slingbacks. A few of them I envied, for their cool, their nonchalance. Jenny, a girl we knew from the Orpheus, was wearing a dress that had been on TV the night before, on *Ready Steady Go!*, the mods' programme. It looked good in maroon. Another girl was still wearing her coat. 'Orange suede,' Sandra murmured. 'Nice.' She was being sarcastic. It was the way mods talked. We manoeuvred our way to the mirrors.

This was almost the best part of the evening, standing here in the toilets, the low throb of music from the hall just discernible, my hair and make-up exactly as they should be, my perfume, 'Wishing' by Avon, heavy and sweet and my beige skirt impeccably ironed. At this moment I knew that anything might happen, a dance, a conversation, a glimpse of someone exciting, a throwaway remark. Whatever happened it would be something to mull over, to savour, to write about in my diary.

Under the harsh fluorescent light we gazed at our reflections. Neither Sandra nor I were pretty, exactly (although sometimes, at home on my own, in the bedroom, I really did resemble Jean Shrimpton, the button-nosed elegant model whose picture was everywhere). But you didn't have to be good-looking to be a mod. You just had to have the right clothes and the right hair, and a smart line on the right occasion. And on Saturday nights, we always did.

I smoothed my hair down with my hands and pulled my fringe straighter. It was almost the Cleopatra look. I inspected my eyeliner and the lines in the sockets, grey to bring out the blue of my eyes, with the white pearlised sheen below my eyebrows and on my lips. All as good as it could be. I smiled.

Sandra ran her tongue over her lips. She was experimenting with a new, flavoured lipstick. '"Caramel Kiss",' she said, pouting at herself.

'You hope.'

'You try it,' she said, handing me the small silver tube. 'Tastes nice. Like Caramac.'

I dabbed a touch of orange onto my lips. 'Mmm. Not bad.'

'Do you think Danny will be here?' Sandra said. Danny was her on-off boyfriend. More off than on. There was a rumour he'd been let out of prison for the weekend.

'Who knows?' I hoped not. If he came tonight it would mean I'd have no one to dance with, and no one to talk to during the slow songs.

'Tonight could be the night,' she said. Her New Year's Resolution was to get engaged, preferably to Danny.

'I'll keep my fingers crossed,' I said.

We walked back through the hall, past the boys dancing neatly to the smooth saxophone of Junior Walker and the All Stars, and out onto the worn stone steps leading down to the street. On Fridays, Chelmsford's market day, the Corn

Exchange was the hub of the town. Farm animals, sheep and cattle, were herded down the middle of the road while business transactions took place inside. But come Saturday night, the Corn Exchange belonged to the mods.

Several scooters were parked nearby. The polished panels of the Lambrettas and the shining bubbles of the Vespas glinted silver, bottle green, navy blue under the street lights. The cool mod scooter boys leaned against the backrests, their pork-pie hats tipped over their eyes, close enough to feel the throb of the music from the hall, waiting for Geno Washington to start his set.

Then Sandra's whole body quivered. 'There he is,' she said.

It was Danny, walking through a crowd of mods, nodding to a few, self-consciously pulling his coat straight. It was a long navy-blue leather coat. And he was grinning.

Sandra turned to me, touching her hair, licking her lips. 'Do I look all right?' She was trying not to smile too much.

'You look fab.'

'So does he,' she said. 'That coat's new. Where'd he get that?'

I didn't reply. Wherever he'd got it I was sure it wasn't legal.

'Now where's he going?' she said.

He hadn't seen us. He was walking away from the Corn Exchange towards Tindal Street. There were several places he could be going in that direction, and they were all pubs, the White Hart, the Spotted Dog or the Dolphin. And that was just Tindal Street.

'Here we go,' Sandra said, and grabbed my arm. We ran down the steps and pushed through a group of boys in parkas into the road.

Mick Flynn and his mate Jeff were sitting with Ray Bales in the White Hart. Like the other pubs in the road, it was an old coaching inn, with a low ceiling and bare wooden floors. 'Have you seen Danny?' Sandra said.

'And hello to you too, Sandra,' Mick said. He was wearing his bottle-green suede coat with the leather collar and his customary dark glasses. Mick Flynn was a local hero. He had been in an accident with a rocker. The story was that Mick had been on his Lambretta, riding past the bus station, showing off his shiny blue panels, waving to his mates when a rocker, with slicked-back greasy hair and a chunky leather jacket, drove towards him on his Harley-Davidson motorbike and a game of chicken began. Neither of them got out of the way and they smashed into each other. The rocker damaged his leg and Mick was blinded. It all happened before Sandra and I started going out in the evenings, but everyone knew about it. And he was still a mod, but now he wore dark glasses as part of his moddy outfit. He made it his business to keep up with all the happenings in Chelmsford. If anyone knew about Danny, it would be him. 'Mulroney? Oh yeah, it's this weekend,' he said. 'Nah, haven't seen him.'

'You sure?' Sandra said.

'I'm not his manager. Didn't he write and tell you where he'd be?' Mick said. 'All his other girlfriends seem to know.'

'What do you mean?' Sandra said. 'What other girl-friends?'

'Oh, just all the girls in Chelmsford.' He was grinning. Sandra turned.

'Don't look at me,' I said. 'I don't know what he's talk-ing about.'

'Is that your mate Linda? The one who looks like Jean Shrimpton?'

'That's right,' Sandra said. She laughed.

I looked at her. 'You told him?' I mouthed.

'But you do, actually,' Ray said. 'Sometimes.'

'Just not tonight,' Sandra said.

'Well, tonight I'm incognito,' I said.

'Tell you what, Sandra,' Mick said, 'if Danny doesn't turn up, you can try your luck with me. But you'll have to wait in the queue, after Linda.'

Sandra pushed him, and his Guinness rocked in his hand.

'Forget about Danny,' Ray said to me. 'Come back up to the Corn Exchange and have a dance.'

I frowned. Ray lived on our estate and wore dread-ful jumpers, jumpers that no proper mod would be seen dead in. I had fancied Ray once, ages ago when my dad started giving his dad a lift to union meetings. Sometimes

I had to go round to his house with a message, changing the arrangements or warning him about an extra meeting, and if Ray answered the door I would talk to him while his dad finished his tea. We talked about the Labour Party (his dad was Chairman of the local branch) or the trade union (my dad was the District Secretary of the Amalgamated Engineering Union) or Del Shannon, who sang 'Runaway' and 'Hey Little Girl'. But that was then, before I was a mod. Ray wasn't really a mod at all, and I had stopped talking to anyone about Del Shannon. It was a bit late for him to ask me to dance now. Why couldn't he have asked me a year ago?

I shook my head and rolled my eyes at Sandra, but I did wonder if he was a good dancer.

Sandra and I walked along the road to the Spotted Dog. Danny wasn't in there, either.

The Dolphin was the last pub in Tindal Street. The public bar was full of men, most of them standing up. There was a smell of spilled beer, cigarettes and sweat. As we walked in there were shouts and the scraping of furniture at the back of the room. A fight was breaking out.

Sandra pulled her shoulders back. 'He's here.' She licked her lips. Then licked them again. 'And if he doesn't like toffee, that's just too bad.'

Everyone was looking towards the door to the Gents. From behind the bar the landlord called, 'Oy, what's going on?' We wove our way through the crowd. There was a crash as a chair fell against a table and legs in jeans flailed through the air. As we got closer I could see a man on the floor. It was Danny, shielding his face with his hands as another man who I didn't recognise, a thin man in a grey suede coat, kicked him in the side. Danny was laughing.

Sandra slid over to him just before the landlord arrived. She elbowed the other man out of the way, grabbed Danny's arm, pulled him to his feet and dragged him towards the door into the saloon bar. Danny grinned and turned back. 'It ain't your night, is it?' he called to the man who was wiping blood from his nose.

The landlord called 'Hey!' but Sandra gave him a look and he turned his attention to the other man, pulling him towards the front door. As he pushed him into the street, the landlord said, 'Out! And don't come back.' Almost to himself, he said, 'That's it. I'm fed up with the lot of you.'

The man in the grey suede coat shouted back through the door, 'We had a deal, Mulroney, and you know what the deal was. Get it sorted out.'

Danny waved his hands in the air as if he was ready to continue the fight, and Sandra hissed, 'Behave!' Danny's arms fell to his sides and he gave Sandra a dazed smile.

I wondered if that was why Danny liked Sandra, because she took control. I wondered if that was why she liked him, because she could.

In the saloon bar Sandra balanced Danny on a stool at a table. The tables and a few tatty rugs differentiated it from the public bar, along with faded prints of horses on the walls.

'All right,' I said, 'I'm going back to the Corn Exchange.' I wanted to see if Ray had meant what he said.

'You can't go yet,' Sandra said. 'What am I going to do with him like this?'

Danny was still grinning, rubbing his side, swaying on the stool. He had a small cut below his eye and blood on his cheek. 'Hello, darling,' he kept saying to Sandra. 'What's your name?'

'My name is Sandra.' She tugged his sleeve as he slid dangerously over to one side. 'I'm your girlfriend.'

'Are you?' He looked at Sandra, then slowly turned his head to me, then back to Sandra. 'Is it my eyes, or are there two of you?'

'It's your eyes,' Sandra said.

'Is that Linda, Little Lindy Lindah?' Danny moaned. 'You still banning the bomb, Linda? Still wearing the badge? What's she wear that badge for, Sandy? Can't she afford proper jewellery? Why do you wear a badge, Linda?'

The Campaign for Nuclear Disarmament and my CND badge were important to me, but I didn't want to talk about that tonight, especially not with someone who was drunk and who had a loud voice. 'Why were you and that bloke fighting?' I said, to change the subject.

'Who? What? Where is he, what's he saying . . .?'

'Don't worry about him. He's long gone,' Sandra said. 'Look at you. What have you been doing?'

'I have been celebrating my release from the worst place in the world, Wormwood Scrubs.'

A couple at the next table exchanged a glance. They both still had their coats on and the woman had a scarf on her head.

Danny leered at them.

'Well! I think someone's in the wrong bar,' the woman said loudly. She prodded her husband and gestured to the door. He got to his feet, picked up his small glass of beer and drained it in one mouthful. 'I didn't mean straightaway, Cyril,' she said, but she stood up and they left.

'Thank Christ for that,' Danny said, and tipped very slowly to his right until his head touched the bench.

'We've got to stay with him,' Sandra said.

'Us?' I said. 'But we've paid for our tickets.'

'Sandy!' Danny shouted, suddenly sitting up. 'Oh, there you are.' Then he crooned. 'Sandy, Sandy. Do you think I'm handy?'

'Not at the moment.' She shook her head at me.

'Do you think I look dandy, Sandy?' He held out his arms as if he wanted to hug her. Then he toppled off the stool and onto the floor.

'Get up,' Sandra hissed.

'Because guess what, I feel randy,' he moaned, and then he laughed. 'Get us a shandy.'

'Shut up, you drunk lump.'

'Oh, Sandy, I love it when you talk dirty. Get me a brandy, Sandy, and then we'll be jamdy.' He laughed again.

'We can't leave him,' Sandra said.

'He's not going to ask you to marry him like this,' I murmured.

'This might be the best chance I get,' she whispered.

Danny was staggering to his feet. 'How about a drink?' he said.

'What shall I do?' Sandra said.

'Let's walk him back to the Corn Exchange,' I suggested. 'See if we can find someone to take him home.'

Sandra grabbed Danny's arm and wrapped it round her neck. He blinked hard and shook himself like a wet dog. 'OK, girl,' he said. 'Let's go.'

Sandra passed me her handbag and slowly we left the pub.

People were milling about on the steps of the Corn Exchange. Mick was chatting to some girls who worked in Boots. Jeff was tinkering with his scooter. I could hear live music, a blaring saxophone and crashing cymbals, and I wanted to be inside.

Sandra tried to lean Danny against a lamp post. 'Go and collect our coats.' She thrust her ticket into my hand. 'We're getting a taxi home.'

I pushed my way into the hall. The place was packed. Geno Washington was singing, 'Oh, Geno!' and people were joining in, swaying and clapping.

I retrieved our coats and elbowed my way back through the throng by the stage, past the smoochers dancing, towards the doors. I was almost there when Ray grabbed my arm and swung me round. 'You came!'

I held out the coats. 'It's home time.'

'Five minutes.'

I didn't want to leave, even if his jumper looked like his mum had knitted it. I might even have danced with him, but I shook my head and wove my way out.

Danny, Sandra and I walked up to the railway station to find a taxi. We would drop Danny at his landlady's and then we'd carry on home, Sandra said. In the queue I held back a little so they could talk. I could see Sandra smiling as Danny stroked her face. When we reached the front of the queue, Danny opened the taxi door with a flourish. I slid into the back seat and Sandra followed, tucking her coat round her to make space, but not too much, so that Danny could squeeze in beside her. Danny bent down then slapped his forehead theatrically. 'Oh Sandy, guess what, I forgot. I've got to deliver some stuff.'

'Now?' Sandra said. 'I thought you won the fight.'

'Yeah, now. No, not to him. Another . . . contact of mine. So . . . bye.' Danny puckered his lips in a kiss, then slammed the door. We watched him stagger into the station.

'Do you want to go after him?' I said. 'Keep him out of trouble?'

'There's no point. I bet he's just going up West.' Most of the boys we knew went up to the West End of London when the Corn Exchange closed, to the Flamingo or the Marquee, clubs where they could hear more music, take more drugs and maybe have another fight or two. 'Danny didn't want to see me home, is the truth of it,' she said sadly. The taxi drove past the bus station. 'He said he'll see me next week. But that could mean anything. Still,' Sandra tossed a coin in her hand, 'he gave me half a crown to pay for the taxi.'

'That's almost like getting engaged, in Danny's terms,' I said. Two and six was a big commitment.

'Of course, I did just lend him five bob.' She looked down at her bare left hand. 'Do you think he'll ever ask me to get engaged?'

I wanted to say, 'You're the Catholic. You're supposed to believe in miracles.' But as we passed a street light I could see her mouth making a funny shape, as if she was going to cry, so I said, 'You don't know. He might. He should do – you'd keep him on the straight and narrow.'

'Yes,' she agreed, 'I would.'

The taxi dropped us at the shops so Sandra's mum and dad wouldn't ask questions. We walked up to her house together, said goodnight and I carried on up the road.

*

The house was quiet when I got indoors. The telly was off, Mum and my sister Judith were in bed, but Dad was still up, sitting in the front room with his bulky faded red copy of George Bernard Shaw's *Collected Works*. I didn't know anyone else whose dad read plays. 'Good time, love?' he said.

I thought about the evening. We had scarcely spent ten minutes in the Corn Exchange. There'd been Danny's fight in the Dolphin, I'd seen a dress I liked, Ray had asked me to dance and Sandra and I had extravagantly taken a taxi home. 'Not bad.'

CHAPTER 2

The Orpheus

Six months earlier

SANDRA'S OLDER SISTER, MARIE, became a mod first, so it was natural that Sandra should be a mod, and even more natural that I should be a mod, too. Sandra and I had been best friends for years, since our family had moved onto the estate. She lived across the road, four doors down, and though we'd always gone to different schools, because she was Catholic, we'd played together after school and in all the school holidays. We went bike riding, we made dens, played schools, put on plays. We'd even written a newspaper, the *Hayfield News*, that we handwrote and sewed together, then delivered to the houses around us.

Marie and her friend Deirdre were three years older than us, but they had been our friends. They would come into town with us on Saturday mornings, and to the pictures, the Odeon or the Regent, on Saturday afternoons. But now we hardly saw them, Marie was courting strong, and when we did see them they were full of snide comments about our clothes – too ordinary, and the way we did our hair – too messy, and our age – too childish.

Sandra and I agreed that if all mods thought like that, who'd want to be a mod? But we did want to be mods. We watched *Ready Steady Go!*. We liked the clothes, we liked the dancing, and we loved the music. We wanted to be part of it, we wanted to be mods. And where we really wanted to go was the Orpheus, the mods' coffee bar in town, with its jukebox and frothy coffee and scooters parked outside. Then and only then would we be able to call ourselves mods. But we didn't dare step into its dark, dangerous depths.

Sandra was almost ready to leave school, and I was a year younger, when we first slid into the Orpheus. We were hovering outside, as we always did when we came into town, pretending to look in the art shop window, trying to catch the atmosphere of the coffee bar below, straining to hear the music, yearning to go inside.

As we stood listening to the final notes of Paul Jones' insistent harmonica on '5-4-3-2-1', rain began to fall. Now we had an excuse for standing there. If Marie came past we could say we were sheltering under the awning of the art shop.

Some mods puttered up on their scooters, parka hoods over their heads. As they parked, one boy's scooter toppled onto its side. As he tried to pull it upright, he fell over too. He stood up, soaked with rain, oil stains on his parka. The others laughed. They were jostling and pushing each other, then they ran inside.

Sandra and I looked at each other. 'If they're going in looking like that, we might as well go in too,' she said, in a natural way.

'We're not even wet,' I said.

We stepped off the street into a dark narrow corridor. On the left was the entrance to the art shop, and at the end of the corridor was another door – the door to the Orpheus. The boys had disappeared, clattering down the stairs. The faint pulse of music came up through the floor. It was the Hollies asking us to 'Stay'. 'It's a sign,' Sandra whispered. She pushed open the door which led to a narrow landing and the staircase down to the cellar. My heart started pounding. This was it. We were here at last. We were going into the Orpheus. This is where the mods were, with their stylish clothes and good music. This is where our lives would change. We held on to the rail and stepped slowly down the steep, twisting staircase.

There was hardly any light, and at first there seemed to be nothing but walls and pillars and a counter. Then I realised I was looking at reflections in the smoky mirrors on the walls. It was much bigger than I'd imagined – it was the cellar area of not one, but two shops. Groups of mods stood around tables or sat on leather benches looking like pictures from the pages of the *Evening News*. Boys slouched in green parkas, in dark suede or leather coats.

They were clean-shaven; their hair was short and smart. There were fewer girls, but they too wore suede jackets and had short, neat hair. One girl in a black leather coat strolled round the room. Her hair was backcombed; it was almost a beehive. That wasn't right for a mod. That was rocker girl hair. Surely she was in the wrong place, she should have been in the Long Bar, the rockers' coffee bar. But people seemed to like her, greeting her, or waving a hand as she passed. The hair didn't seem to matter. Perhaps the mod rules weren't as strict as I thought, perhaps they weren't as strict as I wanted them to be. I gazed round the room. One girl leaned casually against the counter, stirring a cup of coffee. Her hair was swinging and shiny, Cleopatra-style, like Cathy McGowan's from *Ready Steady Go!*, the look Sandra and I were aiming for.

Apart from the Cathy McGowan girl and the girl with the beehive, everyone seemed to be engaged in conversation. They all looked sophisticated and confident. Someone flicked a glance towards us, taking us in, judging us. My brown suedette jacket, which had seemed quite modern and stylish outside, now felt like the cheap imitation it was. This is why we shouldn't have come. We weren't ready. We didn't have the money to carry it off.

Sandra walked casually over to the counter on the right of the staircase to order us a drink, while I lingered at the foot of the stairs, shrinking against a pillar, afraid someone would talk to me, hoping they would. The record had ended and now every eye seemed to be turned on us, the new girls. I wondered where the wet scooter boys had disappeared to. Why was no one looking at them?

But then the thin, high guitar notes of a song that I waited for every night on Radio Luxembourg snaked out of the jukebox, 'Hi-Heel Sneakers' by Tommy Tucker. I knew the words to this record. I loved this record. On Radio Luxembourg the sound was thin and tinny and faded in and out. But here, the song filled the room, rolling over every surface, bouncing off the walls. It was an overture, an introduction.

A boy appeared round the corner, dancing on the tiptoes of his Hush Puppies, his long suede coat flapping, weaving his way between the tables, singing along with Tommy Tucker. He danced up to me. 'Hi-Heel Sneakers,' he sang into my face, opening his eyes wide. He took my hand. I looked round quickly for Sandra, thrilled, terrified, worrying that he would say something about suedette, or my hair, or my age, as he began slowly jiving with me, turning me under his arm. Then abruptly he dropped my hand and danced away.

'That was Blond Don,' Sandra murmured, appearing beside me with two glasses of milk. 'Marie says he pops pills like they're sherbet lemons. You're lucky he didn't push some purple hearts down your throat.'

'I don't think I need them,' I said. My heart was racing from the dancing.

I thought that Blond Don with his long suede coat and his bleached white hair was the epitome of what being a mod was all about: careless, showy, a hint of danger, a good dancer. But that was before I met Tap.

For some weeks we didn't go back. Sandra said the reason no one had talked to us, apart from Blond Don, and that didn't count, was the CND badge on the lapel of my jacket. It was the expensive 2s 6d one, small, black and silver. But it was a badge. She said it let us down. The unwritten rule was that if you were going to wear badges you had to wear a lot on your parka, and you had to be a boy. And you didn't have to care about what the badge represented. But I believed in banning the bomb, and I was proud of the badge.

I said if there was a reason no one spoke to us it was because they didn't know us and because I was wearing a suedette jacket and not a suede one. 'So it was your fault anyway,' Sandra said.

But then the warm weather started and we went, on the train, to Southend. With my saved-up Christmas and birthday money I was able to buy myself mod. I chose a royal-blue twinset and a grey fan-pleated skirt. Sandra bought a pink jumper and a pinstriped skirt. Now we didn't need the second-hand dresses Marie and Deirdre had sold us, with their insecure belts and strange, pale colours, and sunshine meant we didn't have to wear jackets at all. We were set.

We began to go to the Orpheus regularly. We started to recognise the scooters and their owners – the maroon GS, the cream LI with sky-blue panels, the green Vespa with silver bubbles. We said hello to Jenny, the Cathy McGowan girl. One day Blond Don called me by name. 'Hey, Linda, where's your mate Sandra?'

'She'll be down in a few minutes.'

He knew our names. He'd asked about us. We were in. And now it seemed as if we'd never been anywhere else. We went to the Orpheus every Saturday, and on school nights we'd drop in after our tea when our mums thought we were across the road, watching each other's telly. We put records on the jukebox. We chatted to Brenda behind the counter. We looked at strangers who walked in. But I still wore my badge.

I was wearing the badge the day I spoke to Tap for the first time. It was carefully attached to my new nylon mac. Although I was worried about making permanent holes in the lapel, the badge was important. As I walked over to the counter, Mick's friend Jeff came up behind me and asked me to buy him a glass of milk. Then he laughed. 'Only kidding. What do you want?' Jeff was doing a building apprenticeship. A small shower of plaster fell from his sleeve onto the counter as he called Brenda and ordered two glasses of milk.

'I'll have one too.' Tap was suddenly there at my side, looking cool in a pale blue Fred Perry and grey mohair trousers. He was Chelmsford's biggest mod. He leaned forward and brushed a flake of plaster from my shoulder. 'What's this?' he said. 'What are you wearing?'

'It's a badge. A CND badge.'

'Not the badge, girl. The badge is the best part of it. I mean this.' He tweaked my sleeve.

'It's a nylon mac.' Nylon macs were all the go. Navy-blue nylon macs.

'But what colour do you call that?'

I had so hoped it would work. 'It's caramel,' I said. Mum had bought it at a jumble sale. I had altered the hem and changed the buttons. 'Caramel's coming in,' I said, lifting my chin. 'It's going to be really big.' I looked into his eyes. They were very blue. 'That's what I heard, anyway.'

He shook his head. He grinned. 'I think you heard wrong. Where you from? Frinton-on-Sea? 'Cos it ain't coming in here.' He looked at me. 'Well, I suppose if it never comes in, it never goes out.' He stroked another piece of plaster from my shoulder. 'I'll get hers,' he said to Jeff. He put some money on the counter and walked away.

'He didn't,' Sandra said when I told her.

'He did.'

'He must have thought you had dandruff and needed a bit of help,' she said. 'Why would he talk to you?'

'We were discussing fashion.'

'He felt sorry for you,' she said, ''cos you fancy him and you're wearing a brown mac.'

'I don't fancy him,' I said. 'I don't know him.'

'Yes you do, everyone knows Tap. You fancy him! Not that it'll do you any good,' Sandra said.

Tap came and went in the Orpheus. He worked in The Boutique, the best men's clothes shop in Chelmsford, and weeks went by and we didn't catch sight of him.

'See?' Sandra would say, occasionally. 'He's in London all the time. Probably got some fancy bird up there. He can't be doing with girls in nylon macs from Frinton.'

Then we started to go to the Corn Exchange on Saturday nights. All the best groups came, The Who, the Yardbirds, Georgie Fame and the Blue Flames, and the solo singers, David Bowie, Wilson Pickett, Memphis Slim. As the weather got colder Sandra lent me her suede jacket, which she'd had for her birthday, while she wore her leather coat which she'd bought with her first month's wages. And then finally, with pocket money and a loan from my mum, I bought my own suede.

And I pinned my CND badge onto the collar. Sometimes people didn't notice it at all, but then, if I was putting on my coat to go home or to go for a walk round town, someone would ask, 'Ban the Bomb? Do you ban the bomb?' There'd be a pause and then, 'Do you believe in free love?' And suddenly I'd feel serious and out of place. But I still wore it.

CHAPTER 3

Meeting Sylvia

BUT I NEEDED MORE CLOTHES. I'd worn the blue twinset so often I'd had to darn the sleeve, and the fan-pleated skirt was a bit saggy now. My suede was great, even with the big wide sleeves, but you couldn't keep your coat on all the time. I needed cash, but I owed Mum the money she'd lent me for my coat and my birthday wasn't for ages.

'Why don't you do some babysitting?' Mum said. 'You used to babysit with Sandra.'

'We didn't babysit,' I said. 'We didn't go into people's houses. We went out.'

Before Sandra started work, when there was nothing else to do or if we were hard up, we would run errands for people, shopping, posting letters, getting keys cut. Sometimes we took the babies on the estate for walks. We got threepence or even sixpence out of it, but more often just a glass of squash and a big thank you. Once Sandra had the nerve to ask for a shilling, from some posh people who lived in The Lane at the top of the estate with a grand-daughter who had curly hair and always needed to go to the toilet. 'We earned this,' Sandra had said. 'All those pennies we had to fork out down town.'

'Mrs Brady says Mrs Weston could do with a hand looking after her grandson during the holidays,' Mum said. 'And Mrs Weston is a person who really needs some help.'

I knew about the Westons. Mrs Weston worked in the grocer's with Mrs Brady, Sandra's mum. Mrs Weston, her daughter Sylvia and baby Mansell all lived together in the Crescent. When Sylvia was away in hospital, or just 'bad', she couldn't look after the baby. Sandra and I had taken him out once or twice before, and Sandra had sometimes gone to their house to babysit. 'Sandra can't do it now she's at work,' I said, quickly.

'Do it on your own.'

'They must be desperate if they want me to do it. Anyway, it's no fun without Sandra. I need a proper job.'

'Helping out Mrs Weston would be a decent way of earning some money,' Mum said. I was brushing her hair. She had put in the rollers and dried it, and now I was styling it. The theory was that I enjoyed doing this because I was good with hair – but the real reason was that Mum liked having her hair brushed, although somehow she never asked my sister Judith to do it. Mum looked at herself in the little hand mirror and frowned. 'But if you want something to fill your time, and don't want to babysit for people in need, you could always hoover this house, start-ing with the stairs.'

'And are you going to pay me?'

'I think I've been paying since you were born,' Mum said. 'And pocket money doesn't grow on trees. I can't afford any more.' She gave me ninepence a week. Ninepence! 'Alterna-tively, when you're next in the shop, ask Mrs Weston when she would like you to look after Mansell.'

'What kind of name is Mansell?' I said.

'It's the baby's name, and I don't want to hear any jokes. That poor woman has enough trouble already.'

'What do you mean?' I asked. Sandra had given me her mum's version, but I wanted the steadiness of my mum's description. Mum always said we should be good and kind to others who were less well off than us, although I couldn't think who could be less well off than we were. Dad's pay as a trade union District Secretary was not good. But I knew our standards were the right standards. And I knew Mum's way of summing up the Westons would be the right one.

She looked at me in the mirror and sighed. 'There are people who have strong feelings about unmarried mothers, especially those who keep their babies. And Mansell's mum, Sylvia, has ... problems. Often people don't understand –' She stopped.

'What? Don't understand what?'

'Baby blues.'

'Is that what she's got?'

I'd never met Sylvia. I'd never been to their house; we'd always picked Mansell up from the shop. Sandra had reported from her mum that Sylvia had been really bad for the last few weeks, in and out of Severalls, the hospital in Colchester, twenty miles away. Going to Severalls meant you were mad. When I thought of Sylvia I had visions of witches with wild dry hair and wide eyes, their fingers flexed ready to grab my throat. What if she wanted to come out for a walk with me and the baby? What would people think if they saw us together?

'So what does she look like?' I asked Mum.

'It isn't necessarily something you can see.'

'Is that why she goes to the loony bin all the time?'

Mum looked at me sharply. 'We do not call it a loony bin. Severalls is a hospital, a mental hospital. She is ill, in just the same way that you were ill when you had chickenpox.'

I had nearly died.

I stopped brushing Mum's hair. 'I've finished.'

Mum looked at her hair in the mirror and then looked up at me. 'She's not going to jump out at you.' Sometimes she read my mind. 'She's rather sad and lonely. Just be polite and kind.' She looked back at her hair. 'That'll do.' I didn't know if she meant the hair, or if she was underlining how she wanted me to treat Sylvia.

*

The Hayfield Estate was a new estate, built in the 1950s. Our road was the central road, the road that gave the estate its name. There was no pub, which my mum was pleased about – she was a strict teetotaller – but there was a row of shops, down the road from us. The grocer's where Mrs Weston worked with Mrs Brady was in the middle of the row, between the baker's, the off-licence and the newsagent's on one side, and the hardware shop, the greengrocer's and the fish shop on the other.

The grocer's was a large shop with a pillar in the middle where the sterilised milk crates were stacked, next to the large bottomless freezer that was only interesting to us because, among other things, it held ice cream. The owner of the grocer's was Mr Roberts. He owned another two shops in town and hardly ever came to ours. 'Thank Gawd,' Sandra's mum said.

We were in their kitchen. It was the night before I was to take Mansell for a walk. Mrs Brady was leaning against the sideboard, smoking, while Mr Brady was standing on a stepladder, doing something with the fluorescent light bulb. The only light came through the arch from their living room and the lamp that Sandra was holding.

'He buggers up all our systems,' Mrs Brady said. 'It's quicker if we cut the ham in the morning before anyone's asked for it, and I told him they all like the cheese ready wrapped in the greaseproof. He says it's "potentially wasteful". I'll waste him, never mind about potential, cheeky bleeder! And then he doesn't like us sitting on the sacks of sugar in the back room when we take our breaks. "Unhygienic," he says. Unhygienic!' she shouted at Mr Brady. 'It's had more than our bums in overalls sitting on it, I can tell you. It's all because he doesn't like that pram parked in the shop by the biscuits. He says it's bad for business. Mrs Weston says people don't mind it. She says to him it attracts people to the biscuits and makes them buy more, which it bloody well doesn't.' She stubbed out her cigarette in the glass ashtray. 'But he's the boss. Thank Gawd we only see him twice a year. Hold the light where your dad can see it, Sandra, you silly bleeder.'

When Mr Brady had fixed the bulb and the light was back on, Sandra and I went up to the bedroom she shared with Marie. We were discussing the arrangements for the next day. I was to pick Mansell up from the shop and drop him back with Mrs Weston just before they closed.

'But if Mr Roberts is hardly ever there, why have I got to take him out? They needn't tell him he's in the shop,' I said. I was trying to pin her hair up in curls on the back of her head.

Sandra handed me a hair clip. 'They're doing stock-taking at the moment, and Mr Roberts has to come over every afternoon. So Mrs Weston's desperate to get him away from the Maryland Cookies.'

'She'll probably pay me in loose biscuits,' I said.

'My mum said Mrs Weston wanted Sylvia to have the baby adopted,' Sandra said. 'They'd got all the forms and everything, but then just before he was born, Sylvia upped sticks and ran away.'

'Where to?'

'She said she went to France. And that's likely.' Sandra was filing her nails. 'She was only away for the weekend. But when she came back she started calling herself Sylvie. What kind of name's Sylvie?'

'Sylvie's a French name,' I said. If she called herself Sylvie, she might be a bit more interesting. Sylvie Vartan went out with Johnny Hallyday. As a pop music duo, they were all the go in France. The French *assistante* at school had played us one of their records. I liked French. 'She could have gone to France,' I said. 'People do.'

'Yeah, well, pigs could fly. They just don't.' Sandra looked at me in her dressing-table mirror. 'Her mum thought she'd gone to London. My mum reckons she went to the air base.'

'Pregnant?'

'You can ask her when you see her. Anyway, when she got back from wherever it was, Mrs Weston didn't have the heart to make her give the baby up, not after he was born.' She blew on her fingernails. 'While you're at it, try and find out who the dad is. She won't tell anyone.'

'She's hardly likely to tell me. Anyway, I'm not going to see her, I'm only going to the shop.' I twisted a lock of Sandra's hair round my finger. There were many stories about Sylvia. That the father was a married man who lived on our estate; that he lived on another estate; that she spent her time going to dances at the American air base near Braintree, jiving and flashing her petticoats; that she was weird even before she had the baby. 'What have people got against her?'

'I don't know,' Sandra said. 'But it's not fair that she gets to have a baby and no one says a word –'

'Oh, I think they do. You said her next-door neighbours won't even speak to them now.'

'Well, there you are. Not saying a word. All the rest of us get locked in our room and have to say four hundred Hail Marys for even kissing a boy.'

'Really?' Sandra's mum and dad were strict, but I didn't know about the Hail Marys.

'Marie said Deirdre had to leave town just for going out with Mick Flynn.'

'The priest made her do that?'

'No, her mum, but it's the same thing.'

'So have you told the priest about Danny?'

'You have to. That's what confession's about. You're not meant to have any fun, but Sylvie did and she got away with it. You're not supposed to get away with it.'

'Except she's not that well now and people talk about her all the time.'

Sandra shrugged.

'But what should she have done?' I said.

She handed me a hairgrip. 'Got married.'

'Who to?'

'The father.'

'What if he wouldn't marry her? What if he couldn't marry her?'

'Then she should have given it away.'

'Do you really think that? Would you have given it away?'

'I wouldn't have had a choice – my mum and dad would have seen to that.'

'But would you want to?'

Sandra laughed. 'It would depend on the baby.'

The arrangement was that I would pick up Mansell every afternoon that week except Wednesday, which was early closing. Mrs Weston offered to pay me a shilling each time but mum said that was too much just for taking a baby for a walk, so they agreed on two shillings for four afternoons.

'I'm supposed to be making money!' I said.

'The family relies on Mrs Weston's wages from the shop,' Mum said. 'You shouldn't really accept any money at all.'

'So what am I doing it for?'

'Sylvia needs us to show we don't think of her as an outcast.'

'All right,' I said. 'I'll just think of her as someone who ought to be paying me more than two shillings a week.'

Mansell was five months old. He had a round, chubby face and shining lips from all the dribble but he wasn't bad because he smiled at my jokes – which weren't that funny – hiding behind my hands and saying boo, but it was something.

The first afternoon we walked round the estate. When I dropped him back at the shop, just as I had predicted, I got two bourbon biscuits. On Tuesday I took him along Partridge Avenue, beside Piggy Wood and down North Avenue past my mum's church. Wednesday was half-day closing, so I wasn't needed. On Thursday we went round the lanes to my old primary school, and up to the village hall where our Guide meetings used to take place. I explained to Mansell that I had been in the White Heather patrol and had obtained several badges which enabled me to look after him so well, Child Care, Emergency Helper, Cook and Hostess. He blinked at me seriously and then fell asleep.

We walked along the Main Road and up Sperry Drive back onto the estate, but we were too early. As we reached the shop I could see through the window that Mr Roberts was still there, standing at the slicing machine, holding down a huge ham, smiling and chatting. It was only four o'clock. I wasn't going to walk round for another hour. That meant delivering the baby back to Sylvia in their house. Mrs Weston had said Sylvia would be at home all afternoon, so if necessary I could drop Mansell off with her.

The Crescent was a turning off our road, almost opposite the shops. Number thirty-two was in the middle of a terrace of three. It looked faded and grubby. The houses in the Crescent were newer than ours, but Dad said the quality was much lower, as the council had overspent the budget on the brick houses in our road. Their front door was pale yellow and the paint was peeling. The door-knocker wasn't one you could polish, like ours; it was light grey metal and it hardly made any noise at all when I knocked.

I knocked again, and waited. I felt breathless. I didn't know what to expect and it was getting dark.

Beside the front door was a small square of earth filled with flowers, pale lemon daffodils. They looked pretty, they looked normal. I started to calm down. I knocked a third time. Still there was no reply. She wasn't in.

I looked at my watch. Mr Roberts might have gone by now. I'd go back to the shop, wander past, look in casually.

And then the front door opened.

Sylvia was about twenty-five. Or she could have been thirty. She was pale and thin, and her eyes seemed to fill her face. Her thick black hair was pushed back from her forehead with an alice band, and the ends flicked up. And she was tall, taller than me, even considering that I was on a step lower than her. She was wearing a big, grey man's cardigan hugged round herself, a long blue skirt and bright maroon embroidered slippers. I wondered which came first, the depression or the outfit.

I was in my duffel coat but I wished I was wearing my suede, so she'd know that I was a mod and had more style than her. We looked at each other for a minute. 'So you're Linda,' she said, with a little smile. Her voice was a bit posh. 'You're the one saving Mansell from his mum.'

What did she mean? She was his mum, wasn't she? Why was she talking about herself as someone else? 'Well, I'm the one taking him out,' I said. 'Which I love doing,' I added, in case that sounded unkind.

'And where've you been today?'

'We went round The Lane. Past my old school.'

'How lovely. Did you see anybody interesting?'

'It's only a school,' I said. 'And everyone's on holiday.'

'Well, come in, Linda.'

'It's OK,' I said. 'Mansell's fast asleep.'

'No, do come in. Have a cup of tea. The kettle's just boiled.'

Reluctantly I wheeled the pram into the hall. There was a cold smell in the house.

'You can leave the pram here,' she said. 'Mansell will be fine.'

I followed her into the kitchen. The light was on, a bare bulb with no lampshade. It was bigger than our kitchen – there was room for a small flimsy table and two spindly chairs that didn't match. The cooker stood on its own against one wall. Under the window, next to a cupboard, was a sink and a grooved wooden draining board. There was an old calendar for 1962 hanging crookedly on the wall. It said July and had a picture of a brown and white carthorse. The room felt empty and lonely, as if the cheapness of the outside of the house had slipped inside when no one was looking.

Sylvia almost fell into a chair. 'Could you make the tea, chicken?' she said. 'I'm afraid I'm having a bit of a slump.'

'Perhaps I should go home,' I said.

'No, no, it's lovely to have company.'

For you maybe, I thought. I wasn't good at making tea. I took the kettle off the top of the cooker. The kettle was cold. It was empty. It wasn't boiling at all. I looked at Sylvia, but she was rubbing her face with her hands. This was going to take ages. As I filled the kettle, the tap wobbled because the pipe was coming away from the wall. I lit the gas with a match from a large squashed box on the draining board and looked for the teapot.

Sylvia waved a hand towards the cupboard. Crockery was piled inside. The lid didn't match the teapot, and the cups didn't match anything. They were all chipped. I hoped the boiling water from the kettle would kill the germs.

'Where's your fridge?' I said.

'Oh, the milk's in the bucket by the sink.'

I gave Sylvia the nicest cup, ornately shaped with a gold rim and fading roses, because she was the person who wasn't well. I had a green one like the ones in Mum's church. 'That's lovely, chicken,' Sylvia said. She took a mouthful of tea. She shuddered. 'Ooh.'

'It's too weak, isn't it?' I said.

'No, no. It's just – there's no sugar.' She pulled the sugar bowl towards her and stirred in three heaped spoonfuls. She took another sip. 'Ahh, that's better.' She looked at me, hunched on my chair. 'Are you cold? Let's go into the living room. Bring your tea.' Before I could think of another way of saying *I want to go home*, she stood up and walked across the hall.

In the living room another bare bulb lit the room. This didn't look like a room for living in at all. It was like a junk room. There were three different styles and colours of chairs, and everything was faded, greys and greens and browns. Mustardy, cracked lino covered the floor with a matted orange rug in front of the electric fire. Our living room was shabby – we had a hole in the middle of the carpet – but at least our settee matched the armchairs.

And there was a smell of cigarettes and baby sick and a sort of dampness. No wonder Sylvia was depressed.

But she didn't seem depressed now. 'Right,' she said, gaily, 'let's get a bit of atmosphere in here and listen to some music.' She switched on the fire with a loud, empty ping. The fan behind the plastic coals began to whirr and the bars turned slowly red. She pulled the curtains but they didn't meet in the middle. Then she said, 'Turn off the light,' and motioned to the switch on the wall.

She wanted us to sit in the dark! Now I really wanted to go home.

But Sylvia switched on a standard lamp and the glow from the lamp and gradually the red of the fire meant the room looked cosier. 'That's better,' she said. 'A bit of atmosphere. Right, what shall we have?' In one corner next to the TV, on top of an old-fashioned bulbous wooden sideboard, was a record player, green and cream, with a pile of LPs beside it. She slid the records from side to side. 'How about this one?' She held up the cover of a Louis Armstrong record.

I didn't like Louis Armstrong. He wasn't sleek and lean like the Motown artists, and he played the trumpet. When he did sing in that gravelly voice it was songs like 'Hello Dolly', that bounced in a jaunty sort of way.

'Louis Armstrong is a remarkable man, Linda,' Sylvia said, looking at my disdainful expression. 'He is an interesting musician and he paved the way for all those young men I assume you like.'

It did make a difference to know he was a good musician and a trailblazer. I knew black people had had a hard time in America, even though slavery was over, and if he made it easier for Tamla Motown to exist, that was great, but I still didn't like his music.

'Listen to this.' Carefully she moved the arm of the record player and put the needle down on the disc. It was 'Mack the Knife'.

'OK,' I said optimistically, but he was singing it as if it was 'Hello Dolly'.

I looked at a heap of paperbacks on the floor in the corner. 'Do you read?' I said. Instantly I regretted the question. It sounded as if I was surprised, as if I thought she must be stupid.

But Sylvia simply said, 'Yes, that's my library.' She laughed.

'Why don't you have shelves?'

'Because my mother said we needed a pram for the baby.'

According to Louis Armstrong, Mack Heath was back in town. Sylvia threw herself into an armchair, picked up her cup of tea and tapped her foot to the music.

I perched on the edge of the other armchair. The room was heating up. I wanted to take my coat off, but I didn't want her to think I was stopping.

'Have you heard this before?'

'Yes, my sister Judith likes this kind of music. But she's older than me and a bit of a beatnik. Though they do play it on the Aldermaston.'

'The Aldermaston march?' she said. 'Do you go on the Aldermaston march?'

'I've been going for years,' I said nonchalantly. Two years. The jazz bands played as they marched, or sometimes when we stopped for dinner. People even danced sometimes.

'Doesn't that rhythm stir you on, and keep you going?' Sylvia said.

'I suppose,' I said. I would think about that later.

'Your Ban the Bomb badge really is serious, then?' Sylvia put her head on one side and looked at me and the badge.

'Yes.' I wished it was the expensive one, to show how serious I was, but that was at home, pinned to my suede.

'And you believe in it? And you really do go on the march?'

'Yes!' I didn't know why she was asking me. 'I would have gone earlier, but my mum wouldn't let us go when we were young because she didn't want people saying she'd indoctrinated us.'

Sylvia nodded. 'I know several people who go. I wonder if you know them?'

'It's quite a big march, thousands of people.'

She smiled. 'That's true. And you march for the whole four days?'

'The CND group usually go up for one or two days, in a coach. Sometimes on Good Friday to Aldermaston and then we go up to London on Easter Monday. Next year I'll go for the whole march. But however much you do, it's still important.'

'Of course.'

'And you still get blisters.'

'Oh, Linda.' She laughed. 'So you're quite a political person?'

'I suppose so.'

'How does that work at school? Which school do you go to?'

'The High School.'

'Oh,' she said, 'you passed the eleven-plus.' She sounded surprised. 'So what does the High School think about your politics?'

'I was told not to wear my CND badge on school premises,' I said.

'That's a bit much.'

I liked her for saying that. Mum had said what did I expect? I shouldn't have worn it in the first place.

'I should think they'd be pleased that their girls were thinking about important political issues,' she said.

'They don't seem to. I mean, no one in my form talks about it.'

'Would you like it if they did?'

'I'd be surprised. They're all so posh.'

'Some posh people think about politics.'

I looked at her. Was she laughing at me? Her face was serious. 'I don't know. I don't talk to them very much. I don't think they want to talk to me, the council estate girl.'

'Don't put yourself down,' Sylvia said. 'I think you've got a lot to offer.'

I smiled. No one had ever said anything like that to me before. It was a nice feeling. Even if it was Sylvia.

The song ended and Sylvia jumped up. 'What shall we have now? How about a little Frank Sinatra?'

'I thought he was quite tall.'

'That's very good, Linda, but actually I think he isn't the tallest person in the world.' She slid a disc out of its cover and put it on the turntable and Frank Sinatra began to sing 'Fly Me to the Moon'.

The fact she'd got my joke made me feel better. For a few minutes I forgot the smell of the room and the feeling of shabby sadness in the house.

Sylvia watched my eyes gazing round the room. 'Now that I'm back home my new project is to make this room look better,' she said. 'Do you think that's a good plan?'

I was jolted back into her life. 'How?' I said.

'Well . . .'

'You'd have to do quite a bit,' I said. Her face fell. I was being rude. 'But probably,' I added quickly, 'if you got some bits of wood you could make shelves. Or even cardboard boxes, from the shop, for the books. And if you tidied up a bit and put a picture or two on the wall . . .'

Sylvia laughed. 'I like a girl with ideas,' she said. 'Are you the person who designs the rooms in your house?'

'No,' I said. 'No one is. They just happen. Or they happened ages ago. We haven't had a new carpet for years.' Had I said too much? Giving away our family shame? My shame. 'Sandra said you call yourself Sylvie.'

'Do you mean Mrs Brady's daughter?'

'She's my best friend. We've been friends since I was three years old.'

'That's nice,' she said. 'And I do, yes, I do call myself Sylvie. I think it's prettier. It's almost French, you know, like Sylvie Vartan.'

'That's what I said!' I was pleased. 'So should I call you Sylvie?'

'If you like. Yes, please. That would be nice.'

I looked at my watch. 'I'd better go now. I have to help my mum make the tea.'

'And you're taking Mansell out tomorrow?'

'I'm picking him up from the shop at quarter past two.'

'Are you sure that's all right? You seem to have rather a lot on your plate – politics, designing rooms – and I'm sure you have homework.'

'Well, I'm not really a designing person, and I don't do as much homework as I should,' I said. Why was I telling her so much? 'But it's OK.'

'And will you bring him back here?' she said. 'It's been lovely talking to you. We can think about your ideas for the room and listen to some more Louis Armstrong.'

'So you don't really want me to come back.'

She laughed. 'You can bring your own records if you like.'

'We haven't got a record player,' I said, sadly.

'All right, well, you can choose from mine.'

I wasn't optimistic.

'So how was the baby boy wonder?' Sandra was ringing me at teatime.

'He was fine.' I settled myself on the stairs. 'I had to take him back to their house, actually. Sylvie was there.'

'So now you've seen her too! What did you say to her?'

'We had a cup of tea. Which I made.'

'Ooh, get you. So who's the father?'

'Give me a chance. I hardly know her yet,' I said.

'So what do you think?' She lowered her voice. Their phone was in the hall, like ours, so her mum was probably listening from the kitchen. 'What was she like?'

'I don't know. She had maroon slippers on. And she likes Louis Armstrong.'

'There you are.'

'That's what I thought. They're really poor, though. Their house is cold and smells like, like –' I stopped. I was going to say 'like our outside toilet', but it would sound wrong. I didn't mean their house smelt like a toilet, but like somewhere damp and outside with no fire to heat it. Sandra would know what it meant. Their outside toilet smelt like that too. But she might take it the wrong way. I realised I felt protective of Sylvie. 'You know, cold. Just cold.'

I put the phone down. Mum and Dad were in the kitchen, talking, Mum cutting bread, Dad opening a tin of beans. I went back into the living room. Judith, wearing a big sloppy jumper, was lying on the settee with her legs over the arm, reading *Woman's Own*. The fire was burning in the grate with the coal scuttle beside. Our rust-coloured three-piece suite was old and faded but it was comfortable. Hanging on one wall was a painting of Heybridge Basin, the small fishing village near Maldon where my dad came from. There was a mirror on another. The new green-and-silver-striped curtains at the French windows brushed the floor and met in the middle, even if they didn't ripple. The central light had a lampshade that matched the curtains. On the sideboard was a bowl of oranges. Even the threadbare patch in the middle of the carpet looked homely by comparison with the Westons' house.

On either side of the fireplace were the oak bookcases that Mum and Dad had got when they married, just after the war. They were in the Utility style, and were filled with books, including Mum's favourites, *Jane Eyre* and *Pride and Prejudice*, and Dad's, by Ezra Pound and Walt Whitman. On the bottom shelf were their copies of Shakespeare's *Collected Works*, side by side. Dad's was maroon, leather-bound. His mother had given it to him for his twenty-first birthday present. The cover of Mum's was navy-blue cardboard. She'd bought it with her first week's wages, in the war. When Judith and I were young we each took one copy, staggering under the weight, as we put on productions of *The Tempest* and *Much Ado About Nothing* in the living room, wrapped round with sheets, tea towels and Mum's belts, proclaiming loudly with all the wrong inflections and pronunciations.

The books on the shelves were comforting and friendly, even the books about Hiroshima and Apartheid which I read from time to time and which reassured me that I was right when people responded angrily to my arguments about why I didn't eat South African oranges and why I wanted to ban the bomb.

I sniffed. All I could smell was our house, Dad's cigarettes and Lux soap flakes.

But even if we weren't as poor as Sylvie and Mrs Weston, we were still poor. And I needed more clothes. If I wasn't careful I'd look like Sylvie, everything mismatched and odd. I wouldn't be able to go to the Orpheus or the Corn Exchange. You couldn't be a mod if you didn't have style. 'I've got to get a proper job that pays proper money,' I said aloud.

Judith was studying an article illustrated by a photograph of a worried-looking woman talking to someone in a white coat. 'Well, get one.'

'It's all right for you,' I said. On Saturdays Judith worked in the greengrocer's on the parade. 'And you don't need as much money as me. You and your beatnik mates never go out, and you never buy any clothes.'

'Clothes aren't everything. My friends and I drink beer. That doesn't come free.'

'You're too young.'

'So are you.'

'I don't drink beer.'

'That's not what I was talking about. Listen to this letter.' She was reading the Mary Grant problem page.

'"My boyfriend and I have never had full intercourse, although we have engaged in heavy petting. My boyfriend says that I cannot get pregnant this way, even if we are not wearing clothes and he lies very close to me when he finishes." Is that what happened to your friend down the road?'

'First of all, she's not my friend. And second of all, I only met her today, and funnily enough, we didn't talk about it. Why do you care what happened? I thought you believed in free love – you're the beatnik, not me.'

'Yes, but I'm not a man. It's the men who believe in it. Girls don't usually get off free.' It sounded as if she'd given it more thought than I had.

Mum called us into the kitchen. Dad had gone upstairs to change. Judith took the tablecloth and cutlery from the drawer to lay the table in the front room. I had to watch the toast while Mum tipped the beans into a saucepan.

'I hear you met Sylvia today,' Mum said.

'Word gets around!' I said. 'Anyway, she calls herself Sylvie.'

'How was she?'

'All right. Their house is a worse dump than ours.'

'As long as it's clean, you don't need to worry.' She looked at my face. 'But if you think it's not clean, you could always lend them a hand in that department.'

'I'm not sure they can afford a hoover,' I said. I turned the toast.

CHAPTER 4

Power

I HADN'T SEEN SYLVIE SINCE THAT first day, weeks before. I hadn't gone back, there had been no need. I'd gone to the shop on the Friday so Mrs Weston could pay me and I left Mansell there. But now we had a day off school and Mum had somehow arranged more baby-watching for me.

Mansell and I walked to the Main Road and then across into the Avenues, looking at the big houses of all the people who voted Conservative. These were not council houses, and at election time they all had Conservative Party posters in their windows. Then we walked back onto the estate and without thinking I wheeled the pram into the Crescent.

Sylvie was sitting on the wall outside their house. Today she looked completely different. Her hair was pulled back into a smooth French pleat and she was wearing a simple red jumper and blue skirt. She looked like an ordinary person. Two women I vaguely recognised from further down the Crescent were walking towards her. I slowed down. 'Oh dear, Mansell,' I whispered, 'we're going to have to make polite conversation. You're going to have to look sweet. Which you do, of course.' The women were staring at Sylvie and then, instead of smiling and stopping for a chat, they very pointedly crossed over to the other side of the road.

I looked at them and back to Sylvie. If she had noticed, she gave no sign.

'Hello!' I said loudly, in a cheerful voice.

'Linda!' Sylvie said, glancing at the women. 'Am I glad to see you! Bring him in.'

I wheeled the pram into the hall and lifted Mansell out and tucked him onto my hip.

'What was all that about?' I said, gesturing out into the street.

'Oh, some people think there are rules to live by, and they get frightened if the rules are broken.'

'Is this about Mansell?' I said.

'Yes. Well, me really. But you're not worried , are you?'

I frowned and shook my head.

'I knew you wouldn't be,' Sylvie said. 'Now, come into the living room!'

The living room was different. 'You inspired me,' she said. The fire was already on and the standard lamp had a pink bulb which gave out a soft glow. Two faded cotton bedspreads were draped over the armchairs so that at least they matched.

'But I didn't say any of this,' I said.

'I could see it in your eyes,' Sylvie said, dramatically.

I looked at the books, which were now lined up smartly on the floor against the wall. 'That's the library,' she said. 'For very short people.'

'I didn't know Mansell could read.'

'You'd be surprised. He's very bookish.'

We both laughed. Mansell blinked.

'So what do you think of my efforts?' she said.

'It looks . . . nice.'

The records had been tidied into a neat pile on the sideboard. Next to them was a sketch of a jug of flowers.

'And you got a picture too,' I said.

'It's a birthday card.'

'Is it your birthday?'

'No, that's a card from me to my mother. I got it for her this morning. Her birthday was last week, but of course I forgot. You don't think much about happy returns of the day when you're doped up in a locked ward.' She looked at me and I wondered if she was trying to shock me. 'And anyway, there's not much of a selection of cards over there, and you can't get stamps, even if you promise to take all your medicine like a good girl.'

I said nothing. This was what I had been afraid of from the beginning, a discussion about madness. I held Mansell tight.

'I'm sorry,' she said. 'That's what they call an inappropriate topic of conversation, isn't it?'

'Well, it's not really a conversation because I don't know what to say back.'

'That's honest,' she said. 'I don't get a lot of honesty. People usually say what they think I want to hear.'

'I wouldn't know how to do that,' I said. 'I don't know you well enough.'

'They say things like how well I am today, how lovely I look.'

'Oh, I could do that,' I said. 'I like your skirt.' We laughed again. This was better. 'So if you were in – in hospital last week, does that mean you didn't send any Valentine cards?' I asked.

'No, I didn't, Linda. Did you?'

'Yes,' I said.

'So you're a romantic as well as a political animal!'

'I don't know about that.'

'And who was the lucky boy?'

I explained the situation about Ray from down the road, that I had really liked him when I was thirteen but that was ages ago. But currently there was no one else, no one whose address I knew. I told her about Tap, being so stylish and working in The Boutique and about my caramel nylon mac. 'But Sandra sent a card to him,' I said. 'Sandra sent two – well, three. Two to Danny, one funny and one loving, as well as the one to Tap.'

Sylvie frowned. 'I don't understand. I thought you liked Tap.'

'Sandra wants to keep Danny guessing but still interested.'

'Who is this Danny?' Sylvie said. 'Why does she like him so much?'

'Danny.' I sighed. 'Do you really want to know?'

'I love a good story,' she said.

I tried to remember what I'd written in my diary. 'The first time we met Danny Mulroney was one Saturday morning in the record department of the Co-op. It was in the summer holidays, not long after we'd started going down the Orpheus. Sandra was still at school then.

'We were at the counter and Sandra was asking the woman in the orange nylon overall if they had Roy Orbison's latest single, when someone wearing a navy-blue Crombie overcoat and a bluebeat hat came out of one of the booths, shouting at us, "No, no, you don't want to listen to that rubbish, listen to this, listen to this!" He leaned over the counter and moved the arm of the record player back to the beginning of a 45 already on the turntable. The woman stared at him. "Turn it up!" he said. Slowly she turned the volume knob and then stood with folded arms as we listened to 'Madness' by Prince Buster. The man rocked round the counter to the ska beat, his head nodding back and forth like a chicken. When the record finished, Sandra asked the assistant to put it on again. After we'd listened to it twice, Sandra said, "Yeah, thanks," and we left the shop. We had to go home for dinner.

'The next Monday we met him again, in the Orpheus. I'd put 'One Fine Day' on the jukebox and that first single piano note was knocking round the room and we were both singing "Shooby dooby dooby dooby do wup bup" as he came down the stairs. He turned his back to the counter and shouted, "Today we're going to break the sound barrier. Who wants to go for a ride?" Brenda said, "Sorry, Danny, not today." Sandra and I were the only other people in there, and Sandra nudged me and said it would be a laugh.

'I'd rather have listened to the end of the record but I knew Sandra really wanted to go.

'The car was a small black Austin Seven. It was parked outside the Orpheus. Sandra said later she'd guessed straightaway that it was stolen. "I couldn't say anything," she'd said. "You wouldn't have come if you'd thought it was nicked, would you? Think what we'd have missed."

'Danny opened the passenger door, bowing, and I climbed into the back. Sandra sat in the front, laughing and making cracks, smoothing down her skirt. I had to lean forward, straining to hear what they were saying.

'We were going about twenty miles an hour.

'"I thought you said we'd go fast," Sandra said.

'"This is fast for an Austin Seven," he said, revving the engine. He changed gear and there was a loud noise. "And there goes the sound barrier."

'We were driving along the Main Road towards Braintree before he actually introduced himself. Then suddenly he was groping under his seat and pulling out two hairbrushes. "Look at these," he said to Sandra. They had tortoiseshell and silver backs and the bristle was soft and creamy.

'He held one in each hand and turned round to show them to me. Turned round! He was driving! But Sandra just slapped his thigh and said, "Look where you're going."

'He laughed.

'Sandra made him stop at the 311 bus stop. She kissed him goodbye, and that was it. They were courting.

'He got arrested as he drove back into town. We heard that he pleaded guilty at the magistrates' court. He got three months suspended for six months, for taking the car and driving without a licence or insurance, with the theft of the brushes taken into consideration. When he got caught stealing a Mini outside the Corn Exchange two weeks later, they added on the month and he went inside. He's been in prison three times since then.'

Sylvie laughed. 'Well, that's quite a story. But when do you have time to do all these things? Go for drives, listen to music, worry about who's in and who's out?'

'That doesn't take much time,' I said. 'Tap's always In, and Danny's usually In – prison, that is – except when he's Out, which isn't very often. And Ray's always there.' I felt a bit ashamed of being so offhand about Ray. I had sent him the card.

'What about your homework?'

'Oh, I do it.'

There was a silence. I wanted her to ask me. There was more silence. 'Did you get any? Valentines?' I said.

'I did,' she said. 'Just the one.'

'Can I see it?'

'Oh, I don't know where it is, poppet.' She waved her hand vaguely. 'Look in those drawers.'

Still holding Mansell on my hip, I looked in the three drawers of the sideboard. There were photo albums, needles and thread, buttons, shoe polish. In the last, with folded paper bags and little balls of string, I found it.

It was a big card, with a large red padded heart in the middle. Inside, it said, 'You light up my life. May I light up your world?' Which, compared to the cards we'd sent, was pathetic. Underneath, in flowery handwriting, were the words, 'Do you remember?' followed by five crosses.

'Do you?' I said.

'What?'

'Remember.'

'Oh, Linda, there is so much to remember, and much more that I would rather forget.' She was taking the Louis

Armstrong album out of its cover. She'd already forgotten what I thought about that. I was going to say something, but then I thought, what if she'd gone through things at the hospital, like drugs, or electric shock treatment, that had made her mind go blank? If I pointed out she'd forgotten that I didn't like Louis Armstrong it might undo the work of the treatment, or she might just think I was making rude comments. Casually I sat back down. 'Do you know who the card's from?'

'Oh, I don't know. Some deluded individual somewhere. It's not what I'd call an attractive card. Would you like it?'

'No! I – I had one of my own.'

'Oh, Linda! You didn't say. Tell me what it was like.'

'Actually, I've . . .' My hand crept to my bag.

'You've got it with you! Oh, chicken, that's sweet. Let me see it straightaway.'

It wasn't sweet, it was anything but sweet, and I wanted to say *no, sorry, I made a mistake, I left it at home*. But I was sort of proud of it. It was better than hers. I made a show of rummaging in my bag, but I knew exactly where it was. I took it out.

It was handmade, it was painted, yellow and brown lines on a piece of card. On the other side it said, 'What do you think? Will you be my Valentine? I can wait', and three kisses. At first I hadn't known what to think. It was so horrible, it had to be real. Brown and yellow. Lines. Who would have sent me something so wrong? But despite the disappointment of the design and the colour, it was a card and it was addressed to me, and it wasn't entirely stupid. I had wondered if it might be from Tap – perhaps he was a painting kind of person, perhaps it was an ironic comment on the caramel colour of my nylon mac. I couldn't really picture that. And how would he know my address? He hardly knew my name.

Sylvie looked at it thoughtfully. 'This is rather good,' she said. 'You see, I knew you were artistic.'

'I didn't make it myself!' If I had it wouldn't have been yellow and brown.

'No, but it was sent to you because artistic people recognise each other and appreciate each other.'

'Do they?' A shiver of pleasure ran up my back.

'Well, for example, I like you and I hope you like me.'

I hardly knew her, but she hadn't been well, so I said, 'Yes, I do.'

'There you are.'

'You didn't send it to me?'

'No, silly. I don't think I even know your surname, let alone where you live.'

'How do you know I'm artistic?' I said. I loved the thought, but it was a daring question. If I'd asked Sandra or one of the boys down the Orpheus, it would inevitably lead to a short laugh and a sarcastic answer, like, 'Did you say art or fart? I wondered what that smell was.'

Sylvie tilted her head and looked at me. 'Hmm. Let me see. Well, you care about your clothes, and how they match – the olive green of your top and the beige of your slacks.'

'These are about the only decent clothes I've got.'

'You wear them very well,' she said, seriously. 'And there's your neat little Ban the Bomb badge, which means you're a thoughtful girl. And you've got a well-developed sense of humour.'

I smiled into Mansell's hair. I settled back in the arm-chair.

'And you've just received a rather interesting Valentine's card, from someone who knows you will appreciate a piece of original, modern art. Because that's what it is, Linda. You should take care of it.'

'Thank you,' I said. I felt sorry for Sylvie only having received a crude red satin heart.

'And was it from someone you had sent a card to? What were their names? Rap, Tap and Dapper?'

At least she'd got Tap's name right. 'I don't know. But not Danny, anyway. And certainly not Tap.'

'Aha! I see.' She smiled. 'But what about Sandra? Did she receive any cards?'

'Yes,' I said carefully. Her mum worked with Sandra's mum. 'But she didn't know who from.'

'Your secrets are safe with me,' she said, as if she understood. 'No one listens to a mad woman, anyway.'

'But you're not mad, are you?' I said, hoping I didn't sound too desperate. 'Mum says you're just a bit . . . sad.'

'That's a rather enlightened view, Linda, and I thank you for telling me.'

I liked that. She liked my mum, but on my terms. She liked me, she liked things about me I didn't even know were likeable. I was glad I was here, sitting in a room with a lamp with a pink bulb and a fire, listening to music, having a conversation. Mansell had fallen asleep and was a pleasant heavy weight on my shoulder. 'But, what's it like? I mean, I get sad, about school and things. But I don't have to go to hospital.' There was a pause and I thought I'd said too much. Asking her questions, telling her about school – things I never told anyone.

'I think it's different,' she said slowly. 'Everyone gets a bit mixed up when they're in their teens. And as for you and your school – well, political differences can be hard. As for me, I suppose I've gone a few steps further down the line. I think my . . . sadness is part of my make-up.' She looked at my face. 'But you're all right, you know. I have great faith in you.'

I smiled. 'Thank you.'

'And I think the person with the paintbrush thinks so too!'

We laughed. Mansell gave a little snore. 'Shall I put Mansell in his cot?'

'Oh, just pop him into his pram.'

Standing up, heaving Mansell onto my shoulder, I said, trying to make my voice sound casual, 'Could your card be from Mansell's dad?'

'Oh, Linda.' She gave a short laugh, and looked over at me from the pile of records. 'I don't think that's his hand-writing. Not that I've seen much of his handwriting.'

'Handwriting's nothing,' I said.

'Well –' She took a breath and I thought she was going to say something else.

But as I hovered at the doorway there was a sort of click and the light suddenly snapped off, Louis Armstrong's voice slid to a halt and the bars on the fire began to fade. We were in darkness.

There was a shriek. I gasped and held Mansell tight against me.

'Oh, no!' Sylvie shouted. I stumbled as she almost fell on top of me. She must have leaped across the room. She was grabbing at me.

'Don't worry,' I said, my heart racing. 'It's just a power cut. Perhaps there's going to be a storm.'

'Oh, no!' She wailed a loud, scary noise from the back of her throat. And then she began to cry.

My heart was stamping in my chest. I wanted to run out of the front door. I was in a dark room with a scream-ing, shouting person. Mansell began to whimper. I should take him too. 'Perhaps I should go,' I said.

'Oh, no.' She wailed louder.

I wanted to be sick.

'No, no.' She was sobbing. I could see the silhouette of her chest moving up and down. 'It's the meter. The electricity's run out,' she whispered.

Screaming because the meter had run out. I'd like to see what my mum would say about that. 'Well, have you got any money?' I said. 'What does it take?'

'I haven't got any money.'

'Why not?' I said. I was furious. I could see where this was going.

'I don't get my money till tomorrow.' Now she was crashing round the room. 'Perhaps there's some money down the back of the settee.'

I knew how hopeless that would be. 'What does it take?'

'Sixpences, shillings.'

Light from the street was filtering through the gaps in the curtains. With one hand I groped on the floor for my bag and fumbled for my purse. I pulled out sixpence. 'Where's your meter?'

'Under the stairs.'

And now I had to go under the stairs in the dark! I walked back towards the hall, feeling my way, holding Mansell with one arm. I bumped into the pram. 'Do you want to go back in your pram?' I whispered, and before Mansell could answer or complain I laid him down on the soft flannel covering.

'It's at the back,' Sylvie said. 'Behind the bike.'

I moved round the pram and crouched down. Tentatively I put out my hands – there was a bucket and some boxes and something wet that I didn't want to think about and then I stuck my fingers in the chain of a bicycle. I poked through the spokes and found the meter. It was like our gas meter, with a butterfly handle. I pushed sixpence into the slot and turned. With a small metallic crash the sixpence fell to the bottom of the box. The light in the hall sprang on and Sylvie gave a cry of pleasure. Louis Armstrong revved himself up to Jupiter and Mars. I was pleased to hear him.

'Oh, Linda,' Sylvie said. 'Clever, sensible and fortunately rich.'

'Not anymore,' I said.

'I'll pay you back. I'm sorry about that. Shall we have a cup of tea?'

'No thanks.' I looked at Mansell in his pram. He gazed back at me seriously, his hair sticking out in a funny little tuft over one ear. 'I'm going home now,' I said to him. Then I whispered, 'I can't take you with me.' My throat hurt. 'Be good. Be really good.'

As if he knew I was going, Mansell screwed up his face and let out a howl.

Sylvie poked her head into the hall. 'Oh dear.' She picked him up and put him over her shoulder, rubbing his back. He didn't stop crying. 'Will you come and visit us again, Linda?' she shouted. 'It's so nice to have someone sensible to talk to.' Her face drooped. 'I don't see many people, you know.'

What a surprise, I thought. 'Maybe,' I murmured. 'We haven't got any school holidays for ages.' My heart was still beating fast. Then I looked at Mansell screeching in her arms, his mouth open and his face red, and I thought about the trouble he had caused in Sylvie's life, making her an unmarried mother, maybe even causing her illness, making her the subject of gossip on the estate, people pointing at her from the bus. 'I could take him out another time, if you like,' I muttered.

'Oh Linda, are you offering? That would be lovely. And when you bring him back, you could come in and listen to some music. I've got some other LPs I'd like you to hear. And we could have a proper conversation. Linda, that would be lovely.'

Sixpence! I thought, as I walked back up the road. My sixpence! I knew Mum wouldn't let me ask for it back.

CHAPTER 5

Danny's Friend

Now that Sandra was working, I didn't think she would come delivering again. Delivering meant pushing Labour Party election leaflets through the letter boxes on our estate. We did it for most elections. This time, my dad was standing for the County Council. I thought Sandra might make an excuse not to come, but on Tuesday evening Mum called out that Sandra was at the door.

I ran downstairs as Sandra stepped inside onto the mat. 'Aren't you changing?' she said. She had on her new Marks' bottle-green twinset.

'If you wear your school uniform they don't shout at you so much,' I said.

'What about after?'

'I thought tonight was a Danny night.' Danny had been out for two weeks.

'It is, but he's bringing his mate. Just for you.'

'Oh?' I grinned. 'It's not . . .?'

'No, it's not Tap.'

'Didn't think it would be,' I said quickly. 'Who? Who?'

Danny was friends with anyone. He had to be, because people grew fed up with him. He let them down. He cheated them. Whenever he went inside his friends drifted away. When he came back to Chelmsford he would pal up with new people who wanted a bit of excitement, who only knew him by reputation. And he would bring them along on his dates with Sandra. People like Dick, a postman he brought down the Orpheus. Dick had his second delivery sack with him and he was so excited at being Danny's friend he threw all the letters in the river when we walked round town. 'Who is it this time?'

'Cooky.'

'Who's Cooky?'

'If you come, you'll find out.'

'What's he like?'

'Think of Tap, but with curlier hair. And a bigger car. He's – he's nice. I've met him a few times. You'll like him.'

I looked at her.

'Probably. No, it's going to be great. I think Danny might propose tonight.'

'Really?'

'He keeps hinting about rings and things.'

I couldn't believe her. I couldn't believe that Danny wanted to get married. Danny's favourite song was 'Shotgun Wedding', and he put it on the jukebox in the

Orpheus whenever anyone announced their engagement. But she looked so hopeful I said, 'Just as long as I'm your bridesmaid.'

'Just as long as you come out tonight.'

'You won't want me there if he's popping the big question.'

'I know, but someone's got to talk to Cooky or he'll keep butting in.'

'All right, I'll come,' I sighed. 'But I can't go out in my uniform.'

'That's what I said. We'll have to be quick, and then you can change when we've finished. So where are the leaflets?'

I pointed to the telephone table.

'There's loads!' she said. 'Are we doing the whole of Essex?'

'No, the Crescent, the Place, your side of the road and the flats.'

'I wanted to get into town before the pubs shut.'

'We've got to do it all tonight.'

Sandra picked up a pile of leaflets. 'Come on then,' she said. 'Race you to the top of the road.'

Mum was watching *Panorama* and Dad was out at a union meeting, so it was easy to slip upstairs and change into my newest acquisition, a blue skirt that had been Judith's. I'd taken down the hem so that it was the right mod length. I put on a cream cardigan that I buttoned up to the neck.

I glanced at myself in the mirror. Hmm, not bad. Jean Shrimpton on a quiet evening.

Half an hour later we were at the bus station, waiting near the railway arches, where the flower stall stood during the day. Sandra went into the old toilets to change her shoes.

One or two Vespas went past and Sandra waved in case it was someone we knew.

'If I'm not in by half past nine I'm going to be in real trouble,' I said.

'Yeah, yeah.'

'I said I'd do my homework before I went to bed.'

'What is it this time?'

'French. All the tenses of the verbs "to be" and "to have" and to know when to use them.'

'That's easy, I *be* veray borrred and I *'ave* a feeling zis is not going to be a good evernink, after oll.'

'Oh yeah, that's good. I can see Miss Harmon liking that. Do you think I should leave the top button of my cardigan done up? Or should I undo it, just casually?'

She looked at me.

'What if this Cooky thinks it's stupid?'

'Cooky won't care.'

'What does that mean?' I said, but Sandra was looking under the railway bridge.

'Here they are.'

A large green-and-white Corsair drew up. Danny got out of the front and took hold of Sandra's hand. He opened the back door with a flourish. They climbed in.

Sandra hissed, 'Get in.' I hesitated. 'The front.'

I looked into the car. Behind the steering wheel, at the far end of the long bench seat, sat a boy in a red shirt and jeans.

'This is Cooky,' Sandra said as I sat down. The car smelt of petrol. 'Cooky, this is my best mate, Linda.'

'Watcha Linda,' Cooky said, and rolled his eyes at me.

'Shut the door, Linda,' Sandra said.

This couldn't be the Cooky who was like Tap but with curlier hair, who had a car like Tap's only bigger. This couldn't be the Cooky who was going to make it a great night out. This Cooky was wearing drainpipe trousers, and his shoes on the pedals were long, scuffed and pointed. This Cooky had greased-back hair. This Cooky was a rocker. He wasn't even that good a rocker – one or two curls were slipping away from the Brylcreem, flopping onto his forehead. A rocker with curly hair! And his rolled-up shirtsleeves revealed pale freckled skin and on his left arm the tattooed bottom half of a woman's body that moved as he turned the wheel.

I turned and looked at Sandra, my eyes wide. She grinned and gave me a thumbs up.

Cooky slid the gears up and down on the steering column. 'Is there a way we can get out of this place without me turning round?' he said. 'I'm having trouble with my reverse.'

We had to drive through the bus station and halfway up to Westlands Estate because he couldn't turn round, but eventually we were back in town, cruising past Bond's, and Woolworth's, over the bridge and past The Boutique and the Regent, past the Co-op and then round into London Road. Radio Luxembourg faded in and out and Cooky kept banging the dashboard with his hand. When the Bachelors disappeared I said, 'Well, that's one good thing.'

'But I like that one!' he shouted. When Matt Monro dissolved into a hiss, Cooky yelled, 'That's my favourite!'

I leaned against the car door and looked at Sandra, but she was locked in Danny's arms. He was playing with her hair.

The car stopped at the lights at the Shire Hall as Johnny Kidd and the Pirates were singing 'Ecstasy'. Cooky threw a glance over his shoulder and crooned, 'Mmm . . . kisses, mmm . . . this is – ecstasy.'

'Shut up,' Danny said.

'How come you know Danny?' I asked Cooky.

'His mum knows my mum,' Cooky said, 'and as his mum won't have him in the house –'

'My mum's a cunt,' Danny said.

'Danny!' Sandra and I said in unison.

'You don't know her,' he murmured.

'He's staying with us.'

'That's nice of you,' I said.

'And I only had to ask twice,' Danny said.

'My mum thinks he's trouble.'

'Your mum might be right,' I said quietly.

Cooky looked over at me. 'Do you believe in sex before marriage?'

'Why?'

'You know, with that badge.'

'That's not what the badge stands for,' I said.

'Oh, get you. No, just say, just suppose everyone did it. Would you? Do it?'

'Who with?'

'Me.'

'You what? I don't even know you, and you may not have noticed, but I'm a mod.'

'I don't care.'

'I don't care if you care. I care. I wouldn't do it with a rocker. Whether or not I believed in it.'

'You know who you remind me of?' he said. 'That Mandy Rice-Davies.'

'I beg your pardon?' I said loudly.

'What did he say?' Sandra asked from the back seat.

'He wants to know if I believe in sex before marriage.' I couldn't bear to repeat his comment about Mandy Rice-Davies, with her thick make-up, her round face and that beehive hairdo.

'You should watch out,' Sandra said to Cooky. 'Her dad's a magistrate.'

'He's what?' Danny said.

'Nothing,' Sandra and I chorused.

Cooky snorted with laughter. 'Better not talk about your business, Danny,' he said over his shoulder. 'Your little parcels –'

'Your little what?' I said.

'Shut up, Cooky,' Danny said. 'Talking rubbish. What say we go and have a drink, girls?'

'What's the time?' I said. 'Have we got time?'

'As long as we don't have to turn round,' Cooky said. 'I don't know what's wrong with these gears. Here, Danny, isn't that someone you know?'

Walking under the railway bridge were two girls. One wore a long black leather coat. 'Fuck,' Danny said. He slid down the seat, hunching his shoulders. 'Don't look, don't look!'

'Who is it?' Sandra said.

'Don't look!' Danny hissed. 'It's some girl who's got the wrong idea.'

'She must have,' I said. 'How would she know you, Danny? She looks like a rocker.' I looked at Cooky. 'Excuse my French.'

'Was that French? Shall we stop?' Cooky said over his shoulder. He was winding down his window.

'Don't be stupid!' Danny sounded panicked.

'What's up with you?' Sandra said.

'He'll only encourage her,' Danny said. 'Keep driving.'

'Where are we going?' Cooky said.

'We're pointing in the direction of our estate,' I said. 'We might as well carry on.'

Sandra sighed. 'All right. We can park outside the shops for a bit and talk.' She must have thought he'd ask her to marry him outside the fish shop.

I leaned back in the seat as we drove along the Main Road towards Sperry Drive.

'Who was that girl?' I said.

'That? That was Barbara. Oh!' Cooky opened his eyes wide and grinned at me. He put his finger to his lips. He looked in his rear-view mirror at Sandra and Danny.

I wondered who Barbara was. Was she the reason for all the nudges and winks when Sandra asked people if they'd seen Danny?

Cooky parked the car outside the hardware shop. I glanced at my watch – there were ten minutes before I had to be in. Cooky settled back against his door, sliding his knee onto the seat, and said, 'So, your dad's a magistrate? What's he doing living on a council estate?'

'He's a magistrate because he's a trade union official,' I said.

'You Labour, then?'

'Yes.'

'I'm a Conservative,' he said. A rocker and a Conservative. I wasn't doing this again, keeping Danny's friends amused while Sandra tried to keep her New Year's Resolution. It was

March; who cares about New Year's Resolutions in March? If Danny didn't ask Sandra to marry him tonight, I'd suggest she join a convent. 'That's how come I know people like Mandy,' Cooky was saying.

'What?'

'You know, Mandy Rice-Davies.'

'You know her?'

'I don't know her, but I know people like her. You'd be surprised.'

'Yes, I would.'

'We get all sorts at the base. I work at the base. You know, Wethersfield.'

'The American air base? What do you do there?'

'He cuts the grass,' Danny said.

'And I drive the van,' Cooky said. 'Sometimes.'

I snorted.

'What have you got against Americans?' he said.

'For a start, they're American, then they dropped the bomb on Hiroshima, and now they're in Vietnam.' They were killing people they didn't know, men, women and children, destroying towns and cities in a place far away, and no one seemed to want to stop them.

'You take it too seriously.' Cooky slid along the big front seat. 'Looking at you now, you know, you look more like Christine Keeler. She's got nice legs too.' His arm was on the back of the seat and his hand stroked my hair, as he moved his head towards me, puckering his lips.

'Get off!' I yelled. I pushed him away while Danny shouted, 'Down Cooky, down!' and roared with laughter.

Sandra and I watched the tail lights of the Corsair disappear down the road.

'So?' I said. 'Did he ask you?'

'No. But he might have if you hadn't jumped out of the car so fast.'

'It's gone ten o'clock, Cooky's sex mad and you and Danny weren't exactly talking,' I said.

She sighed. 'There's probably no point, anyway. He's up in court again. This time it's a big one, he said.'

We walked to her house and stopped at the gate. 'Who's Barbara?' I said.

She opened her eyes wide. 'Why?' she demanded. 'What did Cooky say?'

Her reaction was so strong, I felt guilty. 'Nothing!'

'Why did you say it then?'

'No reason.'

'Why, though?'

'He just said that's who was walking under the bridge.'

'When?'

'He just said the name when you and Danny were not exactly talking. Cooky's an idiot.'

'But what did he say?'

'It just came up, he was talking about loads of things. Christine Keeler and Mandy Rice-Davies, and Americans.

And it just came up. Her name. That was all. You could have joined in the conversation but you were busy in the back seat.'

'You know who Barbara is, she was down the Orpheus that first day,' Sandra said sadly, 'with her long black leather.'

'But that girl tonight really was a rocker. She had big bouffant hair.'

'So it was her.'

'I don't know. Cooky's probably just stirring it.'

'Danny had a thing with her,' she said.

'Did he?'

'Ages ago. He told me all about it. It's over, but she won't let it go. He said.' She picked at a button on her coat. 'I don't know.'

'What do you mean?'

'I think he still sees her.'

'Why? Why would he? All his friends are mods now – well, except Cooky, but that's just because he lives with him. Anyway, he's got you. Why would he go out with a rocker? He's finished with rockers.'

She was silent, looking down.

'Hasn't he?' I followed her gaze and stared at her new shoes. They were black patent, had a thin, two-inch heel and they were pointed. They were rocker shoes. 'Oh, Sandra,' I said.

'What? What?'

'Is he worth it? He's changing you.'

'No he isn't!'

'He's two-timing you.'

'He isn't.'

'Well, he's messing you about. You're wasting your life with him.'

'No I'm not. You're just jealous.' She was breathing heavily.

'I'm not! He's wasting my life, too.'

'You don't have to come out.'

'Yes I do. You're my best friend. But he's no good.'

'Well, this is my life and I'm going to do what I want.'

We were talking in song titles, but I couldn't laugh. I was angry. 'He makes you upset, he's never there when you need him. He spoils our fun.'

'He's there when I want him.'

'Well, you want him most of the time, and most of the time he's in prison.'

'Shut up,' she said. 'Shut up! Oh God, here we go.'

Her dad appeared from the back of the house. 'Out gallivanting, without mentioning you'd broken your mother's favourite cup. Get indoors!' he hissed at her. 'Now!'

We shared a look, then silently she walked down the path.

CHAPTER 6

The Election

THERE WAS A LABOUR PRIME MINISTER, Harold Wilson, but Chelmsford had a Conservative MP, Norman St John-Stevas. The local elections were always touch and go.

Chelmsford was a boom town, with the firms Marconi and Hoffman's, Crompton's and the English Electric Valve Company. Dad had union members in all the factories in town and beyond. There were a lot of local issues he had to be involved in: wages, job cuts, working conditions, as well as the efficiency and safety of the power station at Bradwell.

I loved the fact that Dad was a trade union official. I loved being Labour. Labour stood for fairness, equality, the National Health Service and proper education for everyone. Labour meant a belief in council housing and nationalising industry so that it was the workers who got the benefits of their labours, not a small group of uncontrolled shareholders. It was so logical and so good. It was a description of how people should behave towards each other, to be fair, to give everyone the same chance, regardless of where they were born.

Dad said his politics came from Karl Marx, who'd said, 'From each according to his ability, to each according to his needs'. Mum said her politics came from Jesus, who wanted everyone to love each other and to be good to each other. Mum was a Congregationalist. Dad wasn't that religious. If asked, he said he was C of E, but he never went to church. Dad's compromise with Mum was to say that Jesus was the first Communist. That made me like Jesus, although I couldn't really forgive him for the fact that I'd spent my childhood in Sunday School. It was only a few months since I had rebelled and said I couldn't go anymore, because it made me feel like a kid. Mum said I could leave Sunday School if I went to another church. I was still deciding which church to go to. The Quakers were in the lead because they had good politics – they supported CND – and they had no hymns.

The election was the last Thursday in March and everyone had a day off school, but Judith and I had to do poll-checking, so it wasn't much of a holiday.

'At least it's the last day we have the "Vote Piper, Vote Labour" poster in the front room window,' Judith said. Although we knew the issues were important, some aspects of Dad standing for the council were embarrassing.

The polling station on our estate was made up of tents, which were put up for the day on the waste ground behind the shops. Poll-checking involved jumping out at voters as they entered or left the polling booths, asking for their voting numbers. If people didn't have their number with them, we had to ask for their address. We had little yellow pads to write it all on, which was stupid as we were Labour and yellow was a Liberal colour.

The afternoon was a slow, lonely time to take numbers. But as it got near to five o'clock, things started happening. People who cycled to work swooped round the curve of the road and propped their bikes against the kerb, nipping in to vote before going home for their tea. Those who'd got off the bus at Sperry Drive arrived in waves.

Then, walking carefully from the back of the shops, came Sylvie and Mrs Weston.

I bent down and retied my shoe. I didn't want their polling number; I didn't want to ask them for it. I knew their address. I didn't need to talk to them. The sound of Sylvie wailing was still in my ears. The desperate way she had clutched at me. They disappeared into the yellow light of the tents.

Some people said that Mrs Weston hadn't been married herself, and that there had never been a Mr Weston. Sometimes customers in the shop waited to be served by Mrs Brady rather than have Mrs Weston serve them. My

dad said that was bally stupid, and once or twice he specifically waited for Mrs Weston to serve him. 'No, no,'
he said, 'I'd like Mrs Weston to cut the Cheddar for me
today.' Or, 'Mrs Weston, you always seem to choose the
best biscuits.' In fact, we never had that much cheese and
there were always too many Nice and not enough custard creams, whoever put them in the bag. But after that
people didn't mind who served them. But they still murmured about Sylvie, crossed the road to avoid passing her
in the street. Sandra said she'd seen someone nearly fall
over on the bus, trying to move when Sylvie sat down
next to her.

I didn't want to be like those people, but I wasn't sure
how Sylvie was going to behave. When she and Mrs Weston
came out of the tent I pretended to be looking across the
field as if I could see a whole gang of people surging forward to put their cross in the box. But Sylvie said, 'It's Linda!
Linda! Hello!'

She had made an effort and she looked quite nice –
for someone with a beehive hairdo. Her maroon lipstick
matched her maroon mohair coat. She was wearing black
high heels and her legs were really long. The Conservative poll checker's eyes followed her across the mud as she
walked towards me.

'Do you want our numbers?' she said. 'I don't know if
we've got them.'

'It's all right,' I said. 'I know your address.'

'Oh, that's good.' She looked round conspiratorially. 'Who are you collecting numbers for?'

'Labour, of course,' I said.

'Of course, of course. And that's good because they've got our vote, haven't they, Mum?' she said. I liked her for that.

Mrs Weston smiled and started to walk away. Sylvie hovered.

'I haven't seen you for a little while, Linda. Why don't you come and see me sometime, as they say in the movies?'

My stomach clenched. I smiled stupidly.

'You don't have to take Mansell out, come round for a cup of tea. You know, I sometimes feel the need to reimmerse myself in the outside world, and you're just the girl to do it.' She paused. 'With the help of Rat, Trap and Dapper.'

I smiled in spite of myself.

'And I owe you sixpence.'

She'd remembered. 'Do you?' I said, carelessly.

'Anyway, chicken,' she said, 'do come. I want to know about that lovely Valentine card. Did you find out who sent it?'

I shrugged. 'I'm not sure. What about yours?'

'Who knows? Will you come?'

'I'll try. I don't know how much time I'm going to have, though, because I'm – I'm trying to get a job,' I said wildly.

'A job! Oh, Linda!' She frowned. 'You're not leaving school, are you?' She seemed genuinely concerned.

'No such luck,' I said. 'I want to get a Saturday job. And other times too, possibly.'

'Well, that's exciting. You see, we have so much to talk about! And I love those trews on you,' she said. 'They're rather French. Come when you can.'

She blew me a kiss and walked over to where her mum stood waiting. Mrs Weston waved her hand limply in my direction, and they disappeared.

Despite the really embarrassing election posters in the windows and the clumsy wooden loudspeaker contraption roped onto the roof, it was comforting to see our car pull up. 'Judith's come to relieve you,' Mum said. 'Bring your pad with you, she's got her own.'

Mum and I drove to the Committee Rooms for our ward. It was basically Ron Bales' front room. Five or six people with their coats on stood looking at the Bales' dining table, which was covered with pages of the electoral roll. The columns were marked with an intricate pattern of blue, red and orange crayon. The colours indicated the party allegiance of the people who had answered their doors to the Labour Party canvassers and said who they were going to vote for.

Ron Bales was a big man who always had a pencil or a cigarette tucked behind his ear. As we arrived he was saying loudly, 'Although many people have been canvassed – and thank you, Joanne and Gordon, for your sterling work . . . oh, and Vera, too, welcome,' he added as he noticed my mum, 'and those people assured everyone that they intended to vote Labour, the numbers that our poll checkers have collected – thanks to all involved – indicate that not many have actually got off their backsides to do it. Everyone available is needed to go knocking up. Get those voters out. They know they want to. The pretty ones' – he looked across at me – 'get to stay behind and continue the all-important job of checking numbers against addresses, which is therefore what I shall be doing. And Linda, you can help me with that.' We all laughed.

He was handing out lists of addresses, matching people who had cars with those who had red rosettes, when Dad appeared. 'The man himself!' Ron boomed. 'And if you've come here looking for a cup of tea, there's no time. It's all going very well, but you and Vera should go out with the loudspeaker.'

I cringed. The loudspeaker again.

'Come on, Vera,' Dad said. 'Duty calls.' There was a smattering of applause as they left.

Half past six was the time when people who had gone straight home from work to have their tea might start thinking about coming out to vote. That's when it began to rain. People came into the Committee Rooms from the polling stations, shrugging the rain off their macs, with half-empty sheets of numbers.

Ron looked through the net curtains to the street. 'Well, there goes Harry's seat.'

Mrs Bales said, 'Ron!' and looked over at me.

'Political reality is a hard lesson to learn,' Ron said to the room in general. 'The sooner you do, the better.'

The atmosphere was damp and depressed. Nobody even asked for a cup of tea. Every now and then Dad's voice sounded outside in the street, 'Vote Labour, vote Piper'. People who hadn't been sent to knock up looked out of the window, gazing at the sky.

Ron said, 'This is why I don't believe in God, because if he exists he's obviously a Conservative.'

His wife looked at him, then looked at me.

'Well, I suppose it could be worse,' he said. 'It could be snowing.'

People laughed.

I was stretching across the table, over the spread of pages from the electoral roll, trying to find the number 3468 when Ray came in. For a moment I forgot that he lived here and I looked at him in surprise. I hoped he wouldn't say anything embarrassing.

'Watcha,' he said to me. 'Nice trews.'

It sounded sarcastic. 'They're French,' I said brazenly. I didn't think he could seriously be making derogatory comments about my trousers, given his own taste in jumpers. But I had liked him once, and in fact, as he stood there in their front room in the midst of all the old Labour Party people, he looked like Little Joe from *Bonanza*. Quite nice. I couldn't continue the lie. 'French-ish,' I said. 'Almost French.'

He grinned.

'Ray, we need someone to go knocking up in the flats,' his mum said.

'I've only come in for my cigs,' he said.

'Take this list.'

'That's what you get for smoking,' I murmured.

'Do you want to come with me, Frenchy, and make sure I don't smoke while I'm talking?' he said to me.

'Linda's doing important work here,' Mrs Bales said. 'Get going.'

I was sorry about that.

At nine o'clock, after the polls had closed, Mum and Dad went to the Count – Mum dolled up with lipstick and powder that always made her smell so nice, and Dad in his big overcoat, his trilby tipped over his left eye. Mum said if we promised not to kill each other, Judith and I could stay downstairs till they got back. She put pillows and a blanket on the settee and we burrowed down in our pyjamas, head to toe, to wait for the result.

It was midnight and the fire had burnt down to grey ash when the sound of the key in the lock woke me up. I nudged Judith with my foot.

'Who's for a cup of celebration tea?' Dad called as he and Mum hung up their coats in the hall.

Judith and I cheered.

'Oh, Harry, it's late,' Mum said.

'Mum!' Judith and I moaned.

'Just this once,' Dad said.

Mum went into the kitchen and Dad laid two extra pieces of coal on the fire and put his finger to his lips so that Mum didn't know.

The fire licked in the grate as we sat with cups of tea and a digestive biscuit and Dad told us the numbers – he'd got 1,791 votes to the Conservative's 1,308.

He took two spoons from the cutlery set in the sideboard drawer and began to play them, which he normally only did at Christmas, clicking them on his thigh, swaying from side to side, going 'Ha–cha!' and Judith and I got up and danced in our pyjamas in front of the fire. After five minutes Mum said, 'It's one o'clock!' and we had to go to bed.

CHAPTER 7

Sylvie's story

I HAD DECIDED I WASN'T GOING back to Sylvie's. It was all so embarrassing and difficult, and having to be so careful not to upset her. But there was something about her, the things she said, the way she listened to me as if what I said was important. I'd never met anyone like her before.

A week later it was raining when I got home from school and I had forgotten my key. Judith was playing hockey. Sandra was of course at work. There was nowhere to go. And I quite missed seeing Mansell. So I left my school bag under an old sheet in our shed and went down to the Crescent.

The house looked grey and cold in the rain. I huddled under the narrow strip of concrete over the door that was meant to be a porch, and knocked. Again I had to wait. I looked down at the daffodils in the small square of earth beside me and realised they were plastic.

The door opened the merest crack.

Sylvie's face peeped through.

'Hello?' Her voice was a croak. She was holding a brown matted cardigan tightly at her throat.

She stared at me, then began to close the door.

'Sylvie!' I said. 'It's me! Linda.'

'Linda? Oh, Linda.' Her face relaxed. 'Linda, hello.' She opened the door and peered out behind me. 'Come in,' she said, and I stepped inside. 'I thought you were the never-never man.'

'In a school beret?' I said.

Quietly she closed the door. 'We are a little behind in our payments.' She looked down. 'I'm afraid you find me rather *déshabillé*. I was just having a lie-down.' A faded petticoat hung limply under the washed-out cardigan. 'What are you doing here?' she said doubtfully.

'I forgot my key and I'm locked out of our house.' Suddenly I felt very sorry for myself.

'Oh, chicken,' she said, 'and you're soaked! Let's have a cup of tea. We can cheer each other up and listen to some music.'

I wiped my feet and looked over at Mansell's empty pram beside the stairs.

'Mansell was having a sleep next to me.' She cocked her head towards the stairs and murmured, 'He's still dozing. You go into the kitchen and put on the kettle. I'll nip up and change into something less comfortable. Then we'll both feel better.'

When she came back downstairs she was wearing a pink sloppy mohair jumper over a tight skirt that showed her knees. She was carrying Mansell on her hip, and looked like an advert for a loving mum with a baby who drinks Carnation milk.

'Don't you think he's handsome?'

Mansell gazed at Sylvie as if she was the only person in the world. I put the cups and the teapot on the table.

'So we won,' I said, picking a milk bottle out of the bucket and looking round for something to catch the drips.

'What did we win?'

'The election. My dad got in.'

'Election?' She thought for a moment. 'Your dad?' She wiped dribble from the baby's chin with her finger and handed me a muslin nappy.

'Yes, you voted for my dad. Well, you said you did.'

'Was that your dad? The Labour candidate? What was his name? Piper.'

'Harry Piper.'

'Yes, yes, of course we voted for him. And he won? Linda, that's wonderful. I'm even more honoured to have you here. We should really be drinking champagne.'

'My mum would go mad.' I stopped abruptly. I'd used the word 'mad'. I shook my head. Sylvie didn't seem to notice. 'When I've poured the tea we can clink our cups.'

'Very sensible.' She sounded as if she'd prefer champagne. 'No wonder you're a political animal. You obviously imbibed Labour politics with your mother's milk.'

'Maybe,' I muttered, embarrassed at the thought. 'I worked a lot of it out for myself.'

'I'm sure you did. I'm not criticising,' she said. 'It's just that there's not a lot of political debate on this estate.'

'There is in our house,' I said. 'All the time. Breakfast, dinner and tea.' I knew our house was different: my dad stood for the council, we took the *Daily Herald*, though now it was the *Sun*, and the *Sunday Citizen*, we had books everywhere in the house and a set of Arthur Mee's Encyclopaedias. Judith and I went to the High School. We would stay on and take exams ... We were so different.

'How lucky you are.'

'Yeah.'

'So your dad's a Labour councillor. That's fantastic.'

'It's not that good.' I knew it was good, but I didn't want to boast. And often talking about it just made me feel even more of an outsider.

'Don't be afraid of being different,' Sylvie said. 'It will stand you in good stead.'

'Maybe,' I said reluctantly. 'You take a lot of sugar, don't you?'

'Well, three,' she said. 'Don't look like that! How many do you have?'

'I stopped taking sugar years ago,' I said proudly, 'because . . .' Suddenly I felt stupid.

'Because what? Are you diabetic?'

'No. Because I thought it was . . . more sophisticated not to take it.'

Sylvie laughed. 'Don't hang your head, chicken, that's the kind of thing you do when you're twelve.'

'I was eleven,' I said.

'Eleven! That's impressive. Well, I was twelve when I started playing poker. I thought that was a very sophisticated thing to do.'

'Poker!' Poker was gambling. Poker was . . . bad. 'I don't play cards,' I said.

'One day I'll teach you how to play poker,' she said. 'But you'd better watch out. It can get you into big trouble. Let's listen to some music,' she said. 'You hold Mansell. I'll bring the tea.'

Mansell was warm and heavy in my arms. I kissed the top of his head; it smelt of baby soap. Sylvie picked up the two cups and led the way into the living room. She put the cups on the sideboard and slid a Frank Sinatra LP onto the turntable.

I took a breath. 'Will you tell me about Mansell's dad?'

Sylvie's face didn't change. 'Are you really interested? Or are you just after the gossip?'

'I know the gossip,' I said. 'I'd like to know the real story.' It sounded clumsy and intrusive as I said it. 'But you don't have to tell me. Only if you want to.'

She picked up the LP cover and stared at it. 'What is the gossip?'

'Oh, you know. That – that you don't know . . . who he is, I mean, that you don't want people to know. That, that perhaps he's someone famous!' I added.

'That last one I think you've made up for yourself.' She dropped into an armchair.

'He could be,' I said. 'Mansell could be Tommy Steele's love child.'

She laughed. 'He wasn't famous. He was . . . American. Let's say.'

'Where did you meet him? Did you meet him in this country?'

'I met him, I met him . . . We should drink our tea.'

I didn't want her to change the subject. 'Did you know him for long before, before –'

'Before Mansell? I suppose it depends what you mean by long. I probably hadn't known him long enough.' She went to the sideboard, picked up the two cups of tea and handed one to me.

'Were you going out with him? Were you engaged?' Suddenly I wanted it to be an ordinary story – they'd been in love, they were planning a wedding and they got carried away. Then she realised she didn't want to marry him and he didn't want to marry her and that was all there was to it. I didn't want it to be dramatic. I didn't want him to be a soldier, a fighter. I didn't want him to be a hero. A dead hero. 'Is he still alive?' I said.

She gave a short, exasperated laugh. 'I'm sure he is.'

'Is he in America?'

'Not as far as I know. Do you really want to talk about this? It's quite a boring story. Why don't we talk about something else? Your future career, or the film that's on at the Select at the moment? With Julie Christie in. What's it called?'

'You mean *Darling*. I'd rather hear about – what's his name?'

She laughed. 'We could play cards. I know, why don't we make today the day I teach you to play poker?'

'In here?'

'Or in the kitchen.'

'You can teach me one day, but tell me your story now. Why won't you? It's Mansell's story too.' Was I whining?

'Yes, I suppose it is.' She sighed. 'I don't know why I'm so reluctant to tell you.' She tugged a loose thread on the armchair.

'I won't tell anyone else.'

'Won't you?'

I thought about it. I would want to tell Sandra. I would really want to tell Sandra. I might tell my mum, if it was a sad story. I looked at her.

'Well, it was, in fact, playing cards that caused my . . . downfall.'

'Cards?'

'At a casino.' The music had stopped. The room was silent apart from the low whirring of the electric fire.

'What were you doing at a casino? Were you working there?'

'Em, no, not then. I did work in a casino once, but not then. I met him when I was on holiday.'

'With your mum?'

'No.'

'What did happen to your dad?'

'Questions, questions. My dad died. In the war. So my mum says. They didn't get married, though he loved her with all his heart. But that makes me a bastard too, as my Uncle Peter would say. It must run in the family.'

'There's nothing wrong with being a . . . bastard.' It was hard to say the word; it was so harsh and ugly, as well as being a swear word. Mansell was asleep trustingly in my arms. It seemed wrong to use a word like that to describe him. It seemed wrong to think of Sylvie like that, or to call her a tart, like the husband and wife from the flats did when they went past the shop. 'It's not your fault. It's not Mansell's fault. Anyone can make a mistake.'

'I wish everyone thought like that.' She laughed. 'Life would be a lot simpler.'

'It's what my mum says,' I said.

'Your mum sounds so nice.'

'To other people. I think she'd kill me if I came home pregnant.'

'She only makes you think that so you don't do it. But if you did, I'm sure she'd be all right.'

I wasn't going to take any bets on that. 'What do you wear to a casino?'

'A very pertinent question. Where do I start? Well, are you sitting comfortably?' Sylvie looked out of the window.

We were staying in a boarding house in Great Yarmouth, me and my friend Janet. It was her auntie's boarding house. We'd just finished our secretarial courses, and Janet's auntie had said we could come up for a few days' holiday as a treat. And then, when we arrived, there were two Americans staying there too – one for each of us, Janet said. But mine was nicer. He was tough and good-looking, like Humphrey Bogart. He had green eyes and a low laugh that burst out when someone said something funny.

I don't really remember the other one. Short and fat, probably. Very different, anyway.

They were airmen, stationed at a base in Norfolk, I don't remember the name. We were only staying for a few days, till the weekend, so we had to work fast. There was a dance in the ballroom in town, and in order to make sure the

Americans went to it, Janet said, 'Why don't we make a leaflet!' So we did. The leaflet said, *Dance! Saturday! Be there or be square!!* and Janet illustrated it with a girl in a skirt with lots of petticoats and a boy in a shirt with rolled-up sleeves, jiving together.

It was pretty amateurish, but she said we had to have something. We couldn't ask them in person – that would have been too brazen. My job was to put it under the door of the airmen's room. But my airman opened the door as I was bending down. I felt so stupid, kneeling there, wearing a top that gaped at the neck.

'Well, hi there,' he said. His voice was smooth, like a film star. 'Or should I say, "Low there"?' He put his hand out to help me up. I remember thinking what a warm, dry hand it was. I stood up, dusting my knees, throwing looks at the rug on the lino, as if I'd been walking along the landing quite innocently and the rug had tripped me up on the polished floor. 'And what's this?' He bent down and picked up the leaflet.

'I don't know, what is it?' I twisted my head round and squinted at the piece of paper as if I'd never seen it before. 'Oh!' I said, 'look at that! It's for the dance at the ballroom in town tonight. Are you going?'

'Are you?'

'Oh, yes, we're going. My friend and I. My friend, Janet. I'm Sylvia . . . Sylvie, by the way. We're going.' Suddenly

I decided to call myself Sylvie – it just sounded so . . . so much more mysterious. And I suppose, in a way, I wanted to be mysterious.

He grinned. 'We'll probably see you there,' he said. 'Perhaps we could have a dance.'

The American way he said 'dance' made me shiver. 'Yes, perhaps we could,' I said, and I turned on my heel, glaring at the rug as I went.

Janet and I spent the afternoon pinning our hair into curls and drawing lines up the backs of our legs. Janet had to sit on a pile of cushions all afternoon, on top of her skirt, trying to press out the creases. I hung my dress by the window to blow out the wrinkles. We couldn't use the iron – we didn't want Janet's auntie asking questions. She was a bit square. She wouldn't have approved.

So, off we went to the dance, looking around the dance floor, but we didn't see anyone we recognised. So we danced together, all sorts of dances – modern, some skiffle, even a bit of Tommy Steele – not in person, in case you're wondering. This was mostly jazzy, and songs from the war. There were people of all ages there, it wasn't just young-sters. There were waltzes, and the cha-cha-cha.

'Did he know how to do those?' I asked.

'I don't know, because he wasn't there – not at first. Nei-ther of them was there. Janet and I were quite downhearted, and I began to think I should have stayed in Braintree with Kenny.'

'Who's Kenny?'

'He was my boyfriend. He wanted to marry me, and I wasn't sure, so Janet had said this would be a good time to think about it, on my own, calmly.'

'Why did you have to think about it?' I said. 'Didn't you know whether you loved him or not? If you had to think about it, it sounds like you didn't.'

'I'm afraid things aren't always that black and white, Linda. Marriage isn't just about love. And love doesn't inevitably lead to marriage.' She looked at Mansell. 'But anyway, I wasn't at home with Kenny. I was in Great Yarmouth, and I danced with a few country lads before I looked up in the middle of a foxtrot and saw the Yanks standing at the door, gazing round the room like two strangers in paradise.

'I apologised to my partner, I pretended I'd hurt my foot – which I had really, since he kept stepping on it – and I limped away. Of course, I stopped limping when I got to the edge of the dance floor. And I put on my smile and I walked round to greet them.

'"And don't you look good enough to eat?" he said.

'I knew I was looking nice. My hair was behaving itself, and my dress was simple but pretty, blue cotton with a yellow and blue pattern, a few petticoats underneath to make the skirt stick out, and I'd picked a flower from a display on the front as we walked to the hall, and I'd put it behind my ear.'

'What was his name?'

'His name. Well, I didn't know his name at that point.' She stretched. 'We'll do some more next time. And now I will put on a record to make you swoon. Johnny Mathis.'

'Perhaps I should leave now.'

She laughed. 'Don't make that face. You'll like it when you listen properly. But yes, you put Mansell down, and I'll switch on the hi-fi. It'll take a little while to warm up.'

'But that's rubbish,' Sandra said dismissively. We were upstairs on their landing, folding the washing, holding the ends of the sheets, moving backwards and forwards, making neat squares, almost dancing. It was a way of making up for our argument. She'd rung and asked if I wanted to have a good time. It was sorting laundry. She'd done the ringing and I was helping with the folding.

'Why is it rubbish?' Their sheets were pink, slithery Bri-nylon.

'For a start, when do people go to secretarial college? They go when they leave school, when they're fifteen or sixteen. Not when they're twenty-six or thirty-six, or however old she is.'

'They might do.'

'Yeah, that would look good, wouldn't it? "Take a letter, Miss Smith." "Ooh, sorry, I can't pick up my pencil, I've got rheumatism."'

'Twenty-six isn't that old. Do you think she's lying?'

'My mum says she lies to the doctors about when she's feeling well or ill, so no one knows what's going on.' Sandra put a folded sheet over the banister. 'And who's this Janet? I've never heard of her.'

'It's her friend. She probably hasn't heard of your friend Halina.'

Sandra grunted.

'Well, I don't care,' I said. I paused. Did I care? She was so much older than me, and lovely and sad that actually, no, it didn't matter to me. 'She's like a film star, like Audrey Hepburn or someone, talking about her last film,' I said. 'Perhaps it's true, perhaps it's not. It's a story. I just want to know what happens in the story. It doesn't matter if it's true. The stories don't hurt anyone.'

'You're the one who's always going on about telling the truth.'

'That's my mum.' I paused. 'Well, I suppose I think the truth is a good thing a lot of the time, but people don't always tell the truth. Danny lies to you all the time.'

'Oh, don't start that again.' She lifted up the pile of folded laundry. 'Nobody believes anything Danny says. If they do, they're stupid.'

'And I like Sylvie.' Sandra looked at me. 'She's different. She says interesting things.'

'That's nice.' Sandra's mouth turned down.

'And you're at work all the time. I have to talk to someone!'

'And you want to know who the dad is, don't you?'

'Not really.' But I was just being contrary. I was intrigued. Hearing the story of how they met was romantic. I wanted to find out as much as I could. I picked up the end of a trailing pillow case and followed Sandra downstairs. To find out would mean I'd have to keep going round there. But my mum would approve of that.

CHAPTER 8

'Good Morning Little School Girl'

ALL OF OUR YEAR HAD TO GO INTO the hall to hear a talk by the careers lady and then, later, go and see her individually.

The day she spoke to me I reeled home from school. I'd said stupid things. I felt stupid.

Sylvie was wheeling the pram out of the shop as I walked up the road. 'Hello, Linda!' she said, squinting in the watery sun. 'What a nice surprise. Have you got time for a cup of tea?'

'I don't think I'll be very good company.'

'Oh, chicken, why ever not? Bad day at school?'

'The careers lady came.'

'Oh, that's interesting.' We walked into the Crescent. Sylvie unlocked the front door. 'Now you push the pram in – gently, or he'll wake up – and I'll put the kettle on and then you can tell me all the exciting things they've suggested to you.'

'It's not what they suggested to me. It's what I said to them.'

'Aha! They didn't like it, I can tell.'

I slumped into a chair at the kitchen table and tore off my beret.

'So.' Sylvie was filling the kettle at the sink. The water hitting the aluminium base made a hollow roaring sound. 'Did you tell them you were going to follow your dad into politics?'

'Not likely. All those meetings he has to go to.'

'Did you tell them you wanted to be a racing driver?'

'No!'

'Be a woman of importance?'

'Huh!' I said.

'What did you say?'

'I said I wanted to be a housewife.'

Slowly Sylvie put the kettle on top of the stove. When she turned round her face was a mixture of curiosity and concern.

'Don't look like that,' I pleaded. 'I didn't mean it. I didn't know what to say, I didn't know what she wanted me to say. I always feel wrong at school. So I said what I thought everyone in the class was aiming for. Their mums don't go to work. They all talk about getting married and having children. And I know I could do it – I got all those badges in Guides.'

Sylvie began spooning tea into the teapot. I got the feeling she wasn't listening, but I carried on speaking to myself, in a bitter whisper. 'It's what they all talk about all the time. I never join in. I'm always on the outside, with my CND badge and being bad at games and my dad being a Labour councillor. I don't care, but when you're face to face with someone . . . If I'd said what I really want to be, she'd have thought I'd got ideas above my station.'

'Oh, Linda!'

'And then it turned out everyone else said things like teacher or librarian or air hostess, even. They looked at me as if I was . . .' I stopped. 'As if I was strange.' Sylvie was pouring boiling water into the pot. 'What do you think?' I said.

'Well, I think housework is probably not the best use you can make of your time. But then, you only need to look round this house to know I think that. What do you really want to do with your life?'

I looked at her. Could I tell her? Should I tell her?

She was waiting. All the possibilities I dreamed of, that I wrote in very small writing in my diary – journalist, actress, traveller – seemed stupid. Would she think they were hopelessly out of my reach, a girl from a council estate who didn't know her place? I shrugged. 'A teacher, probably.'

'Teaching! That's good,' she said. 'But what else could you do? Let's think.'

I looked at her. She was being serious. Hesitantly I said, 'A journalist. Perhaps. A journalist in Africa.'

'That's an extraordinary thing to want to be.'

I blushed. I should have kept my mouth shut.

'No, I mean, that's a wonderful thing to want to do. How exciting. You could go to North Africa, Morocco or Algeria – and then, oh, you could go to the Sahara Desert. Or how about the Belgian Congo? Or the Ivory Coast?' She was really excited. 'There's so much to write about. Not a lot of women do it.'

I wished I hadn't said it – I knew almost nothing about Africa. Was Morocco really in Africa? 'It's just an idea,' I muttered, before she asked me anything, like where Nairobi was or the Panama Canal.

'But why is it just an idea? It could be a reality. You're smart, and you're very good with people.'

'Am I?'

'You talk sensibly to them and you get people talking to you. Look at me! I'm telling you all sorts of things.'

'Are you?'

'And then – well, what's your favourite lesson at school?'

I thought about it. 'French? English?'

'You're halfway there! You could write about the people you meet. If you're in France, or even one of the French colonies in Africa, you can speak to the people in their own language, find out their stories and then float down the rivers, or climb the mountains. You could write about the food. Or the clothes, even. You'd like that, wouldn't you?'

I wasn't sure. It was the first time I'd said it out loud, and it sounded different from the way it did in my head. I needed time to think about the implications. 'You should be the one to go,' I said.

'I would if I could,' she said. 'Oh, I would if I could. But I can't. So that's why you've got to do it.'

'But I'm just me,' I said. 'A mod from Chelmsford.'

'Everybody was somebody else at the beginning.'

'I don't even know where half those places are.'

'I don't know what they do teach you at that school of yours,' she said.

'Not very much at all,' I said. 'But that's not their fault, necessarily. I've dropped geography.'

'But that's the best part of it. You don't need geography lessons. You'll get to find out about places by actually being there. How do you think I know about Paris? Paris would be a great place to start. It's so easy to get to. You take the night train from Victoria Station in London. And you get off at Dover and walk onto the boat. It's so exciting.' She sighed as if she was remembering a journey of her own. 'Let's go through into the living room. You bring the tea, Dr Livingstone,' she said. 'I've decided my job will be to complete your education in the subjects they don't teach you at school.'

'I have quite a lot of homework,' I said uneasily, following her.

She was looking through the pile of LPs, which was messy again. 'Do you like modern jazz?' she said.

'I don't know.' I did know – I didn't like it – but I also knew that was not the right thing to say.

'This is Miles Davis.' She put the record on the turntable and the sound of a mournful trumpet filled the room.

It felt so lonely, it made me feel sad and almost anxious, but I didn't know if that was because I'd spoken aloud about my dream future, or if I was worried about Sylvie listening to the music.

'So, you like travelling.' She settled herself in an armchair. Then she spoke almost to herself. 'I'm so pleased you want to travel.' She looked at me. 'What other languages do you learn at school?'

'German,' I said. 'Latin.'

'So you've got French and German, that's good. And Latin will help you with other languages. So they say.' She leaned over the arm of the chair and knocked over a pile of books and slid them around. 'Look,' she said. 'This is a book I am reading at the moment, and I think you might like it. It's called *The Second Sex*.'

'Really?'

'Don't you know who Simone de Beauvoir is, my little radical?'

'Is she something to do with . . .?' I hoped Sylvie would fill in the gap.

'Jean-Paul Sartre. She's French.'

'Oh, it's the way you said it.'

She laughed. 'Very good! She's the leader of the new generation of suffragettes.'

I scoured my brain. 'That's votes for women, isn't it?'

'Yes, feminists. There are still countries where women don't have the vote. Switzerland, for example. Imagine that!' She looked at me with her eyebrows raised, to make sure I'd understood. 'But suffragettes didn't only want the vote, they wanted freedom and equality. Think about it. Until quite recently women teachers who got married had to stop teaching. Boom, just like that. Which is shocking, isn't it?'

It was shocking. We were living in the twentieth century. How could people not have the vote? Why should women not be able to teach if they were married?

'So you and I think it's shocking,' she went on, 'but surprisingly, that's very controversial, which is what we like, isn't it?'

I wasn't sure. I wasn't sure what she meant.

'The library had to order this book specially,' she went on. 'The librarian was looking all around as she gave it to me. I think she wanted to wrap it up in a paper bag.'

'Have you finished it?' I said, picking it up gingerly. It was a thick book and the print was small. Perhaps she'd only just started it and there wouldn't be time for me to look at it before it was due back at the library. I looked in the front. Oh no – there were two weeks to go. I thought hopefully that Mum wouldn't want me to read a book the librarian disapproved of, although Dad probably wouldn't care. He'd say, 'If it's printed on paper, read it. But with a question on your lips.' Oh, I knew I should read it. I knew it was important to fight injustice. I'd read a book about Elizabeth Fry, who had campaigned to reform prisons. I'd really liked that. But it was a much shorter book. Perhaps Sylvie could just tell me what it said.

'So did you meet Simone de Beauvoir when you went to France?' I said.

'France? Oh, no,' she said. 'Janet and I were so young and so innocent when we were in Paris. I don't think we would have had much to say to Simone.'

'Was that before or after you met Mansell's dad?'

'What? Paris?' She gave a short laugh. 'Oh yes, that was the trouble. In Paris we got a taste for all things exotic.'

'Like Mansell's dad?'

'A bit.'

'Was this before your secretarial course?'

She cocked her head to one side. 'Hmm, deep, probing questions. I'm sure there's a job you could do that requires that skill. You could be a detective.'

'Yeah, of course,' I said, but I toyed with the idea for a minute. WPC Piper. Then I said, 'So you and Janet were in France . . .'

'Do you know, I really don't remember much about Paris. It was another of our mad dashes . . . We'd decided we were singers. We went into a million bars asking for work until the *patron* of a tiny place, I think it was near the Sacré Coeur, said we could step in for one night. And so we did, there and then. His usual person had let him down. The accompanist was there – he had an accordion and smelt of sausage and garlic.' She paused and looked over at Mansell's pram in the hall. 'We had hardly any songs in our repertoire, songs that we knew the words of, that is. There was . . .' She looked up at the ceiling. "Every Time We Say Goodbye". And . . . I think . . . "You Do Something To Me", and, of course, "I Love Paris". The rest we just la-la'd our way through.'

'Were there lots of people?' I wasn't sure if it was true. In spite of what I'd said to Sandra, I wasn't sure I wanted to hear completely made-up stories.

'It was a room hardly any bigger than this, just like in all the films, dark and shady, with little orange lamps and full of French people all drinking wine and eating horse.'

'Horse!'

'I don't know, probably. And we didn't start till about ten o'clock at night. I was almost asleep. We were so young.' She was smiling. 'We'd put on lots of red lipstick and very tight black dresses we'd got from C&A in Oxford Street.'

'That's where I got my suede,' I said.

'That's nice.' She wasn't interested. I was interrupting the flow.

'What did you call yourselves?'

'Sylvie and Jeanette. It was the first time I'd called myself Sylvie. It was so much nicer than Sylvia.'

'But how did the man with the accordion know what to play?'

'Fortunately, he was an Ella Fitzgerald fan. "Ah, Ey-La!" he said every time we suggested something, although he played a bit strangely.' She smiled again and shook her head.

'And how did it go?'

'It went very well. We got lots of tips, and they asked us to come back.'

'And did you?'

'No, that night we got back to our hotel so late the manager wouldn't let us in. He shouted at us through the door.' She laughed. 'The trouble was, we had met some marines in the bar. We should never have taken them with us. The manager mouthed, "*Putains!*" through the glass, which means, as you probably haven't learned at school, prosti-tutes. So we had nowhere to stay, and of course, we'd spent all our tips, which meant we had no money, and nor did the marines, and so when they asked us to go down to Nice with them, we said yes.'

'You didn't!'

'No, we didn't. We said we'd meet them at the Gare d'Austerlitz, but we skedaddled.'

'Was that Mansell's dad?'

'Oh no, these were French marines. Or perhaps they were in the Foreign Legion.' She frowned. 'So after a night on a bench at the Gare du Nord, we came home. Back to dear old Chelmsford. And I was sick on the boat all the way down my coat.'

'But what about your things? At the hotel?'

'Oh, we donated them to the manager's wife. Somewhere in North Paris is a woman who is probably still wearing a St Michael's vest and a green cardigan with an unravelling sleeve.'

'When was this?' I could hear Sandra asking the question.

'It was a long, long time ago.'

'Years?'

'Oh, yes.'

'How many?'

She yawned. 'I really can't remember.'

It was time to go. I stood up.

'Don't forget the book.' She picked it up and followed me into the hall. The haunting trumpet wafted after her. I put the book in my school bag.

'I love that beret,' Sylvie said, as I clipped it back on my head.

'You're joking, aren't you?'

'Well, perhaps a little bit.' She leaned against the door and fluttered her hand in a wave as I walked down the path.

'You're getting very matey, aren't you?' Sandra said that evening. We were on the bus into town. 'I don't know why you want to hang around with someone who's so old.'

'She's not that old. And I don't hang around with her. I just talk to her. She's . . . she's lent me a book.'

'Well, just watch out. I mean, when did she actually decide to call herself Sylvie? When she met the French, or when she was expecting?'

'I don't know.'

'Well, when did she go to France? And all that about the marines, did she show you any proof? A sailor's cap or a tattoo or the coat she was sick on?'

'It wasn't that kind of conversation. Anyway, it was years ago. She told me that much. It was just a story.'

Sandra sighed.

I'd told her about my afternoon at Sylvie's, but I hadn't told her about my experience with the careers lady. I could have told her I'd said I wanted to be a housewife. But I couldn't tell her how upset I was that I'd said it. A housewife was what Sandra would be once she got married to Danny, and she knew what I thought about that. I certainly couldn't tell her what I really wanted to do, because she'd laugh. And she'd be jealous. We both still talked about our dream of getting away, the two of us on a scooter, driving around England, getting jobs where we could, spending the summer by a beach. We both knew it would never happen.

Danny was coming out of the Orpheus as we were crossing the bridge in London Road, and seemed as surprised as we were. He wasn't meant to be here. He frowned. Then he said, 'It's my best girls! Hey, tell you what – let's go up to Moulsham! It's their youth club tonight.'

'Moulsham?' I said. 'We've just got off the bus. We're going down the Orpheus.'

'Shut up, you,' Sandra said.

'Yeah, come on, girls. You don't want to go down there. We can get the bus.'

'But Moulsham!' I said. 'By the time we get up there, it'll be time to go home.'

Nobody said anything.

'For me to go home.'

Silence.

'So I might as well go home now.' I said. 'Cheerio, then,' I said. I could have stayed, but I knew it would be at least a shilling to get up there, then we'd have to pay to get in, and unless there was someone with a scooter who'd passed his test we'd have to pay to get home and probably end up getting a taxi. I couldn't afford all that. Not if I wanted to go to the Corn Exchange on Saturday. And I did have some Latin verbs to learn. If I went home now I might even have a chance of remembering them for tomorrow's test.

As Sandra and Danny crossed the road, Sandra turned and grinned at me. Behind his back she waved the third finger of her left hand. She hadn't given up the plan. Then she tucked her arm through his and they disappeared round the corner.

I watched them for a moment, then walked back along London Road and turned into Tindal Street. Though I couldn't understand what she saw in him, I could imagine how nice it would be to have someone, someone you cared about so much you wanted them to put a ring on your finger. But here I was, on my own, with no one. I felt sad and abandoned, but I quite liked it. Sometimes it was good to be alone in town, on a cold clear night like tonight. The evening felt full of possibilities; anything might happen, even just walking home. I could meet anyone.

And there he was.

At the far end of the cobbled street, right by the Corn Exchange, was Tap, leaning against the passenger door of his Mini, his suede coat bundled around him, smoking.

This was my chance. I would talk to him. It was fate. But it was terrifying. What would I say? Would he even reply? He might be waiting for someone, and not want to be seen talking to me. But he might say hello. We might even chat. Why not? Linda Piper the fearless, probing journalist wouldn't be intimidated, nor would Linda Piper the mountain-climbing, desert-crossing traveller. At the very least I'd have something to tell Sandra.

How should I start the conversation? Hello, Tap, I rehearsed in my head. Hi Tap. Watcha Tap. Remember me? I'm the girl with the caramel-coloured nylon mac, but look at me now! Look at my suede! I bought it in London. Up West.

'Hi, Tap,' I said.

He stared at me.

'I'm Linda.'

He looked at me. I wondered if he recognised me at all.

'I'm a friend of Sandra's.'

He nodded slowly.

'Danny Mulroney's girlfriend.'

He snorted. 'Which one are we talking about? You're not a mate of Barbara's, are you?'

Barbara again! 'No, Sandra.'

He shook his head. 'Danny Mulroney's girlfriend Sandra. Interesting.'

'Yes,' I said, uncertainly.

'So, Danny Mulroney's girlfriend Sandra's friend . . .'

'Linda . . .'

'Linda, what can I do for you?'

'I wondered if you'd seen her, Sandra.' It sounded lame, even to me.

'Not sure I'd recognise the girl.' He glanced up and down the empty street as if he was looking for her. 'What's Danny up to these days?' he said, conversationally.

'You know, the usual. Fighting, getting drunk, winding people up.'

He laughed. 'That sounds about right. If you see him, tell him he owes me five quid and then some.'

'OK,' I said, doubtfully.

'Who do you say he's going out with now?'

'Sandra.'

'Well, well. Is that your mate – the one with the brown leather?'

'Yes.' He did know who she was. Who I was.

'No, I haven't seen her.' He looked up and down the street again.

I stood uncomfortably, not sure what to do. 'Are you waiting for someone?' I said.

He looked at his watch. 'Not anymore. You're Linda, right?'

'Yes.'

'Where you off to now then, Linda?' he said.

'The bus station.'

'Get in,' he said. 'I'll drive you up there.'

He opened the passenger door for me – no one had ever done that before – and I got in while Tap walked round to the driver's side.

The Mini smelt of leather and new seats. It was pristine, clean and uncluttered, not like our car with sweet wrappers and elastic bands everywhere. Tap got in, carefully tucking his coat round him, and started the car.

Expertly he turned the steering wheel with the flat of his hand. In silence we drove into Market Road, round the back of the Golden Fleece, past the posh bogs and into Victoria Street. I sat neatly, trying to be calm and cool sitting next to Chelmsford's top mod.

As we drove under the railway bridge, he said, 'You meeting someone up here?'

'Unless you mean the driver of the 311, no,' I said. 'I'm going home.'

'Where do you live?'

'The Hayfield Estate.'

'All right then, Lorna, I'll drive you home,' he said.

'Linda. Thank you.'

We sailed past the bus station.

'So, Linda, where do you work?'

I hated this question. I hated answering it; it made me feel about twelve. Sometimes I wished I could just leave school and work in a bank. Or even become a housewife. At least then I'd have something to do. I took a deep breath. 'I'm at school. I'm – I'm staying on.'

'A schoolgirl,' he said. '"Good morning, little school-girl".' He tapped the beat of the song on the steering wheel. '"Good morning, little schoolgirl".'

I wondered if he was high; why else would he be taking me home and chanting a song at me? People said Tap was a dealer. I didn't know if that was true, but I knew about drugs, knew the names – purple hearts, black bombers – and what they did, uppers, downers. But I didn't take them, nor did Sandra. Nobody ever offered them to us. I didn't even know what they looked like. But I knew people who took them, and I knew what they looked like when they did. Tap didn't look wide-eyed and loose. He fumbled in the pocket of his suede and pulled out a packet of Embassy cigarettes, flipped open the pack and shook one into his mouth. 'Smoke?'

'No,' I said. 'Not at the moment.' As if I'd ever smoked.

He pulled out a box of matches. 'Light this for me, will you?' he said.

I tried to remember the cool way to strike a match, towards you or away from you. Which way? I struck the match towards me, cupped the flame in my other hand and moved across to him. As I held the match towards his mouth I smelt Brut aftershave, sharp and cold. He put his hand over mine and steadied the match. He sucked on the cigarette.

I pushed down my window and threw the match into the street. I wanted to stick my head out and shout that I was having a cigarette with a mod in a Mini. Not just any mod. Tap! From The Boutique!!

'Do you like having a Mini?' It was something to say.

'I'm going to get rid of it,' he said.

'What for?' I couldn't think of anything better than a Mini.

'Something bigger. I've got my eye on an American Chevy up at the air base.'

'With the steering wheel on the other side? Are you allowed to drive cars like that?'

'Yeah. Why not? If they stopped me I could say I was American, couldn't I?' He put on a Jimmy Cagney accent. 'Just give me the money, you dirty rat.'

'Well, you could . . .'

'Gee, thanks.' He pushed down his window and with a twist of his wrist flicked ash from his cigarette.

'Is that how your manager talks?'

'Eddy? Nah. He's London through and through.'

'From what people said I thought he was American.' Everyone in the Orpheus was talking about the new manager in The Boutique, Eddy – his clothes, his walk, his voice. 'What's he like?'

'He's all right. He's just taken my job, that's all.' He inhaled sharply.

The atmosphere had changed.

'Did you want to be the manager? I mean, did you apply for the job?'

'No, mate, it was all done over my head. They just told me he was starting the next Monday.'

'But what about you?'

'They said I was the stylist. I'm the one who has to bring in the young customers.'

'But that's good, isn't it? Because you are a Stylist.' Stylists were the really big mods.

'Yeah, I know.' He nodded. 'We've got some good Ben Shermans in at the moment, that I chose. We sold six today.'

'There you are.'

'You sound like my nan.'

'Oh.'

Tap switched on the radio. It was Radio Luxembourg and 'Please Please Me' was playing.

'Like this?' he said.

'Not really,' I said.

'No, nor do I.' We both laughed.

'I like blues,' I said hesitantly. What if he said he didn't?

'Me too,' he said, easily. 'Who do you like?'

'Howlin' Wolf,' I said, 'Muddy Waters.' I'd heard them on Radio 390, a pirate radio station.

'Yeah! All right!' he said. He turned and looked at me.

I directed him off the Main Road, onto our estate. As we approached the shops, I said, 'You'd better park here.'

He pulled up in front of Roberts'. I wondered if he would switch off the engine or keep it running while I got out. He switched the engine off. Otis Redding was singing 'I've Been Loving You Too Long'. 'I like this,' I whispered.

'So do I,' he whispered back. He leaned across and put his arm round me and pulled me to him. He kissed me lightly on the lips. He put his head back and looked at me. He smiled. 'I remember this.' He flicked my badge with the tip of his finger. 'Ban the bomb, then. Do you go on the marches? Have those sit-down protests?'

'I go on the marches. I haven't done much sitting down. Except, you know, when I have my tea. But that's not really a protest. Except when it's sardines.' It was a joke. I hoped he got it.

'I'd join you in that one.' He laughed. 'How old are you?'

I looked at him, his face so close to mine, the sharp aftershave smell in my nostrils. 'Old enough.'

'Really?' He kissed me again. His tongue licked my lips but I kept my mouth closed, and he moved back in his seat and started the car.

The lift was over. 'Thanks for bringing me home,' I said, not sure if I was relieved or disappointed.

'Yeah,' he said. I got out of the car. I pushed the door closed.

'Hey, Lorna!' he said.

I opened the door.

'Did you send me a Valentine's card?'

'Why?'

'I got some mad card.'

So Sandra had sent a stupid card. 'No, it wasn't me. If I'd sent you a card it would have said "You're a real Stylist. Be my Valentine".'

He laughed. 'That's not very romantic.'

'I don't know you very well.'

'We'll have to see about that. Bye.'

The Mini drove off up the road.

'When, though? When will we see about that?' I said to myself, walking up to our house. The street was empty and silent.

I was opening the garden gate when the Mini came back. It screeched to a halt and Tap pushed down his window. 'How the fuck do I get out of here?' he shouted.

I opened my eyes wide. Everyone in the street would hear. I crept up to the car and whispered, 'Down there, turn right, turn left and then you're at the main road.'

'OK, babe. Come into the shop sometime. Nice coat, by the way. Better than the mac.'

He couldn't remember my name, but he remembered my mac. It was something.

CHAPTER 9

Poetry in Motion

THE NEXT DAY IN SCHOOL, after lunch, Miss Reeves, our old form teacher, walked through the dining room. 'Have you wiped the table?' she said.

'Yes.'

'What's this then?' She held up her hand.

'Looks like three fingers with water on,' I said. I was still cheerful from the night before, and I was showing off to the others. Cray, my friend Christine Ray, snorted.

Miss Reeves said I was impertinent. She gave me a five-minute lecture on the meaning and importance of respect for one's elders. She then said I had to go and see her just before lessons started that afternoon.

Her class of second-years stared at me as I stood at her desk. She asked me my name. She'd been my form mistress, but she didn't remember who I was. I wondered if it was because she hadn't seen me sitting at the back of the class, or that I rarely said anything, or simply that she didn't like me. She lectured me again about the need for politeness. She said I had to learn a poem.

It made me late for French. I tried to slip into the room while Miss Harmon was writing '*le hoquet*' on the blackboard. Everyone was laughing because Julia Gilbert actually had hiccups, but Miss Harmon turned with the chalk in her hand and gazed at me. She looked at her watch. '*Bienvenue*, Mademoiselle Linda,' she said.

'*Je m'excuse d'être en retard*,' I muttered. The apology for being late was one of the first sentences in French I'd had to learn. I went to the empty seat next to Cray.

'*Et pourquoi es-tu en retard?*' she said.

I looked desperately at Cray. '*Pourquoi*' meant why, that much I had made out. Cray stared back at me, wordlessly.

'Because . . .'

'*En français, s'il te plaît.*'

'*Parce que j'ai des problèmes?*' I said.

'Oh,' Miss Harmon said. '*Partage tes difficultés avec la classe, s'il te plaît.*'

What on earth had she said? '*Je ne regrette rien*,' I said, hopelessly.

'La Vie en Rose *est un peu trop pour toi, je crois.*' Miss Harmon sighed, and so did I. I had no idea what she was saying. 'You're a lazy little monkey, Mademoiselle Linda.

You could do so much better. You're good at French, but you do no work.'

I blinked at her.

'Yes, and I'm bothered,' I whispered to Cray when we were doing an exercise. 'There are two types of bothered, bothered and bothered, and I'm bothered.' Cray didn't understand moddy talk. But I was sorry Miss Harmon was disappointed, because French was my favourite lesson, even if I wasn't in the top division and even if people laughed when I tried to speak with a French accent. Did she mean I could be good at French? Did I have it in me? Was I clever? I hadn't been clever since I left primary school, where it had all been so easy. Sylvie thought I was clever. Was she right? Could I travel the world speaking French, have adventures, write about them?

At home after school Judith was sitting in the living room, reading. There was an hour before Mum got home. She had a temporary coding job at County Hall. 'The hoover's in the hall,' Judith said. 'And don't look like that, I've done upstairs already.'

'I wasn't born to do housework,' I said.

'Try telling Mum that.'

'I've had a horrible day at school –'

'Which was doubtless your own fault.'

'And hoovering the stairs is not going to make it better. I'm going out.'

'Someone has to clean everything,' Judith shouted after me.

I stomped out of the house. I wanted to talk to someone. I realised the person I wanted to talk to was Sylvie. I knocked on Sylvie's door.

'Thank goodness you've arrived,' Sylvie said, as if she'd asked me to come. She hung my coat in the hall and I followed her past Mansell, sleeping in his pram, into the living room. There was a swathe of red-and-white material on the floor. Flimsy pieces of paper pattern were pinned haphazardly onto it. 'It's a dress,' Sylvie said, waving a paper packet at me. On the front was a sketch of a very thin woman in pointed shoes, posing with her hand on her hip. She wore a dress with a tight bodice and a full, gathered skirt.

I frowned.

'I'm on an economy drive and I am henceforth going to make my own clothes. But I can't make head or tail of these instructions.' Sylvie handed me a large piece of paper with pale words and diagrams. 'Can you understand it?' She cocked her head on one side. 'If you decipher the code, you can borrow the pattern.'

I looked at her. I'd never wear anything in that style. 'You've chosen the hardest one,' I said. 'It's *Vogue*. They hardly tell you anything.' I knelt on the floor. 'You're supposed to cut the pattern into individual pieces first.' I raised my hand. Silently Sylvie handed me some scissors.

As I cut through the paper, following the faint outlines, Sylvie said, 'So how is your life? If I may say, you look a little disgruntled. Is that because you disagree with *Vogue*? Or have they moved you to the housewives' class in school?'

'Don't,' I said. 'Everything's horrible. I got into a load of trouble with two teachers today and they've both given me poems to learn.'

'Poems? That's a good thing to do. You must know poems.'

'But it's two.'

'If they're for different teachers, couldn't you just learn one? You must know one poem.'

'One of them has to be in French. I don't think my English teacher would appreciate a French poem. A French poem!'

'There are some lovely French poems, very romantic, passionate poems. You'd like them.'

'I don't think our French teacher would. I was thinking of "*Frère Jacques*".'

Sylvie made a face. 'I think we can do better than that.'

'And the English one has to have at least three verses, and I've got to do it by Monday.'

Sylvie wrinkled her nose. 'Shakespeare?'

'No.'

'I know – "How They Brought the Good News from Ghent to Aix".'

'Isn't that a really long poem? I'll be there till Christmas if I have to do that one. It's all just so boring.'

'Oh, chicken, I'm sure it's for your own good. The High School is a highly respected school. It's the best you can get. You really should make the most of your schooldays. Enjoy them, relish them.'

'Learning poems? If I apply for a job and they say, "What can you do?" and I say, "Not much, but I know two poems, one of which is in French," do you think they'll give me the job?'

'We-e-ell, it depends what it is.'

I rocked back on my heels. 'They're all so posh, the teachers, the girls. Even my friend Cray is posh. I don't want to be posh. I'm working class, and I'm proud of that.'

'I know it's not easy, but you should take as much as they will give you. And then you can show them! You can be a working-class success.'

'Yes, that's likely. The trouble is, I don't want to be a big swot. The girls who are swots have terrible hair and they don't care what their uniform looks like.' I reached for a jam jar of pins and looked for one that wasn't rusty. 'I suppose I just want to know everything, but not have to do all the work.'

'What a wonderful world that would be, if we could do that,' Sylvie said. 'Look, promise me you will try, do some homework, read those books.'

I looked at her. What did she want from me?

As if she'd read my mind, Sylvie said, 'It's not for me, it's for you. For your future.'

I was still rooting round in the jam jar. I stabbed myself in the finger. 'Ow!'

'And now you're bleeding. Chicken, you are in the wars. What can I do to cheer you up?'

I sucked my finger. 'You could tell me some more about how you met . . .'

Sylvie glanced over to the door. She could see Mansell in his pram. He was still asleep. She looked back at me, tilting her head on one side. 'You're such a funny one, getting me to tell you all my secrets. All right. Now then, where had we got up to . . .?'

I knew exactly where we'd got up to. They were at the dance, and he'd just arrived with his friend. So she said. Did I really want to know more? What strange and mysterious things would she tell me? But it was such a romantic story. I did want to know. 'You were just about to dance with him.'

'Oh, but I didn't.' She settled herself on the settee.

As I walked off the dance floor towards him, all smiles and looking forward to an interesting evening, a group of girls arrived, laughing and giggling and smelling of hairspray and perfume and Mum deodorant. They completely surrounded our two Yanks, and even though I sat out the next dance, waiting for him, he didn't come and find me. I thought, well, that's it. I threw my cardigan round my shoulders and slid across the floor to Janet, who was dancing with someone who looked like a vicar, and told her I was going home. I walked back to the boarding house on my own, under the stars, listening to the sound of the waves rushing onto the shore.

'But it can't have ended there,' I said.

'Patience, my little chickadee,' Sylvie said.

It was the next night. Janet and I went to the pub near the boarding house. I was wearing my favourite red lipstick, 'French Passion' it was called, and a halterneck dress. The skin on my back was quite tight and hot from the sun. And lo and behold, he was in there with his friend. I had no idea he'd be there. Janet went straight up to the bar to order the drinks. She stood right beside them. Suddenly I felt shy and I crept over to the corner and perched on the edge of a bench seat.

'Two Martinis, please,' Janet ordered in a loud voice. She was always the pushy one.

The barman turned towards the row of bottles behind him.

'You don't want a Martini, gal,' one of the Yanks said. 'There's no point, there's no ice in this country.'

'OK, cancel that,' Janet said, without looking at them. 'I'll have two glasses of wine. White wine. *Vin blanc.*' We'd been to France, we knew the lingo.

The barman turned back and looked at her with a frown. 'You mean, ginger wine?' he said.

'Ginger wine! That sounds exciting,' one of the Americans said. 'Hey sweetie, are you old enough to drink?'

Janet said, 'I'm old enough for a lot of things.' She glanced across at me. 'We both are.'

'OK then, let's all have ginger wine.'

Janet turned and winked at me. I didn't know what to do with my face. I was thrilled he was there, but I was afraid he'd think we were chasing them. Janet came back and scolded me for my lack of effort. 'I was doing all that work for you,' she said, handing me a glass.

It tasted like cough medicine. 'This is revolting,' I said. 'Why did you get this?'

'It's a drink, isn't it? It was all they had.' Janet sipped from her glass. 'Oh, it is horrible. Ooh.' We began to laugh.

Then, to top it all, the barman brought over two more. 'From those jokers,' he said. He tipped his head towards the Americans. I noticed a ten-shilling note poking out of the top pocket of his shirt.

The Americans bowed at us and raised their glasses. Janet raised hers and hissed, 'Smile!' So I smiled.

The men sauntered over. 'Oh God, now we'll have to drink it,' I said to Janet.

He came and sat beside me. I moved to make room for him and scraped my back on the rough material of the seat. 'Ow!' I squeaked and I jumped, almost onto his lap!

'What's up?' he asked in that smooth American voice.

'I've got sunburn.'

'Oh, don't you have cream?' He looked really concerned.

'Cream? We don't have anything,' I said. 'We've only just got rid of our ration books.'

'No, no.' He laughed. 'I mean, cream to rub into that smooth, perfect skin of yours. It's called – oh, heck, what is it called? Help me out here, I'm trying to soft-soap you and I can't remember my lines.' He looked at me so helplessly, with his eyes so green and strange.

'Are you talking about suntan lotion?' I said.

'Something like that.' He grinned. 'My mom has a special recipe. It eases away all your pain.' His voice was soft and intimate, and just for me. I knew what his game was, and I liked it. And the fact that he was so open about it, and so inept, was very appealing. 'Let me show you,' he murmured, and he leaned towards me.

As if I was hypnotised, I moved my shoulder towards him and his fingers grazed my skin. So lightly, but it felt like – like fire. I gasped and and jumped away.

He laughed. 'OK. Maybe later. Let's have a proper drink. Do you like this stuff?'

'If this is all there is, I'd rather have a glass of orange,' I said.

'OJ sounds good. I'll join you.'

His friend said, 'Well, that's a new one on me.'

The time flew by and suddenly it was ten o'clock. Janet and I had to get back. 'It's lucky you're staying at our boarding house,' Janet said. 'We can all go back together.'

'OK,' he said. 'Let's go.' He looked at his friend, who shrugged. We all stood up and strolled out into the chill night air. Janet nudged me and whispered, 'All right? All right?' Then she dropped back and I could hear her talking to the other one. Something about sugar beet, I think, which, as you know, is a Norfolk crop.

So there we were, walking and talking, as if we'd known each other for months. He was a pilot in the US Air Force and his name was . . . Bob. Bob Stanferd.

'Bob?' I was sorry; it sounded so ordinary, so unromantic.

'That's exactly what I said.' Sylvie shook her head. 'So boring.'

'"You never heard of Bob Mitchum?" he said.'

He came from the South, he said. His friend, Gary, was from Wisconsin. They were in Great Yarmouth for the week. He said he had seen me swimming; he was impressed. He said I seemed different from other English girls.

'All the girls at the dance, I suppose?' I said.

He frowned. 'At the dance?'

'Did you kiss the girls and make them cry?' I said.

'I lost you! You disappeared,' he said. 'I hope I didn't make you cry. We're under orders to maintain good relations with our host country.'

We both laughed.

As we approached the front door of the boarding house, Janet murmured, 'We'd better go in first.' It wouldn't do for her auntie to see us with the Yanks.

Gary looked at Bob.

'OK, I guess we'll just take another walk around the town,' Bob said. 'Take in some more of the sights.' Then he whispered to me, 'I'll see you tomorrow, gorgeous. We'll go to a little club I know. It's a kind of a casino. Make yourself glamorous.'

'A casino!' I said. 'Is that why you play poker?'

'No, it actually isn't,' Sylvie said, and yawned.

'So, did you make yourself glamorous?'

She gave a short laugh. 'What do you think? I had no money and very few clothes. And I wasn't about to run up a little number from the curtains in our room.'

I looked at the material on the floor. 'No.'

'I bet you could have done something.'

I smiled. 'I bet I could . . . something dramatic with an interesting waistband.'

'How lovely that sounds.' She stood up and ruffled my hair. I smiled at her. Sometimes I really liked her. 'Anyway,' she said. 'No more today. What about these poems of yours?'

'Well, perhaps I will do a –'

Sylvie said, 'I've got an idea! Give me a moment.' She ran upstairs.

'– love poem.' I stretched over the material, pinning on the pattern pieces, thinking about the story, about Bob's soft American accent, the way he joked with Sylvie, the way he'd been looking for her at the dance. It was lovely. Would it ever happen to me? Might I have that with Tap? I sat back on my heels and examined the material, wondering if it mattered that I'd pinned the last piece on back to front. Sylvie came into the room and held out a thin paperback.

'Larry Fabbrona. He's a Beat poet,' she said, settling herself back on the settee. 'Anyone who wants to be hip should know the Beats.'

Sitting in Sylvie's living room, making her clothes, sharing her love story, I did want to be hip. I opened the book. The paper was very thick and some of the pages wouldn't even turn but there wasn't any obvious love poetry.

'It's a French edition,' Sylvie said. 'But it's in English. And a couple of the pages still need to be cut.'

'Perhaps I could learn one of these and convince Miss Harmon it's a French poem.'

'I don't think that would work,' Sylvie said. 'But you should like the Beats, they're like us. They're free thinkers. We're different from the rest.' Sylvie thought I was a free thinker. I didn't think like everybody else, I was different. Did I want to be different? Yes, I did. Different from the posh girls, proud of my accent, proud of my family. My stomach curled with pleasure. This is why I liked her. This is why I didn't care about the story being totally true. It was the things she said. The way she made me feel better about myself.

'The Beats live on the road, they experience things, they express themselves freely. They love passionately.' She drew her knees up under her chin. 'They don't want to live a boring suburban life.'

I thought about it. As a free thinker I should say what I felt. I said, 'But we live a boring suburban life, don't we?'

'We don't live in suburbia, chicken,' she said softly. 'We live on a council estate.'

In French I stood at the front of the class and recited '*Les sanglots longs, des violons . . .*' It was an easy choice – it was at the back of our textbook. I spoke slowly and sadly. There was a hush as I finished and then a spattering of applause.

'*Tu vois,*' Miss Harmon said, '*tu peux le faire quand tu fais un effort.* You can do it if you try. I want to see more of that, Linda Piper.'

At the end of the day, after the last bell, I went back to Miss Reeves' form room, still glowing from Miss Harmon's compliments. I peeped through the glass door. Miss Reeves wasn't there, but a load of girls were sitting on the desks. They were from all different years, including the sixth form. Some of them I knew by sight, but there was no one from my form. Silence fell and one or two looked surprised as I walked through the door.

'You haven't all got to do poems, have you?' I said. It could take hours; there was bound to be someone who'd recite the whole of *Hiawatha* or *The Pied Piper of Hamelin.* I slunk to the back of the room and sat down.

The door opened again and a girl from my sister's year walked in. Suddenly everyone was friendly and smiling.

'Hi, Rosemary.'

'Where've you *beeeeen*?'

'We were waiting for you.'

Rosemary looked round the room, smiling. She noticed me and stopped. 'A new face! Hooray. Have you come to join us?'

'I've come to do a poem.'

'A poem? That's good. We'll take that. Anything's OK for an audition as long as it shows us what you can do.'

'I'm not doing an audition.'

'The rule is stay and do an audition or exit stage left, I'm afraid,' Rosemary said.

I looked at them all afresh. 'You're the drama group, aren't you?'

Rosemary nodded.

'Well, I can't. Exit, that is,' I said. 'I'm in enough trouble already. I'm waiting for Miss Reeves.'

'Is Reevesy coming back? We're supposed to be safe in here on Wednesdays and Fridays.' Rosemary sighed. 'Come on then, like the wandering minstrels that we are, we shall have to find another room.' With a big gesture Rosemary beckoned the others to follow her. 'Sure you don't want to come? You're Judith's sister, aren't you? We could use you.'

'I'd better stay here,' I said. I watched them file out of the room. I wondered what it would be like to be in the drama group, to be part of a group where everyone knew you and people were pleased when you walked into the room and you worked together to do something.

I waited for twenty minutes. Miss Reeves didn't come. Perhaps that was the punishment.

The next day I went to Miss Reeves' form room at break time. She was marking a pile of books.

'I have a poem for you,' I said indignantly. 'I had it last night. I learned it.'

'Oh,' she said, vaguely. 'Oh yes, you're the girl who wore a lot of jewellery into school, aren't you?'

She'd forgotten. 'I was the girl who made a joke,' I said. 'We had a conversation in the dining hall.'

She frowned at me. Her thick grey fringe almost covered her eyes. Her hair was even worse than my mum's. It was completely straight, but not in a good way. Plus she had a clip in it. 'Well, you'd better recite your poem.'

I straightened my shoulders, looked just across her right shoulder and began.

Out in the wind, like the hobos say, the saints and outcasts
of the jungle night, the jungle camps and lean-tos
along the tracks and the sidings where the billy club guards
prowl and whack, brutal authority under the moon and that sky
wide as America, wider than the darkness stretching out and across
the small towns and the big cities, packed and jammed, loose and straggling
until the emptiness begins, the sky into and out of night,
and then all there is is mountains and deserts and the sea

everyone is heading for, out in the wind and the
   whistle blowing and blowing.

And the jazz guys lick their lips and lift their horns
   and blow
the breath of eternity out of the silver and gold cor-
   nucopias
free as air, a puff becoming melody, rhythm, dancing,
   dancing,
in all the upstairs rooms and downstairs rooms, the
   cellars
and attics tucked away, the clubs in all the jammed
   and packed
cities and little towns scattered in the emptiness of
   the night,
the windows glowing and friendly, smoked and
   spangled.

And now, right now, this music moment, there is no
   tomorrow,
there is no punching the clock, no tick-tock
of the working day keeping track, the patter and
   clatter
of the kettle drum of enforcing authority, the boss
   and routine,
in this moment's eternity, trumpets and saxophones

and the eyes of girls shining in the shadowed corners,
their legs and faces pale and bright as stars,
and everyone floating, floating, free as a bird.

As I said the lines Miss Reeves' mouth puckered into a shape of distaste and her eyebrows lowered. By the end her face was almost folded in two.

'And where did you find this poem? If it is a poem, which is debatable.'

'It's by Lorenzo Fabbrona, he's a Beat poet.' I liked the poem now. I wanted to defend it. It had taken ages to learn and I'd been worried she might say it wasn't three proper verses, more like three sentences, but that didn't seem to be the problem. 'You should read the book,' I said, dragging it out of my bag.

She hardly glanced at the cover. 'It's not what I had in mind.'

'But they're really famous. They're American.'

'I know who they are.' She looked at me. I wondered if she was weighing up whether she cared enough to make me learn another one. The classroom was filling up with chattering first-years.

She shook her head. 'These poems may be considered interesting. But only because they exist. They're temporary, ephemeral. Their purpose is just for now. They will not stand you in good stead in life. When you are thrown into a prison in some exotic land, for having breached some minor rule of etiquette, this poem will not raise your spirits in the way something such as a Shakespearean sonnet would do.'

'If I was in prison in some exotic land, I don't think reciting poetry would be top of my list of things to do.'

'I wouldn't be so sure.'

The first-years were staring at us.

'And if I did, I think these poets would be quite handy,' I said. 'They're free thinkers. That's the whole point. They experience things. They don't want to live a boring suburban life.' I looked at her with pity. Her face was wrinkled all over, her eyes, her mouth, her neck. Pale pink powder flaked from her cheeks. She looked like an old dusty ghost.

'I wonder if you are taking advantage of the opportunities this school offers. A girl like you should be grateful to be here.' She smiled sadly. 'You can go now.'

I looked at her. I had done what she asked. And I was a free thinker. I lifted my chin and walked proudly out of the room.

'You have to feel sorry for her. Her fiancé was killed in the war,' Judith said, as I put out the light in our bedroom.

I padded back to bed. 'He should have been a conscientious objector, then he wouldn't have been killed. Anyway, why does she take it out on me?'

'We're the working class. They don't like us being there. We clutter the place up. How many council house girls are there in your class?'

'Just me. Nadine Brown's in 4P, and there's a couple of other girls, I think.'

'Out of, what, a hundred and twenty? hundred and thirty? in your year? Not many. They just don't like us.'

'Perhaps she thinks if more working-class soldiers had died in the war, her fiancé would still be alive.'

'Probably. But before you get into more arguments you should know that conscientious objectors got killed in the war too.'

'Now she tells me. How do you know?'

'I've read about it.'

'She said I'd end up in prison.'

'With friends like yours you probably will. I hear you tried to join the drama group.'

'I didn't.'

'That's what I said to Rosemary. I couldn't imagine you doing something that productive.'

'Shut up.'

'For what it's worth, she said she liked your voice and they'd find a part for you in their summer production, if you want one.' I heard her turn over and pull the blankets up. Then she was asleep.

I put my hands behind my head and reflected on the day. The drama group wanted me for my voice. Miss

Harmon said I was good at French and Miss Reeves thought I might end up in a foreign country. I liked the idea of it. I liked all of it. What would become of me? When would it start? A foreign country. Which one? Would I be there on holiday, or would it be part of a job? Did Miss Reeves think I would have a job in a foreign country?

At least I had two poems to recite if I got stuck in a prison.

Prison. Why would I be in prison? For some noble cause, I hoped. I wondered if Sandra would come and visit me in prison. Or would Sandra be in prison too?

CHAPTER 10

The Shire Hall

SOME WEEKS BEFORE, WE'D BEEN called into assembly in the middle of the day to be told our headmistress had been awarded the MBE. And today we had the day off school to celebrate. And I had somewhere to go.

I looked at the clothes on my bed. It was obviously important to wear the right outfit when you were going to court to support your best friend, whose boyfriend was due to appear, especially when that boyfriend, in this case, Danny, might be sent to prison. People would look at Sandra with interest, and if I wasn't careful they'd wonder who the ragbag beside her was.

There wasn't much choice. I really needed more clothes. Today I would wear my cream straight skirt and blue twin-set. I looked at my stockings. One small ladder. It would have to do. I wasn't Danny's girlfriend.

'Do you want hot milk with your Ready Brek, or are you happy with it going cold?' Mum called up.

I ran downstairs as the post fell through the letter box.

There was an envelope with a French stamp for me, from a new penfriend in Marseilles, and one for Mum. The other letters were for Dad. As I handed them to him I said, 'Dad, do you know anyone who needs a person who is bright and cheerful and good at almost anything, to work for them?'

'But I've got a job,' Judith said, and laughed. Today she was wearing her hair in bunches and I was glad I wouldn't have to walk to school with her.

'I could ask Wainwright in the Milk Bar if he needs someone.'

The Milk Bar! The Milk Bar was in the centre of town, halfway between the Orpheus and the Corn Exchange. Sandra and I had gone into the Milk Bar regularly before we started going to the Orpheus. Interesting arty-type people went in there, as well as Dad and his union members and his mate Jimmy Peecock, from the *Essex Weekly News*, and Judith's beardy folk friends.

The Milk Bar was the kind of place the Beatles would go to if they ever came to Chelmsford. The Beatles weren't mods – not in those jackets – so they would never go to the Orpheus. I didn't really like the Beatles, but I wouldn't mind serving them a coffee and a Chelsea bun. John, who, if I had to choose, was my favourite, probably wouldn't ever come to Chelmsford, but Paul might.

'Could you really get me a job in the Milk Bar?' Already I could envisage a new life on Saturdays. I would be working.

'Yes, I have a job.' 'Yes, I work in the centre of town.' 'Oh, I can't see you tomorrow, I'll be at work.' I'd be earning cash. I'd be meeting new people, smiling.

If I went to work in the Milk Bar, Saturdays would never be the same again. Sandra and I would never again catch the quarter to ten bus into town on Saturday mornings. We would never listen to records in the Co-op record department. We would never again gaze at eternity rings in Walker's on the way back to the bus station to catch the twelve o'clock bus home for dinner.

Dad was glancing at a letter he had just opened. 'When I see him, I'll ask him,' he said absently.

'So who's coming to Wethersfield on Saturday?' Mum said, looking at her letter. Wethersfield was the American air base, where Sylvie apparently went. One year the local CND groups had had an alternative Aldermaston march from there.

Judith and I groaned.

'That's enough,' Mum said.

'I'd have thought you'd want to go,' Judith said. 'It's all about talking to the boys there.'

'Do you really talk to them?' I said to Mum.

'Yes,' she said, 'if we see them. They're not allowed to come out and meet us specifically, and we're not allowed in. But when people are going in or out, we have a bit of a chat. I think a lot of them are homesick.'

'And they want someone to be nice to them,' Dad said, tucking a letter back into its envelope. 'And they don't come nicer than your mother.'

Mum sniffed.

'How can you talk to them?' I said. 'They're Americans. They're just about to go off and kill people in Vietnam.'

'And very likely to be killed themselves,' Mum said. 'Though, hopefully, not all of them.'

'But it's war. Against some small country, thousands of miles away, that's got nothing to do with them.'

'Unfortunately the American government considers the country rather important,' Dad said.

'A lot of these young men don't know where they are or what they're doing. And a lot of them are very scared,' Mum said.

'Then they shouldn't be in the army.'

'It's the Air Force,' Judith said.

'And for most of them it's not a choice. Most of them have been drafted,' Mum said.

'And there's such a thing as draft-resisting,' I said.

'Draft dodgers!' said Judith, relishing the words.

'I think that's a very hard row to hoe, love,' Dad said to me. 'You have to leave everything you know – your family, your friends, your Milk Bars.'

'Sometimes people have to do what they're told,' Judith said. 'Like we do. Go to school, eat breakfast, go to war.'

'Whose side are you on?' I said to Judith. She wore a CND badge too. 'I don't know why you bother going,' I said to Mum. 'They're already on the way out there.'

'Well, of course, we want them to know there's another way of looking at things. But it's not just about them. It's about highlighting the issue. Helen Grenville is always trying to get the press interested when we go because if there's an article, the general public learn about CND, and the bomb, and Vietnam. It gives them another point of view. They might realise that there are other valid ways of thinking about the issue. They may even change their opinion.'

'That's not going to stop the war.'

'It's a start.' Mum sighed. 'All right, you don't need to come this time.'

Dad opened another letter. A page fell onto the table. 'I tell them I can't sit, but they never seem to remember,' he said. 'In Chelmsford the law certainly is an ass.' I felt a quiver of anxiety. On the table was a list of cases to be dealt with in the magistrates' court.

'Are you on the Bench today?' I asked. A list was always sent to Dad in the week that he was going to sit. Halfway down the page I could see Danny's name. Dad would be sentencing Danny. What would Sandra think as my dad sent her boyfriend to jail? And what would Dad say? He didn't mind the friends I had, but he might view it differently if I sat in his actual court saying hello to criminals as they came in. I didn't want to upset him just when he was trying to get me a job in the Milk Bar.

Dad picked up the list and glanced at it. 'Oh, no!' I said before I could stop myself. Tap's name, Peter Tappling, was halfway down the second side. He was charged with . . . I peered casually . . . obstructing a police officer. When had that happened? This meant Dad would be passing sentence on Danny and Tap.

Judith looked at my face and glanced at the list in Dad's hand. 'I thought you were going to Cambridge today,' she said to him, inspecting one of her bunches and wiping off some marmalade. 'You said I could come.'

'I am and you can,' Dad said. 'I'll have to ring them.' He folded up the letter, tucked it into his inside pocket and smiled at me. Mum, Judith and Dad finally left the house. I was alone. The house was quiet, as if even I wasn't there. Silently I cleared the breakfast table, I shook out the tablecloth at the back door and then I ran up to the bedroom. I was going to see Tap, so I changed into my best, unladdered stockings. I looked at myself in the mirror and smiled. Did I look like Jean Shrimpton? As good as.

People were standing outside the Shire Hall. One or two I recognised from the Orpheus. And then I saw Tap. He was standing apart, smoking, inhaling hard, staring at the ground. He looked thin and pale. But he was really smart – in a grey mohair suit and a white shirt and dark knitted tie.

'Hello Tap,' I said.

'Hello Lorna,' he said.

'Who's Lorna?' Sandra murmured. 'Seen Danny?' she asked.

Tap shrugged.

'Good luck,' I said as we climbed the stairs.

He raised his eyebrows.

Danny wasn't in the large entrance hall. We looked at the lists of cases pinned to the wall, then walked up the stairs to Court Three, where Tap and Danny's cases would be heard.

The courtroom was full of men in suits and policemen in uniform. Everything was dark and worrying. Two mod girls stuck out like Dinky toys on the top of a birthday cake.

A policeman with a clipboard called out Tap's name and Sandra and I looked at each other. Tap walked into the courtroom with his hands behind his back, the Duke of Edinburgh stroll. He looked smart and confident. As he stepped into the dock I looked at his hands. They were trembling. A man at the front stood up and said, 'I represent Mr Tappling this morning.' Tap rolled his shoulders. He stood up straight as the charge was put to him: obstruction of a police officer. After a nod from his lawyer, in a careless voice he said, 'Guilty.' A police officer then began speaking. He had seen a man he now knew to be Peter Tappling in Tindal Square, speaking to another man and acting in a way that led him to believe he was in possession of amphetamine pills, known as purple hearts. He followed the said Tappling until he reached the Orpheus coffee bar, a venue frequented by so-called mods, whereupon he spoke to him. He asked Tappling for his name and address and asked to search his pockets, when, without warning, Tappling pulled off his coat (believed to be a light brown suede material) and threw it into the crowd of onlookers, one of whom caught it and drove off with it on a Lambretta scooter, amid much laughter. Peter Tappling had then been arrested and charged.

Tap's lawyer said his client was behaving out of character because his mother had been ill and he was anxious about her. The chairman of the magistrates (who should have been my dad) gave Tap a lecture about pills, scooters and bad company. Then he gave him a conditional discharge.

As he stepped out of the dock Tap looked round. When he saw me, he winked. It was a sad wink, I thought. He wanted to show that what the lawyer had said about his mum was just any old rubbish. He hadn't needed him to say that. But I was the only person he knew to wink at. And he didn't even know me.

'Lorna, you are a lucky girl,' Sandra whispered to me, looking at Tap then back at me. I took a chance and beckoned to him to come and sit with us. He walked over and grinned at me. He looked as if he was near to tears.

He took my hand. 'Thanks for coming,' he whispered.

His hand was thin and bony and cold. Without thinking I covered it with my other hand and gently rubbed it. With his other hand he stroked my cheek. I wanted to kiss him. I think he wanted to kiss me.

Sandra nudged me. They were calling Danny's name. 'Daniel Mulroney, Daniel Mulroney!'

'Here we go,' she said.

'Daniel Mulroney! No reply,' said the police officer with the clipboard.

The chief magistrate leaned over to the man at the table in front of the Bench, the clerk of the court. I heard the word 'warrant'.

'He's here,' Sandra called.

The chairman frowned. 'Who said that?' He looked round.

'He's here,' Sandra said, less confidently. I nodded vaguely, which could have meant, 'She's right', or, alternatively, 'Fancy shouting in court!'

'Could you try once more, officer, please?'

The police officer left the court and we heard the cry, 'Daniel James Mulroney!' echo down the corridor.

'He's got to be here,' Sandra murmured. 'If he doesn't turn up, I'll kill him. I've taken a day off work because of him.'

Then Danny sauntered in, laughing, as if he was in the middle of a good joke.

'Stop smiling,' Sandra hissed. He didn't have a lawyer, so she had to tell him what to do.

He was charged with forging four cheques belonging to Mrs Pamela Cook, his landlady. He'd nicked money from Cooky's mum. That was terrible. And stupid. Had Sandra known? I looked at her. Her face was expressionless.

The clerk of the court said, 'How do you plead?'

Danny said guilty.

The chairman asked him if he had anything he wanted to say. Danny looked round the room and licked his lips. His head ducked forward. 'They were charging me too much rent.'

He got six months inside.

Everyone stood up as the magistrates left the courtroom. Sandra gripped the bench in front of us. Tap slid along the seat and out of the door.

CHAPTER 11

Birthday Presents

'HAPPY BIRTHDAY!' JUDITH SHOOK my arm but I wasn't asleep. I'd been awake for ages. I struggled out of the sheet and sat up. This was going to be a great birthday for so many reasons. The Easter holidays had started. My stars in *Woman's Own* had said, 'Adventures of the heart will bring happiness. Money prospects are good'. And in the paper bag that Judith was holding out was the handbag I'd asked for, long and brown, with a big gold clasp and two handles. I'd seen an article about it in the *Evening News* and Judith had said she'd see what she could do.

On the breakfast table was a small pile of presents. The straight shiny grey skirt from Mum and Dad I had chosen from Sandra's mum's catalogue. There was a book of plays by John Osborne from Dad, and a book about the Match Girls' strike in 1888 that I had asked for.

Dad said, 'And there's something else.'

We all looked at him, including Mum.

'Well, I don't know if this is going to be a good birthday present because it will eat into your very important weekends, but Mr Wainwright said that from this weekend there will be a job for you in the Milk Bar.'

'Really? That's fab!' The Milk Bar. The centre of town. 'When, when can I start?'

'It will be every Saturday, and sometimes in the school holidays. He said you could start on Saturday if you wanted, but I thought it might be a bit soon as you have other things to do.' It was the Aldermaston march. 'He said you can start the day after Easter Monday. And if you get on all right it will be permanent.'

'That's fantastic!'

'How much is she going to get paid?' Judith asked, obviously worried I might earn more than her.

'It's not a whole day,' Dad said. 'I think it's about ten shillings, twelve and six perhaps.'

I could hear showers of coins raining down from the sky. I would be rich. I would have different clothes for every night of the week if I wanted. 'I must tell Sandra.' I ran to the phone.

She answered on the second ring. 'Oh, it's you. Happy Birthday.' It could have been Danny calling her from prison. When I told her the news she said, 'Does that mean I'll have to start going to the Milk Bar again? It'll be funny asking you for a strawberry milkshake.'

'It's not the whole day,' I said. 'I finish at half past two. So we can still go down the Orpheus in the afternoon.'

'And now you're earning, you can buy the drinks,' she said. 'What a great birthday present. See you later.' Sandra was coming to tea.

'What do you want tonight?' Mum said, as she went out of the front door. We were allowed to choose our favourite meal on our birthdays. I didn't have to tell her. 'I'll get some eggs on the way home from work. I think we've got enough potatoes for the chips.'

Judith said, 'Do you like the bag?'

'It's fab,' I said. 'Do you want to come down the town with me and show it off?'

'I'm going round to James's,' she said. 'Why don't you go with Sandra?'

'She's at work.'

The whole birthday stretched ahead of me. I wondered what to do till the delight of fried egg and chips at teatime.

Sylvie answered the door quickly. She looked lovely, in a straight emerald-green shift dress that came down to her knees, and her black high heels. 'Hello, Linda. What are you doing here?' she said.

'It's my birthday,' I said.

'Happy Birthday!' she said. 'You should have told me.'

'Didn't I?' I hadn't told her because I hadn't seen her.

'So what are you going to do on your special day?' she said.

'I don't know.'

'Well, I've got to be in town a bit later, why don't we go in now? Do some window shopping, drop in to the library. We could have a birthday cup of coffee. You can tell me all about your poetry recitation.'

I looked at her. 'There's not much to tell. What about Mansell?'

'He's in the shop with Mum. I've got the day off.' She smiled.

'Does that mean I ought to go and take him for a walk?'

'Oh, no!' she said. 'Mr Roberts is on holiday. They've all gone to Butlin's. So Mum's safe, and anyway, it's your birthday! Is that a new outfit? It's lovely.'

I smiled down at the new skirt. 'Yes. Thank you. And you look nice,' I said, generously.

'Thank you, Linda. Coming from you that means a lot. I know you have very high standards.'

I made a face at her.

'I mean it!' she said. 'Just give me a minute to powder my nose.' She ran upstairs.

On the bus she asked me how I was getting on with *The Second Sex*.

'Well, I liked the bit about housework. How it's a tyranny.'

'Exactly!' she said, and clapped her hands.

I knew she'd be pleased I'd read that part. 'I tried telling my mum.' Mum hadn't been impressed. She'd said, 'Yes, housework is a filthy job. Unfortunately it's a necessary job. And sometimes that job falls to you.'

'What I thought was so . . . inspiring about the book,' Sylvie said, 'was how she absolutely puts her finger on what is wrong with our lives, we as women, I mean. Marriage is just a way of keeping women in their place through motherhood.' She was speaking too loudly and people were looking. 'I mean, motherhood is OK, of course, but how it ties women down, how they are seen as mothers and only that. That's how people see me, isn't it? And a bad mother at that.'

I looked at her. She was right. People saw nothing about her except that she'd had an illegitimate child. The people who were staring now, who were judging her, that's all they saw. They didn't see the Sylvie I knew.

'Whereas you,' she went on, 'you will be more than that. And by the time it comes for you to have children the world will be a very different place.'

I had never really thought about having children; getting married, yes, talking it over with Sandra, planning the day. But not children. I wouldn't like to think that having children changed me as a person, or changed how people saw me.

'Penny for your thoughts,' Sylvie said.

I smiled and shook my head.

'Where shall we go for our coffee?' she said. 'Shall we pop into the Milk Bar?'

'Oh, no,' I said. 'I'm going to start work in there soon.'

'You got the job!' she said. 'Hooray! Linda, that's marvellous. You can show me round.'

'No!' I said. 'I don't want to go in till I start.' What if they didn't like me? I didn't want people to see that happen.

'Ah, quite right,' she said. 'Save all the embarrassing meetings till you actually work there.' I did like that about her, that she understood.

We went to the Amber Tea Bar near the cathedral. Sylvie ordered us both a strawberry milkshake.

'Are these milkshakes as good as Wainwright's?' she said.

I took a long, thoughtful suck on my straw. 'I don't think so.'

'That's what we want to hear,' she said. 'You will be working in the emporium that serves the best milkshakes in town. And because it's your birthday, how about a bit more of our story while we are enjoying the second-best milkshakes in Chelmsford?'

'OK,' I said. The fact that she wanted to tell me the story and I hadn't even asked her made me feel that we were almost friends.

'Are you sitting comfortably?' she asked.

I nodded.

'Then I'll begin.' She sat up straight and pushed her empty glass to one side.

I stood in front of the mirror in the small wardrobe in the bedroom, sighing. I was desperate. How could I be glamorous for a casino? The skirt I was wearing was made from an old dress of my mother's. It wasn't bad, cotton with a contemporary design, and it was clean, but it was hardly glamorous.

'Here.' Janet tied the ends of my blouse into a bow at the front, so that it looked more fun.

'I look like a harlot.'

'You look fabulous,' Janet drawled in an American accent. She was staying in to wash her hair.

I ran down the stairs.

We were meeting in the Queen's Head at the end of the road. I looked through the window of the pub and saw them standing at the bar. Bob was wearing a shirt and tie, carrying a jacket hooked over his shoulder. He looked splendid and mysterious and like no one I had ever known. I stepped up behind him and tapped him on the shoulder – he was at least four inches taller than me – and he spun round. He hesitated and I had a pang of anguish – was he disappointed in me? Then he smiled and put his arm round my shoulders.

His friend Gary murmured something and laughed. Bob pulled me towards him and rubbed his fingers up my neck. It made me shiver. They ordered me a beer, because that's what they were drinking, though Bob complained it wasn't cold enough.

'It's beer,' I said. 'What do you expect?'

Gary seemed disappointed that Janet hadn't come, and said he would go to the pier to see what there was to see. 'You kids have fun now,' he said, putting his empty glass on the bar.

The air was hot as Bob and I walked through the streets. He held my hand and told me about his day with Gary, swimming, walking and finding themselves participating in a football game. He called it soccer. 'I didn't know the rules, but apparently I scored three goals,' he said, 'and a couple of bruises.' We seemed to be walking for ages, passing through alleys, round dark corners. We had almost left the town when we came to a high wall with two large wrought iron gates. Through them I could see a drive and small lamps guiding the way up to an enormous house. I was wide-eyed with excitement. Bob rang a bell and a man in a commissionaire's uniform, all gold braid and buttons, stepped forward and ushered us in. The front door of the house was suddenly flung open and the light was dazzling. Two chandeliers hung down low from the ceiling. Again I was conscious of the odd material of my skirt and the silly knot in my blouse. I stepped over the threshold like a timid mouse, clutching my handbag in front of me with both hands like a shield, trying not to care.

Bob exchanged some money for plastic chips and guided me towards another room where it was dark, just a few lights hanging low over gaming tables, so now nobody would see the wretched skirt. At first he did nothing, moving from game to game, watching. People milled around us. It was another world. It was so exciting. My cheeks were throbbing with heat. He came up behind me and stood very close, then he breathed in my ear, 'When's your birthday?'

'The fourteenth of October.'

He reached forward and put a small pile of chips on square number fourteen. The wheel spun round, the ball clattering.

'*Rien ne va plus.*'

I leaned closer to him, all the time trying to focus on the wheel and to keep sight of the ball as it whirred round. It shuddered to a halt on fourteen. Chips were pushed towards him. He played again and again, so calmly, bending forward, putting down the chips, standing quietly. But his sweat changed, I could smell it, through the soap, as though his body was tense, even if he wasn't showing it.

Without looking at me he said, 'Here. Try your hand with these,' and he gave me four chips.

I was in a casino with a beautiful man and I had chips to play with. I put them on two squares and six chips were pushed back towards me. It was wonderful and I clapped my hands with joy. He laughed at me. And then, of course,

I immediately lost them all. He squeezed my hand and said, 'Don't worry, honey, I'll win for both of us.'

And he did. He won a lot more. He relaxed, his shoulders loosened. We strolled back over to the cashier and he exchanged chips for wads of paper money.

'You've brought me luck,' he said. He peeled off notes. One pound, two, three, ten, twenty pounds. 'Here you go.' He gave me a huge grin. 'Buy yourself something beautiful to wear. Tomorrow' – he looked at his watch – 'no, tonight! we'll come back and play again.'

It was two in the morning. The streets were empty and there was a chill in the air. He took off his jacket and draped it round my shoulders. The notes were almost throbbing in my handbag. I'd never had so much money in my life before.

The boarding house was in darkness as I slid the key into the lock. As the door swung open he whispered, 'Are you thirsty? Why don't you come to my room, for an orange juice?' Oh, he was such a charmer!

'What about Gary?' I murmured.

'He's a big boy, he'll find himself a place to stay for the night.'

I looked at him and he stroked a strand of hair from my face. He seemed almost sad. He was an airman, far from home. He could go off to war at any moment and never come back. 'All right then,' I said.

The door to his room clicked shut behind us. He didn't switch on the light . . . He was very gentle, asking about the sunburn on my back, as he slipped the top from my shoulders. Then he said all those soft American words. 'Honey', 'baby', 'crazy'.

Sylvie fell silent. She had almost forgotten I was there. 'Do you know what he asked me? He asked me if it was my first time. I think he was really worried. I said no, because I didn't want him to think I was just a silly girl. But it wasn't true. It was my first time. I don't know if he believed me. He looked at me seriously and said, "You are so sweet. Thank you." And I looked at his beautiful face, and his soft lips and the creases round his eyes when he smiled, and I thought, I should be thanking you!'

She laughed.

'So, then what happened?' I said. I wanted her to move on, get out of the bedroom. It was too embarrassing.

'Ah, well, the next part – perhaps that isn't quite a birth-day story. Whereas today is your special day,' she said. 'How lovely to be young.' She rummaged in her bag. 'Just a moment.' She rummaged some more, then handed me a small white paper bag folded in half.

I opened it. It was a hanky, fine white cotton with deep red roses embroidered in the corner.

'It's from a set my grandmother gave me when I was about your age.'

It was so pretty and so soft. I loved it. 'Are you sure?' I said.

'Oh, I've had it for ages in the back of my dressing-table drawer. I never use it. It's much more appropriate for someone of your age.'

I folded the handkerchief carefully back into the bag. 'If you could go back, would you have done things differently?' I said.

'Hmm, good question . . .' Thoughtfully, she wiped the straw round the inside of her glass. 'Am I allowed to change everything? I'd like to have had an ordinary life. Because if I could have, I would certainly have chosen a different family.'

'But your mum's nice, isn't she?'

'Oh, my mum's not so bad,' Sylvie said. 'It's her brothers. In particular, my Uncle Peter, who lives too close.' I knew he and his wife Rita lived in the same road as Sylvie. 'Ironically, they're the reason we moved here, all the way from Braintree.' She licked her straw. 'My grandmother's not much better, even though she once gave me that lovely hanky.'

'What's wrong with them?' I asked. Sandra's mum had said the rest of the Weston family were low life and gave our estate a bad name.

'Let's say they don't understand me.' Sylvie gave a small laugh. 'There's nothing wrong with Rita, she's got a good heart, but Peter thinks he has to act as my father, as well as drinking rather too much and therefore finding it difficult to hold down a job. The others still live over in Braintree, which is good, but unfortunately not far enough.' She sighed. 'They just don't like me.'

'They're your family,' I said. 'They have to like you, don't they?'

She sighed. 'It's a long story. They dislike practically everything I've ever done.'

'Do you like them?'

'Good question. Probably not.'

'Which came first?'

'Well, chicken, it could have been the egg, but in Peter's case it was more likely the beer. It's hard to know. But – oh, look at the time! I'm meeting Rita at two o'clock. She's coming with me to a doctor's appointment at the hospital.'

'The hospital? Are you still . . . unhappy?' I said, worried.

'Oh, chicken, no no no!' She paused. 'No. And I've just spent a lovely morning with my special girl!' She stood up. 'Wasn't there something else?' She frowned. 'I know! I still owe you money!' She held out a sixpence.

I took it. 'That's the third present you've given me.'

'Well, it's not really a present, since I owed it to you. But in return, if you like, perhaps you could . . .'

I held my breath.

'Come round and help me with my dressmaking.' She looked at my face and said, 'Don't worry, there's no rush. If it isn't finished this year, I'll wear it next year.'

I shrugged. 'OK.' I wondered how far she'd got since I'd helped her cut it out. I hoped she didn't want me to do the zip. Zips took ages. She smiled and slid out of the café.

The shops were opening up after the dinner hour. I had missed dinner, but there was no one at home and it was my birthday. I could do what I wanted. I could . . . go to The Boutique. Why shouldn't I?

As I stepped inside there was no sign of Tap or the manager. The Boutique was dark except for bright spotlights shining down on the racks of suits and rows of Fred Perrys. On the record player the Crystals were singing 'He's A Rebel'. I walked quietly round the room touching the clothes on the racks. They smelt fresh and biscuity, as if they'd crunch between your teeth if you bit them.

Tap came through a door at the back. He was folding a grey sweater. I remembered how his hand felt under mine in court.

'Hello!' he said. He seemed pleased to see me. 'You come to buy something? I'm supposed to be tidying the stockroom.'

'It's my birthday,' I said.

'Oh, Happy Birthday,' he said. 'Nice to see a friendly face in here. I'll just put this away. You could put on another record.'

I flicked through the pile of records. I picked out a Four Tops single. I loved the Four Tops. They clicked their fingers and yearned, 'Baby I Need Your Loving'. I swayed to the music.

Suddenly Tap's hands were on my hips. 'Let's dance.'

He pulled me back against him and we swayed together. He drew me closer and echoed the aching voice of Levi Stubbs in my ear.

'Come into the stockroom with me,' he whispered. 'I'll give you a birthday kiss.'

I turned to look at him.

'Oh, those big, trusting eyes,' he said.

Then the door opened and Eddy his manager walked in. Tap jumped away from me.

Eddy laughed. 'Back to work,' he said. He walked into the stockroom, shrugging off his jacket.

Tap frowned, then went behind the counter. 'Here!' he hissed. 'Happy Birthday!' He tossed a crackling cellophane packet to me. I could see that it was a Fred Perry, a maroon Fred Perry. I really wished we'd kissed.

'Thank you,' I began.

He put his finger to his lips and winked at me.

'And he just gave it to you, just like that?' Sandra said. We were in our front room after tea, with a slice of birthday cake. I was telling her about my day.

'It was a birthday present.'

She looked at the Fred Perry. 'It's a bit good, isn't it? Since when does Tap give you presents?'

'Since today. He threw it at me!'

'Well, there you are,' she said. She was envious, I could tell. So I didn't tell her about the swaying or the offer of a kiss. I didn't really understand it myself.

Then we had another piece of cake and I told her about Sylvie's story and the romance of the casino.

'Sweat changing? Creases round his eyes?' Sandra said. 'She's making it up. Who smells sweat changing?' she said.

'Obviously not you,' I said.

'She should have just said BO! And been done with it. When exactly was this?'

'Well . . . Mansell's about six months old, and add on another nine months and you've got –'

'Rubbish, that's what you've got. You can't tell me she went to Norfolk in January. Nobody goes to Norfolk in January and gets sunburn.'

Miserably, I realised she was right.

CHAPTER 12

Football

SANDRA AND I WALKED INTO TOWN. We were going to see Chelmsford City play.

No one we knew was about; the interesting people had all gone to Clacton, where there was supposed to be a mods and rockers battle on the beach. But then opposite the Orpheus, sitting on the back of Jeff's Lambretta, looking cool in his bottle-green suede, was Mick Flynn.

'Watcha Mick,' Sandra called.

'Sandra!' Mick said. 'I'd know that foghorn voice anywhere.'

'Where you off to?' she said, as we crossed the road.

'We are going down Clacton, my dear,' Mick said.

Jeff looked up from where he was tinkering with the front wheel.

'Funny time to go to the seaside,' Sandra said. 'Won't it all be over?'

'It's never over,' Mick said. 'I'm going to pick up the pieces, and if we hurry, we'll catch ourselves a plate of fish and chips and a couple of girls to kiss-me-quick on the pier.'

'Seen Tap?' she said. I pinched her.

'He's never much of a one for a bundle on the beach. But if I do see him I'll tell him you were asking.'

'It's not for me, it's for Linda here.'

'Hello, Linda,' Mick said. 'All right?' He wrapped his coat round himself, Jeff revved the scooter, kicked the stand and, waving in our direction, they swooped away.

Suddenly the street was quiet.

'See what I do for you?' Sandra said.

'But it's embarrassing.'

'Mick doesn't care.'

Chelmsford City football ground was quite full, compared to most weeks, because it was the last game of the season and Chelmsford were playing Yeovil, who'd won the league the year before. Sandra and I walked through the park, paid our money and passed through the turnstile. We wove our way through the Chelmsford fans – groups of old men with scarves and flat caps standing on the terraces, smoking roll-ups, with the *Daily Mirror* sticking out of their pockets; some dads with little boys with caps on, and mods from the Orpheus in parkas and

Crombie overcoats. It was a cold afternoon, and the sky was filled with grey clouds, threatening rain at any minute. A group of Yeovil supporters huddled together at the far end.

We were standing with boys from Sandra's old school, but Sandra was hoping that Danny would turn up, which was always a possibility, she said. Ray and a few of his mates leaned against the concrete and corrugated iron wall at the top of the steps behind the goal. We'd said hello to them on the way in, and I was conscious of Ray behind us throughout the first half.

At half-time Sandra wandered off to look for Danny. Five minutes later she returned with a thin, scruffy man with greased-back hair.

'This is Peter,' she said, almost triumphantly. 'He's Sylvie's uncle.'

'You're kidding,' I said.

'This is Linda,' Sandra said.

He looked me up and down.

'Where did you meet him?' I said to Sandra.

'He just jumped out at me,' Sandra said. 'He thought I was you.'

'Cheek,' we said together. There was a pause. Sandra was looking at me as if I was the person whose job it was to say something.

'Do you know what the score is?' I said.

He roared with laughter, and the sour smell of beer on his breath was smothering. 'That's a fine thing,' he said. 'You go to a fancy school and you can't tell the score in a football match. What do they teach you?'

'Not to drink before dark,' I said. I didn't mind smelling beer on a Saturday night, with my friends, when we were all having a good time at the Corn Exchange, when the smell was fresh and almost sweet, but here, with him – he had to be over thirty and it was only ten to four – I didn't like it.

'I hear you're a friend of my niece Sylvia.' He made a face.

'Sylvie's very nice,' I said. I wasn't going to say anything bad about Sylvie to a man in an ancient car coat with a button missing and oil stains down the front. 'She's very interesting. She knows a lot.'

'Oh yeah?'

'And she's been to a lot of interesting places.'

'You what? Like where?'

'Paris.'

'Come off it. She ain't even got a passport.' He grinned. One of his side teeth was missing. 'She's never been anywhere apart from Wethersfield air base. She ain't right in the head.'

'She's been under a lot of stress. From her relations,' I added under my breath.

'Stress? That's the first time I heard it called that. She's been under a lot of things, darling, particularly Yanks, but stress, well, that's a new one on me.'

'You obviously don't understand Sylvie,' I said.

'And I suppose you do? That makes sense – she thinks she's Brigitte Bardot, and your dad thinks he's Lord of the Manor. Oh, and your mum thinks she's the Virgin Mary.'

It was like a punch in the stomach, though I'd never been punched before. I gasped and stared at him. Was this what people thought about my mum and dad? I was having trouble breathing. 'Yeah, well, you're not Pope Pius, from what I heard.'

He stepped towards me. 'Yeah, and what have you heard?'

I hadn't heard anything. His face and his breath were two inches from my nose.

'I don't have to hear anything,' I said. 'I can smell it.' I gazed at him, trying to keep my breathing under control.

Peter stretched out his long thin dirty fingers and with a pointed black nail he flicked me. Then he did it again! I stepped back a pace and tripped on a step. Sandra said 'Hey!' as she caught me. I wanted her to say something funny, like, 'Seconds out!' or 'You can't fight here, you haven't got your gumshields in', to make it feel less threatening.

'What are you playing at?' I shouted. 'These steps are concrete. Someone could get hurt.'

'Yes,' Sandra said, 'and that person could be you!' She poked him in the stomach.

Sandra and I stood side by side. Peter's face twisted into a grin. 'Oh, got your friend to protect you now, have you?' he leered.

Sandra laughed.

Someone came up behind me. 'Watcha, Frenchy. Ready for the second half?' It was Ray. 'They're coming back onto the pitch. All right, mate?' he said to Peter.

Peter eyed Ray. 'What's your fucking problem?'

Ray looked at me and Sandra, then back at Peter. 'Sounds like you're the one with the problem.'

Peter swayed gently, his lips still curled in a sneer. No one said anything. Ray stood beside me, tense. Peter moved back and Ray straightened as if he expected Peter to throw a punch. Something had to be done. I opened my mouth.

'Your flies are undone,' I said to Peter.

His head snapped down. I turned away and walked up the steps. Ray followed and Sandra trailed behind. At the top we began to walk round the perimeter of the ground.

'It's all right,' Sandra said. 'We don't have to walk to Witham. He's gone. And I've got the wrong shoes on.'

We stopped near the drinks stand. 'What was all that about?' Ray said. 'I come over to talk to you and I'm in the middle of a fight.'

'It was nothing. He was being rude about Sylvie, you know, Mrs Weston in the shop – her daughter.'

'Oh, don't worry about him.'

'But all those things he said about my dad. And my mum! I don't even know him.'

'Forget it. He probably votes Conservative. You gave him as good as you got. Better.'

We stood together till the end of the match. I couldn't stop thinking about what Peter had said. He'd been so rude. I wasn't used to that.

Sometimes Ray put his arm round me, sometimes he took out a cigarette and smoked. My stomach gradually relaxed. It was nice to be with him. At the end of the game he said, 'I'll walk you up to the bus station in case he's still around.'

It felt good, walking through the park in the middle of the crowd, knowing I'd stood up to a bully, and being with someone who wanted to be with me. He kept his arm lightly round my shoulders and tried to explain why a corner was better than a free kick. Even being bored was comfortable. For today, I could like this.

As we approached the bus station Sandra said, 'Wonder who's in Snows?' Snows was the other coffee bar that mods went to – especially ones without scooters because it was handy for the bus station, being directly opposite. I could see Blond Don sitting astride a shiny Lambretta, chatting to some lads from Kelvedon. A group of other people were leaning against a bottle-green Mini, Tap's Mini. I saw Tap. He looked up as we drew level. I could see him looking at me and then at Ray. My shoulders sagged. I wished Ray's arm wasn't there.

Tap strolled across the road. 'Watcha,' he said.

'Watcha Tap,' said Sandra, but he didn't look at her.

Tap was staring at me. 'Nice Fred Perry,' he said.

'Yes. Thanks.'

His eyes slid across to Ray. Then he glanced back at me. 'I see,' he said and turned and crossed back to his car. He said something and people laughed. I wanted to run after him and say, 'What do you see? And what was so funny? This isn't what it looks like.' But something stopped me. Up till a minute ago I'd liked Ray's arm round me. And anyway, what would Tap say if I did go over to him? He was still laughing.

The driver of the 311 was climbing into his cab. Ray, Sandra and I all got on the bus. We went upstairs. Sandra walked to the front, Ray and I sat at the back and Ray paid my fare. As we passed the boys' grammar school, he said, 'You're not still thinking about that bloke, are you?'

'Which one?'

'The one at the football . . . Oh, you're thinking about that fella, Tap. What was that about?'

'What do you mean?'

'Why was he looking at you like that?'

'I don't know.'

'Is there something I should know?' he said.

'No!' I said, thinking, it was just a Fred Perry. I didn't even kiss him.

'You sure? The way he looked at me, I thought there was going to be another fight. Blimey, the people you hang about with!'

'What do you mean?'

He hesitated. 'People in the Orpheus, Tap, Danny Mulroney. That bloke at the match.'

'I don't know that bloke at the match. But you go into town. You know that lot too.'

'I'm just saying. You should be careful. Some of them are . . . tricky.'

'Don't you start.' I knew he was right, but I didn't need him to tell me. 'They're just friends. They're not going to be my friends for the rest of my life.' As I said it I felt I was being disloyal to Tap. He'd given me a Fred Perry. I hadn't even said a proper thank you.

'No, but it's now. They're, they're . . .'

'What? They're what?'

'I'm just saying. Tap is the person people go to for their pills.'

'Well, I don't take drugs.' I was getting hot.

'I didn't say you did, but –'

'And who are you? My dad?'

'No, no.'

'So where should I go? Down Baddow Road in the Long Bar with the rockers? Is that where you go?'

'No, no. I'm just – just concerned about you.'

'Yeah, well, don't be!' I shouted. I didn't know what to say. He was talking about my friends, Sandra's friends. He was here and Tap wasn't. 'I'm sorry,' I said, 'I think I got on the bus with the wrong person. This is my stop.' I stood up and rang the bell and ran down the stairs. Sandra called out, 'Linda!' The bus stopped opposite First Avenue and I jumped off, pushing through the queue waiting to board.

Sandra was standing at the next bus stop, by Sunrise Avenue. 'What's going on? I paid to go to Sperry Drive,' she said. 'Ray was going to get off, but I told him I'd sort it out.'

'Nothing,' I said. 'He was going on about Tap.'

'I'm not surprised, Tap looked ready to punch him.'

I still couldn't believe it. 'I don't think he would have done, he was wearing his nice suede. I don't know who Ray thinks he is.'

'What did he say?'

'He said I – we – should watch out.' Now I hesitated. I didn't want to tell her he'd included Danny. I didn't want her to hate him. 'He said people who go down the Orpheus are tricky.'

'That's why we like them,' said Sandra.

'Yes,' I said. I knew what Ray meant and I knew what Sandra meant, and I didn't know what to think.

CHAPTER 13

Aldermaston

'WHAT SANDWICHES HAVE YOU GOT?' It was half past six on Monday morning, the day of the London stage of the Aldermaston march, and I wanted to eat my lunch already. I had been awake since five, when Dad had brought us a cup of tea. After breakfast Sandra arrived and Dad drove us all down to the Friends' Meeting House. He wasn't coming on the march. 'I shall keep the home fires burning,' he said, which is what he always said when we went somewhere he didn't want to go, like the Sunday School outing or shopping trips to Oxford Street.

'Spam and pickle.' It was her usual.

And I had mine – corned beef and tomato. I knew they'd be squashed and a bit soggy, even now, which made them delicious and chewy and I couldn't wait.

Sandra and I had never really talked about CND, but this year Sandra had said she wanted to ban the bomb and she'd like to come on the march and Mum said she could. She'd told Danny, and she said he was enthusiastic. She'd thought he might be jealous of her doing things he couldn't do because he was inside.

'He'd never go on a CND march,' I said.

'That's not the point.'

Something in the back of my mind told me that wasn't logical but it was like chewing gum, stretching and popping in my brain and I couldn't work it out.

Mum had first gone on an Aldermaston march in 1958. Aldermaston was where research into nuclear weapons was carried out. I'd known about the H-bomb and the A-bomb for years, particularly about what happened to Japan in August 1945, when the Americans dropped A-bombs onto Hiroshima and Nagasaki. We had discussions round the tea table and we had CND leaflets, but the books on our bookshelves were the most informative. The description of the effects of the bomb had stayed with me – the noise, the flash, the people falling in the streets, the outline of their bodies left on the ground, how some seemed all right and then when they were touched their skin came off like gloves. Like gloves.

Mrs Grenville from the CND group was standing on the pavement by the coach counting everyone in.

The coach wasn't empty because they'd already picked up people from Witham and Boreham. We found a seat in the middle of the coach, and I let Sandra sit by the window as this was her first time on the march.

The Spratts, the Van Gazen family, who Dad called the Star Gazers, Mr and Mrs Germaine, Beryl and Jeremy Husband – most of the Chelmsford CND group – clambered onto the coach. Ken and Robert Sadd were already sitting at the back. Ken and Robert were beatniks who lived near Boreham. Everyone knew that Robert fancied Judith. When she got on the coach he waved wildly at her. I found it hard to believe that people could like Judith, but he had a beard so he was clearly desperate. Judith sailed smugly down the aisle of the coach to join them, followed by her brainy friend James, who was frowning but trying to look nonchalant.

People settled themselves into seats. Mr and Mrs Germaine argued softly about putting their rolled-up macs in the rack above. Some Labour Party members were laughing, telling them to hurry up, comrades. The coach was almost full.

Mrs Grenville was beckoning urgently down the street. It was Ron Bales and Ray. Ray was wearing a faded navy-blue donkey jacket with the collar up. They spent five minutes on the pavement arguing with the driver to open up the luggage compartment on the side of the coach so they could put the banner in.

'If you want to go and sit with him, that's all right,' Sandra said, 'I'll have this seat all to myself.'

'Not likely,' I said. I knew she didn't really mean it. And nor did I.

Ray walked down the aisle towards us. He nodded at me and hesitated as if he was going to say something. Perhaps he'd say he was sorry about the row; that I was right, it was nothing to do with him, and I'd say, that's OK, tell me some more about the rules of football. Then a girl's voice called, 'Hey, it's Ray!' and he shook his head and walked on to the back of the coach.

'Who was that, calling out?' Sandra said. 'You might have a bit of competition there, Lin.'

'I don't care,' I said. I willed myself not to turn and look but Sandra swivelled round and stared over her seat at the back of the bus. She shrugged. 'Can't see. Fingers crossed, though.'

Mrs Grenville stepped up into the coach and counted everyone. 'There's just one more to come,' she called, frowning down at her list. Some people at the back were rumbling the tune of 'Why Are We waiting?'. Mrs Grenville took a step down and hung out of the coach door, looking anxiously along the street. 'Oh, here we are! Quickly!'

'You never said she was coming,' Sandra said.

I shrank into my seat. 'I didn't know!'

Sylvie clambered up the steps into the coach. She was wearing her maroon coat and her hair was pulled back into a pony tail. She didn't look too bad, not showy, not extreme, but she shouldn't have been there. Mrs Grenville was smiling at her, checking her name on the list. 'Better late than never,' she said, patting her arm. Sylvie looked down the aisle of the coach, frowning slightly. Ken Sadd shouted out, 'There's room at the back for a little one,' which I thought was uncool for a beatnik. But Sylvie gave a big smile.

'Have we got to march with her?' Sandra said.

'I don't know. I don't know why she's here.' I felt sick; I was the one who gave her the idea.

Sylvie was coming down the bus.

'Don't look, don't look,' I hissed. 'Look down. Down!'

'Hello, Sylvie,' Sandra said loudly.

'Hello Linda, hello Sandra,' Sylvie said, and carried on walking.

'Oh no,' I said.

'She's gone,' Sandra said.

'But did she hear? Did she hear me? Oh no.' I wrapped my arms round my stomach, doubled up with guilt.

Sandra twisted round again, gazing at the back of the coach. 'No, she's saying hello to a load of people. She's sitting down between the one who shouted and some thin bloke with a beard. Oh, they've all got beards. Nice.'

'What's wrong with us, then? Why doesn't she want to sit with us?'

'Because we haven't got beards. And there's no room. I thought you said she didn't have any friends.'

'That's what she said.'

'Well, she's laughing and joking like she's known them a hundred years.'

I looked round. Sylvie was comfortably squashed into the back seat with the beatniks. Ray was sitting three places away.

'Let's have a sandwich,' Sandra said.

As the coach drove along, I heard Sylvie laugh a lot. I thought I heard Ray's voice. Someone took out a guitar and someone had a banjo, and the back of the bus erupted into song, 'Ban Ban Ban the Bloody H-Bomb'.

'I wouldn't mind, but it's only half past seven in the morning,' Sandra said.

'Is Judith playing?' I asked.

Sandra squinted at the back of the coach. 'No, it's that grammar school bloke of hers. I suppose he has to have a guitar because he's only got half a beard.'

'Judith says he's got a lot of brains.'

'Is that supposed to make it better?'

They were singing 'It Takes a Worried Man to Sing a Worried Song', driving along the A12, just past Romford, and it was getting a bit much. Sandra said, 'If I'd known there'd be singing I might have brought my transistor. Remind me why we're here – tell me your story about the bomb.'

'That wasn't about the H-bomb, or even the A-bomb. And it's not my story.'

'It was about a bomb, and we're against all bombs, aren't we? In case anyone asks me.'

'No one'll ask you. They'll assume.'

'Tell me anyway.'

I told her the story of the German bomb that flattened the house that my mum and her sisters had been sleeping in, in 1940. It killed her mum and dad and her sister Honor, but all the other girls, my mum and my aunties, were pulled out of the rubble without a scratch.

'That was so sad,' Sandra said. 'That could have been your Auntie Sheila, or your Auntie Rita.' Sandra knew my aunties, like I knew hers. 'Why haven't they banned all bombs already? If they'd done it before the war you'd have grandparents.'

'But I probably wouldn't have come from Chelmsford.'

'And we wouldn't be on this coach with this lovely singing. They really should have banned the bomb when they had the chance.'

We got to West London at about nine o'clock. We were joining the march which had started on Good Friday. We would march into Trafalgar Square for the rally at two in the afternoon.

As we stepped off the coach, Ron Bales was carefully unrolling the banner, watched politely by the two Star Gazers that Mrs Grenville had enlisted to carry it. Ray sloped off with some of the Boreham people. Sandra said, 'Why don't you say something to him?'

'There's nothing to say. Anyway, he's gone now.'

'Run after him.'

'Yeah, that would look good.'

One of the Star Gazers climbed into the belly of the coach to find the banner poles. He and his brother slid them into place, in the loops on the sides of the banner. They staggered a little as they lifted it up. It was black and white and read CHELMSFORD CND, WORKING FOR PEACE.

'I wouldn't mind carrying that,' Sandra said.

I looked at her. She obviously hadn't been on a march before. 'It's really heavy,' I said. 'When it rains it gets heavier and if the wind blows, look out. You almost get blown away because it hasn't got any holes in. And why is that? Because Robert Sadd is artistic and didn't want holes in it.'

Witham had their own banner which said WITHAM AGAINST THE BOMB.

'Ours is better,' Sandra said.

'But theirs has holes in.'

I was still worrying about Sylvie. She hadn't got off the coach yet. I felt responsible for her but I didn't know what to do.

Sandra said, 'Why are we waiting? I want to start marching. Hup two, three, four,' she sang, just as Sylvie came down the steps of the coach, laughing. She was followed by Ken Sadd, carrying the banjo.

Sylvie gave us a little wave and they crossed the road and went into a café.

'Is that how you ban the bomb?' Sandra said. 'Going for a coffee?'

'If you do it peacefully,' I said. 'Perhaps they're going to give out leaflets.'

We could hear chanting and bands playing. The Star Gazers lifted the banner and the Chelmsford group stepped off the pavement in a higgledy-piggledy gang. The Witham group followed.

'Aren't we going with them?' Sandra asked.

'No fear,' I said. 'I'm not marching with my mum.'

We stood on the side of the road, watching the march go past. A boy in a college scarf came up to us and said, '*Avez-vous lu votre* Peace News? *Seulement neuf pence.*'

I laughed.

'What's he say?' Sandra asked.

'Peace is cheap.'

A boy in a duffel coat was weaving through the crowds handing out leaflets about a Regional Seat of Government. He put his finger to his lips and said, 'Shhhh, it's a secret.'

You could tell the people who'd done the whole march because they looked messy and worn out. I felt too smart and out of place in my suede coat. I wanted to look tired and experienced.

We walked along the pavement, overtaking Chelmsford, till we found a group with a jazz band. It was Ilford. We stepped into the road and joined them. Strangely, in this setting the jazz sounded just right, rousing and important, not like when Acker Bilk played on the *Billy Cotton Band Show*, when it was plump old people being self-satisfied. Behind their banner this group looked the same as the Chelmsford group, men in overcoats and tweed jackets, women in plastic macs and beatniks in donkey jackets and black jumpers. We were the only mods. After we'd sung 'When the Saints Go Marching In' three times, Sandra said, 'Do you think there's another group, like Romford or Southend, that's got a band playing more of a pop selection?'

'You mean, one that sings "I Never Felt More Like Banning the Bomb"?'

'"Listen, Do You Want to Ban the Bomb?"'

'"Needles and Bombs".'

'"Anyone Who Had a Bomb".'

We had our dinner in Hyde Park. Sandra and I sat under a tree and took out what was left of our sandwiches.

'They look like us,' Sandra said. 'Squashed and limp.'

'And delicious,' I said.

'Shall we take our shoes off?'

'We might never get them back on.'

'I don't care.' Sandra eased off her Hush Puppies. 'Oh God, look at that.' She had a huge blister on her heel. And another on the joint of her big toe. And one across the arch of her foot. Her feet were covered.

I groped in my duffel bag for the little plastic pack of plasters that Mum had given each of us that morning. 'If you had a few more plasters you'd look like the Invisible Man,' I said.

'If I was the Invisible Man I wouldn't be here, I'd be in Wormwood Scrubs.' She wiggled her toes. 'There she is again.'

Sylvie was walking daintily across the grass.

'Do you think she's been following us all the time?' Sandra squinted at her. 'She hasn't got any shoes on.'

'Nor have you.'

'What are you doing?' Sandra said.

I was waving.

Sylvie flapped her hand and tottered over. She was holding a pair of plimsolls. 'Hello, girls, I wondered where you were,' she said. 'What a wonderful spread.' We had laid the sandwiches out on the leaflets we had been given along the route. Sylvie sank to the ground beside us and lay flat on the grass. She closed her eyes. 'I am exhausted. Thank goodness it's lunchtime.' She said that, but she didn't have any food with her.

'Do you want a sandwich?' I asked her.

Sandra punched my arm. I was letting the side down. She glared at Sylvie. 'Didn't you bring anything to eat?'

'Actually, I'm not that hungry.' Sylvie yawned. 'We had egg and bacon earlier.'

'Yeah, we saw,' Sandra said. 'We didn't have time to stop off at cafés, we're banning the bomb the proper way. Marching.'

I still felt responsible. 'Do you want an apple?' I said to Sylvie.

'Thanks.' Sylvie took a bite and looked around her. 'Oh, there they are. See you later, girls.' She handed me back the apple and scrambled to her feet. 'Oh, have this.' She threw a bar of chocolate into my lap, and then ran across to where the Chelmsford group was entering the park.

'So our apples aren't good enough for her,' Sandra said. 'I thought you were going to ask her about her passport.'

'Give me a chance! I'll ask her next week.'

Sandra looked at the chocolate Sylvie had thrown. It was a big bar, a sixpenny bar. 'Make sure she doesn't think that chocolate makes up for the money she owes you.'

'She paid me back. It was another birthday present.'

'Hanky and sixpence. Not bad. No wonder you don't want to ask her difficult questions.' I looked over at Sandra. She was lying on her back, gazing up. 'There's a lot of sky in London, isn't there?' she said.

The last pieces of chocolate were melting in our mouths when the march began slowly shuffling back onto the road. We walked round the park to find the Chelmsford banner. Its poles were stuck in the grass, working for peace under a large oak tree. Ray was still nowhere to be seen. Judith's friend James was playing a Spanish tune on his guitar, and Judith was sitting beside him, doing that fast-clapping thing, which was embarrassing. People were easing their rucksacks onto their backs and Mrs Grenville was picking up litter. There still weren't any mods, but by this stage even the beatniks didn't look too bad. Someone was wearing a beret, someone else had a PVC mac.

'From a distance, if you ignore the old people, and almost close your eyes, Chelmsford looks all right,' Sandra said. She still fancied carrying the banner and went over to Mrs Grenville. Mrs Grenville asked Ron Bales. I could see him nodding and grinning. Together he and Sandra carefully pulled the poles out of the ground. So now we were marching with Chelmsford.

We walked down Park Lane shouting, 'One, two, three, four, we don't want war, five, six, seven, eight, we say negotiate,' and Ken Sadd began a shout: 'Yankee agressors,' and the answer from the march came, 'Out!' 'US in Vietnam,' 'Out!' 'Polaris,' 'Out, out, out!'

'What's Polaris?' Sandra asked me.

'Something in Scotland, that they doo-na want,' I said.

'And what's he doing?'

Ken Sadd was holding hands with Sylvie. He wasn't even one of the beatniks who looked all right.

'I thought you said he fancied Judith,' Sandra said.

'That's his brother.'

Sandra shouted 'Blisters!' and everyone shouted 'Out, out, out!' and laughed.

Mum said, 'Linda!'

We looked up at the people in the hotels watching us, and someone called up to them, 'Ban the bomb! Join the march!' Along Piccadilly we sang, 'Och, och, there's a monster in the loch,' and in Piccadilly Circus, 'It's a long way to Trafalgar Square.'

Sandra was still carrying the banner. 'How much further?' she said. 'I've got blisters on my gloves. Next time I'm going with Witham.' But she was grinning. She shouted, 'What do we want? To get to Trafalgar Square! When do we want it? Now!'

Suddenly I felt very happy. This was where it all made sense. This was what I wanted. Sandra and I, together on the march, agreeing about politics, not arguing about Danny. People being involved but funny, believing in something and doing something about it. And some of them were wearing really quite nice clothes. These were the people who would probably come into the Milk Bar, people who wore a CND badge, people who voted Labour. We might have conversations about books and music and Apartheid and pacifism. And Simone de Beauvoir. This was fantastic.

Then Sandra started looking at her watch.

Chelmsford limped to the end of the Haymarket and round into Trafalgar Square. The speeches had already begun. We were right at the back.

Sandra handed the banner to Mrs Grenville. 'We're late, aren't we?' she said.

I shrugged. 'You never know what time you're going to get to Trafalgar Square.'

'I-I need to go to the toilet.'

'But it's Bertrand Russell.'

'Who?'

'The speaker, the man himself.'

'Can you see him?'

'A bit.'

'Can you hear what he's saying?'

'No.'

'Read it in the paper tomorrow. I've got to go.'

I sighed. 'But this is why we're here. We're trying to change the world.'

'Well, that's likely to happen.'

'But if we don't do something, who will?' I wanted to stay, I wanted to be part of it.

Sandra laughed. 'Well, everyone's going to have a horrible journey home if I don't go soon.'

I sighed. 'All right.'

It took time – finding the toilet, looking for pennies, struggling through the turnstile, queueing, and then we had to find a phone box and four more pennies so she could make a phone call. She pushed me out of the phone box. 'It's personal,' she said.

'You're not ringing Danny?' I groaned.

'Funnily enough, no, because, newsflash, Danny's in prison.'

'Who, then?'

'No one you know.'

I watched her as she took two pieces of paper out of her bag. She put the pennies in the slot, dialled a number I couldn't make out, and then I heard the clatter of money as she pressed button A. A red double-decker bus rolled past and I couldn't hear her first words, but then I heard 'Chelmsford, Essex ... When? OK.' She said goodbye, but stood holding the receiver, staring across the road.

I pulled open the door. 'Who were you ringing?'

She jumped. 'No one, nothing. It doesn't matter.'

'That's not what it looks like. Your face!'

'It's nothing to do with you. Or me, really. It's just ... nothing.'

'Tell me. You had two bits of paper.'

She sighed. 'They were both the number. One part came in one letter and the other part came in the next one.'

So it was Danny. My stomach churned. I didn't want to know anymore.

But she carried on. 'He had to send it in two parts, otherwise the screws would have found it.'

'You're mad. If he's sending you letters with a secret phone number there must be something wrong with it, something you could end up paying for.'

'What was I supposed to do? He asked me.'

'Well, he didn't ask me! The letters come to our house. And my mum's here today.'

'But that was the thing. He was protecting us all. If I made a phone call in London it couldn't be traced to him or me. Or you.'

I shook my head. It still didn't feel right.

'Oh, Linda, leave off. It's just a phone call.'

'Sandra –'

'Come on, we've got to hurry. Your mum will go mad.'

'Yeah, she probably will,' I said. 'About everything.'

CHAPTER 14

The Milk Bar

IT WAS FIVE TO EIGHT ON THE Tuesday morning after Easter – I'd never been in town this early before. It felt strange and empty, as if I was on a film set, waiting for the director to shout 'Action!' so the posse could gallop down the High Street. Even the air was different, fresh and unused. I walked past the Golden Fleece and the Corn Exchange into Tindal Street and past the White Hart, the Spotted Dog and the Dolphin. It was a two-minute walk – if you weren't Danny. If you were Danny, it would take several hours.

The Milk Bar was on the corner of Tindal Street and London Road. It had two entrances. I tried the glass door on the angle of the two streets; it was locked. I went to the London Road glass door. That too was locked. Perhaps it had all been a joke, there was no job, the Milk Bar was closed, permanently, and a Wimpy Bar was going to open in its place. I shook the door in frustration and it rattled loudly.

'Hold your horses,' a voice called from inside. A woman stepped out from behind the espresso machine. She had silver permed hair with a clip in the side, and she was wearing a red-and-black check pinafore apron over a white overall. She waved a large bunch of keys at me and unlocked the door. I walked in and she locked the door behind me.

'Nice and early, that's good,' she said. 'You're Linda, aren't you?'

I nodded.

'I'm Elsie.'

I'd seen her before, though I'd never known her name. The place was the same as ever with its cream and green walls, the long counter with high wooden stools, the low bench along the length of the glass walls that looked out on to London Road. The espresso machine in all its chrome magnificence was sitting on a special counter almost under the stairs, with its own particular supply of glass cups and saucers. The staircase curved up to the tables on the first floor, and beside it was the dumb waiter that ran through the whole building from the kitchen at the top to the counter on the ground floor. All this I knew.

But today the Milk Bar felt very different, because now I worked here. It was quiet and empty and I was talking to Elsie.

Or rather, she was talking to me. I was staring at her in silence. 'You don't have to be scared of me. Although I do the expressos. And that can get dangerous.' She cackled with laughter. 'Except when Mr Wainwright's in. He does the expressos then. Stands by the machine all smooth and nice. That's when he talks to people like your dad. And he's still got all his teeth.' Later she told me the espresso machine was the reason her two front teeth were missing, because once the handle had shot back so fast it had smacked her in the mouth. Then she laughed, so I didn't know what to think.

Elsie was looking me up and down. 'Try these.' She picked up a pile of crisp, ironed clothes from the counter and handed it to me. The clothes mirrored exactly what she was wearing. I hung up my duffel coat on the hooks in the far corner beyond the stairs and changed into my uniform. I looked down at myself. I loved it: the stiff white cotton overall and the simple, contrasting red-and-black apron.

Two more people came in – Val and Noelle. Noelle worked there full time and was small and pale and Irish. Val was a Saturday girl like me; she was at the Tec, which was next to Sandra's school, although I'd never seen her. She was pretty in a brown-wavy-hair, grey-eyes kind of way. They said hello, hung up their coats, picked up their piles of overalls from the counter, put them on and got to work, all within about thirty seconds. Methodically, Val lifted clean white Pyrex cups and saucers out of the dumb waiter and put them on shelves. Noelle took two huge chrome teapots from under the counter and began measuring tea into them from an enormous grey tin of tea leaves. While Val checked the number of milk churns at the end of the counter, Noelle filled one of the teapots with hot water from a tap that hissed and spat. My stomach churned. Noelle and Val were so efficient and useful. How would I ever know the right thing to do?

Doris came in, the cook from the kitchen. She was short and dumpy and she smelt funny. 'This is our new girl,' Elsie said. Doris nodded at me without speaking. She heaved herself up the stairs and disappeared. 'The smell is Germolene, she has bad legs,' Val whispered to me. We both snorted and coughed and she nudged me, and I felt better.

Elsie asked me to sweep the floor. The broom was large and unwieldy and suddenly the room seemed three times as big. We never swept at home, certainly not with a broom, and I wasn't sure what to do. I had to crouch down to reach under the benches and the broom got stuck behind the table legs and I banged my head. There didn't seem to be any point; I couldn't see any dust. Gradually the others all stopped working and stared at me, smiling. Elsie cackled, 'Go the other way, you're treading in it.' I wanted to say, 'If you gave me a hoover there wouldn't be any treading and I could do it twice as fast.' I wanted to say, 'I'm going home now.'

But I couldn't; I'd made such a fuss about getting the job. I just hadn't thought there would be cleaning involved, apart from perhaps giving the tables a swift, efficient wipe with a damp cloth. I wanted to smile charmingly at people and give them golden-coloured cups of tea and offer them their change. I carried on sweeping, turning the broom this way and that, until there was a small pile of dust in one corner and the floor was apparently clean. Everyone cheered. 'She's really getting the hang of it,' Elsie announced, and gave me a hug. 'They all start off hating the broom,' she said to me quietly, and I felt I'd passed a test and I started to enjoy myself.

It was Noelle who showed me how to balance two cups of tea in one hand and how to work the till and, as the sandwiches arrived in the dumb waiter, sent down by Doris in the kitchen, she told me how much the different fillings cost: egg, fish paste, salad. I was muttering prices under my breath when she said the best thing. 'Now you're going to make milkshakes.'

'Really?' I breathed. I had always watched the magic of the process when I ordered milkshakes, and now I was weaving the spell myself. I took the silver metal flask, poured in a measure of rich-coloured syrup, added the milk and then hooked the flask onto the heavy yellow electric whisk on the wall. I stood holding my breath as the whisk hummed thickly, transforming the mixture into a foaming, pale pink milkshake. I poured it into a glass.

'You'd better drink this one,' Noelle said. 'Otherwise we'll just throw it away.' She opened her eyes wide, so I knew it was a treat. Elsie was carrying a tray of glass cups to her den under the stairs. 'Drink it quick,' she said. 'It's almost half past eight. I want to open the doors.'

'There's too much,' I said, gulping, pointing at the half-full flask. Noelle emptied the flask into another glass and Val swallowed it in one go. I longed for my break so that I could make a proper one, all for myself, one that I could savour. I might even put ice cream in.

Elsie unlocked the doors and people trickled in. By ten o'clock we were busy and I was running up and down behind the counter carrying plates and cups and money and change, just as I'd dreamed. Then the owner, Mr Wainwright, came in. He put on a short white cotton jacket and said, 'Welcome, Linda.' He spoke with a really posh accent, which I thought was funny for someone who worked in a milk bar. 'I am sure you will enjoy working here,' he said in a calm, low voice. 'You will see the difference in our service, compared to the other cafés in the town. Here we like to foster the art of quiet conversation. There is no jukebox. I hope that poses no problem for you.'

I shook my head.

At dinner time Sandra came in and ordered a glass of milk.

'The state of you and the price of fish,' she said, looking at my overall. But I knew she was jealous.

At a quarter to three, after another humiliating session with the broom, I walked out of the Milk Bar and along London Road, humming 'Oh Boy'. My precious brown paper envelope containing 12s 6d, my first pay packet, was lying warmly in my bag. I felt mature, part of the real world, a person with her own money.

CHAPTER 15

Dress Sense

WE WERE ALMOST HALFWAY THROUGH the summer term and I was starting to worry about my exams, when the letter came.

The house was empty and the envelope was on the shelf in the hall, propped against the little wooden telephone box that read, *To keep the bill small, please pay for your call*. Mum's friend Rene had given it to her. I recognised the flimsy bluey-grey prison envelope before I recognised the handwriting. It was from Danny, addressed to me, intended for Sandra. She came over to collect it after tea.

Sitting on my bed, she opened the envelope and took out the yellowy lined prison writing paper covered in his neat curly handwriting. Another piece of paper fell onto her lap.

Sandra glanced down and then looked up, her eyes shining. 'It's a Visiting Order. He only wants us to go and visit him in the Scrubs.'

'Who?' My breath disappeared. 'He wants who to go and visit him?' I was playing for time, hoping that if I strung out the question long enough, the answer I feared would change.

'Me and you.'

'He wants me to go? I'm not old enough to visit someone in prison.'

'Yes you are. Look, he says since we are his loving cousins he would be very pleased to see us –'

'But we're not his cousins.'

'And could we bring some cigs.'

'I thought you said he was giving up.'

'Yeah, but they use them, don't they? They swap them.'

'Is it allowed?'

'Of course it is, or they wouldn't let him put it in the letter. Ooh, what shall we wear?'

'Yes, and my mum's likely to let me go. I don't think.'

'Just say we're going to Oxford Street. You want to buy that nightshirt up there, don't you?'

'Yeah, but I don't want to go to prison for it. Anyway, I'm at school, remember.'

'You have holidays, don't you? It's half-term soon, isn't it?'

'I don't know.'

'That's when we'll go.'

'I'll be at work,' I said. 'Probably.'

'I thought you were on a probationary period.'

'I am.'

'You might not even have a job then.'

'Thanks.'

'But Mr Wainwright might not need you.'

'It's a holiday, we'll be busy.'

'But you need a holiday. You said we could go up to London in your half-term. You said that. Oh, go on. Please?'

'Oh, Sandra.'

'All right – just come up on the train with me, to Liverpool Street. Then I'll go to the prison on my own. And we'll both be able to say we're going to London for the day, which will be true.'

'Why? Why does he all of a sudden send you a Visiting Order? I thought he was coming out soon.'

'He is.'

'But he's never done it before.'

'He's lonely. And I'm his girlfriend.'

'So why doesn't he just say that in the Visiting Order?'

'Because that way you wouldn't have been related to him and you couldn't come.'

'But I'm not coming.'

I knocked on Sylvie's door.

'Linda! What a lovely surprise. Have you come to take Mansell for a walk?'

'No, I just . . . came to see you.' *And I have a big worry in the pit of my stomach*, I didn't say.

'That's nice,' she said. 'Come in, I've just made a pot of tea.' She put her finger to her lips. 'The boy's asleep.' We walked past his pram. I went into the living room while Sylvie brought two cups of tea from the kitchen. 'How's the new job?'

Job, the word almost made me smile. 'It's good,' I said. 'It's hard work.'

'Good training for the rest of your life. Have any of the Beatles been in to see you yet?'

I laughed. It was embarrassing that I had ever thought that. And that I'd told her. 'I don't think so,' I said. 'Unless they were in deep disguise as two blokes who sent back their pie and beans because they weren't hot enough. But that would have been George and Ringo, so I don't care.'

'I haven't seen you since the Aldermaston march, have I?' she said. 'Did you enjoy it? Did it give you any ideas?'

'What kind of ideas?'

'About your future. About the people you might get to know. The ones who might come in to the Milk Bar and get chatting.'

I didn't want to talk about that now. I wanted to tell her about the Visiting Order, but I didn't know how to put it. There was a pause.

'School all right?'

'I've got my exams soon.'

She looked at me expectantly, as if she knew I had something to say.

Hurriedly I said, 'How's that dress you were making?'

'Oh, it hasn't got much further.'

'Do you want me to look at it?'

'Would you? Really?' She ran upstairs and came down with a large carrier bag.

I pulled out the white and red material from the bag. It was almost finished. Then a zip fell into my lap. A zip. It was my own fault. I sank down onto the cushion of the settee. I found a reel of cotton and a needle case. I would tack the zip into the back of the dress. That's all. Carefully I began pinning the thick cloth of the zip to the seam of the dress. 'Sandra wants me to go Wormwood Scrubs to see Danny with her,' I said casually, then looked up at Sylvie to gauge her reaction. She had a thoughtful expression on her face. 'And I don't want to go,' I added quickly, before she could say how thrilling that sounded and what a wonderful experience for me, and how she wished she'd been able to do something like that when she was my age.

But she smiled. 'Oh, I say.'

'I'm not going.'

She examined my face. 'But . . . you feel you should go?'

'Yes, except I shouldn't. I mean, I should go for Sandra's sake, but I shouldn't go on my mum's terms.'

'And what about your terms?'

'I don't know!'

She raised her eyebrows. 'All right. Here's my advice – if you want it?'

I nodded miserably.

'Don't think about it, and make a decision only when you have to.' That seemed so simple and sensible. 'When is all this meant to happen?'

'At half-term,' I said. 'Two weeks.'

'All right,' she said. 'When the bus into town arrives, decide at that point whether you'll get on it, or simply stand at the bus stop and wave Sandra off with a jaunty smile.'

'Oh, I'm definitely getting on the bus. I'm going to London. It's what happens when we get there, that's the problem. I want to go shopping, she wants to . . .'

'. . . to visit Danny. Oh well, chicken, just see how it feels at the time, if it feels right, or wrong, or silly, or interesting. And then choose,' she said.

I looked at her. 'I have chosen,' I said. 'I'm not going to the prison.' I wanted to see what she said, see if her face fell, see if she was disappointed in me.

'That's fine,' she said. 'It's your decision. And you've made it. That's something.' She paused. 'But you're troubled, aren't you? Don't think about it anymore today. Now, what can we do to lighten the mood?' She looked over at the record player.

She must have seen me wince. 'I know,' she said, 'let me tell you about the casino.' She arranged herself in the armchair, tucking her skirt under her knees. 'So, where had we got up to? Ah, yes. I was just about to tell you what happened after I won all that money.'

'I thought you lost it again.'

'Did I? Oh yes.'

'And then you had your night with . . .'

'With Bob, my night of passion. Of course! I had quite forgotten I'd told you about that.' She sighed.

'And he gave you some money.' Surely she remembered. It was her story.

'Yes, yes, that's right. Now this part has got some fashion in it,' she added. 'Quite a lot, actually.'

'Go on, go on,' I said.

'Are you sitting comfortably?' Sylvie said. She put her head back and closed her eyes.

In the morning over breakfast – very nice sausages, I remember, and very, very good crisp fried bread, Janet asked her aunt's advice as to where we might buy a dress that was a little out of the ordinary, something with a bit of style, for a special event I had coming up in Chelmsford. Janet kept smirking, and her aunt looked at us suspiciously, but eventually she said she knew a shop that might sell the sort of outfit we were after, although it was rather high-class.

'Perfect,' said Janet.

It was a hot day. Janet and I pushed our way through the crowds in the main road, the tourists wandering aimlessly, eating candyfloss and licking sticks of rock. We had something very important to do. The thought of it made us laugh. Thinking back, I suppose I was a little hysterical – the memory of the night before, the things he'd said, it was all so wonderful. We couldn't find the road. It took ages, up and down, round and round. I was sweating. Finally, we turned into a shadowy dark street.

'Here we are,' Janet said, stopping outside a door that looked like the door to a house, not a shop.

'Are you sure?' There was no one in the street; it all felt unreal.

'It's high-class,' Janet said. 'That's what they're like. In you go.' She gave the door a push. The bell pinged and we were inside.

'I need a dress,' I said to the assistant.

'It's got to be glamorous, and she needs it for tonight.' Janet sat down in a small, ornate armchair and crossed her hands over her stomach. She looked much more confident than I felt.

The assistant hesitated. We must have looked a sight, our faces so red and our hair all windswept. This was a very swanky establishment.

There wasn't much of anything ready-made. I tried on a dress. It was grey, and it was too big.

'You look like an elephant,' Janet said.

I tried on two more. They were black. Janet shook her head. 'Sorry, doll, you don't look what I'd call gorgeous in those.'

The assistant pursed her lips. 'I'm afraid that's all we have.'

'How much money have you got, Sylvie?' Janet asked.

I pulled out the handful of notes from my bag.

The assistant's eyes widened. She said, 'Ah, well. Perhaps we have another dress. A lady was meant to be picking it up last week, but she didn't come. It may fit you.'

It was blue, sapphire blue. I slipped it on. The heavy crepe fell over my hips, skimmed my knees. I looked at myself in the mirror and I was transformed. I looked lovely. Down to my ankles, that is. 'I haven't got the right shoes,' I moaned, looking at my feet, which were very dusty.

'How about these?' The woman produced a pair of high, strappy gold sandals. I slid them on, and my goodness, the difference they made. My legs looked two feet longer and very, very slim.

Janet put her head on one side. 'Turn round . . . Sylvie, you are gorgeous. Just right.'

The dress was 18 guineas, the shoes were 25s 11d. We scrabbled in our purses for the change for the last four shillings.

'So you've paid for some of it yourself, which means you're not exactly a kept woman,' Janet said, putting the penny change in her bag.

I have to say that I could hardly tear myself away from my reflection, and I took the dress off very slowly and carefully.

'You look like the cat with the cream,' Janet said. I was smiling to myself, thinking about him, his face the night before, what his face would say that night when he saw me.

When we got back to the boarding house, I scurried upstairs with the expensive carrier bag while Janet told her aunt that we hadn't seen anything we liked. If she'd suspected I was going out that night in an expensive dress she might have asked too many questions. If she'd thought I was going out with one of her lodgers, she might even have stopped me going. That's what it was like in those days.

After the evening meal, I walked down the stairs, my raincoat draped over my shoulders, covering the dress. Janet walked behind me. We said goodbye at the door, grinning like mad at each other. We'd said I was going out with a friend from Chelmsford to a youth club she knew. Janet was going to put her aunt's hair in rollers as a treat for letting us stay in her boarding house for such a reasonable price. I felt a bit guilty that I was having all the fun and Janet kept staying in. 'Don't worry,' she said. 'Auntie and I have got all sorts of excitement planned. After the hair-washing, we'll have a few rounds of gin rummy and a little whist. We might even play for money. It will be our very own casino, right here. Sure you don't want to stay?'

At nine o'clock I walked into the pub, my raincoat over my arm, conscious of the dress moving with me, making me graceful, gliding. My hair was pulled back, all shiny and, what do you call it? tumbling down to my shoulders. I could feel people's eyes on me as I approached the bar. I glanced round the room, smiling at everyone, heady with anticipation, then turned back to the barman. He studied my face with approval, I felt, and my smile got even wider. 'You're the lady who was in here last night, aren't you, with the Yanks?'

I nodded.

'You're looking very nice tonight,' he said.

'Thank you,' I said. I noticed he had a pound note sticking out of his shirt pocket.

His expression changed. He frowned as he handed me a folded-up piece of paper. 'I've to give you this.' He almost spat the words, and I couldn't think why. Did this man not like Americans? Did he think I was a loose woman? I looked at him. But he was polishing a glass, his face turned studiously away from me. I looked down at the folded piece of paper and I felt ever so slightly sick. I knew I wasn't going to like whatever was in the note. Slowly I opened it and I read the words:

I'm sorry, honey, we have to go back to base. You were great. I'll remember you. B

I looked up at the barman. Now he was wiping the counter, but glancing at me, not really looking. He said, almost to himself, 'Yanks, eh?' I was having difficulty breathing. Then he said casually, 'Do you want a drink? On the house?' He was so kind, the tears almost spilled over. I shook my head, I couldn't speak. I turned and left the pub, trying to keep at least a little smile on my face. I put the raincoat on and dragged myself back to the boarding house. I walked upstairs to the room, kicked off the shoes and ripped off the dress.

Janet came in. 'You don't have to say anything. I know.' Twenty minutes after I'd gone, she said, the Americans came down to pay their bill. Her auntie nearly died. The Americans were peeling off the pound notes, and there she was with a scarf tied round her head, hiding four rows of rollers.

I laughed. 'Tell her she needn't have worried.'

'I'll tell her she should have charged them twice as much.' Janet straightened the gold shoes and put them neatly beside the wardrobe. She came and sat on the bed and put her arm round me. She said, 'Can I borrow the dress for my sister's wedding?'

I smiled, but tears were rolling down my face.

I couldn't bear it. I couldn't bear that it had ended like that. I was furious. 'But how could he? You and he ...'

I looked at Sylvie's face, but she seemed calm, just picking a bit of fluff from her skirt.

'These things happen.' She gave a little smile. 'Let's talk about something else.'

I didn't know what to say. 'Janet sounds nice,' I said weakly.

'Janet's been with me through thick and thin.'

'But when was this?' I said, keeping my eyes on my stitching. Sandra's comments were playing in my head.

'Oh, don't bother trying to do the sums, you'll only get a headache,' Sylvie said. 'But yes. Bob played his part. And now there's Mansell, and for that we must all be truly grateful.'

The way she said it, I wasn't sure she meant it.

'I have to say that,' she said, as if she'd read my mind, 'or people think I'm a terrible mother. But if things hadn't happened the way they happened, and if he hadn't been born, well, he wouldn't have been born.'

'But did you see Bob again? Does he send you money? For Mansell?'

'Bob? He hasn't got any money.'

'I thought all Americans had money – even in the war they were giving everyone nylons and chewing gum, weren't they?'

'I think that, relatively speaking, those weren't expensive. And Bob was what they call white trash. He lived in a trailer.

A caravan. A lot of poor Americans do it. Being in the Air Force was a great thing for him. Any spare cash he had he sent home to his dear old mom. That's what he said, anyway.'

I was so confused. Was Bob a good thing or a bad thing? He was an American serviceman, but he was poor and he loved his mum. Did Sylvie like him or not?

'Why don't you care about . . . Mansell's father?'

'It's not me who doesn't care, it's his father who . . . who doesn't show his feelings.'

'But what if Mansell wants to know him?'

'Well, that might be a hard one. His dad is very good at making himself scarce. As you see, I have very little company. Except for you, of course, and I wouldn't be without that. If his dad wants to know Mansell when he's older, I shan't stop him. But basically, children need the people who love them and care for them. It doesn't have to be their parents. It could be like the children of the kibbutz.'

I didn't know what a kibbutz was. It sounded like a made-up word. It sounded mad.

'Naturally,' Sandra would say. 'That's because she is mad.'

But today she didn't look mad; today she looked thoughtful and lovely.

'So would you have given him away? To be adopted?'

'No! A kibbutz isn't about giving children away, it's about the community caring for them. I've seen it in action. In Israel.'

'Abroad? Did you go there? Have you got a passport?'

'All these questions! No, I didn't go there, I saw a film. So I didn't need a passport. But the kibbutz system works very well. It's a shame we don't have them here. I was, in fact, under a lot of pressure to give Mansell away. People said he'd have a better life if he was adopted, but I wouldn't. I wouldn't do it.'

'Do you think he would have been better off adopted?' I said, before I realised what I was saying. 'Oh, I mean, I didn't mean he's not well off . . . he's . . . he's growing so well.'

'What does it mean? Better off,' Sylvie said thoughtfully, taking my question as just a question. 'Materially, yes, he might have been. But he's not adopted, and he never will be.' She looked over at Mansell. 'He's mine.'

Quietly I folded up the dress and put it back in its bag.

'Well, what an afternoon!' Sylvie said. 'We've talked about a lot of things, haven't we? But I've rather enjoyed it.'

I looked at her. We both had tears in our eyes. 'So have I,' I said. 'Thanks for the advice. About the Visiting Order.'

Sylvie took the bag and held it against her. 'I don't think I said anything you hadn't already thought yourself,' she said. 'I know it's a tricky one.'

I picked up my coat and walked to the door. I realised I felt better than I had for a long time.

CHAPTER 16

A Day Out in London

SANDRA WAS WEARING HER CREAM straight skirt and her bottle-green twinset. I was wearing my straight grey skirt and my twinset because Danny had called us his cousins, which meant we were technically sisters, so we ought to look as if we were related. But this was just for the train. To get Sandra in the mood. I wasn't going to the prison.

She came with me to Oxford Street. She wanted her hair done and she didn't know where else to go. There was a place called Chez Janine that we'd noticed before, at the top of a narrow fire escape in an alleyway near Oxford Circus. I left her climbing the metal stairs while I went into British Home Stores and looked at nightshirts.

When we met up again I hadn't bought a nightshirt but she'd had a lot of backcombing done. It was a beehive.

'My friend Sandra, the rocker,' I said.

It looked surprising, but I knew why she'd done it.

'He'll like it like this,' she said.

There was still time to spare – she wasn't due at the prison until two o'clock – so we decided to have egg and chips in Littlewoods.

We put our trays on the table and hung our coats carefully over the backs of our chairs.

Sandra leaned across the table for the tomato sauce. 'I want to get a new suede,' she said. 'They've got some really good navy-blue ones in Sacks and Brendlor's. It'll go nicely with Danny's leather.'

'If he's ever out long enough for you to walk down the street together.' I was irritated. She kept looking at her watch. She was yearning to get to Wormwood Scrubs. 'Why do you want to get engaged to Danny, anyway? He's in and out of prison like a bad game of snakes and ladders. And you can't really call him a mod. He's never had a scooter, and he hasn't got a car except the ones he nicks. He hasn't even passed his driving test. And look at all the backcombing you've had done, just for him.'

She pointed her knife at me. 'You think too much about mods. It's not just about that, you know.' She put down her knife and fork. 'All right, this is why I like Danny.' She held up her hand and pointed to her fingers in turn. 'One, he's different, he's beefy and strong. Two, he's exciting. Had you ever been in an Austin Seven before? No. Have you ever had a letter from a boy in prison? No. And – newsflash – I'm not going to end up marrying someone who wears glasses.'

'Nor am I! I don't know anyone who wears glasses.'

'Not yet. But you know you will. You'll go off to college and meet lots of interesting people. Danny's the most interesting thing I've bumped into since I fell over next door's sausage dog. I know that's not saying much, but we do live in Chelmsford. And,' she held up her hand again, 'three, four and five – he's a good kisser.' She crowed with laughter.

'But you could do it too.'

'What?'

'Go to college.'

'Yeah, my mum and dad are likely to let that happen.' She picked up her knife and fork.

'Or, I don't know, come up here to London, to get a job. I could go to college here. We could share a flat or something. That's what Cray's going to do. Lots of people are doing that now. Do you really want to get married to a jailbird? You could do loads of things. You could get a job in one of the big hotels, on the reception desk.' Sandra knew that was a job I'd quite like myself. 'Or what about working in Carnaby Street? You'd probably get the clothes cheaper. They like people who chat. You chat. The Beatles might come in.' I was seeing the life we could have, swinging London girls in fashionable clothes, jumping onto a red London bus to get to work. There were so many possibilities.

She shook her head. 'I like our life in Chelmsford. Don't you?'

'Yes.' It was true, I did like our life.

'Well, then.'

I knew I couldn't have both. I didn't know what to think.

'What time is it?' Sandra said.

I said I'd walk her down to Tottenham Court Road Underground station.

We stopped at a kiosk on the way for her to buy some cigarettes and chocolate. As we got to the Underground, she said, 'Oh, come with me. I can't go on my own, they'll ask me where you are. We do look like sisters, and that eyeliner makes you look much older.'

I'd known all along she'd say this. And I had sort of known all along that I would go with her. She needed me to go with her, and I wouldn't have known what to do on my own for three hours.

Then she added reluctantly, 'And Danny asked me specially to bring you, in the letter. He underlined it.'

'He underlines everything.' But I was pleased.

We got on the Central Line train and travelled to Shepherd's Bush. The platform was dark and grimy, and the tunnels on the way out were long and empty. I wasn't sure it was worth it.

'Wormwood Scrubs?' said the ticket collector incredulously, when Sandra asked the way. 'Wormwood Scrubs?

It's not here.' He laughed, looking across at the ticket office, and said loudly, 'Why would anyone think Wormwood Scrubs is at Shepherd's Bush?'

I could see Sandra thinking, Because that's the postmark on his letters. But she said nothing. I was thinking, We don't have to go, we can't find it, we don't have to go.

'You've got to get off at East Acton if you want to go to Wormwood Scrubs.' He was still laughing. The laughing was a bad omen. He knew who we were. He could tell we weren't sisters, he knew we weren't going to visit our cousin. He was enjoying our stupidity. 'East Acton is two more stops.'

Sandra said, 'Well, give us our tickets back, then, so we can go there,' as if it was his fault we'd got off too early. 'Cheek,' she said, and I felt better.

East Acton wasn't underground at all; there were trees and gardens. And signs to the large grey stone prison. We followed a trickle of women with children in pushchairs through a narrow side door.

As we handed in the Visiting Order I remembered the chocolate. As well as the two packets of cigarettes, Sandra had bought Danny a large liqueur chocolate wrapped in silver paper, laughing, saying, 'He'll get a surprise when he eats this.' And I had laughed too, thinking I wouldn't be there, imagining the look on his face as unexpected alcohol dripped down his throat. Now we were inside the prison walls. We were taking alcohol to a prisoner, which had to be illegal, and we weren't related, to him or to each other, and despite everything she had said, we probably were underage to be visiting a prison. What if they searched us and found the chocolate? What would they do to us? What if they separated us and grilled us? What would Sandra say? What would I say? Would they keep us in Wormwood Scrubs, or would they haul us off to a women's prison?

They scarcely even looked at the soft, creased piece of rag which the Visiting Order had become in Sandra's hands, and we were directed to a large, airy room like a seaside café, with frosted glass windows. We sat down at an empty table. Around the room men in royal-blue cotton overalls were chatting quietly to women. Two small children chased each other around the seats. Then Danny came in, laughing and joking with the warders. Sandra stood up and pushed back her chair. She and Danny kissed for a long time, with their arms round each other. It was like being in Chelmsford bus station on a Saturday night.

When Sandra and Danny sat down she gave him the cigarettes. And then she brought out the chocolate. It had grown since it had been in her bag. It was the size and shape of a hand grenade. Danny unwrapped the silver paper slowly, looking over at Sandra from time to time, and then carefully put the silver paper in the ashtray. I sat rigid. Carefully he bit off the tip of the chocolate, tilted back his head and swallowed the contents. Sighing with pleasure, he put the empty chocolate shell on top of the silver paper in the ashtray and we all watched it rocking gently to a standstill.

A warder came up and said, 'Everything all right, Danny?'

Danny burped. There was the sweet smell of rum. My mouth went dry. 'Yeah, how's yourself?' he said. The warder nodded and moved away.

'The screws love me.'

'Why's that, Danny?' I said.

'Because everyone loves a lover.'

I rolled my eyes.

'That reminds me,' he said. 'I've got something for you, Linda.' Sandra stiffened. Danny turned in his chair towards the tea trolley. 'Oy, Trevor,' he called. Another man in a blue prison uniform, holding a cup under the tea urn, looked up and waved. Danny said, 'That's Trevor. He's a bit lonely and I said I'd fix him up.'

'With me?' I said. Someone for me? We were in a prison, lying about who we were, smuggling in rum and now I was being set up with a criminal! If this was Chelmsford life, I didn't want it.

Trevor smiled at me. He had short brown hair and a thin face like a weasel. In different clothes he would have looked like a mod from Chelmsford. In really good clothes he could have come from Mile End. I smiled back uncertainly. He looked twenty or even older. I wondered how old he thought I was.

Sandra said, 'Who's he?'

Danny said, 'Trevor's an old mate of mine.'

Trevor laughed. I wondered if we had seen him before. There was something very Chelmsford about him.

'No one writes to him.' Danny winked at Trevor, who was placing a cup of watery tea on the table in front of me. 'All right, Trevor?' He slid a packet of cigarettes across the table.

I couldn't think why he was giving cigarettes to Trevor. He should have been giving them to me, because I was the one doing Trevor the favour. If I ever did do him a favour. If I smoked Embassy. If I smoked.

'All right, Mulroney.' Trevor sat down next to me. 'So you're the famous Linda,' he began. 'Very nice. Take sugar?'

'No thanks.' We sat in silence and looked at Sandra and Danny. They were holding on to each other's arms, murmuring.

Trevor looked at his watch. He was bored. 'Don't let me hold you up,' I said, looking over at the tea trolley.

'It's all right,' he said. 'They can serve themselves. Keep the screws busy.' He looked at me. 'So you're from Chelmsford. Is it still a whole scene going down there?'

'We get some good groups, if that's what you mean,' I said. 'We've got Wilson Pickett on Saturday.' I wanted to have a normal conversation, I wanted to look normal, I didn't want anyone looking too closely.

'Oh yeah? Lucky old Wilson,' he said.

I heard Danny say, 'Good girl, thanks.'

'You've got a nice little figure,' Trevor said. He leaned over to another table to get an empty ashtray.

'Have I?' I looked down at my twinset. Danny was stroking Sandra's stiff hair.

Trevor offered me a cigarette. I shook my head. He held the packet out towards Danny. 'Danny tells me you haven't got a boyfriend.'

'Danny doesn't know everything,' I said.

At the mention of his name, Danny looked up. 'That's right, I forgot,' he grinned. 'There's always Tommy Steele, or is it Mark Wynter now?' He took a cigarette. Sandra slapped his arm and he put it behind his ear.

'I'm actually into blues, if you must know,' I said. I had liked Tommy Steele when I was much younger, but I had never liked Mark Wynter. 'Do you like blues?' I asked Trevor.

'I get the blues,' he said.

'Do you have the radio in here?' I said. 'You should listen to Mike Raven's music programme. Radio 390.' Trevor said nothing. 'On Wednesdays.' I wondered if I was talking to myself. But I wanted him to understand. 'It's the emotion of the songs I like, and the sound, as if they've been recorded in a toilet,' I said.

'This one likes toilets,' Trevor said to Danny. 'Is that what gets the girls going in Chelmsford?'

I could feel the blush rise up my cheeks.

'What's she saying now?' Sandra frowned at me.

'Nothing,' I said. 'We're talking about music.'

Sandra turned back to Danny.

'It's the way the records hiss because the recording's so scratchy.' I wanted to explain myself. 'It's not just the sound, it's the rhythms.'

'Oh, I like rhythm. I'm a great one for rhythm, me.' He took a drag on his cigarette.

I knew he didn't care but I wanted to get the word toilet out of the air. 'They sort of ache with sadness and despair.'

Trevor looked round the room. 'Yeah, there's a lot of that in here.' He yawned. Danny settled Sandra into the crook of his arm.

'And the records he plays, in his programme, sometimes it's people who play at the Marquee.'

Trevor stretched his legs. 'If you say so.'

I felt stupid. 'In Soho,' I finished uncertainly.

'Oh, Soho?' Trevor sat up. 'So you go to Soho? Is that where you work, then?' He laughed and pulled his chair closer to mine. His eyes were small and his eyelashes pale, almost invisible.

'No,' I said. I knew what he meant. 'That's where Tin Pan Alley is, isn't it?' He looked at me. He wasn't yawning. 'And the Two-i's? Where Tommy Steele was discovered? I think Cliff Richard started there too.' I made a face, to show that although I knew the history, I didn't really care about Cliff Richard. He had always been too smooth, his voice too posh to be a real rock and roller.

'I like Cliff Richard,' he said.

'Oh.' That was disappointing.

Sandra and Danny were talking intensely, their heads close together.

Trevor put his arm along the back of my chair. There was a smell of sour sweat as he tucked the St Michael label back into my cardigan, brushing my neck with his fingers. My back tingled. 'When I get out, Linda, perhaps you and I could go to Soho.'

'Yeah, perhaps,' I said, thinking, not if you like Cliff Richard, we couldn't. You'd have to be wearing really, really good clothes if that was ever going to happen.

A bell rang. Sandra's eyes got red. She took a hanky out of her pocket and blew her nose. Danny stood up and wrapped his arms round her. 'Bye-bye, Sandy,' he whispered. She clung on to him, burying her head in his chest. Danny looked over at Trevor and winked.

Trevor stood up. 'You're lucky she's got good legs, Mulroney,' he said over my head, 'or it would be more than one packet of fags.'

'I told you you'd like her,' Danny said.

'All right, Mulroney, we'll see,' Trevor said.

I stood up and Trevor leaned towards me. The sour smell was strong. He put his face near mine, bumping my nose. 'Can you do something for me, dear?' he murmured.

'What?' My heart pounded, what did he mean? A convict wanted me to do something? a job for him?

'Nothing illegal.' He laughed. 'Just see she gets home all right.'

'Who? What do you mean?'

'It's not so much for me, it's for Mulroney there. He wants you to tell her.'

'Tell her what?'

The bell rang again, loud and persistent, like a fire alarm bell.

Trevor looked over his shoulder. Sandra and Danny were still kissing.

'What?!'

'Shh! He's – he's finishing with her. He doesn't want to go out with her anymore.'

I jerked my head back, angry with relief that it was nothing illegal. 'You're making it up. Are you a friend of his, or what? Look at them.'

'That's just for show. Don't forget, me and Mulroney go back a long way. We have what you might call an understanding, even if we have our ups and downs.' He almost laughed.

'Why doesn't he tell her himself?' I said. 'Or if you're such a good mate, you tell her.'

He pulled me tightly towards him. 'He doesn't want a scene.' He muttered into my ear, 'He thought she might get upset.'

'I think she might. Why? What's it all about?'

Danny was touching Sandra's cheek, tenderly, with his thumb. Could Trevor really be telling the truth?

Trevor looked round, then began to stroke my hair as if I was his girlfriend and we were saying a sad goodbye. 'It's the other girl, you know. Brenda? Belinda? What's her name? B . . .'

'Barbara? Do you mean Barbara?'

'Shh! Yes, you got it! He said you were a brainy girl. Look, between you and me, Barbara's in a bit of trouble, if you get my drift, and Mulroney's the – the person who needs to sort it out. He wants you to tell Sandra, though not about the – ah – trouble, obviously. He knows you'll think of the right thing to say. Don't tell her till you're at home. Understand?'

I looked at him, furious.

'Ooh, look at her, wrinkling her nose,' he sneered. 'Don't blame me, mate. I'm just passing it on. She'll get over it, don't worry. There's plenty more fish in the sea. And you'll do it, won't you?' He put his face close to my ear and whispered, 'I hate it when people don't do what I ask them to, don't you?' He moved away and smiled. 'Anyway,' he said in a normal voice, 'this is your lucky day, you've met me and we've got that date in Soho, yeah?' He picked up the packet of cigarettes from the table and gave me a little shove towards the exit.

Sandra and I walked to East Acton station. I was silent as she dabbed her eyes and blew her nose, and I stayed silent as she grew brighter, talking about the romantic things Danny had said and all her plans for the future. I wanted to say, 'What about what Trevor said?' But was it true? He might simply be holding a grudge against Danny. He said they'd had their ups and downs. Should I tell Sandra? I wanted her to know so we could discuss it. But he'd said to wait till we got home. What if he had someone watching us?

As our train pulled out of Liverpool Street Station, Sandra wrote the word 'Danny' on the misted-up window of the carriage. 'Cheer up,' she said. 'We didn't get arrested, and you've got yourself a nice boyfriend.'

'I don't think so.'

'Actually, I should probably tell you,' Sandra said, 'he's up for armed robbery. He's supposed to have shot someone.'

'Oh great,' I said. 'I've just spent the afternoon with a killer.'

'He didn't kill him, he shot him in the leg.'

'Shot him!'

'It was only an airgun. It was self-defence. Apparently.'

'Well, that's all right then.' I didn't know what to do. I wrote 'Tap' very small in a corner of the window. The train was leaving Romford Station when Sandra said, 'So go on then, what did he say to you?'

'Who?'

'Trevor.'

I shrugged. 'Nothing. About Soho and stuff.'

'No, at the end, what did he say to you?'

I shook my head. 'Is he really a friend of Danny's?'

'Danny said he was. He said he met him years ago. I think that means they met in borstal. And that was him in the fight that night in the Dolphin.'

I shivered. 'He didn't look much like a friend then.'

'But Danny said Trevor gave you an important message.' So it was true.

'Go on, tell us,' she wheedled. 'He said I shouldn't ask till we got back to Chelmsford, but go on.'

I took a breath. 'He said I had to look after you and make sure you got home all right.'

'You? Have to look after me? Why?'

'That's what I said. He said – he said that Danny was finishing with you.'

Her face went white. 'What?'

'He said –'

239

'I heard. Are you saying he's packed me up?' she hissed.

'It's not my fault,' I said. 'Perhaps it's not true. Trevor could be making it up . . .' My voice trailed away.

'He's not making it up, it's true. I knew it. I knew there was something. He was being so nice. How could he? How could he?' She plunged her hand into her bag and pulled out his last letter. She squeezed the pages into her fist. 'Why?' she said. 'Why would he want to do that?'

'I don't know.' I hesitated. 'Trevor said something about Barbara.'

'Barbara? Bloody Barbara? Look at this! Look at this!' She held out the pieces of paper. '"I love you . . . I can't wait to see you . . . You're the best girl". Yeah, after bleeding bloody Barbara. Who was it ringing up weird people, delivering messages for him?! It wasn't bloody Barbara, was it? It was me.'

'What do you mean? What sort of messages? Do you mean that phone call? Is that what we were doing today? Passing messages? Sandra! What if your dad found out? What if the police caught you? We could both be in so much trouble.'

'Well, it's done now.' She started to tear the pages. 'He didn't have to write all that love stuff. Why couldn't he just finish with me in the letter, like a normal person?' She pulled down the window and threw the scraps of paper back along the track. There were tears in her eyes.

I couldn't keep on at her. 'Perhaps he thought it was better to tell you face to face.'

'But he didn't! He told Trevor to tell you to tell me.' Sandra was breathing on the window. The word Danny was just readable, the letters disappearing into tears of condensation. She wiped her hand across the glass. Danny was gone.

She opened her bag again. 'Do you want a bit of chocolate?' She pulled out the empty grenade and handed it to me.

'I didn't see you pick that up,' I said. I spread a hanky on my lap and cracked the chocolate. I gave Sandra a piece.

'At least he drank the rum. I hate rum,' she said.

We chewed the chocolate in silence, through Shenfield and Ingatestone and past the lights of the Chelmsford City football ground. As we stepped out onto the platform, she linked her arm through mine. 'He'll probably change his mind when he gets out,' she said.

'But you won't?'

'We'll have to see,' she said.

'Oh, Sandra,' I sighed.

We were passing the grammar school when a green-and-white Corsair glided past and then stopped.

'All right, girls?' Cooky said. 'What have you been up to today?'

'You don't want to know,' Sandra said. 'Take us home, will you?'

Cooky drove us up to the shops where we got out and he drove away.

'Why's he so friendly all of a sudden?' I said.

'Who do you think sent that Valentine I got?' Sandra looked up the road as Cooky took the long way out of the estate.

CHAPTER 17

Sylvie Tries

EVERYTHING SEEMED CALMER AFTER THE trip to Wormwood Scrubs, and now I had to focus on my exams which were a week away.

When I got home from school Mum was ironing in the living room. She was having a week off. A heap of washing sat on her armchair. 'Ah, there you are.' She heaved a sheet across the ironing board. 'I was in the shop this morning and Mrs Weston mentioned that as it was early closing this afternoon, she was taking Mansell over to Braintree for a visit.' She straightened the edges of the sheet. 'She wondered if you would like to go and sit with Sylvie.' Mum gazed at me. 'It's a good thing to do.'

'What about my exams?' I said. 'I've got to revise biology. It's the ear. The ear is complicated.'

'It's a shame you didn't use your holiday to do it,' Mum said.

'I was working,' I said, bitterly. 'Earning money. It's not just about hearing, you know, it's about balance and giddiness and all sorts.'

'It sounds as if you know it already,' Mum said. 'But if you're so anxious to revise, take your books with you. I think it's important that you go. Have a slice of bread now and then you won't need any tea.'

I had to knock three times. Then a tired voice called, 'Coming.' Sylvie pulled open the door. I stared at her. She looked cold, her skin was almost, what was that word? translucent. In fact she looked quite nice, what my mum would have called 'pale and interesting', in her plain green shift dress and her hair brushed back from her face in a French pleat. She smiled at me and silently beckoned me in.

I followed her into the kitchen. She put the kettle on, while I pulled out a chair and sat down.

She leaned back against the sink and held on with both hands. 'It's so lovely to see you,' she said, the first words she had spoken. 'I haven't seen many people lately. So what have you been up to?' She spoke as if it was a strain, as if she was trying to swallow the words.

I shrugged. 'Nothing.' She looked at me with a slight frown. I felt uncomfortable. 'Going to school.'

'And how's school?' Her lower lip was moving strangely. I shook my head. 'We've got exams coming up.'

'That's good.' She poured boiling water into the pot. 'And how's Tap?' she said. 'That bad boy, what's he up to?'

I smiled. It was nice to hear his name. It was nice to see her. 'He still works in The Boutique. But because of my exams, I can't really go out much.'

'Lovely.' She kept swallowing. 'How's school?'

'We've got exams,' I said again.

Sylvie sat down, putting the teapot and the cups on the table. 'Ah, you must be working hard.'

'Sort of.'

'Oh dear.' Her face stretched into an odd shape.

'Are you all right? I'm sorry I haven't been round lately.'

'Well, I haven't been here.'

'Good job I didn't come,' I said.

She smiled. 'Do you know where I've been?'

I shook my head. I had a feeling I didn't want to know where she'd been. I poured the tea. Sylvie heaped spoonfuls of sugar into her cup, three, four. Finally, in the thick silence, I said, 'How are you?'

'I stuck my head in the oven.'

I stared at her.

'Our oven, it's a gas oven. I turned on the taps and put my head in there.'

She'd tried to kill herself. No one had said anything about that.

She lifted her eyes to mine and I looked away sharply. All I'd said was 'How are you?' I only asked because I was trying to be polite, and then this came out! She stuck her head in the oven. I couldn't even begin to wonder why she had done it. I knew why she had done it. She was ill. But why did she have to tell me? What did she want me to say? Is that why I was here, to stop her trying to kill herself again?

'And do you know what my mother's first words were when she came in and found me? This will make you laugh.' I doubted it. 'The first thing she said when she was flinging open the windows, before she dragged me up off the floor, was, "I hope it was your money in the meter".' She laughed, her little cracked laugh.

I wanted to say, 'Well, at least it wasn't mine,' but I also wanted to say, 'I don't want this cup of tea, thank you, I want to go home.' I didn't want to talk about this. She shouldn't be telling me about it. There was a funny little smile on her face that wasn't meant for me. 'Always practical, my mother,' she said. 'I half-expected her to say, "And when you've woken up a bit, could you give the oven a clean?" Which I should say, from close examination, it could do with.'

'But you don't like housework, do you?' I said.

'Ooh, is that a little criticism, Linda?'

'No, it's what you said.' It wasn't fair. 'It was in the book.' I didn't know how to talk to her. I scrabbled in my bag to find *The Second Sex*. I'd brought it back.

'The thing is, Linda, it's quite hard to gas yourself, as well as being very uncomfortable, kneeling on the floor bending your head to get the right angle to fit in the oven.

And before that you've got to fill in every possible gap and hole in the doors and windows. Which I have to say, was my undoing. It took me so long to make the room airtight that by the time I had done that and then got my head in position, Mum was back from work. Before I'd even drifted off. I hadn't realised what a very draughty house this is.' She was swirling the tea in her cup.

'My dad said these houses weren't as well built as the ones in our road,' I said.

She nodded. 'And he would know.'

There was a lot of saliva in my mouth.

'Of course, it's not illegal, not now,' she said. 'But they do still make a fuss. Because, of course, to the church it is a sin.'

'Not in our church, it isn't,' I said. 'My mum's church.'

'What do you think?' she said.

I didn't think anything. There were other people I'd heard about on our estate who had killed themselves, the man who was having an affair with the lady over the road. He did it, then she did it. Mum had said we should feel sorry for all of them. Those who had died because they must have been really desperate, and those left behind because they would be so sad. 'My mum said people don't try to kill themselves unless there's something really wrong, or at least they think something is really wrong in their life.'

'That's a sweet thing to say,' Sylvie said. 'Unfortunately a lot of people don't care about that. After she'd opened all the windows, Mum rang Dr Gardner. He drove me to the hospital in town. They let me sleep it off. But he didn't say anything about suicide – he told everyone it was an accident in the home.'

Dr Gardner was our doctor. I liked him for that.

'So I'm not bad, I'm just a bit mad.'

She didn't look mad. She looked lovely, lovelier than I'd seen her before, with her eyes really dark blue against her pale skin and her lips just the red side of pink.

'Well, I think you're just . . . sad,' I said.

She smiled. 'Perhaps you're right. I do worry. About everything. But mostly, I worry about Mansell.'

'Why? Is he ill?'

'No, no. I worry that I'm going to lose him.'

'What do you mean? Why would you?'

'Because I'm a useless mother.'

'Everyone says that.'

'Do they? Oh no, do they?'

'I don't mean about you,' I said quickly. 'I mean about themselves. Every mother says "I'm a terrible mother".' I'd read that in *Woman's Own*. 'You're just – just anxious. Why would anyone take him? You look after him all right.' It would be terrible. I would never see him again, that little face, that little smile. And if I felt like that, what must Sylvie feel?

She looked out of the window. 'I don't live an entirely conventional life,' she said. 'I don't have a husband. There are my trips to my personal sanatorium. There's . . . me.' She tucked a loose strand of hair behind her ear and shook her head. 'The hospital pumped me full of pills, most of which slow me down and a few that speed me up.' She waved her hand over to the windowsill, where four small brown bottles were arranged in a row. 'I have to take three every four hours. They're rather hard to swallow. But if I jump, I rattle.'

'Better not jump then,' I said. 'Not if Mansell's asleep, anyway.'

'You are funny, Linda. Oh, it's good to see you.' She looked into her cup as if she was reading the tea leaves. She lifted her head. 'Sorry, that was a bit of a conversation-stopper, wasn't it? What would you like to do? Do you want to listen to some music?'

'You don't have to entertain me,' I said. I didn't want to hear any Frank Sinatra or Louis Armstrong. Or that piercing Miles Davis. I didn't know what to suggest.

'All right.' She smiled. 'We'll sit here quietly, drinking our tea. And we won't talk about . . . what I did.'

'You're not thinking about it at the moment, are you?'

She laughed that little cracked laugh again. 'No, not right now. You're here, and I am full of Largactyl, so I wouldn't be able to turn on the gas, let alone block up the windows.'

'Perhaps you should get an electric cooker,' I said, stiffly.

She looked at my face. 'Oh, Linda, have I frightened you?'

'I don't know,' I said. 'What about the people you might have hurt, didn't you think about them? Your mum, Mansell, Mansell's dad?'

'Oh, I'm just a worry for my mother. It would be a relief to her if I went. And Mansell? He's as happy with her as he is with me. He wouldn't miss me. And as for Mansell's dad . . .' She laughed. 'Well, he probably wouldn't know. Nope – no one would really care.'

'Well, what about me? I'd miss you.'

'Linda!' Tears filled her eyes. I'd upset her. What would she do now? 'Linda, that's the loveliest thing that anyone has said to me in a long while.' I hadn't meant it to be that lovely. 'Would you be sad?'

'Yes.'

'Oh Linda, this is not what we should be doing at teatime on a Thursday. Sitting on hard chairs in my kitchen talking about this sort of thing. Let's listen to some Acker Bilk.'

'That might make me want to kill myself,' I said, then wished I hadn't.

But Sylvie laughed. 'You make a fresh pot of tea, and I'll put on something that will tickle you.'

As I walked into the living room with the tea things, Sylvie was fiddling with the record player, humming to herself.

She must be feeling better, I thought. I felt pleased.

She waggled an LP cover in my face. 'Shelley Berman.'

I poured out the tea and carefully Sylvie put the needle onto the record. There was no music, just a man talking. About a night out, smiling a lot, then getting home and looking in the mirror and seeing spinach on his teeth. And then describing waking up, the morning after, feeling terrible. He had a husky, confident American accent. And it did make me laugh. 'Who is he?' I said.

'He's a comedian.'

'I've never heard of him. He's not on telly.'

'He's American.'

'So's Perry Como, and he's on all the time. Is that all he does? Tell stories? Does he sing?'

'Oh no.'

I liked that. I liked the idea of it. Telling jokes and people roaring with laughter, and not having to say, 'And now here's a little song that I sang at my mother's knee.'

'Can you play it again?' I said. 'The one about the Alka Seltzer. I want to remember it – to tell Sandra.'

'Take it home with you,' she said. 'Bring it back next time you come.'

She'd obviously forgotten that we didn't have a record player. She stretched her arms in the air. 'Do you mind if we put the telly on?' she said. 'I'm a bit tired all of a sudden. Not very good company, I'm afraid.' She fell back on the settee.

'Shall I go home?' I looked at my watch. 'It'll just be the news.'

'No, stay. I don't mind – whatever's on,' she said. 'I'll curl up here and close my eyes for a moment.' She lifted her feet onto the cushions, put her head on the arm of the settee and within seconds was breathing heavily and regularly.

Lying there, asleep, in her simple green dress, strands of her hair drifting softly round her face, she looked like something out of a fairy story. I wished she could always look that peaceful, not worrying about her problems; I wished she could be happy. She was so interesting, she knew so much, she'd done so much. She had a lovely baby that she'd fought hard to keep, in spite of what everyone else thought. And yet always she seemed so fragile, as if she might break at any moment, for any reason.

I stood up and quietly put *The Second Sex* on the sideboard. Then I put Shelley Berman back on the record player and walked round the room listening to the record and practising the routine so I could repeat it later. 'Good evening, ladies and gentlemen. I want to tell you a story.'

'Have you heard of Shelley Berman?' I said to Judith as we lay in bed in the dark.

'Is he one of your important blues singers?'

'You obviously haven't heard of him. He's a comedian.' I repeated as much of the Alka Seltzer scene as I could remember. Judith laughed.

'Wouldn't it be great to do that for a living?' I said.

'What?'

'Be a comedian. Standing on a stage, making people laugh.'

'If you want to be on the stage, you should join the drama group at school.'

'They're all posh,' I said.

'They're not all posh, Rosemary's not posh. Go and see if you like it.'

'I've got too much to do,' I said.

'Like what?'

'Keeping Sandra out of trouble.'

'Then you'll never have time to join anything,' Judith said.

CHAPTER 18

The Fair

IT WAS CHELMSFORD CARNIVAL DAY. The excitement seemed to infect the town. Crowds of people came into the Milk Bar, talking loudly to each other and laughing raucously.

I was coming down the stairs after my mid-morning break, smiling, when Ray came in. I hadn't seen him since the Aldermaston march, before I started work. I hadn't actually spoken to him since the row after the football match. As he positioned himself on a stool, I remembered the warmth of his arm round me that day, and then the argument at the back of the bus. My smile faltered.

Val nudged me with her hip as I slid back behind the counter. 'Yours or mine?'

'Mine.' Cheek! Ray was mine. Wasn't he? I saw him through Val's eyes, his smiling, open face and thick dark hair. And you couldn't see any jumpers under his donkey jacket. I squeezed behind her and went to serve him.

Ray looked at me for a moment, taking in my uniform and my attempt at a pinned-up hairstyle. 'Hello,' he said. It was good to hear his voice. 'So – this is your new workplace.'

'Yes.'

He looked round. 'Very nice. You too.'

I smiled. 'Don't you ever work on Saturdays?' He worked in a garage on Broomfield Road.

'I'm their star employee, so I can choose my days off.'

'Lucky old you,' I said. 'What would you like?'

'That's a loaded question!' he said.

'So, one tea, then,' I said.

'Yeah, for now.' He grinned.

As I gave him his tea, he said, 'Are we all right?'

I could have pretended not to understand, but I wanted him to smile at me again. 'I think so,' I said carefully.

'Are you going to the fair?'

'Of course.'

'I might see you there.'

'You might.'

'We could go for a drive on the dodgems.'

I raised one eyebrow, took his sixpence and went to serve a customer at the far end of the counter. When I'd finished, Ray had gone.

'Nice,' said Val. 'Very nice.'

I looked at Val and I wondered how Ray saw her. She was small and pretty. I felt a pang of something, in my stomach. Surely it couldn't be jealousy. This was Ray from down the road.

I always had tea at Sandra's house on Carnival Day, and then we went to the fair.

Tea was ham salad with a lot of cucumber. And there was tinned fruit and tinned cream for afters. Not my favourite, but as much cream as you wanted.

After tea we went upstairs to her bedroom to change.

Getting ready to go out, doing something normal, felt good after all that worry over Sylvie, not to mention Ray and Tap. Sandra sat down at her dressing table to do her hair. She pulled up handfuls to backcomb, sighing. She was thinking about Danny. She had hoped he would pop back into her life and carry on as if the Trevor conversation had never happened. But there had been no Tuesday letters recently, and no one had any news about him.

'Do you think Danny will come back to Chelmsford?' I said.

'If he's coming he'd better get a move-on.' She pushed down some hair with her comb. 'He's not the only fish in the sea.'

'Isn't he?' I said.

She smiled and started to backcomb again. 'I might change my mind about him.'

'Why don't you miss out the middle heartache and change your mind about him now?'

'Because that wouldn't be any fun.'

Sometimes I wondered if she was really serious about him, or if it was just about seeing how far she could go towards getting a fiancé. 'What about our coats?' I said, to change the subject. 'Are we wearing our coats?'

'Of course. It's our mod shorthand.' She had started day release, doing shorthand and typing. 'The place will be jam-packed with rockers. So when they come flooding towards us, wanting to take us on the dodgems . . .' My heart did a little quiver when she said the word dodgems. 'Instead of having to say, sorry, we're mods, so leave us alone, they'll just see our coats and get the message.' We were laughing. 'It's quicker,' she said. 'Plus it'll be cold by eleven o'clock.'

The light was fading as we got to the bus station. We joined the crowds flowing down the street beside the railway arches, towards the entrance to the park. First came the smell, candyfloss, hot dogs and diesel, then we felt the throb of the generators and, as we turned into the park, we heard snatches of our favourite records, Sam the Sham, the Animals, the Four Tops.

We passed the last of the dads and mums sweating under the dazzling lights of the sideshows as they shot, balanced and threw balls to win goldfish, plastic ducks and coconuts for their kids before they took them home to bed. We stepped gingerly across the grass, over the thick, rubber-cased wires, past the generators pulsing out their greasy engine smell, past the tall test-your-strength machine and the huge wooden mallet leaning against it, and made our way towards the roundabouts in the centre. We stood on the steps of the waltzer. As the ride went round, the wooden floor rose and fell and the seats swirled. Bruce Chanel and his harmonica blared 'Hey Baby' from loudspeakers tied roughly to a pole. Boys in dirty jeans with slicked-back rocker hair and the collars of their shirts turned up stood easily on the heaving wooden boards, pushing the chairs round to make the girls scream and their skirts fly up. I wanted to go on, and I knew our straight skirts wouldn't move, but I also knew it would make me feel sick.

'Do you think Bruce is a rocker name?' Sandra said.

'I don't know. It makes me think of Bill Haley,' I said, 'so probably, yes.' We were just making conversation, passing time, looking around.

'There's no one good here,' Sandra said. We moved on.

We walked past the swing roundabout, the seats hanging on long, long chains which splayed out higher and higher the faster they went round. 'It's all rockers!' I said. At every turn were boys with greasy hair and girls with stiletto heels sinking into the grass. Peter and Gordon were singing 'A World Without Love' and Sandra said, 'Well, that's all they deserve.'

We stepped past a group of girls with petticoats so full their skirts were almost horizontal with their waists. 'They must have used pounds of sugar to get them sticking out like that,' Sandra said. Once upon a time, before we were mods, we had stiffened our petticoats with sugar water, so we knew all about it. And seeing them now, standing in the lights of the sideshows, with their bouffant hair, their cardigans done up to the neck, their legs lean and tan, waiting for sneering boys in leather jackets and white t-shirts to whisk them into the ghost train, I thought it might be quite exciting to be a rocker. You could certainly go faster on the back of a motorbike. If we'd been rockers, we'd have wandered down Baddow Road to the Long Bar in the evening, not London Road to the Orpheus, and we'd have stood at their big Wurlitzer jukebox to choose a record. But we'd have to have hated mods. And we wouldn't have worn suede coats and Fred Perrys.

'Big Girls Don't Cry', a song we both liked, was belching out from the cakewalk. Sandra said we might as well have a go, till the mods arrived. We paid our money and jumped on. Everyone was trying to stay upright and move from one end of the tramway to the other, as the floor shifted back and forth. Sandra was mucking about, walking backwards and then running forward to catch up, banging into people, making me laugh. She nearly fell off, between the bars, and I had to drag her back in, which I almost couldn't because I had such a pain in my side from laughing. A couple of rockers said, 'All right, girls?' and Sandra said, 'You'll be lucky!' and we jumped off.

We walked across to the old-fashioned roundabout with big wooden horses. Their manes were flying as they went round and round and up and down while blaring horns announced Bob & Earl singing 'Harlem Shuffle'. It was a song they played at least twice a night at the Corn Exchange, so we hummed along, tapping our feet, shrugging our shoulders, and then, on a small patch of squashed, oily grass, we started dancing.

'This could catch on,' Sandra said. 'People might mistake it for the Corn Exchange and they'll all flock over.'

'We could charge,' I said.

'How much do you reckon?'

'Well, it's only records, so . . . four and six?'

And then, from behind a candyfloss cart, Cooky appeared.

'Fancy seeing you here,' he said. The look on his face made me think he wasn't surprised at all. I suspected he'd been following us. The only real surprise was that he wasn't driving the car. 'Fancy a ride?' He jerked his head towards the horses.

'No fear!' I said.

'I wasn't asking you,' he said, mildly. The horses were slowing down. He looked at Sandra. 'Well?'

She only said yes! I wondered what she was up to. As they flew past, I could see Cooky pretending to slide off his horse and Sandra laughing. It wasn't fair. It made me feel sick just watching, and not only because they were going round and round. I didn't particularly like Cooky, with his big Corsair and all that talk about sex before marriage and the fact he'd sent Sandra a Valentine card – she said – but even so, I did think he should have asked me first. He and Sandra shouldn't be having such a good time together. What about Danny? But for Sandra, perhaps engagement was the thing. From the way Cooky was looking at her now, getting engaged to him would be as easy as falling off a horse on a roundabout. But he was a rocker. But she was laughing.

I sighed. She was so certain about her future. Weren't we too young to be making those big, final decisions?

I walked away from the roundabout towards Bobby Darin singing 'Dream Lover'. The music was coming through the loudspeakers on the dodgems. Bobby Darin was a bit of a rocker, with his short, shiny black hair, but a smart rocker, in an Italian mohair suit. I walked up the steps.

And there was Ray, leaning on a post at the side, watching the cars go round.

'Watcha,' I said.

'Hallo, Linda! How's it going?' He was wearing the horrible turquoise jumper. He wasn't even trying. But it was lovely to see him.

'All right.'

'Where's your mate?'

'Don't ask me.'

Bobby Darin was still singing as the cars slid to a halt. 'Fancy a go?' he said.

I looked at him. There was the jumper, and what he thought about all my friends, and I had hoped Tap might turn up and offer to take me on one of the rides. And what if someone I knew saw me? But Sandra was down there on that roundabout with Cooky, and Tap was nowhere to be seen, and actually I wanted to go on the dodgems and I wanted to go on with him. So I said, 'Yeah, all right.'

We walked round the edge of the track. There was the smell of burning rubber, and little sparks from the electrical connections overhead. 'This one's a good mover,' Ray shouted over the music as we reached a blue-and-black car.

'You only like it because it matches your jumper.'

'You wait and see.' We climbed in as the Shangri-Las began talking to each other, wondering if she was really going out with him, and the singer was explaining where she'd met the Leader of the Pack. I wondered if it was a bad song to drive to. It didn't end well. Perhaps I should beg Ray to go slow. I turned to him, but the music was loud and he was busy dealing with a man in a red check shirt who was hopping from car to car collecting money, and I forgot what I was going to say.

Over the loudspeakers the Leader of the Pack revved his engine and we slowly set off. Ray was a careful driver, squinting through the smoke of the cigarette between his teeth. We drove quickly and smoothly round the track, avoiding the other cars, overtaking on the inside, veering to the right. Then a red car bumped into us and someone shouted, 'Oy, Ray!' and we sped after him, our car squealing, and with a lurch we skidded into the side of the rink. We caught up to the red car and rammed into it, jumping forward in our seats. A Shangri-La began screaming, 'Look out! Look out! Look out!' and I grabbed Ray's arm. He took his hands off the wheel and shouted, 'You take over.'

'I can't drive!' His hands were still in the air and someone banged into us from behind and the car spun round. I grabbed the wheel and turned it sharply left but we had no power. 'What do I do?' I yelled.

'Accelerate! Put your foot on the accelerator!' I squashed my foot down onto his, and the car jumped into the centre of the rink.

'Watch out!' he shouted, laughing as we crashed into an empty car. He put his hands on top of mine, and held them there as we moved back into the flow of cars.

'I think you've broken my foot,' he said, as we slowed to a stop.

'It's your own fault, I told you I couldn't drive.'

'Want another go?'

'Only if you want me to stamp on your other foot,' I said. *It's too expensive*, I could hear my mum saying. *You shouldn't let him*.

He helped me out of the car. 'How about a toffee apple?'

'No thanks,' I said. Toffee apples were a nice idea but they were never as nice as you wanted them to be; the toffee was always too hard and the apples always too soft.

'We can go on the big wheel if you like,' he said.

I laughed. I almost clapped my hands. I loved the big wheel. When you stopped at the top it was always freezing cold, and it was just you up in the air, but you could see the whole of the fairground, the roundabouts all lit up and the people moving about, unaware of you up in the sky, looking down on them, and you held your breath and sat as still as you could and hoped the person you were with did the same so that you didn't fall out.

'I might just agree to that,' I said.

He laughed. We wandered past a long queue of rockers in front of the test-your-strength machine. The sound of Chris Montez singing 'Let's Dance' drifted through the air.

'Look,' he said, 'do you want to go out sometime?'

'With you?' I asked.

'What do you think?' he said.

'It depends.'

'On what?' He was smiling.

'Whether or not you get a decent jumper.'

'That's a bit shallow, isn't it?'

'You know what I mean. But why do you want to go out with me? You don't like my friends, you hardly know me . . . and you think I'm shallow. So what do you want?'

'Oh, Linda. What I want is you.'

A small electric shock ran through my body. That was so direct and so unexpected. 'Really?'

'Yes.'

'But my hair looks so horrible at the moment.'

'What's that got to do with it? I fancy you.'

'Oh, shut up. Where've you been since Easter?'

'Well, I've been here. But I thought you wanted to be somewhere else. Why, did you miss me?'

'You're bonkers.' I couldn't stop myself smiling. It was probably the most romantic thing that had ever happened to me. But it was Ray. But it was romantic. And what about . . . the rest of the world out there? What would people say? What about Tap? I hesitated. Perhaps it didn't matter.

'Look, I don't want to marry you,' he said, 'just, you know, do nice things together, go to the pictures, go to London, go for a walk.'

'Walking! No thanks.'

'Whatever you want. I mean, I've just given you a ride on the dodgems, haven't I?'

'You made me drive.'

He sighed. 'You are hard work,' he said.

'Am I?' I shook my head.

'We could go out for a meal. Or go to the theatre.'

'Don't go mad. I'll think about it,' I said, though it sounded quite good. I looked at my watch. It was half past ten. I hadn't seen Sandra for nearly an hour. Normally at this time we'd be thinking about the last bus, but tonight everything was different. 'I've got to find Sandra,' I said. 'Otherwise I've got nowhere to stay tonight.'

'You could stay with me.'

'No, I couldn't. They've got electric blankets at their house. Have you got electric blankets?'

'No, but I could keep you warm. You could share my jumper.'

'This?' I said. I pulled at the hem. 'If that's your best offer, we'd better find her fast.' I noticed a spot of yellow paint. Examining it, it looked the same colour as the paint on the Valentine's card.

I heard a shout. And another. I looked round. 'Up here!' It was Sandra; she was on the big wheel. And she was still with Cooky. He was rocking the seat and she was laughing and bashing his arm.

'There you are,' Ray said. 'She's safe and sound.'

'I'm not sure you can say that when Cooky's involved.'

'What shall we do now?' Ray said. We were standing by the rifle range.

'You could try your luck on here,' I said.

'What shall I go for?' he said. 'How about that doll?'

'If you like.'

He paid for four shots. The first two didn't hit anything. Then he hit a target and won a bag of dolly mixture. 'This time the dolly mixture, next time the doll,' he said, looking at my face as he handed me the sweets.

'Just give me the gun,' I said. I aimed at a bobbing mechanical duck. There was a ping of metal. The stallholder passed me another bag of dolly mixture. I held it out to Ray. 'And here's some for you.'

'Thanks,' he said. 'So you can drive, and you can shoot. I'm learning a lot about you. And it's all lovable.'

'And there's so much more,' I said.

'Oh, really?'

I wasn't sure, so I didn't say anything. We joined the queue for the big wheel.

'So how's the Milk Bar? Next time I come in you could give me a free drink.'

'That's not how it works,' I said. 'You come in, you pay. But I do like it, actually.' I tore open the packet of sweets he'd given me and poured some into his palm. 'Do you like working in the garage?'

'Yes,' he said, seriously. 'I enjoy it. I'm quite good with a spanner, you know.'

'Get you.'

'What I'd really like to do is art, not that you can earn a living that way. But it was my best subject at school. I've got a painting in the Arts Festival, in the exhibition in the library. You could go and see it.'

'I didn't know you painted.' I felt a sting of envy. He was doing something artistic and I wasn't. 'What do you paint?'

'All sorts. The one in the exhibition is a still life. But I do portraits. I do life drawing. Naked bodies!' he hissed. The people in front of us turned round.

'Shhh,' I said. 'Keep your jumper on!'

He put his arm round my shoulder and whispered in my ear, 'I'll paint your picture if you like!' I pushed a sweet into his mouth.

We were nearly at the front of the queue and we both had our mouths full of dolly mixtures, when I saw Danny. He was on his own, his hands in the pockets of his leather coat, his shoulders hunched.

Sandra was still on the big wheel with Cooky. I didn't know what she would want me to do. The last time she had seen Danny he had finished with her. Would she want me to punch him on the nose, or should I try and persuade him to take her back? From the corner of my eye I could see Sandra and Cooky, rocking slowly a few feet above ground. The ride was over and gradually people were being let off. Sandra shouted, 'Yoo-hoo!' and then stopped. She'd seen him too. She turned away in the seat.

'Watcha,' I said to Danny. 'Fancy seeing you here. Do you want a dolly mixture?'

'I wanna dolly bird,' Danny said, and laughed. I could smell the beer on his breath. I wasn't sure he recognised me.

'Sandra's around somewhere,' I said, looking across to the dodgems as if she might be there. As I turned back I caught a glimpse of Sandra, pushing back the bar across her seat as it swayed to the ground.

'Oh yeah?' he said. He looked round as if there might be someone else he'd rather talk to.

'Are you back for long?' I gabbled.

'Just for a couple of days. Send her my love if you see her.' He turned to move away, but slowly, as if he didn't really want to go. He was on his own. Perhaps he was lonely.

Sandra was hurrying towards us.

'Say I'll see her down the Orpheus later,' he said.

'At this time of night?'

'Oh, all right.' He shrugged. He pulled out a packet of cigarettes. 'Anyone got a light?'

'I've got a match,' I said, and opened my bag. Since lighting Tap's cigarette I had taken to carrying matches round with me. Just in case.

'Well, hello,' Sandra said coldly. But she had tidied her hair. She took the box of matches from my hand. 'What's a nice boy like you doing in a place like this?' She said it sarcastically. She wasn't going to give in straightaway.

Danny almost jumped. Then he laughed. 'I was looking for you, sweetheart,' he said.

'Oh yeah?' Sandra folded her arms, but I could tell she was pleased.

Danny took the box of matches from her in a gesture that was almost a caress. He lit his cigarette and inhaled. 'You seen Cooky around?' he said. I had to stop myself looking at Sandra.

I pointed to the big wheel. Cooky was almost at the top again, sitting alone in his seat.

'Cooky! Oy, Cooky!' Danny called. 'What's he doing up there on his own?'

'Getting away from you, probably,' Sandra said.

'Cooky needs a girlfriend, Linda,' Danny said. 'How about it? You know you like him.' It was as if Ray wasn't even there.

'It's not going to happen,' Sandra said.

'All right, Sandra!' I said. It might have done. 'I'm doing all right, thanks,' I said to Danny. Ray squeezed my shoulder.

'What are you doing here?' Sandra almost shouted at Danny.

'I told you – looking for you. You coming?' He jerked his head towards the big wheel. The ride was slowing down. 'We can squeeze in with Cooky. Give him a thrill.'

'If you think I'm going on there with someone like you, you've got another think coming,' Sandra said.

'Come on, Sandy,' he said, 'don't be like that.'

'Like what? I'm not sure I even remember who you are, and my mum told me not to talk to strangers.'

'They don't get much stranger than me,' Danny chuckled.

'You can say that again,' Sandra said shortly. But she was puffing her hair up.

'I just wanted to share my forty-eight hours of freedom with you,' he said.

'Two days,' Sandra murmured. I could see she was thinking of forgiving him everything, imagining long, smoochy hours with him in the Orpheus, or in one of the pubs in Tindal Street.

'So when do you have to go back?'

'Tonight.'

'Tonight! Where've you been for the last day and a half?' she demanded.

Shrugging, he said, 'I've been here, I've been there, I've been everywhere, man.' He swayed. Then his face changed colour, as if the eerie white light from the ticket kiosk was reflected on his face. But it wasn't. He was looking behind me. I turned.

It was Barbara. She was standing by the rifle range, staring at Danny. Her hair was a real beehive, her eyelids were heavy with black make-up and she was wearing dark red lipstick. Her long black leather coat hung almost to the ground, and she stood straight and still. Sandra turned and followed my gaze. The smile slid from her face, replaced by an expression of complete shock and then determination. She looked at Danny. He gave a watery grin.

His eyes swivelled between the two of them, Sandra, Barbara, Sandra, Barbara, then me. Me! He blinked slowly. Barbara walked up to him and grabbed him by the arm. She pulled him so that his face was level with hers. 'What's all this?' she hissed.

'What? What?' Danny said.

'I've been waiting over an hour for you.'

'I told you, I had to get back.'

'Oh really, via the Dolphin and the Spotted Dog? I only knew where you were because I bought Mick Flynn a drink. And now you're at the fair?'

'It's the quickest way to the station.'

'And you picked up a couple of tarts on the way? That's handy.'

'You what?' said Sandra.

'Me?' I said.

'Oh, Danny,' Barbara sighed. 'That's so typical of you.' She looked down at her shoes, half-submerged in mud. She shook her head. Then she took a deep breath, as if she had decided something. She looked up and slapped his face with a great crack. 'That's it!' she said. She shook the hand that had hit him. 'I don't care what you want, I don't care how much you need me. I just don't care.' Her voice was getting louder. 'And if you ever, ever try to come near me again, I will break every bone in your body!'

Danny rubbed his cheek. 'Babs,' he said in a wheedling tone, 'don't be like that.'

'I'll be any way I fucking like,' she said. 'And don't think this means you don't have to pay me the fifty quid you owe me. It was all your fucking fault.'

Sandra and I looked at each other. Fifty pounds. Big money.

'Fifty quid?' he said. 'I thought we were square.'

'No, you didn't. I told you to bring it today.' She clenched her fists at her side. She turned to Sandra. 'I knew there was someone. I just knew it. Well – you're welcome to him! I only hope you like losers. And you!' She swivelled round to Danny again. 'You can just – just fuck off! All of you!'

She turned and squelched away past the shooting range, knocking someone's arm so his shot went wild and he shouted, 'Hey!'

Danny watched her go. Then he said, 'Right!' He rubbed his hands together. 'What shall we go on now?'

'We're not going on anything,' Sandra said stiffly. 'There's a funny smell round here. Come on Linda, we've got to – to catch the bus. We don't want to miss it.'

I stared at her. We both knew her dad was paying for us to take a taxi home. She returned my glance. I understood. A taxi we could get any time; the bus would require a departure now. She needed to make a point. I loved it when we had these silent conversations. I loved that she'd stood up to Danny for once.

Danny turned to Ray. 'Fancy a drink?'

Ray looked at me. 'That's OK,' he said to Danny. 'I'm just going to walk her up to the bus station.'

'I'll come too,' Danny said.

'No one is walking anyone up to the bus station,' Sandra said. 'Linda and I are going on our own.'

Ray frowned and so did I. I rolled my eyes, trying to tell him that it wasn't my idea at all. He bent down and kissed my cheek. 'I'll be seeing you, Linda.'

I turned my face quickly and kissed him on the mouth. I could see his eyes open in surprise but he kissed me back, putting his arms round me and pulling me to him. Danny murmured, 'Ooh, lovebirds.' I slid my arms round Ray's waist. It was a long kiss. A lovely kiss. Gently, his tongue played on my lips. I opened my mouth. I pressed my tongue against his. I opened my eyes. We looked at each other.

'Bye,' he said.

'Come with us,' I whispered.

'I'll walk up to the bus station with you,' he said aloud. 'I'm going that way anyway.'

'Not you,' Sandra said to Danny, giving him a little push.

Ray, Sandra and I made our way back over the cables and through the mud to the railway arches. Sandra glanced behind us.

'Come on, then,' she shouted. Danny shambled up to her side and draped his arm round her shoulder. She shrugged it off. 'I'm not speaking to you for another two minutes,' she said.

Oh, Sandra, I thought, this is just so . . . so boring. I wanted to shake her. I wanted to say, 'At least Cooky's not a jailbird. At least you know where you are with him. Even if he is a Conservative.'

As we approached the bus station Danny said, 'Hey, Sandy, what about these shoes?' They ducked into the deep doorway of Finch's shoe shop. 'The two minutes isn't up yet,' I heard Sandra say. Then there was silence.

I looked at Ray.

'We could find a shop doorway of our own,' he said.

'We'd better stay here,' I said. 'I've got to make sure she's all right.'

'Does she really like him?' Ray said.

'Oh, don't start that again.'

He put his arm round me and kissed the top of my head. 'I like you.'

I turned towards him. I was about to say, 'And I like you,' when Danny shouted, 'What's the time?'

'It's half past eleven,' I said. 'And we're still out in the open air, having an exciting evening.'

'You what?' Danny said.

'Out in the –' I started.

'Half past eleven? Fuck me, my train!' He set off running towards the station. Sandra ran after him, and Ray and I followed Sandra. Danny was grabbing at his jacket. 'Where's my travel warrant?'

Sandra said, 'It's here.' She picked up a piece of paper and he snatched it from her hand.

'Gotta go, gotta go. Be good,' he said. 'See ya!' and he disappeared through the ticket barrier and up the stairs.

'What happened there?' Sandra said. We were still standing under the railway bridge. I knew she'd been hoping for the big Goodbye scene, the kiss, the love, the promises.

I turned to Ray. 'We're actually going home in a taxi,' I said. A taxi rolled towards us.

'Sure?' he said. 'I meant it when I said you could sleep round at ours.'

'Yeah, yeah.' But staying at Sandra's didn't seem quite so thrilling now. 'You could come in the taxi with us,' I said uncertainly.

'No, it's OK. I've got to see a man about a dog.'

'Well, you can open the taxi door for us if you like.'

He clipped his heels together. 'Yes, ma'am!' He pulled my fringe. 'See ya.' He kissed my forehead. 'I had a good time tonight,' he murmured, and he was gone.

In the back of the car I said, 'How can Danny be going back to prison at this time of night?'

'Don't ask me,' she said. 'At least we know he hasn't gone off with Barbara. She had to be serious – no one would walk into that mud in those shoes just for show.'

We were both silent for a while. I was thinking of Ray and laughing and being on the dodgems, and how I'd kissed him. 'I never got to go on the big wheel,' I said.

'You chose the wrong bloke,' Sandra said, looking out of the window.

'I didn't. You did,' I said.

'Not necessarily.'

The taxi drove along Broomfield Road, past our school. I said carefully, 'That all sounded a bit serious with Barbara. And what was the fifty pounds about?'

Sandra did a little flick of her head. 'I don't know, and nor did he. He's just trying to close the door on that part of his life. She's upset. He's upset.'

'So, what's happening?' I said. 'Between you and him?'

'Quite a lot, actually. I've got this.' She fumbled in her pocket and pulled out a large battered-looking ring with a small dull glass stone. She felt at the neck of her cardigan and pulled out her silver chain. 'Undo this for me,' she said.

'What's this? Whose ring is it?'

'Mine.'

I unfastened the chain and she threaded the ring onto it. She wound the chain back round her neck.

'He actually gave you this?' I said.

She smiled.

'That was quick. Where was I?'

She grinned. 'I don't know. Being crazy with Ray? Linda likes boys in blue jumpers!' she crowed.

'No, she doesn't,' I said. 'Well, it depends on the blue.'

The taxi was passing the Avenues. 'Remember when we came along here in the car with Danny?' Sandra said. She slid the ring back and forth on the chain. She started to hum the Wedding March.

'So is that it?' I said. Could this really mean she'd get married, move away and have kids? With Danny? She couldn't be serious. 'Are you engaged?'

'Yes!' She paused. 'Well, unofficially engaged.'

'What does that mean?'

'I know and he doesn't. He knows I've got the ring, he gave it to me, but he doesn't know we're engaged.'

As the taxi turned into Sperry Drive she gave a little sigh. She spoke almost to herself. 'I don't care about Barbara. She's out of the picture. And now I've got this.' She slid the ring back and forth on the chain.

'It looks a bit scratched,' I said. 'A bit, you know, second-hand.'

'It was his mum's.'

'You hope.'

'I don't care where it came from. I've got it now.' She rubbed the ring between her fingers, smiling to herself. 'I said I'd look after it for him.'

'So is that your New Year's Resolution resolved?'

'No, that's still on the go. He's got to get down on one knee for it to be really real.'

'What about Cooky?'

'Who knows? Cooky's nothing, really.'

'He looked a bit more than that on the big wheel,' I said.

'I suppose he's a sort of back-up. You know, if Danny gets life for something.'

'But you just left him there.'

'They'll chuck him off when they close up.' She turned to me. 'Don't look like that, he knows where he stands. He knows all about Danny. Well, he should do, he's been driv-ing him round in his car long enough.'

The taxi pulled up outside her house. We clambered out. Sandra tucked the ring back under her cardigan. She unlatched the gate and held it open for me.

I wanted to say, *what was Danny doing walking round with a ring in his pocket?* but I didn't want to talk anymore about Danny or the ring or Cooky. I was staying the night. We began to talk about the best music played at the fair.

CHAPTER 19

The Search

My appointment at Wanda's hairdressers was for five o'clock. Although I had decided to grow my hair – a lot of people were doing it, Cathy McGowan was even doing it – it wasn't really working. I needed to tidy up the ends, and I had to do something definite with my fringe. After school I walked into town with Cray. When she'd caught her bus there was an hour before I needed to be at Wanda's. I had time to go into the library.

I loved our library. I loved the quietness and the *sock sock sock* of the librarian's heels on the wooden floor as she moved round the shelves putting books back into their rightful places.

Today she was sitting at her desk, sorting membership cards. I leaned across the counter and whispered, 'Do you have street directories of America?'

'Whereabouts in America?'

I shook my head. Such difficult questions, so soon. 'Arizona? California? Where do they have white trash?' I floundered.

She frowned. I didn't know anything. I didn't know where he lived.

I wanted to find Bob. Sylvie needed him. Mansell needed him. If I found him he could explain himself, he could shoulder his responsibilities and maybe they would fall in love again and Sylvie would be happy and Mansell would be safe. 'Would a telephone directory help?' she said.

I didn't know if he was on the phone. I didn't know if they had phones in caravans in America. They certainly didn't in Clacton.

'Well, we don't keep American directories here, and we can't order them in unless we know some of the details. And there are hundreds, probably thousands of directories, just in the states you've mentioned.'

'Well, I know he's not Canadian.'

'That's something, dear, but it's still not enough, I'm afraid.' She had a thin face and wispy pale brown hair, but I still felt stupid. I wondered if she knew anything about love.

'I think his surname's Stanforth or . . . Stanferd.' What had she said? 'He was a soldier, in Great Yarmouth. Or Wethersfield.'

'An airman, then,' she corrected. 'Well.' She paused. A small frown creased her forehead. 'Well . . . if you don't have much to go on, your best bet may be to ask there.'

'Where?'

'Wethersfield.'

'The air base? But who would I ask?'

'A commanding officer?'

The task seemed enormous. 'I don't even know where Wethersfield is,' I said. I knew it existed, I knew it was an American air base, I knew my mum had marched from there and that sometimes she and other CND members went up there to talk to the servicemen. But I didn't know where it was.

'Ah, well that is something I can help you with,' she said. She led me out of the lending library into the reference room. This was an altogether more serious room. The books were all huge and the silence was thick. The smell of floor polish filled the air. The librarian reached up to a shelf and pulled out a book about Essex. She found a map and I stared at the expanse of green her clean, clipped nail was pointing to. I read the words 'Wethersfield aerodrome'. I still didn't know where it was, but then I saw the words 'Braintree' and 'Halstead' nearby. Braintree was where Sylvie's grandmother lived. Braintree and Halstead were the final destinations of the buses we caught home on Saturday nights. If our buses dropped us off then lumbered on to Braintree at eleven o'clock, it couldn't be too far. I felt I was almost there.

I walked to Wanda's feeling like someone out of *77 Sunset Strip*. I wanted to click my fingers. I was on the trail.

'You paid three and six for that?' Mum said, staring at my newly cut hair. 'There's hardly any difference. How much did she take off?'

'Some.' I wasn't concentrating. I had a journey to organise.

We were in the kitchen and Mum was frying eggs. I was standing at the side of the cooker, keeping an eye on the toast under the grill. 'Mum,' I said casually, 'you know Wethersfield?'

'Yes.' She slid an egg into the pan.

'Will CND be going up there soon?' I hoped I sounded as if I was interested in going with them.

'I'm sure they will.'

'Will you go?'

'I've told Helen I'm not going for a while. There are a lot of church meetings coming up. If you want to go you should ring her, they're always pleased to have new recruits.'

That was good. I didn't want my mum there. So I had two possibilities – to ring Mrs Grenville and ask to go with the CND group on a visit to meet the USAF, and then somehow drop in some questions. Or to go with Sandra.

I rang Sandra to tell her about my afternoon at the library.

'Well, if you're talking about Bob Stanferd,' she said, 'he comes from Texas.'

'How do you know?'

'Mrs Weston told my mum.'

'Why didn't you tell me?'

'Why didn't you ask?'

I felt really stupid. 'What else does Mrs Weston know?'

'Nothing. You know more than she does. She just says Sylvie said something about Texas once.'

'And Bob's the father? Does he know?'

'Probably not.'

'Don't say he's the unofficial father.'

'I don't know if he is or not. Mrs Weston doesn't know. But he is American.' We were both silent, remembering what Peter had said at the football match.

'It is Bob. It's got to be Bob. But was he at Wethersfield?' I said.

'We'd better go there and find out.'

I hadn't even asked her. I'd hesitated because I expected she'd say she was too busy planning an engagement party or writing letters to Wormwood Scrubs, but now she said it would be a laugh, why not, and we had nothing else to do. She was happier now she had the ring.

The next Saturday afternoon, when I finished work, Sandra and I caught the 311 to Halstead. When we got off the bus we followed a sign that said USAF Air Base. It was advertising an Open Day, but not today. We walked through the countryside. 'Do you know where we're going?' Sandra said.

'Maybe.'

'Wouldn't it have been easier to go with the CND people?'

'Well, CND don't go into the base. They stand at the entrance, demonstrating. You said you wanted to come.'

'I didn't know we'd be actually walking to America. It's so hot, and I've got ladders in both stockings. Are you sure there's a public entrance?'

'They have dances and this Open Day thing that anyone can go to. There must be a way in.'

'You hope. And when we get there, what are we actually looking for?'

'I don't know – his address, or a phone number, or some way of contacting him. We might even find Bob himself.'

'Why didn't you just ask Sylvie?'

'I don't think she has that information. Anyway, it's a surprise.'

'Do you think she'll like it?'

'Everyone likes surprises.'

'Not if it's a horrible surprise. What if she doesn't want to know?'

'She does.'

'You sure? He might be the reason she put her head in the oven.' Sandra couldn't decide how outraged she was that Sylvie had tried to commit suicide.

'No, he wasn't, she would have told me,' I said, although I wasn't convinced that was true. 'And Mansell needs to know his dad.' I stretched my toe to pop a tar bubble in the road. 'I know Sylvie tries not to sound concerned about him, but that's just the way she talks. When she tells me her stories you can hear how much she loved him.'

'Right. Loved him. Then. In the past. Like you used to love Tommy Steele.'

'I wouldn't mind meeting him now, though.'

'All right. Say we find him. Not Tommy Steele, idiot. What are we going to do then? Are you going to invite him round to Sylvie's to have a cup of tea and meet the baby?'

I wasn't really prepared to actually find him, in person, flesh and blood, in his uniform. I hadn't really thought past getting the 311 at the bottom of our road. But how could Sylvie not want to meet him again, after all she went through? 'You think it's all rubbish anyway,' I said. 'How they met, who he was, where they were.'

'All right, I know she's been to Great Yarmouth. Mrs Weston said something about that. But then I've been to Yarmouth too. And I didn't come back with a baby. But I could make up a good story about it. Oh well, fingers crossed we've got the right bloke. And you never know, we might meet some interesting Yanks of our own,' she said, perking up. 'As long as they don't care about a few ladders. And here we are.'

We turned a bend in the road and there ahead of us was a wire fence that seemed to stretch for miles. There was no gate to be seen. And there was nothing inside the fence except very short grass.

'Cut like a GI's hair,' said Sandra, 'like Elvis when he went into the army.' We'd seen *GI Blues*. 'That's what Cooky does.'

'What, cuts hair?'

'Grass. He cuts grass. He told you, that night.'

'Really? He obviously doesn't cut it here,' I said. The grass on our side of the fence was long and filled with cow parsley and occasional buttercups. 'Or perhaps he likes wild flowers.'

'If he was cutting it today he could give us a lift on his mower. Where do we go in?'

'Let's follow the fence,' I said. 'There must be an entrance somewhere.'

'And what are you going to do when we get inside?'

'Ask people if they know him.'

'Good plan, all five thousand of them. That'll take ... how long? What time does the last bus go?' she said.

'They run every day.'

'As long as we're home for Christmas.' We both snorted with laughter. Sandra was stepping carefully round the flowers. 'How come you were so petrified of going into Wormwood Scrubs when we had an actual invitation, and now you're quite happy to stroll into an air base when we're probably breaking about a hundred laws just looking at it?'

I looked up at the sky. 'I suppose this is something I want to do, I'm not just being dragged along like a big gooseberry. I'm pleased you've come.'

She pushed my arm and said, 'Yeah, yeah.' But I knew she was pleased I'd said it. 'Anyway,' I said, 'an air base isn't exactly like a prison. People go in and out all the time.'

'Except your CND friends.'

'Yes, but I've got you with me.'

We walked beside the fence for five minutes. Under my breath I repeated, 'Bob Stanferd, Bob Stanferd, Bob Stanferd.' I didn't want to forget it.

'From Texas.' Sandra wiped some mud off her shoe. 'Is that a gate?'

I didn't want it to be a gate. Now I didn't want to go in. 'Are you sure Mrs Weston doesn't know anything else? She must do. We should have asked her.'

'That's right,' said Sandra. 'We should have gone into the shop and said, "Hello, Mrs Weston, a packet of custard creams please, and as much information as you've got on the American." I told you – she's just guessing.'

We were approaching two high wire gates. Ahead of us a smooth roadway led up to a small cabin. I wanted it all to disappear like a mirage.

'Hadn't you better take your badge off?' Sandra said.

I slid my CND badge into my pocket. 'We don't need to do this,' I said.

'I thought you were all of a doo-da because it's not fair that Mansell's got a dad he doesn't know.'

'But now I know where he comes from, so I can go back to the library to find out all the rest.' I stopped.

'It won't be that easy,' Sandra said. 'And we're here now.' She looked at me. 'Are we going in or not?'

We walked along the smooth roadway. There were two men in the cabin. One of them came out. 'OK, gals?' He spoke with an American accent.

My heart began pounding. Sandra said, 'We're looking for someone. She's looking for someone.' She rolled her eyes so he thought I was in love with an airman, and he laughed.

'I'd like to help you, honey, I mean ma'am. But you can't go in. We've had a deal of trouble recently.'

'But we really do need to find him,' she said. 'And we're no trouble. I've always wanted to go to America. All those lovely accents and your big cars. Oh, go on,' she pleaded, touching his arm.

'OK.' He grinned and went back into the cabin and lifted a telephone receiver. He murmured something into the phone, then he dialled and redialled numbers. The other airman laughed. Then our airman came out and told us we were being taken to see an officer.

*

We were in front of a bored man whose uniform looked as if he'd put it on in the dark, the shoulder seams in the wrong place and one button undone. Sandra said we were there for the Open Day, and we'd obviously got the date wrong. I turned to her gratefully. Of course, that was the thing to say.

He seemed tired. 'I heard you were looking for someone.'

'She is.'

'You were looking for an American airman?'

'Not really.'

He gazed at me.

'Well, yes, in a way. For a friend.'

'Do you have a name?'

'Sylvie.'

The officer sighed. 'His name.'

'What is it?' My mind was empty. I wanted not to be there. 'It starts with T.'

Sandra turned to the officer. 'Stanferd. His name's Bob Stanferd.' She looked at me. 'Starts with T!'

The officer frowned. 'Is anybody here pregnant?'

'No!' we said in unison.

He shook his head. 'That's something. So you're looking for a couple of nice American boys.'

'Well, just one really, but two would do,' said Sandra. 'That's why we wanted to come to the Open Day.' She smiled.

He picked up a phone and said some names, none of them Stanferd or anything like it. 'To my office, now.' He looked at us for a moment then straightened some papers on his desk. 'OK, ladies, you will be escorted from the base. You may find your escorts friendly and they may tell you when the next dance is.'

I wanted to say, look, if we really wanted to nab an American we would have dressed up a bit more, not come in like this, covered in mud and brambles, so you needn't sneer, but we were leaving, which was what I wanted more.

As we walked through the base with our guards, other airmen whistled and called to us. 'Hey gals, can I call you up sometime?' 'Are you English birds?' 'Are you from Liverpool?' Some joined us. It was almost a gang, and we were in the middle. Sandra was enjoying this part, laughing and making wisecracks. 'Go on, say somethin' else,' one with black hair said. Sandra said, 'I will if you will.'

'These chicks crack me up,' he said. 'Go on, talk to me.'

'What's it worth?' Sandra said.

They all roared. 'Lucky, lucky Droberg,' someone said.

As we were walking back to the bus stop, Sandra said, 'Well, I found out something that you might be interested in.'

'What?'

'One of those men came from Texas.'

'Really?' I was sure my heart had stopped. 'Was it him?'

'No, stupid. I asked him if he knew a Bob Stanferd who had a friend called Gary from Wisconsin and he said yes.'

'Really?'

'Well, vaguely, and I said . . .' She looked to make sure I was hanging on her every word, 'I said could he give him a message?'

'What? A message? What do you mean?' A message. That was . . . that was awful. It was dawning on me that this might not have been a sensible thing to do. What effect would this have on Sylvie? And what would Bob think? What would he do?

'Well, he scratched his head and said he hoped it was a short message because he couldn't guarantee he'd remember, and then he said he'd do it. And so then I said, I just said, someone in Chelmsford needed to speak to him.'

My mind was whirling. Was it all right to say Chelmsford? Was it too much? 'Are you sure that's all you said? Did you give him her address?'

'I'm not stupid.'

'But did you give him her name?'

'Yes.' She looked at me. 'Your face!'

'You didn't.'

'Why? Why shouldn't I? At least that gives him some idea of who's looking for him, and if he wants to be found. Otherwise, what was the point of doing all this? You don't have to say thank you.' She looked hurt.

'I don't know if I am grateful.'

'You're still thinking about that boring old general, or whoever he was.'

'Yes, but –'

'You've been planning this for ages. You thought it was a good idea right up to the moment we clapped eyes on that entry sentry, so it probably still is.'

Was it?

She read my face. 'It was a good idea. So you can say thank you.'

'Thank you.'

'Don't thank me, buy me something. Preferably a new pair of stockings. Oh, we've got to stop, I've got something in my shoe.' She leaned on my shoulder and slid her shoe from her foot and shook out some grit. 'Where's the bus stop?' she said. 'When's the next bus?'

'I don't know.' Going back this way, everything looked different. Trees and fields stretched ahead of us. 'Is this even the right road?' I still felt anxious; my stomach was churning.

'We should have chalked marks on the trees.' Sandra looked at her watch. 'We are going to be so late.'

'There's a bus stop!'

A 311 sailed past. 'And there goes the next bus. My mum's going to kill me.'

But it wasn't missing the bus that got her into trouble.

When I got home everyone had had their tea and the table had been cleared. 'I was at Sandra's,' I mumbled when I walked into the living room.

Mum didn't seem to care. She was preparing for her Sunday School class, putting all the pieces of cardboard she saved from Shredded Wheat packets into a bag with some blunt scissors, crayons and glue. 'I'm hungry,' I said. 'Still hungry, I mean.' I turned to go to the kitchen.

'Before you do that,' Mum said. I stopped. What? What? 'I was talking to Mrs Weston in the shop this afternoon.' What had they talked about? What did Mrs Weston know? But Mum was calm. 'It's Mrs Weston's bingo night tonight. Would you like to go and sit with Sylvie and Mansell? Apparently it went very well last time,' she said, putting a rubber band round a pile of pieces of card.

I looked at the ceiling. What would I say to Sylvie when she asked me what I'd been up to? 'You don't even agree with bingo!' I said to Mum. She considered it gambling.

'Alternatively,' Mum went on, 'you can cut out pictures of animals from *Woman's Own*, for the class.'

We hadn't found him. We'd only met some people who might know him. And Sandra had only said Sylvie's name to one of them. It wasn't too bad. We hadn't found him. And I hated cutting out.

I said yes, I'd go and sit with her. Perhaps doing a good deed would make up for what we might have started this afternoon.

Sylvie said I could give Mansell his bath. She dragged out an old tin bath from under the stairs. We had a tin bath at home, that once upon a time we had bathed in, when we were very small, but now we kept it in the shed and Dad used it to aerate the water in the goldfish bowl. 'You can fill it with water from the tap,' Sylvie said. 'Don't worry if you spill it.'

She was really happy this evening, and she looked nice. She was wearing the dress I'd helped her make. The zip didn't fit very well, I noticed, but only because I was look-ing closely. The dress was white with large red flowers, and the gathered waist made her look curvaceous and mys-terious, like Gina Lollobrigida. She was humming as she went upstairs to get some clean pyjamas for Mansell.

I half-filled the bath and staggered with it across to the table. Sylvie ran down the stairs and put a faded yellow sleeping suit over a chair. She handed me a new bar of Johnson's baby soap. I unwrapped the white waxy soap, while she sat down and lit a cigarette. I rolled up my sleeves and lowered Mansell into the bath. Straightaway he smacked his hands into the water, laughing.

'I've been to Wethersfield,' I said, to assuage my guilt, to see how she'd react.

'Oh, have you?' she said. She inhaled deeply on the cigarette. 'Did you like it?'

'It was all right. It's very big.'

'Did you see the shop? They have such wonderful things in there! What were you doing up there?'

'We were escorted off the base.'

'Linda, what a girl you are! Whatever for?' She looked round for an ashtray, then tapped ash into the palm of her hand. As I searched for an answer that would be truthful but not revealing, she said, 'I was once escorted out of a nightclub, but I don't suppose it's the same. I had had rather too much absinthe, I think. You probably didn't have that excuse. The thing about absinthe is that it makes you very maudlin.' She tipped the ash into the cigarette packet. 'Not real absinthe, of course. It was pastis. But it all tastes of aniseed. Mmm.'

'Aniseed?' Sometimes her tastes made me lose all sympathy with her. Who would willingly drink aniseed?

Absently she handed me a towel. 'Juliette Greco,' she said. 'Yves Montand, Edith Piaf, Larry Fabbrona. They were all there. All dressed in black. They were celebrating something or other. Juliette Greco and Piaf did a duet. There was a lot of laughing. When I started crying they said I was spoiling the fiesta. And out I went.' She smiled and shook her head.

When Mansell was dried and powdered and swaddled in clean pyjamas, I laid him in the pram in the hall. Sylvie put on the television. It was the *Billy Cotton Band Show*. We watched in silence. Just before Peter Cook and Dudley Moore's programme started, Mrs Weston came in. She was breezy and chatty. She'd won £25. She went into the kitchen and filled the kettle.

I stood up and put on my coat.

Sylvie followed me to the front door. As I opened the door she said, 'So what were you doing at the base?'

'Oh, nothing. It was a sort of protest.'

CHAPTER 20

Result

I WAS IN THE MIDDLE of the exams. I'd had Bible Knowledge in the morning and Maths in the afternoon. Now Dad had brought Mr Robinson home for tea. Mr Robinson was a union man from London and he was going to speak at Dad's branch meeting. He deserved a good tea, Mum said, and I had to go down the road for three cod and chips. But this was like another exam. If there are five people for tea, how many chips do you need? Mr Robinson would have one whole piece of cod and a portion of chips, Dad would have a piece of fish with the end cut off, I would have Dad's cut-off piece but most of his chips, and Mum and Judith would share one fish and chips between them.

I arrived at the chip shop just as a green-and-white Corsair pulled up. Cooky was giving Sandra a lift home from work. She hadn't told me he gave her lifts home.

I wondered if it was a regular thing – both the lifts and her not telling me. Oh Sandra, I thought. Is this it? Is this where we start separating?

Sandra stuck her head out of the passenger window. 'Oy,' she said. 'Where are you going?'

'I'm going to the chip shop.'

Cooky leaned across her and put his head out of the window. 'Get us some lemonade,' he said.

'She's not going to the off-licence,' Sandra said.

'Get us some chips then,' Cooky said.

'She doesn't want to get you some chips,' Sandra said. 'She's getting something for their tea.'

'I only asked,' he said.

'Well, don't,' she said.

They sounded like a married couple on telly, and with their heads in the window, they looked like it too, moaning at each other but loving it. And I thought Sandra would surely be better off with Cooky instead of Danny, despite Cooky's curly hair and tattoos.

'Wait, I'll come with you,' Sandra called. Their heads disappeared back into the car. I turned away. I didn't want to see, in case she was kissing him goodbye. The car door slammed and Sandra wiggled her fingers at Cooky. The Corsair made a laborious turn in the road and Cooky drove away. Sandra and I went into the chip shop and I placed my order.

'It'll be a few minutes,' the woman said. She poured a crate of chopped potatoes into the fat with a wet, sizzling roar.

'So what's going on with you and Cooky?'

'Nothing. You don't come out in the evenings, with all your exams and everything. What am I supposed to do?'

'Shouldn't you give Danny back his ring?'

A little smile trembled on her lips. 'What's the point? I don't know where he is. He doesn't know we're engaged. Anyway, I don't want to give it back.' She drummed her fingers on the counter. 'That's the trouble. I really want to get engaged to him.' She held out her left hand.

'But why? You and Cooky seem to get on better than you and Danny ever do.'

She looked at me sadly. 'If you must know, Cooky gets on my nerves, him and his car. And he's always talking about his job. Grass! I mean – grass. As if he's the only person who's ever pushed a lawnmower.' She made a face at me. 'All right! I know – he is generous, and the car is handy. But he's not very funny. He doesn't make me laugh, not like Danny.'

We were silent. I looked at the large jar of greenish liquid on the counter, half-full of hard-boiled eggs. Was she running Cooky down a bit too much?

'Three cod, was it?' The woman lifted golden pieces of fish out of the fat. Sandra and I leaned over the counter and watched as she slid them onto greaseproof paper and shovelled chips beside them and then wrapped them in pages of the *Daily Mirror*. I passed over the money and took the large warm parcel.

We had finished our final exam of the year. It was French. 'What did you put for "*haussé ses épaules*"?' I said to Cray as we filed out of the gym where we'd sat for the last hour and a half. 'I put "braced his knees".'

'Well,' said Cray, '"*épaule*" is shoulder. I got that.'

'Braced his shoulders?'

'I put "straightened".'

We looked it up. '*Haussé*' meant shrugged. Shrugged his shoulders. Why didn't I know that? Cray had got it half right, and she wasn't meant to be as good at French as I was.

We had the rest of the day off. I walked home repeating 'braced his knees'! It didn't even mean anything.

At home I went upstairs to get changed. I ripped off my tie – *ma cravate*, my shirt – *ma chemise*, my skirt – *ma jupe*. I knew all those words, they just hadn't come up in the exam. Why did this always happen? The other exams had been fairly bad – in the English exam I'd answered the question about *Pygmalion* by saying that Henry Higgins was too posh to be any good for Eliza and she should have refused to play his game from the start. It wasn't an approach we'd studied in class. I was bound to be marked down. In History I'd forgotten the year for the Diet of Worms. I'd messed up one whole equation, if not all of them, in Maths. And, possibly my mum's fault, I'd mixed up the bones in the inner ear in Biology.

All of that I'd almost expected, but French was one of my best subjects. The results had started to come in and my average so far was 61 per cent. So much for going off exploring, or writing about life in Africa. I'd be lucky to get a job in a bank, which was what Cray was talking about. Perhaps I should try to get a full-time job at the Milk Bar.

I took my ski pants and twinset out of the wardrobe. They felt comfortable as I pulled them on. I knew where I was with them. I picked up the shopping list from the telephone table and walked down to the shop. I thought Mrs Weston was going to kiss me when I walked in. Mr Roberts was due at any minute, she said. Sylvie was at a doctor's appointment, could I take Mansell?

'But we've got half a day off,' I said. 'I wanted to – to do something else.'

'Oh.' Mrs Weston's face fell. 'Sylvie's very well at the moment. And Mansell loves going out with you.'

'It's the end of exams,' I said. 'It doesn't happen at any other time of the year.'

She was biting her bottom lip so hard the skin round it had turned white. I looked at Mansell. He wasn't going to throw my uselessness at languages at me; he wouldn't ask me for mashed banana in French; he wasn't going to say anything except *mum* and *dog*, as Mrs Weston proudly told me. So I said yes. Mrs Weston put a Wagon Wheel and a bottle of fizzy in with the shopping.

Mansell and I walked round to Sandra's old school and up Partridge Avenue, towards the church and my old Sunday School. We came back and strolled past the shop, but Mr Roberts was still there. I looked at my watch. Mrs Weston had said Sylvie would be home at half past four. I'd have to walk about in the street for ten minutes.

I turned into the Crescent. It was empty except for a man I didn't recognise, walking up and down, stepping off the pavement into the road, looking at the houses, frowning at the windows. He was wearing jeans and a beige windcheater. He had dark hair, very short, not greasy. He was altogether good-looking – I wondered what he'd got cooking. I was older now. Perhaps he'd like to cook something up with me. He was walking towards me. I slowed down.

It was just he and I in the world.

'Is that a baby you have there?'

If he hadn't looked so nice I would have said, 'No, it's a bar of soap.' If he hadn't had an American accent I would have said, 'This one's not mine, but we could make one together.' I would never have said that. In my head

I was hysterical. It was a crew cut, he was American, he was outside Sylvie's house, he seemed really, really nice, the kind of person you'd fall for at a dance or in a casino. The kind of person you'd want to make yourself glamorous for.

'Do you live in this neighbourhood?'

I gazed at him, knowing who he was, wishing it wasn't him.

'Do you speak English?' he said.

'*Mieux que le français*,' I said. Much better than French. He frowned.

'Yes, yes. Yes, I do. I do.'

'I'm looking for a friend,' he said.

What would Sandra say? Something smart. Something funny but endearing. 'So am I,' I said. 'But only people who like Del Shannon.'

There was a pause.

Oh, not smart enough. A lot of people didn't like Del Shannon these days. Something about his hair and his jumpers, and his yodelly voice.

'Del Shannon fan, huh? Me too.' He smiled. He had a dimple in his cheek.

I grinned. He just looked so nice. And he liked Del Shannon! I really wanted to say, 'Forget about Sylvie, take me.'

'Which one's your favourite?' he said.

'"Hats Off To Larry".'

'Good choice.'

For a moment we both stared at each other. His eyes travelled up and down my body. What was he thinking? Of course, my CND badge. Would he think I hated all Americans because of Hiroshima and Vietnam? I gripped the handle of the pram. It was almost impossible to stop my hand creeping to my lapel to cover the three searing white lines. 'I don't live in this road,' I whispered and walked on as if I had business elsewhere.

I reached the first curve of the Crescent. I stopped and fiddled with Mansell's blanket, then as casually as I could, turned and looked back. The American was sitting on the wall of the house next to Sylvie's, his legs stretched out in front of him, his hands in the pockets of his windcheater, his head bent low. It had to be Bob. He was so handsome, and now I thought about it, his eyes were similar to Mansell's. I imagined what he and Sylvie must have looked like together, that first night, well matched in height and looks, smiling at each other and the world. Like Sophia Loren and Marcello Mastroianni, or Jean-Paul Belmondo and Jean Seberg.

But what was he doing here?

We'd done it. In the room with that officer, giving Bob's name, and then Sandra talking to those airmen, dropping big hints about why we were there, telling them Sylvie's name. We'd set in train a series of events, so that he ended up here, outside her house. I tried to breathe deeply. I remembered Sylvie wailing that she thought she would lose the baby, that his father might take him. Is that why he'd come? To take Mansell away with him? It had been his first question. 'Is that a baby you have there?'

I'd tried to put him off the scent. Hadn't I? I'd cleverly manoeuvred the conversation round to pop music and old hits. Had it done the trick? I quickened my pace and walked on. What if he ran after me? I'd casually turn to speak to someone. But the street was empty. There was no one to talk to, no one to help. But what would I say anyway? 'There's an American behind me who likes Del Shannon!'

I couldn't turn round and go back to the shop. That would mean meeting Bob again. What if he recognised the likeness in Mansell?

I carried on, following the curve of the road. I kept walking till I was out of the Crescent and back on our road. Children were playing, people were chatting at the bus stop. It was all normal and ordinary. But over at the top of the Crescent sat an anonymous, exotic, threatening man with a lovely smile. What should I do? I looked at my watch. The bus was due any minute. What if Sylvie got off and saw me and called out and he heard her and turned to find out who she was calling and realised it was me and that I had the baby? He might rush up, snatch Mansell and jump on the bus, away, away from us all. I decided to walk quickly up to the shop and tell Mrs Weston. Let her deal with it.

If there was anything to deal with. Perhaps it wasn't Bob at all, just a tired passer-by who needed a garden wall to sit on for a moment's rest. Perhaps he was a figment of my imagination. Resolutely I pushed the pram along the road. When I turned into the parade, I glanced over to the Crescent. The wall was empty. He'd gone. A bus went past. Had it taken him away? Had it brought Sylvie? Had they met?

It wasn't my problem. He'd gone, that was all. I turned the pram and wheeled it back to the house. I knocked on the door. There was no answer. I checked my watch. It was twenty to five. According to Mrs Weston, Sylvie should have been home by now. I looked up and down the road. There was no sign of her or Bob. I knocked again. I pushed open the letter box and called, 'Sylvie! It's Linda.' From inside Sylvie's voice called, 'Coming!'

When she opened the door her cheeks were pink and she looked radiant, beautiful. She looked as well as you could possibly be. She didn't look as if she'd just got back from the doctor's. 'Linda!' She was clutching her cardigan closed at the neck. She had a straight black skirt on and no shoes. She looked back down the hall. 'I wasn't expecting you.' Her eyes glittered strangely. 'Are you all right? You look a little flushed.'

I wanted to say, *me? You're the one who's meant to be ill.*

'Well,' she said, almost reluctantly, 'do you want to come in?'

I did – I wanted to tell her about Bob lurking around. I wanted to talk about my terrible exams. I wanted to hear Sylvie say, 'Exams don't matter. What matters is what you make of yourself.' And I wanted to hear her say, 'Don't worry about Bob. I can handle him.'

'Yes, please,' I said.

She breathed out sharply. Then she waved her arm and gave a slight bow. 'Well, step right in.'

'How was the doctor's?' I said politely.

'Oh, don't let's talk about that,' she said as she watched me park the pram in the hall. She shepherded me into the kitchen. 'Let's talk about something pleasant.'

I couldn't think of anything pleasant. My mind was full of my exams and Bob sitting on the wall. I said, 'You know Bob, did you ever see him again?'

'What?'

'After that night. After you came back from your holiday.'

She frowned. 'Holiday?'

How could she forget? 'In Great Yarmouth. Staying at Janet's auntie's house. The blue dress.'

She laughed. 'Oh, goodness, you have got a good memory, my little elephant.'

Elephant? 'Did you?'

She gave a sort of snuffle and a funny smile spread over her face. 'Well, it really is a long story. And we don't have time for that.' She was pulling out a tray from behind the milk bucket.

'If you don't want to tell me, I suppose you don't have to. But what would you do if he came knocking?'

She spun round. 'What? Who?'

'Bob.'

She breathed in sharply. 'I'd tell him politely to go away because I am entertaining an important guest. And you too.' I laughed, but she was putting three cups onto the tray. There was someone else, an important guest.

What was going on? Who else was here? It couldn't be her mum; she was in the shop. Was it Bob – had he slipped indoors behind the bus? Perhaps it wasn't Bob I'd seen. Perhaps he'd been inside while Gary from Wisconsin stayed outside. Perhaps Gary was the one who liked Del Shannon. Perhaps she didn't want me to be here. 'Do you want me to go?'

'No, no,' she said. 'Look, I've put a cup out for you.' She poured boiling water into the teapot. She put the sugar bowl onto the tray. She took the milk bottle out of the bucket, wiped it slowly on a tea towel and put it on the tray. She stood looking at the tray as if she was about to play Kim's Game and she would be required to remember everything that was on there.

Who was it? Who was here? I wanted to know, but I didn't.

I followed her into the living room. It was tidy, no dirty nappies, no old newspapers. The LPs were in a neat pile by the record player on the sideboard. And beside the record player, earnestly reading the back of a book that looked like *The L Shaped Room*, was a thin man with a wispy brown beard wearing a beige sloppy jumper. He looked up at Sylvie with a smile, and then almost jumped when he saw me.

I knew who this was. He'd been on the Aldermaston coach, at the back with all the other men with beards. It was Ken Sadd.

Sylvie put the tray on top of the pile of LPs. She handed Ken a mismatched flowery cup and saucer.

'This is Kenny,' she said.

Kenny? Ken? Kenny? Surely this wasn't the Kenny from the story of how Sylvie met Mansell's dad? The Kenny she'd been thinking of marrying till she met Bob? She'd dumped him! Hadn't she? Could this really be him? Had she even been to the doctor's?

Kenny looked at his cup of tea as if he couldn't remember how it got there, then hesitated before he put it down precariously on the arm of a chair, and we shook hands.

'Kenny, this is my friend Linda. She has great aspirations for her future and, perhaps more importantly, she makes me laugh.' Sylvie handed me a green cup without the saucer. 'Linda, this is Kenny who likes black polo-neck sweaters, which I think we must all agree are the royal family of sweaters, although he isn't wearing one today, and sometimes he wears glasses, which I don't think he really needs, because he thinks they make him look more intellectual, which I seem to remember is something that you like.'

'Sylvie,' Kenny and I said together.

I looked at Kenny. 'I saw you on the march,' I said politely. 'I was sitting in the middle of the coach, on the left-hand side as you walk down. With my friend, Sandra . . . who said the thing about glasses. Not me.' He looked at me blankly and I could hear Sandra saying, 'That's interesting. Why don't you tell him what we had in our sandwiches?' I felt myself blushing. 'Anyway, I can't stay. I only came to . . . bring Mansell back!'

Sylvie was smiling, but she was breathing fast. 'You see, Kenny, Linda is not just a marcher and a demonstrator,' she gabbled, 'she's also an exceptionally good child-minder, for which she has badges from the Girl Guides.' Her chest was rising and falling rapidly. Why was she in such a state?

I stood up.

'But you can't go yet,' Sylvie said. She was almost shouting. 'You haven't drunk your tea.'

I was moving backwards towards the door. 'I've got things to do. I've got to go out. I'll come back another day,' I said.

CHAPTER 21

Post

THE PACKAGE ARRIVED AT OUR HOUSE on Tuesday, when everyone was out. My dad found it in the outside toilet and gave it to me saying, 'Late birthday or early Christmas present?'

'Probably,' I said, trying to be casual.

I walked upstairs, carefully, being natural, taking off the brown paper wrapping. I knew it couldn't be meant for me. My penfriends were dull. Exciting correspondence with my name on was only ever for Sandra. But Danny didn't usually send parcels. He never sent parcels. This parcel couldn't be from him.

So perhaps it was for me. Perhaps it was a late birthday present, perhaps it was ... I unwrapped it. There was another layer of wrapping underneath with another name. But it wasn't addressed to Sandra. This small square parcel, that looked like five or six packets of cigarettes, had Danny's name written on it, in strange square handwriting. It wasn't from Danny, it was *for* Danny. Which of Danny's friends knew my name and address?

Oh Danny, I thought. Why did this have to happen? Why did you have to come back now? Sandra had been quite happy recently. She seemed to like being driven around in Cooky's big car. And now she was going to have to deal with this parcel, whatever it was: cigarettes, cheques, more hairbrushes. I really hoped that's all it was, but I knew in my heart it was going to be much more serious.

After tea I went over to Sandra's, the parcel stuffed into my brown birthday-present bag. Her mum was in the living room reading the paper and watching *Emergency Ward 10* and her dad was pottering about in the garage. Sandra and I went silently up to her bedroom. When I took the package from my bag, she gasped. I gave it to her. She dropped it onto her lap. 'It's not mine. It's got your name on it.'

'It always has my name on it.'

We stared at the outer layer, my layer. We couldn't read the postmark but it obviously wasn't Shepherd's Bush. 'But the next layer has Danny's name on it,' I said. 'And it isn't Danny's handwriting. Why send it to me? Why not just send it to Cooky's house?'

'Because he doesn't live with Cooky anymore. He lives with an old lady on the Main Road.' She picked up the parcel and threw it on the floor.

'Careful!' I said. 'Don't break it.'

'Why? Do you know what it is?'

'No! Do you?' I said.

She sighed. 'He said it was all over.'

'What?'

'You know that person I had to phone. After the march.'

Well, I don't know. You didn't tell me.'

'It was a friend of Trevor's.'

'Trevor!? Is this what that was all about?'

We both looked at the parcel on the floor. It had to be something really illegal. Trevor was a bank robber. He'd shot a man.

'I don't know,' Sandra said. 'It might not be. It probably isn't. Did you give Trevor your address?'

'No!'

'Danny might have given it to him.'

'Oh, Sandra! Are you going to open it?' I asked her.

'No. I don't want to know. It's got Danny's name on. It's nothing to do with me. But –' She bent and picked up the parcel. She smiled. 'I'll have to give it to him, won't I?' She ran her finger over Danny's name on the parcel. 'I'll go tonight.'

'Where?'

'I'll find him. Don't worry, I'm not asking you to come with me.'

She knew what I'd say if she did.

Sandra looked at her watch. 'I can't go yet. He'll be out.'

'Shouldn't you just take it to the police?'

'Then we all get in trouble,' she said. 'Don't worry. I'll go later.'

'Well, give me that,' I said. Sandra had started to wrap the parcel in the paper with my name on. I snatched it from her and tore it in little pieces which I put in my bag.

I had to go. We had a French test in the morning, a list of vocabulary I had to learn, in preparation for next year. I stood up. 'Why don't you just forget Danny and concentrate on Cooky?'

Sandra laughed. 'I think I can deal with both of them at the same time.'

'Well, tell him to stop being stupid.'

'But then he wouldn't be Danny.' Her expression changed. 'I don't think he's got a choice.'

'Trevor,' we said together.

'Oh Sandra, be careful. This is really serious.'

'I know,' she said.

On Thursday, the second parcel came. This time I was at home when the postman knocked. I took the package from him and saw my name in the same strange square handwriting. I felt sick. I ran upstairs and ripped off the top layer of brown paper. There again was Danny's name. I sat on the bed in despair. What was I going to do?

Judith walked in. 'Come on, just because you've finished your exams, we still have to go to school.' She was hoping to be a prefect so she was practising bossing me about. 'What's wrong? What's that?'

'Nothing! It's Sandra's.' I felt guilty immediately.

'Is it her birthday?'

'No, it's . . . it's something I borrowed. I've got to take it back to her.'

'We're going in five minutes,' Judith said.

I shoved the package under the bedclothes with my nightdress.

After tea I knocked on their back door. 'She's up in their room,' her mum said.

I ran upstairs. Sandra was combing her hair, switching the parting from side to side. 'Did you give him the parcel?' I said.

'Yeah.'

'Did he tell you what it was?'

'No, but he was very, very pleased to get it. Why?'

Suddenly I was furious. 'Another one's come!' I took the parcel out of my bag and threw it on her bed.

'Oooh.' She picked it up. 'Oooh. This is good.'

'No it's not,' I shouted.

'Shhh!'

'It's terrifying. You've got to stop him. Even if you don't care about your future, I care about mine.'

She picked the parcel up. 'This one he's going to have to bargain for. He's going to have to make me an offer. He'll have to, let's say, propose. And then perhaps I'll give it to him as an engagement present.'

'Isn't that called blackmail?'

'No,' Sandra said, 'this is life. I want him, he wants this. Everybody wants, everybody gets.'

'But it must be something illegal. What if someone finds out?'

'How? Have you said anything to anyone?'

'No!'

'No one will know. And once I make my bargain with Danny, he gets the parcel and we'll be in the clear.'

'I'd rather we were in the clear now.'

She was smiling. She looked happy. 'It will all be fine. A wife can't give evidence against her husband.'

'But how does that protect me?'

'It's nothing to do with you now. Forget it. It's all over.'

'Sandra!' It was her dad, shouting up the stairs.

We exchanged a look. What could he want? 'Quick, give me that other bit of paper, the top bit!' Sandra said. Roughly she rewrapped the parcel and thrust it under her pillow.

'Sandra!' Her dad sounded angry. 'Get down here!'

'What? What?' she whispered. 'You don't think he saw it, do you?'

'No,' I said. 'He wasn't in the kitchen.'

'Sandra!'

'Shall I come with you?' I said.

She shook her head and ran down the stairs. Five minutes later she raced back up. 'I've got to tell you to go home.'

'What? What's happened?'

'Someone saw me.'

'Who? What?'

'That stupid Uncle Peter of your friend Sylvie. When I took the parcel to Danny. He was outside the pub. He just told my dad. Apparently he said I was hanging about with criminals. Which is a laugh. He was the one who was as drunk as a skunk. He kept asking Danny for money.'

Her dad's voice reverberated up the stairs. 'Sandra!'

She slid back down the stairs. She started talking as she walked along the hall. 'I wasn't doing anything.' The kitchen door closed and I couldn't hear any more.

But then the shouting began. There were arguments in Sandra's house, I knew. Her mum and dad were always having a go. But this shouting was different.

What were they saying? I crept down the stairs and hovered on the bottom step. I could run back up quickly enough.

The words slut, criminal, cheap, in Mr Brady's voice, ricocheted off the walls. Sandra murmured something and Mrs Brady wailed, 'Stupid tart! We should have put you in a home. I told you, we should have put her in a home.'

Mr Brady said, 'You are not going out of this house again.'

'Oh, and what about my job?' Sandra shouted. 'Do you want me to give up work? I can give up work if you like.'

'That's enough cheek. You're not going out.'

'You can't tell me what to do,' Sandra said. 'I earn my own living. I pay my way.'

'You think what you give your mother pays for everything? You're very wrong.'

'You can't keep me in. What's the point?'

'We can keep you from making an exhibition of yourself. Bringing the family into disrepute, flinging yourself about like Sylvia Weston. What about your sister's reputation? And your mother has to work in the shop.'

'Yeah, I've got to serve everyone on the estate. They'll love that, talking and laughing behind my back.'

'What about Linda? When am I going to see her?'

I shrank back against the wall.

'Linda! Christ knows what her mum would say if she knew who you were hanging about with,' Mrs Brady said.

The kitchen door burst open and I flew back up to the bedroom, followed by Sandra. She was crying as she stomped back into the room. 'My dad's going to meet me at dinner time and come home with me every night, and that's the end of my life.'

'Who are you talking to?' Mr Brady's voice came up the stairs. 'Is Linda still here? I told you to tell her to go home! You won't be seeing her for a while.'

We looked at each other. Angry tears were in Sandra's eyes. 'I hate them,' she said. 'I hate them. I give them all my money, I cook the dinner, I don't do anything wrong. Well, they're not going to stop me seeing Danny. They're not going to ruin my life.'

'You'd better be getting off home now, Linda,' Mr Brady called. His tone was gentler to me. 'It's time you went home.'

I stood up.

And then the phone rang.

Sandra and I stared at each other in horror. We both ran for the stairs. But Mr Brady was there already. He picked up the receiver.

'Sandra? No, you can't. And if that's one of her criminal friends,' he said, 'you can just drop dead.' His Irish accent was more pronounced when he was angry. 'Don't get brazen with me, mister. No, I will not give her a message. She will not be meeting you tonight, or any night. And do not call here again.' He slammed the receiver down.

'You are just ignorant!' Sandra called down the stairs. 'That was my phone call. You can't choose my friends.'

'While you are living under my roof I can choose whatever I want. Come on, Linda.' He beckoned to me. 'It's time for you to be off.'

'I bet that was Danny!' Sandra whispered to me. She looked at her dad. 'I'm going out!' she shouted.

'If you think you're going to meet the ratbag who was just on the phone, you've got another think coming.'

'I've got to go out.'

'If you leave, you don't come back.'

I could see Sandra weighing up the pros and cons. 'You'll have to go,' she whispered.

'I'm going.'

'No, to meet him.'

'What, now? Sandra!'

'Off you go, Linda,' her dad said.

Sandra looked at her watch. 'Yes.'

'Where?'

'Try the Clock House. That's where he drinks now. Say I'll see him on Friday night, straight after work. I do have to stay late sometimes on a Friday. My dad won't wait for his tea, he'll want to get straight home.'

'Where? Where will you meet him?'

'I don't know. The bus station. I must be allowed to go to the bus station, unless they want me to walk home. Tell Danny I'll see him in Snows.'

'Are you sure?' I said.

'Yes. Quick. Hurry.' She ran into her bedroom and came back with the parcel. 'And give him this.' She thrust it into my hands.

'What if he's not there?'

'He'll be there.'

The Clock House wasn't far, just past the 1930s bungalows on the Main Road, on the edge of the estate. But somehow it seemed further and the parcel felt heavier and more dangerous than when I'd crossed the road to Sandra's house an hour earlier. And what if he wasn't there, what would I do with it? I'd just throw it away, anywhere, in someone's dustbin.

But he was there, sitting on a wall outside the pub, with a pint of beer in his hand.

As I approached, Danny looked up. 'Fancy seeing you here,' he said. 'Where's Sandra?'

'She's at home.'

'Really? I just had a very funny phone call with her dad.'

'Well, you've only got yourself to blame.' I sat down beside him. I gave him her message. Then I said, 'I've got something for you.'

'Thank Gawd,' he said.

I opened my bag and was pulling out the parcel when Danny stiffened. A plain dark saloon car was pulling into the pub car park. Two men got out; one wore a grey raincoat and the other was wearing a uniform, a police uniform. He flipped a peaked cap onto his head as he walked towards us. I crammed the parcel down into my bag and stood up. 'I don't care what her name is, she can have you!' I shouted and pushed Danny so that he almost fell over the wall. 'And don't try and ring me up!' Danny stared at me open-mouthed. I was breathing heavily. I hoped the police officers thought it was a lovers' tiff.

'All right then,' Danny said, catching on.

'Make sure you lock him up,' I said to the policemen, hoping it sounded angry and meaningless, and I stalked away, praying they wouldn't call me back. But I could hear Danny laughing. Laughing! I almost turned back and told them what I had in my bag, but I knew that could be dangerous. As I got to the corner I looked round. Danny was shaking his head, holding out his arms, opening his jacket as if he was asking to be searched.

I heard one man say, 'Lucky this time, Mulroney. But remember, we're watching you.' A car door slammed and then the car drove away.

I walked straight to Sandra's house. I knocked on the back door and Sandra opened it, with soapy washing-up hands. 'What?' she hissed. 'Go away.'

'My mum said I had to give you back the . . . cardigan you lent me. Here, she wrapped it up.' I handed her the parcel, sliding off the top layer of paper. 'I told her you wanted to . . . wear it on Friday.'

We stared at each other and she closed the door.

I walked home quickly and asked Mum if I could have a bath. I wanted to wash it all away: the package, Sandra's mum and dad, the police.

CHAPTER 22

Sandra Takes Steps

On saturday i was in the milk bar, making a banana milkshake, hooking the beaker onto the whisking machine, when Sandra came in.

'Watcha,' she said. She pulled a stool across and climbed onto it.

I stared at her. She wasn't meant to be here. I'd nearly got arrested because she wasn't allowed out, and now she walked in as if everything was normal.

'What are you doing here?' I said, reaching for a glass, keeping my eye on Mr Wainwright. 'Do your mum and dad know?'

'According to them I'm at work. We're doing the annual stocktaking in our office at the moment. They don't know I'm not part of it.'

'Is everything all right?' I went to unhook the milkshake beaker.

'We're getting married.'

I stopped. 'What do you mean?'

'Danny and I are getting married.'

'You mean, you're engaged?' The whisk kept turning.

'No, I mean we're getting married.'

'Does he know?'

'Of course.'

'He's asked you to marry him?'

'Yeah.'

I hadn't expected this. 'When? When did all this happen?'

'Last night. Don't act surprised, you arranged it.'

'I arranged a cup of coffee in Snows, not a wedding.'

Mr Wainwright was looking at me. I unhooked the beaker, poured out a glassful of foaming pale yellow milk and took the glass and the beaker to the customer at the far end of the counter. I'd been handling stolen goods for a criminal and she was getting married. Married. We'd joked about it; yes, we'd made New Year's Resolutions, but not really, not seriously, not Danny.

I gave the customer her change and went to serve Sandra. 'What do you want?'

'I want to marry Danny.'

'To drink.'

'Oh, a glass of milk.'

We'd run out of clean glasses. I stood at the dumb waiter for a tray of steaming hot glasses to arrive from Doris in the kitchen and Sandra dragged her stool along the floor to sit opposite me. She watched silently as I unloaded the tray.

I stared her in the face. 'Do you think he means it?'

'He gave me this.'

She stuck out her finger.

'You had that before.'

'Yes, but he'd forgotten I'd got it. This time it's for – for real.'

The ring was still too big. 'I don't understand. What does your mum say?'

'She doesn't know.'

'You're wearing the ring.'

'I don't wear it at home.' She beckoned to me and I leaned towards her over the counter. 'He said we could elope.'

'What?'

'Run away, elope.'

'Really? You're going to elope?'

'Shh! Yeah.' She looked around carefully. 'Why not? It'll be a laugh.'

No it won't, I wanted to say. *It'll all go wrong. He is a criminal. Your mum and dad will disown you.* I took a glass over to the milk machine. As I watched the milk bubbling into the glass, my stomach was churning. This was going too far. It was stupid. She was crazy. But even though I knew that, I felt alone and left behind. I slammed the glass down in front of her. Mr Wainwright was looking across at me. 'That'll be sixpence,' I said.

She paid me and gulped down her milk.

'When's all this meant to happen?'

'Linda!' Mr Wainwright called. 'Customer!'

'You'd better get back to work.' Sandra slid off her stool. 'Just don't say a word.'

'I've got nothing to say. I don't know anything. When will you tell me? I'm not supposed to talk to you, remember, because of your criminal friend Danny. Did he tell you the reason I didn't give him the parcel was because the police came? The police. They searched him. They're after him.'

For a moment she looked worried.

'You haven't given it to him, have you?' I said. 'You've got to.'

'It'll be OK.' She waved her hand, the engagement ring slipping round her finger. 'And now I've got to go and buy my trousseau. Sorry, I mean, go back to work to finish the stocktaking.' She winked at me.

If this had been one of her usual mad Danny plans, I would have said something about stocking up on stockings and we'd have laughed and arranged to meet later in the lingerie department in Bond's or Bolingbroke's. But there was no time to joke, no time to enjoy the prospect of a wedding, to mull over the pros and cons of a negligée versus two nightdresses, a new girdle versus two suspender belts. She was going to buy her trousseau without me. Our trousseaux were something we'd always planned together, discussing the length of our petticoats, the need for a bedjacket, white bras or black, dark stockings or light. It would have been such fun. But she was going to do it on her own.

If she was buying her trousseau today without waiting for me, it must mean she was planning something really imminent. I wanted to call after her. I wanted to tear off my overall and catch up with her and find out what was happening. But Mr Wainwright was still looking at me and I'd had my break at half past ten.

I stared at her as she crossed the road towards the High Street. I hoped that wasn't the bargain – the parcel for an elopement. She slipped into Bond's. I wondered what she'd buy.

I was taking an egg sandwich out of the display cabinet when Ray came in. 'Watcha,' he said, grinning. 'I've come for that drink you promised me.'

'No, if I remember rightly, I didn't,' I said.

'OK, you're right.' He looked at my face. 'What's the matter?'

I wanted to tell someone; I felt full to the brim with it, but it was such a secret. I was afraid just thinking about it would somehow get back to Sandra's mum and dad. I couldn't smile. 'What did you say you wanted?'

'I didn't, but I'll have a tea.' He settled himself onto a stool and drummed a tune on the counter. 'Cheer up,' he said. 'It might never happen.'

'I bet it does,' I said.

'Am I bothering you?' he asked. 'I could just go.'

'No, no. I'm sorry, no. I don't know. Everything's funny today.' I put his tea in front of him. 'That's fourpence.'

Val came over and nudged me. She stretched her hand out to Ray across the counter. 'I'm Val, I don't think we've been properly introduced. I'm very pleased to meet you.'

'Likewise,' he said, shaking her hand.

'Linda!' Mr Wainwright called. 'Could you clear a few tables?'

'Well, bye then,' I said to Ray.

'Do you want to go to the pictures tonight?' he said. 'I'm celebrating.'

I looked at him blankly. 'What is there to celebrate?'

'I passed my test! We can go out on the scooter.'

'Linda!'

I shrugged.

'If she doesn't go with you, I will,' Val said.

'Right you are,' he said.

Unhappily I squeezed past Val. I picked up a damp dishcloth and walked over to the table by the stairs. When I finished clearing and wiping, he'd gone.

Sandra was holding a large cream carrier bag when she came back in. She settled herself on a stool. 'Glass of milk, please,' she said. 'That'll be my second one of the day. Do I get a discount for buying in bulk?'

I looked at her. 'Don't you have to be somewhere?'

'Like where?'

'I don't know, at work, shopping, Gretna Green?'

'Och aye the noo. Actually I do.'

My throat ached.

'I'm going to confession. I thought I'd come and see you before I go. Can you keep this?' She held up the carrier bag. 'Actually, can you keep it till I go?' She winked at me again. It was as if I didn't know her.

'I can't leave the counter,' I said. I didn't want to touch the bag. I could see other bags inside it. I didn't want to know what was in them, or take them home. I didn't want any part of this. But I did want to know what she'd bought. I wanted to see her holding up each item and saying, 'What do you think?' I wanted her to share it with me, not just dump me with it.

Elsie was behind me, reaching for a Chelsea bun on the shelf. 'Do you want to leave that?' she said to Sandra. 'Here, give it to me. I know little Linda's a delicate flower. She'd probably drop it in the teapot. I'll put it up behind the expresso machine.' She smiled at Sandra and leaned past me to take the bag.

'And this.' Sandra held up a small brown suitcase. 'I got it in the market. It was really cheap.'

'Ooh, someone's going on holiday,' Elsie said, taking the suitcase. But she didn't ask any questions and I knew she wouldn't make any comments, whatever she was thinking.

'What is it?' I said to Sandra, as we watched Elsie tuck the bag and the case behind her stool.

'It's my trousseau.'

'I know that, but what?'

'Trousseau things.'

'Are you really going to elope? Whose idea was it?' I put the milk in front of her.

'I don't know. I mean, it came out of the blue. I hadn't said anything about getting married.' She handed me sixpence. 'It was him. I was just telling him about the parcel and how we hadn't opened it but I had an idea what was in it.'

'What?' I asked.

'I don't know, I just said that. But that was why I didn't want to bring it with me. Then I told him how my dad called me downstairs and had a go, and I made it sound like it was all about the parcels, and my dad was probably about to call the police, and he said, and these are his precise words, he said, "You don't have to put up with that, Sandra. You don't."

'And I said, "What choice have I got?"

'And he said, "Live somewhere else."

'And I said, "Yeah, where?"

'And he said, "With me."

'And I said, "Is that a proposal?"

'And he said, "Yeah. Yes, Sandra, it is." And he got down on one knee, if you must know – in the middle of Snows! – and he said . . .' She couldn't stop herself smiling. 'He said,

"Sandy darling, be mine." And then he burst out laughing. And I said, "Do you mean that?" And he said, "Yes." And he said, "Let's go out and get the ring", but of course, it was after five o'clock, nothing was going to be open, which he'd probably worked out. I wanted to dash off there and then, and break into Walker's and grab a selection, 'cos knowing him, he could change his mind. But I said, "What about your ring?" And he said, "Oh yeah." And he was fumbling about in his pockets, looking for it, all panicked. He thought he'd lost it.'

Or that he'd given it to someone else, I didn't say.

'So I put him out of his misery. I took off my chain and gave him the ring and he put it on my finger and he said, 'We'll get you a new one as soon as the shops are open. Then we'll just go and do it.' And then he kissed me. When I got home everyone was still bawling and shouting about the shame I'd brought on our family, Marie saying it was going to ruin her chances; and I still had to make the tea, and I thought, I'm just a slave. They think they've got me where they want me but that's all they know. And I went out this morning and bought this.' She pulled a small box out of her handbag. I was wiping the counter round her glass, trying to look busy. She prised open the box. Inside was the wedding ring we'd both been gazing at for months, a thick band of fine rose-tinted gold that would look lovely on anyone's hand.

'There was no point wasting money on another engagement ring. And he wasn't at the bus station this morning anyway, so I just went straight down to Walker's and got it. If he doesn't like it, that's too bad. He's got to go through with it now.'

I hesitated. 'So what did he actually say about the parcels?'

'Nothing.'

'And you've still got the one that nearly got me arrested!'

'But you didn't get arrested. It's all right. It's going to be my wedding present to him. At least we'll have one wedding present to open.'

I looked at her. How could it be a wedding present? It was stolen goods, contraband; a rare painting folded up small, or an ancient Egyptian manuscript. 'But we could all get into so much trouble.'

'Not you. You took the wrapping away with your name on. And he said there won't be any more. So it's nothing to do with you now.'

I wasn't so sure. 'And once you're actually married, where exactly are you going to live?'

'Somewhere. He's got plans. And if he doesn't do something, I will.'

'What about Cooky?'

'Cooky? That was never going to be anything.' She shuffled on the stool. 'Roll on Monday.'

'Monday! You're going on Monday?'

'I wish it was tomorrow.'

'Is Danny really, really serious?' I said.

'We'll just have to see.'

She grinned. Perhaps it didn't matter what happened. She was so happy now. She slipped off the stool and out of the door.

'So are you going to the pictures with Ray?' Val was sweeping the floor. It was the end of the day.

I was collecting cups. 'I might as well. I haven't got anything else to do.'

'But I mean it, if you don't want him, I'll take him off your hands.'

No you won't, I thought. 'I'll let you know,' I said.

I trailed home with Sandra's bags. As I walked up Sperry Drive I realised there was something I should have done before I came home. I was her best friend and in spite of everything, the least I could do was buy them a proper wedding present, something other than the so-called wedding present she'd already got, which would be awful to open on your wedding day, whatever it was. It had to be today, because tomorrow was Sunday and then nothing would be open at all. I considered the shops on our parade and what I could buy there. Baker's? Nothing. Off-licence? Absolutely not. Sweet shop? Chocolate?

Three sixpenny bars of Cadbury's Dairy Milk, please. No. The grocer's? Mrs Brady, do you have anything suitable for a wedding present? What do you think your daughter would like? Oh, whoops, I wasn't meant to say. I don't think she'd have much use for a Betty Crocker cake mix, anyway. Greengrocer's? Apples? Fish shop? Yes, a couple of pickled eggs please, wrapped in your finest newspaper. The hardware shop. Maybe.

I went into the hardware shop. I looked around hopelessly. I didn't really know what a wedding present should be. I could hardly buy her a watering can or a tin of Ajax. Candles were too cheap. A hairdryer was too expensive. A set of spanners might be useful, but Danny would probably use them on a job. Quickly, before someone I knew came into the shop and asked questions, I chose a torch. 'They take two batteries,' Mr Lambert, the manager, said. 'I'll put them in if you like.'

I watched him. 'Have you got any wedding paper?' I asked.

He looked at me strangely, looked at the suitcase and the overflowing carrier bag. 'We don't sell that here.'

I left the bag and the case in the shed, tucked behind the bikes, while we had tea. When everyone was watching the boisterous opening number of the *Billy Cotton Band Show* I ran out and dragged them upstairs. For once I was pleased that he shouted, 'Wakey wakey!' so loudly. Judith came into the bedroom as I was trying to close the wardrobe door. 'Running away from home?' she said.

'When I've saved up enough.'

'I could you lend you some money,' she said.

I looked at my watch. No sign of Ray. I felt a sting of worry. Perhaps he'd gone to the pictures with Val. I should have been clearer. It would have been good to think about something other than elopements and parcels. I went into the kitchen and put the kettle on. 'Anyone want a drink?' I shouted.

No one replied.

I was listening to the hiss of the coffee powder dissolving in the boiling water when there was a knock on the door.

Ray! Thank goodness. 'At last,' I smiled, opening the door.

But it wasn't Ray. It was Sandra. 'I've come to pack,' she whispered. 'I'm meant to be delivering a pair of shoes from my mum's catalogue to someone in the flats. I can't stay long.'

I stared at her in silence. She looked like a stranger, a strange rocker. She'd obviously been to the hairdresser, but this was much more extreme than when we went to Wormwood Scrubs. Her hair was standing out round her head in a tawny beehive like the girls in the Long Bar. She looked like Barbara.

We crept up to my bedroom. She was so excited, she couldn't stand still. She kept walking over to the dressing table and smiling at herself in the mirror.

I heaved the case and the carrier bag out of the wardrobe.

At the sight of the bags Sandra's face lit up. She explained her plan. She would pack the case from the things in the carrier bag, leave all the empty bags in the back of our wardrobe and hide the case out in the shed, where she would come round for it on Monday morning before anyone was awake.

'What are they going to say when you don't come home from work?'

She put the case on my bed and opened it. 'I've told them I'm going to Halina's for a couple of days because her mum's not well and she has to get up in the night with her. Silver End's far enough.'

'And they believed you?'

'Oh, her mum sent a letter! All in weak, wobbly writing. Which I wrote because she's so ill. They don't know that. And Halina rang from a phone box and spoke to my mum. Halina hasn't got a phone, so they can't check. She hasn't got a mum, actually, not an ill one, anyway. They're just pleased that I'll be out of town, out of trouble. It'll give us a day or so.'

'And then?'

'Then it'll be too late.' She danced over to the dressing table, singing, 'Here comes the bride'. She puckered her lips at herself in the mirror and murmured, 'Gorgeous.'

'So what happens after you pick up the case from our shed?' It didn't seem a very romantic way to start a wedding.

'Then I catch a bus down to the railway station. If he's not there, I'll meet him at Liverpool Street.'

'He isn't even going to London with you? You're eloping. He's meant to be carrying you off.'

'He might. He probably will. He said the problem is that someone might see us together, and try to stop us. Anyway, he's going out tonight to see who's saying what in the town. Although the only people who might remotely care about us going are my mum and dad, and I don't think that's very likely. In fact they probably paid him to ask me, to take me off their hands.'

I remembered the part of the big argument when Mrs Brady had said they should have put Sandra in a home. They'd been saying that to her ever since I could remember. Did they really wish she was in a home, or at least not in their home? Or perhaps it was just something people said. Not that anyone ever said it in our house. 'All right, so you get to London, then what?'

'He's booked us into a hotel. A hotel! If he's not at Liverpool Street Station, he'll come and meet me there. It's near Petticoat Lane. I could do a bit more shopping for the trousseau. I need a new jacket, really. Ooh, I could get a hat. With a veil!' She moved her shoulders at her reflection.

'After the hotel, then what?'

'We catch the train to Scotland.'

'What time's the train?'

'I don't know. Shut up. He's arranging the London part. I just have to get up to Liverpool Street. We didn't have that much time to go into all the details.'

'What if he doesn't come?'

'He'll come. I know he'll come. I've got the parcel, for one thing. And he gave me twenty quid to buy all this lot. And for Danny, that's as good as getting married just by itself. Anyway, I don't care. I'm eloping. And if he doesn't come, I'll elope on my own.' She lifted her chin at herself.

'What are you wearing for the actual ceremony?' I said. I had a good idea, because I'd looked in the bag on the bus home, but I wanted her to show me so we could talk about it.

A large pale pink carrier bag bore the name of the exclusive dress shop in Baddow Road. Tissue paper gave an expensive rustle as Sandra pulled out the dress. It was Nottingham lace, cream and fitted with darts at the waistline. I was so jealous. We both loved Nottingham lace.

'And I've got these shoes.' She wrestled with the box in a Dolcis bag and drew out a pair of beige quilted leather slingbacks. They had chisel toes and Louis heels. We'd been looking at them in the Dolcis window for weeks.

'You're so lucky,' I said.

'I know,' she whispered. Carefully she laid the shoes in the new suitcase. 'And . . .' She pulled a Bond's bag from under her coat. 'I mustn't forget to take this.' She took out a package wrapped in pale blue paper covered in silver horseshoes. 'My wedding present to him. Looks better like this, doesn't it?' She delved into the carrier bag again. One by one she threw some light, crackling packets onto the bed. 'A new girdle, three new pairs of stockings and – ta-da!' She pulled out something gauzy and flimsy. 'Some sexy baby doll pyjamas.'

They were pink nylon. I didn't want to look at them. Not because I was jealous, but because I just didn't want to hear about sex. Somehow it was always there. Cooky wanting to know how I felt about sex before marriage; Tap asking me how old I was; Trevor talking about Soho. Even Ray, looking at me so intensely. I wanted to know but I didn't.

'Don't make that face. It's no big deal. I might as well tell you, we've already done it.'

That was shocking. 'When?'

'Oh, ages ago.'

'And you didn't tell me?' I knew it!

'There wasn't much to say.'

'Where was I?'

'I dunno. Looking after your suicidal friend Sylvie or something.'

'Don't. But is that why you're marrying him? Because you're . . .?'

'In the club? No. Well, I'd better not be.'

'What was it like?' I said.

'All right.'

'Did it hurt?'

'A bit. I don't know what all the fuss is about. Especially if you haven't got anywhere nice to do it. The back of a car isn't exactly Buckingham Palace, I can tell you.'

'You did it in a car? Not Cooky's?'

'No! Danny gets cars. But if it had been Buckingham Palace I might still have had trouble.'

'Yeah, you might have had to marry Prince Charles.'

'But then you could have been my bridesmaid in a big fancy dress and held my train and caught my bouquet.'

'Oh, can't I come and be your bridesmaid?' Tears suddenly welled in my eyes.

'Don't be daft,' she said, folding the baby doll pyjamas with precision. Carefully she pressed them into the case. Without looking at me she said, 'I wish you could, too, but we couldn't afford the train fare.' She closed the lid. 'Let's take the case downstairs before they notice I'm not back and start suspecting the worst.'

We concealed the bulging case under an old sheet in the shed. Danny's parcel was back at our house. I tried to tell myself that if it was in the shed it was not my fault. Anyone could have put it there.

I walked her to the gate. We didn't say anything about what would happen in the next few days. I just said, 'Here.' I gave her the torch that I'd wrapped in Christmas paper. 'It's another wedding present,' I said.

'I'm so scared,' she whispered.

'Don't go,' I said.

'I've got to.'

'Stay there a moment.' I ran back into the house and up the stairs. I pulled open the top drawer of my dressing table. Under my best petticoat was a box that held my jewellery. In the box, underneath the bangles and brooches I'd had for years, was a small bundle of money, my carefully saved wages, ready for our next trip to London, ready to exchange for some wonderful mod clothes, ready to change my life.

I ran back out into the garden, where Sandra was hopping from one foot to the other, anxiously looking up and down the street. 'Here.' I crushed the notes into her hand. 'Take this. Hide it in your shoe or in your washing bag. Don't tell Danny. This is for you.'

She gazed at the fifteen pounds. 'But what about that dress you wanted? Those shoes?'

'I've still got some left,' I said. I had twelve shillings and sixpence. 'I'll earn some more.'

We looked at each other.

'I've got to go,' she said.

'Good luck,' I whispered.

CHAPTER 23

Confessions

I HAD NO CONTACT WITH SANDRA on Sunday, not a note, not a phone call. I watched from the window in case she went to post a letter. Nothing.

And now it was Monday morning. When I had shaken the tablecloth outside the back door after breakfast, I looked in the shed. The suitcase had disappeared. All trace of her elopement was gone, and so was the parcel. I could stop worrying about being arrested in the night. I could start to worry about the elopement. She must have come really early. I wondered if she'd caught the bus at the top of the road, or walked down Sperry Drive to the Main Road. I wondered how often she'd had to put the case down, how often she'd swapped hands.

The summer holidays stretched out endlessly, emptily, before me. What was I going to do without her?

I was going to work.

But at half past three I was back on the estate with nothing to do. Perhaps I could take Mansell out. If I was lucky they might even pay me. Mrs Weston was busy serving as I went over to the pram. Mansell grinned at me and said, 'Mama.'

'Linda,' I said. He crowed and clapped his hands. 'Mama.'

'Linda,' I said. He didn't understand the concept. I looked over at Mrs Weston and pointed at the pram. She smiled and nodded at me.

During our walk, Mansell sat up and looked at dogs and gurgled at trees and grizzled till I gave him his bottle, but he didn't say anything else.

Without thinking I wheeled the pram back into the Crescent. I hadn't seen Sylvie since the day I'd seen Bob, and Sylvie had behaved so oddly when Kenny was there, making comments about glasses and politics. But I realised I wanted to see her, even if she made me furious. I wanted to talk to her. I needed to talk to her.

She answered the door in a petticoat and her old brown cardigan. 'I was just having a little nap. So you've come at the right time for a cup of tea.' She looked at my face. 'Are you all right? Come in, let's put the kettle on. You can give Mansell a bit of banana.'

I sat down with Mansell on my lap while Sylvie made the tea. 'Now then,' she said. 'Tell me all about it.'

I wanted to tell her everything about Sandra, but her mum worked with Sandra's mum. I wanted to tell her about Bob and Wethersfield, but I didn't dare. I said nothing.

'What is it?' Sylvie said.

It was too much. She was being too nice. 'It's Sandra,' I said. 'She's eloped.'

Sylvie's eyebrows rose slightly. 'Well!' she said. 'Who with?'

'Danny, of course,' I said.

'When did she go?'

'This morning.'

'And you're not going with her?'

'I wanted to, but . . .'

'Yes, I don't think three is a good number at an elopement,' she said. 'Does her mum know?'

'No. You won't tell her, will you? You won't say anything to your mum?' Even as I said it, I wasn't sure I meant it.

Sylvie looked at me doubtfully. 'On condition that you keep me posted about what's happening, my lips are sealed. Tell me as soon as you get any news. Give or take a few hours of sleep, of course. Or if you're at school.'

'It's the summer holiday. Till September. She'd better not be away that long,' I said. 'She's coming back. She said she's coming back.'

'Oh, chicken,' she said. 'Didn't you try and stop her?'

'I did, but she was so excited and thrilled. She bought her trousseau and a wedding ring and everything.'

Sylvie's eyes widened. 'She bought the ring?'

'And there was a parcel.'

'A parcel?'

'There were two. One she gave to Danny. Your Uncle Peter saw her and told her dad . . .'

'Oh,' she said. 'So that's what that was all about.'

'The parcels came to our house, because all her letters come to our house.'

'I see. What was in them? The parcels, mean'

'I don't know, but it must be something illegal.'

'And what happened to the second one?'

'Sandra's got it. I tried to give it to him and the police arrived. I could have been arrested. Now she won't give it to him till they're married.'

'And you think . . .?'

'I think he's only saying he'll marry her because of the parcel. What if the police find them before she gives it to him? She could go to jail.' I wanted her to say I was being foolish and that the parcel was probably nothing illegal at all.

'That all sounds rather unsatisfactory.' She gazed at me. 'They came to your house.'

'They had to, because of her mum and dad.'

'But parcels! That's a bit naughty of her.'

'I know, I know,' I said. 'But she's my friend.'

'There comes a time when friends have to part.'

'I know that too,' I said sadly. 'I think we've both been thinking that. We'll probably go to separate prisons.' I wanted to cry.

'Oh, cheer up, chicken. Now then, have you told any-one else?'

'No!'

'Well, you've told me now. I won't tell anyone, unless you want me to. But I will keep your story here.' She put her hand on her chest. 'So you can relax.'

'But what if . . .?'

'We will cross any bridges that need crossing, when and if we come to them.'

I knew she was just saying that. I knew that her having my problems in her heart didn't actually make them disappear. But I felt better. I felt lighter. 'And there's something else,' I said.

'Yes?'

'It's about that day we went to Wethersfield.'

'Yes?'

'Well – we asked about Bob.'

'I don't understand.'

'I was trying to find him for you.'

'Really?'

'You were afraid you'd lose the baby because you didn't have a husband.'

'Was I?'

'You said. That day, after you . . . after you tried . . .'

'Oh yes. I was very sad then. But I don't . . .'

'And then he came to your house.'

351

'He did?'

'But you were out, and he left.'

'Oh, that's typical. But chicken, I knew where he was. He knows where I am. He writes to me about once every two or three months. A postcard. Once he even sent a letter. Oh, and that awful Valentine's card we laughed about.'

'We didn't! You didn't say it was from him. Why didn't you tell me?'

'I didn't think it was important to you, chicken. Or perhaps I didn't want it to be important.'

'Of course it's important. Why do you always say that? Mansell's important, so his dad's important.'

'Well, he didn't think so at first, that's for sure.'

'When did you tell him?'

'Almost as soon as Mansell was born. It seemed only right he should know. I hadn't seen him for a little while.'

'How did you know where he was?'

'I went to the base. At Wethersfield. There was a dance, and I went with Janet. I'm sure I told you that part.'

'No. I would have remembered. You certainly didn't say you'd seen Bob there. Or anywhere, apart from Great Yarmouth.'

'Oh, didn't I? He was there. For a moment or two it was quite civilised. He's a very good dancer.'

'What do you mean, he's a very good dancer?' I shouted.

'He dances well. Why are you so upset?'

I gulped. 'It's because I feel so stupid. We went up to Wethersfield. We got hauled in front of some general. Sandra ruined her stockings.'

'Oh, sweetheart.' She put her arms round me and pulled me to her. She rocked me back and forth. Her breasts were going up and down as she tried to control her laughter.

'But what are you going to do?' I said.

'What do you mean? Nothing. I have Kenny.'

'But what about Bob? Doesn't he deserve some consideration? For Mansell's sake, if for no other reason.'

'The question doesn't arise,' she said crisply.

'But I thought that's what you wanted. To be with Bob. The way you told the story.'

'That's because it's a good story. I like to tell it. Not everything in it is absolutely true. But you enjoyed it, didn't you?'

I felt young and stupid and clumsy. I felt I was ten foot tall and weighed twenty-five stone and filled up the kitchen with my stupid clumsiness. I stood up to go.

Sylvie followed me into the hall.

I put my hand out to open the door, then, 'No!' I said, 'No, it's not just a story. You loved Bob.'

Suddenly it felt like a dangerous thing to say. A strange look passed over her face, as if she was seeing something far away. She said nothing. We stood in silence. I didn't know what I expected her to say, but I didn't want to leave until she'd said it.

353

She took a breath. 'All right, yes, I loved him. And yes, I suppose I still do. But I was pregnant, Linda! You can't talk about love when you're pregnant. You have to talk about a house and clothes and baby food.' Her voice trembled. 'And when you've had the child, you need security and someone beside you.'

'I think that's second best,' I said.

'Oh Linda, don't say that. I'm doing what I can.'

We stood in the hallway looking at each other. 'Kenny's a good man,' she said gently. But there were tears in her eyes.

CHAPTER 24

Without Sandra

THE WEEK DRAGGED ON. When Mum got in from work on Tuesday I was watching *Five O'Clock Club* on telly. Although *Five O'Clock Club* had been a programme that gave the Beatles one of their first TV appearances, it was a children's programme and I didn't normally watch it. Mum said, 'Why are you lolling about looking so miserable?'

'No reason. I've got nothing to do. Sandra's gone away.' I sat up straight. 'To stay with a friend,' I added quickly. 'For a few days.'

'Well, if you really are at a loose end, why don't you go to the CND meeting tonight? You enjoyed it last time, didn't you?'

'Is there a film?'

'No, it's a talk tonight, Helen Grenville was saying.'

I sighed.

'I think it's Pat Arrowsmith. She's one of the founders of CND. She's a good speaker, I've heard. She doesn't just talk about nuclear disarmament. She's been to prison for her beliefs, and I think she's even been force-fed, rather like the suffragettes. So she talks about prison conditions, too, which should interest you.'

'Are you going?'

'No, it's our Women's Fellowship meeting tonight. And anyway, it's being organised by the Youth CND group, so I don't think they'd appreciate older folk.'

'So I'd have to go on my own?'

'Well, you know where it is, and you're sure to know one or two people.'

'Yes, people with beards. The question is, do I want to know them?'

'Don't be so silly. Lay the table.'

As the tablecloth billowed across the table, I remembered the Aldermaston march. I remembered the singing and the banners, and the feeling of everyone fighting for something they believed in, the sense that I might be part of something that was actually making a difference. I thought of the conversations we'd had, about politics, but also about music and even telly. I remembered the jokes, the laughter. I wanted to have those conversations regularly, not just once a year on the march – I wondered if going to the Youth CND meeting would be like that.

I caught the bus into town. During tea I'd thought about what to wear. I was always pleased with how I looked as a mod, but I didn't always fit in. I had decided to wear my big thin black jumper and my brown and white dogtooth check skirt. Combined with my moccasins, I felt I was still being true to mod, but not too mod. And I thought the duffel coat was sensible.

The Friends' Meeting House was in Rainsford Road. When I got off the bus at the bus station, I stood uncertainly on the pavement. Suddenly I really wanted to turn left, stroll into the centre of town, along London Road and slip down into the Orpheus, say hello to a few people, buy a glass of milk and put 'Hi-Heel Sneakers' on the jukebox. But I knew I had to move on. I had at least to try something different. This could be a new part of my life. Perhaps it was only because Sandra had gone that I could do this.

I turned right and walked towards the low neat modern building that was the Friends' Meeting House.

I walked up the steps and into a wide, light foyer which seemed to be full of beatniks. The men all appeared to have beards. The girls all wore sloppy jumpers, but not like mine – theirs were thick and patterned, not thin and plain. There was a lot of backcombed hair. It was like the back seat of the coach to the Aldermaston march.

As the doors closed slowly behind me the conversation in the foyer stopped and everyone turned to look at me.

A girl I thought I recognised walked towards me, smiling. She was holding two glasses of water. 'Linda? You're Linda, aren't you? How nice to see you.' It was Olivia Pearson from school. She was in the year above me. I was surprised she recognised me. I knew her because she always looked very stylish in her school uniform; she managed to make her skirt swing really elegantly, and she had metal tips on the heels of her shoes that clicked in a really cool way when she walked out of assembly. She was wearing a straight black dress that came to her knees and thick black stockings. Her curly hair was pulled back into a pony tail. 'This is your first meeting, isn't it?' she said. 'Come with me.' As she spoke to me the conversation in the room began again.

We walked into a large, light room. Olivia put the glasses of water onto a table at the front of the room, then guided me to a seat in a middle row and sat down beside me.

She looked at her watch. 'I think they'll give it a couple more minutes. One or two haven't arrived yet.'

'Do I have to sign in or anything?' I asked.

'Not at the moment,' she said. 'I'm so glad you're here. I remember when you wore your CND badge to school. I was really impressed.'

'Really?'

'Yes, and I've been hoping you would come to the meetings.'

'But I haven't seen you on the Aldermaston,' I said.

'Ah, that's because I usually march with Hertford CND, because my sister and my dad live there.'

I looked around the room. People were wandering in. 'Do you think meetings like this can change things?'

'If we didn't have meetings like this we wouldn't have the numbers of people that come on the march. It's all about organisation. If we all do something, then big things happen.'

A man with a thick black beard and black horn-rimmed glasses walked in with a woman in jeans and a big over-coat, with short dark hair. The man called the meeting to order, told us he was Don, the chairman of the group, and introduced Pat Arrowsmith.

It was a small meeting – there were only fifteen of us – and there were empty seats in the front row. Later Olivia said that was an excellent turnout. Pat Arrowsmith didn't seem concerned at the size of the gathering and thanked the group for inviting her. She spoke about Hiroshima and Nagasaki and the terrible long-lasting damage caused by nuclear weapons. Some things I knew already, other things were new to me: children being born with deformities, strange illnesses appearing in people who had been in the vicinity. Then she talked about being arrested and what prison had been like, not just for her as a political campaigner, but for the ordinary women prisoners. And she talked about what we could do – demonstrate, write letters, have discussions, if necessary get arrested.

I was enthralled by everything she said.

At the end of the meeting one or two people asked questions, about CND and whether the campaign went far enough. A girl with long straight hair asked whether CND was doing enough about the Vietnam War. Someone else called out that they were doing too much. Pat Arrowsmith answered carefully and said you couldn't divide the two because of the power the Americans had in the world and in the arms race. There was a short discussion about unilateral disarmament, could it ever work and shouldn't we push for all countries to ban the bomb, not just our own. Then someone at the back asked why were there always trad jazz bands on the Aldermaston march – a question I appreciated – and someone said it was because modern jazz wasn't loud enough. Everybody laughed. Then Don closed the meeting and thanked Pat Arrowsmith, who had to leave to catch a train back to London to speak at another meeting.

The time had flown.

'I need a pint and a smoke. Let's go up to the County Hotel,' said someone in a tweed jacket with leather patches. He had been holding a pipe during the meeting.

'That's Guy,' Olivia whispered. 'He's a poet.'

A poet! Yet he looked so ordinary. Apart from the pipe.

'The one who made the joke was Greg. He's got a Morgan.'

'What's a Morgan?'

'It's a crazy car, and it's always breaking down and he's always trying to mend it. He does tend to smell of oil and petrol. But he's very good at offering lifts.'

The group of about ten people ambled up to the County Hotel, still talking about the meeting. I didn't know if I was dreading the possibility of seeing someone I knew or if I was proud to be in this new group. I decided I rather liked it.

'So? What did you think?' Olivia asked as we walked into a small lounge area. 'Will you come again?'

'Yes, I will,' I said. 'I enjoyed it. It was . . . inspiring.' I sat down beside her. Greg asked people what they wanted to drink. Everyone was reaching into their pockets or purses for money. 'It was just what I wanted.' I took out half a crown.

'Put it away,' Olivia said, 'this one's on me.'

CHAPTER 25

Sandra's Story

I WOKE UP WITH A START. What? What was it? My heart was beating like a Dave Clark Five record. What had woken me up? Was it Mum coming into the bedroom to have another go at me for arriving home late for tea? Or was it Judith, complaining I'd been wearing her skirt? Or was it Mr Brady, shouting from across the road that he knew Sandra hadn't gone to visit Halina and demanding the truth?

But it was the middle of the night. I could hear Dad snoring next door.

I closed my eyes and curled into the blankets. Then something knocked against the window. It was something outside, in the back garden. It happened again, a *tap tap* on the glass. My heart thudded.

'Judith,' I hissed. 'Judith.'

'What?' She turned over.

'There's someone outside.'

362

'No there isn't.'

'There was a noise. In the garden.'

'It's raining.'

'Not that noise.'

'It must have been a hedgehog.'

'No, it wasn't. Will you look out of the window and see?'

'No, because I don't care. Go to sleep.'

There was a spatter against the window, like hail.

Judith sat up. 'You look out the window.'

'All right, but stay awake. In case . . .'

'Well, hurry up.'

The garden was in darkness but I saw a movement in the shadows, by the shed.

'It's someone,' I whispered, scarcely able to speak. 'There's someone down there!'

'What do you mean? I'm going to get Dad!' Judith threw back her covers.

I saw a flash of beige. 'Don't,' I said. I squinted through the window. 'I think it's Sandra.'

'What's she doing down there?'

'I don't know, she's supposed to be married.'

'What? What are you talking about?'

'Nothing. Nothing. What shall I do?'

'I don't know. Open the window?' She tucked her legs back under the covers.

'What if Mum hears?'

'All right, leave her out there. She's your friend.'

I opened the window and leaned over the windowsill. It was definitely Sandra, standing in the rain. We looked at each other for an instant.

'What are you doing here?' I whispered.

'Can I come in? I can't go home.'

'She wants to come in,' I said to Judith.

'Then let her in. Hurry up, it's cold.' She pulled the blankets over her shoulders.

I closed the window and put on my slippers.

I padded down to the kitchen with mixed feelings. Turning up in our back garden in the middle of the night in the pouring rain was not a sensible thing to do, but she was back. She was back. But what did it mean?

In the kitchen I closed the door behind me before I switched on the light. As I turned the key to open the back door, I suddenly panicked – what if she'd brought Danny with her? His laugh was so loud.

I opened the door and Sandra stepped into the kitchen. She looked terrible. She was soaking wet. The Nottingham lace dress clung to her legs. My eyes flicked behind her. 'Is Danny . . .?'

'Oh, don't worry,' she said. 'I'm on my own.' She sagged against the sideboard and drops of rain from her hair dripped onto the red and white Fablon covering. I handed her a towel from the rail on the back of the broom cupboard. Roughly she rubbed her hair.

'Are you . . . are you married?' I whispered.

She said nothing.

'Where's your suitcase?'

'Back in your shed,' she said bitterly.

'Why aren't you in Scotland? Where's Danny?'

She looked at me. Her eyes were huge in her face.

'Was he there to meet you?' I asked.

'He was at Liverpool Street Station. And we went to a hotel.'

'A hotel?'

'It was horrible. The toilet was miles away from the room and there were all these really rough men walking around.' She hung the towel back on the rail. 'Then he disappeared. And then the police came.'

'The police!'

'They searched the room. They were looking for something, of course.'

I knew what she meant. My heart was racing.

'They asked me if I had any packages. I said I had a wedding present.'

'You didn't!' Those parcels had come to our house, they had had my name on them. I was implicated. This was terrible; it was the end of my life. I tried to speak. There was a gurgle in my throat.

'I was terrified,' she said. 'It was the middle of the night and these two big policemen were going through everything in the room.'

'Did you tell them how you got it?'

'No!'

I whispered, 'What happened?'

'They opened the drawer in the dressing table and, of course, there it was.'

My heart was pounding. 'What did they do?'

'They opened it.'

'What was it?'

'Well, if you don't know, I don't know who does.'

'It was nothing to do with me, it just came to our house. I didn't . . .'

'It was a torch, stupid. A torch! It was the present you gave me. It's all there was. Danny must have taken the real present.'

I wanted to laugh with relief, even if she was implying that my present wasn't real. 'So what did they say?'

'They said I was a very lucky girl not to be involved. So we're both in the clear. They could see it was nothing to do with me. He'd taken everything, all his clothes and his slippers. He'd brought his slippers! And the parcel. He'd taken five pounds out of my bag, which was all I had, and he took the wedding ring. He didn't need to – it was money in those parcels, you know, piles and piles of ten-pound notes. It was Trevor's. It was, what do they call it – money-laundering, going through Danny. And he took it all and he just disappeared.'

I wanted to ask her about the fifteen pounds I'd given her.

'Can I stay here?'

'Here?' Sandra never stayed at our house.

'I'll go home before anyone knows I'm here.'

'What will you say to your mum and dad?'

'I dunno. I'll tell them there's been a miracle, Halina's mum's cured.'

'Oh yeah?' I wanted to laugh out loud. She was back. 'You'll have to share my bed unless you want to sleep on the floor. Do you want something to wear?'

She shook her head and tapped her bag.

I locked the back door. We crept upstairs and Sandra slid into the bathroom. She came out in the baby doll pyjamas and climbed into bed beside me.

She pulled the covers up to her neck. There was silence. We were lying back to back and I thought she'd gone to sleep.

'If it hadn't been for your money I wouldn't have had anything to eat and I wouldn't have been able to get back to Chelmsford. Thank you.' Her voice was small. 'There's some change.'

'Who are you talking to?' Judith murmured.

'No one,' I said.

We were silent.

Later I woke up and she was crying, sobbing quietly into the pillow, her back towards me. I put my arm round her and then I went back to sleep.

When I woke up in the morning, Sandra had gone and there was only the small lump of the baby doll pyjamas under the bedspread.

'What did Sandra want?' Judith said.

'Don't ask me.'

I shook out the tablecloth after breakfast and checked in the shed. Her case was there. I covered it properly with the old sheet.

I thought she might ring me before I caught the bus to work; I thought she might come into the Milk Bar. But by the time we closed at half past two she still hadn't appeared. And she wasn't waiting outside.

On my way home I dropped a note through Sylvie's door. 'S is back. She had a nice time. Nothing happened.'

CHAPTER 26

Changing

IT WAS SEPTEMBER AND TIME to go back to school. But I wasn't as reluctant as usual because now I was in the fifth year. This was the year things got serious, the year for O levels. At last I got to wear a white shirt, not the pale blue one of the first four years. The shirt said everything about who you were. It made me look different. And I felt different, wearing the white shirt and my navy skirt with a swing and a sheen from years of wear, and my tie with its special knot. It all added up to being someone in the school, someone important.

We were in a new form room, one that I had always thought was for the impossibly senior pupils; and now that was us. Our form mistress was Miss Beasley, the most respected teacher in the school. Her subject was history, one of my subjects. I'd got 75 per cent for that in the exams, out of my final average of 65 per cent. I wanted to get serious. I wanted to get good marks.

Cray and I were on our way to English when Judith's friend, Rosemary, stopped us. As well as running the drama group, she was the new head of our house, Tancock. The Tancock colour was unfortunately yellow and if you wanted to, you could wear a badge on your tie that was an enamel strip of sunshine. I didn't want to. But Rosemary wore the diagonal yellow stripes of the house tie, which only members of the sixth form were allowed to wear. 'Could I have a word?' she said to me.

'Why?' I looked round.

'They probably want you to join the house hockey team,' Cray murmured. Although this was inconceivable, unless the roof of the gym had fallen in on every other member of Tancock, I still had a small thrill of hope.

'Your sister Judith . . .' Rosemary began.

'Judith?'

'. . . says you're free in the evenings after school.'

'Does she?' Oh God, what did they want? Would they ask me to clean the hockey sticks? Prepare the pitch? Pick up litter?

'She says you're funny. Can you come to a meeting of the drama group tomorrow afternoon?'

'The drama group!' I said to Cray, as we walked into English. I hadn't expected that. It wasn't what mods did, but I was quite excited.

'Get you, funny girl,' Cray said.

*

Casually I walked past the noticeboard where the school societies put up information. There it was. 'DRAMA SOCIETY, PANTOMIME AUDITIONS'. The word Thursday was crossed out and replaced by 'TONIGHT! ROOM 31'.

After school, back in Miss Reeves' classroom with the drama group, I half-recognised a few of the girls. Some of them even said hello to me. Rosemary was there and seemed delighted to see me, which made me feel better. Then I noticed she was thrilled to see everyone as they came through the door. She described the roles that needed to be filled and then she handed out the script to each of us. It was two sheets of paper.

'Really?' I said hesitantly. 'It's going to be a very short evening.'

People laughed.

'It's a draft,' Rosemary said. The play would develop as the weeks went by, she said. It was going to be a modern take on an old favourite – *Cinderella*. She wanted input from everyone, those who wanted to act and those who would work backstage. Everyone had ideas, what Cinders should wear, what music might be good, who would do the scenery, and then Rosemary said, 'What about a mod view?' Everyone turned to me.

I wasn't expecting that. 'Erm. Scooters? Prince Charming could wear a parka.'

'Ooh, yes!' said a little first-year, clapping her hands.

'The Ugly Sisters could be rockers,' I said.

'Ye-e-es,' said Rosemary. 'We were hoping we could get teachers to play those roles. Not sure what they'd think about having beehives.'

'Miss Soames has one already,' I said. 'She just hasn't mastered the full leather-jacket-with-chains look yet.' People sniggered.

'Miss Reeves would look good in American tan,' said another girl with short blonde hair and a sixth form tie. American tan stockings were what rocker girls wore. There was someone in the group who got the joke!

'And white stilettos look good on anyone,' I said. We looked at each other and laughed.

It was half past five. The time had gone so fast.

Rosemary said, 'Charlotte, can you collect the drafts?'

'OK.' It was the girl who'd talked about American tan. 'Can I have all the drafts and your lists of ideas,' she shouted.

I handed in my papers. I'd scribbled a note about a possible double act. Charlotte glanced at it, then turned back to me. 'Perhaps we should do something together.'

I nodded. 'All right.'

CHAPTER 27

Birthdays

IT WAS A COLD, SUNNY Sunday morning in October and it was my first Quaker meeting. Finally I had decided which church I wanted to attend, and now I was walking into the Friends' Meeting House.

I stepped hesitantly through the door. To go in on a Sunday morning, I realised, was a different thing to attending CND meetings here. In the foyer was a table with a vase of bright red and purple anemones and some leaflets. A woman I didn't know approached me, smiling quietly, and welcomed me. Then Mrs Grenville came out of a side room carrying a bowl of large pink and red roses. 'Linda!' she said. She introduced me to two or three people who all smiled in a kindly way and seemed pleased to see me. Mrs Grenville took me with her into the meeting room. It was the same cool, light room, filled with pale wooden furniture, but set out in a different way. Now the table was in the middle and Mrs Grenville put the bowl of flowers in the centre. Around the table were rows of chairs. I sat down at the back near the door. Gradually the room filled as people silently took their seats. Olivia from the YCND group came in. When she saw me she opened her eyes wide and smiled.

I knew there would be no hymns or formal prayers or a sermon, but the effect of the silence I hadn't expected. All was calm and seriousness. The words contemplation and peace came into my head. Two people spoke, referring to something that had happened to them in the week that had made them think about love. An older woman who was sitting beside the table said a short prayer. I wasn't sure what I should think about. My mind drifted across what had happened over the last few months with Sandra and Danny, their chaotic love affair, and Sylvie, with her sadness and her illegitimate baby and her love for the father who wasn't there, and now choosing Kenny. And me – who did I love? My stomach rumbled. Then the woman by the table shook hands with an older man sitting next to her, and people began to cough and stand up. There was quiet chatting. Olivia came across and gave me the date of the next YCND meeting. She didn't ask me why I was here, and I liked that. People shook my hand and said they hoped they would see me next week, and I said I hoped so too.

I walked home along Buxton Avenue, behind the Clock House. Sylvie was almost upon me, pushing the pram, before I saw her. 'Hello stranger,' she said. 'We are off to the weekend chemist's.'

'Why? Is Mansell all right?'

'He's got a bit of a cough, and Mum said I'd better get him some medicine. Do you want to come? I don't see you so often these days, Miss Linda.'

'Well, I've got rehearsals. And I've joined CND. And there's the Milk Bar . . .' I trailed off. It was true I hadn't been to see Sylvie since Sandra had returned. I still felt stupid about trying to find Bob, and confused that she wasn't even going to give him a chance. But I knew she was afraid he might take the baby away. She was too complicated.

There was a silence. I made faces at Mansell.

Then Sylvie said brightly, 'What are you doing tomorrow after school?'

'Why?'

'It's Mansell's birthday.'

'Oh!'

And he wants to put up the Christmas decorations.'

'Does he?'

Mansell looked at me from the pram and gave a little throaty cough.

'But Christmas is weeks away yet.'

'It's his first birthday and his first proper Christmas. The tree is already up, we've got lots of glitter and tinsel. He loves it. Tomorrow it will be cake and candles and paper chains, and we need you with your artistic know-how to come and assist. Don't we, Mansell?'

'Mama?' he said, looking at me.

'Linda,' I said. 'I'll try.'

I liked Christmas. I liked Mansell. I liked birthday cake. And there were no rehearsals.

'Hello, chicken!' she said when she opened the front door. 'Come in. We are very grateful you can spare us the time from your busy schedule. And you have balloons!'

I'd bought them in the sweet shop and blown them up as I crossed the road.

I followed her into the living room. The floor was littered with strips of coloured paper. Mansell was sitting up in his pram near the settee, watching everything. There were birthday cards on the sideboard. Some had teddy bears and clowns on, but some had flowers and pictures of birds. I picked one up. It was to Sylvie.

'Sylvie – is it your birthday too?'

'Yes,' she said absently.

'The fourteenth of October,' I said. It had been in the story. I should have remembered. I had a present for Mansell, but not for Sylvie.

'Don't worry, chicken,' she said, looking at my face. 'I don't advertise the fact.'

I gave Mansell the paper bag containing the soft ball I had bought as a special present. I tied the two balloons onto some pieces of string and attached one of them to Mansell's pram and handed the other balloon to Sylvie. 'Happy Birthday.'

'Thank you!' she said. 'A balloon on a string is a perfect present.'

Mansell was tearing at the bag.

'How is he?' I said.

'He's fine, the chemist gave him some cough mixture. I've been giving it to him religiously even though, quite frankly, I think it's just green sugar-water, but it makes Mum happy. Right. Now you've arrived . . .' She rushed out into the kitchen and and when she came back she flicked off the light and stood in the doorway in the glow of a single candle, stuck into the thick icing of a home-made cake.

'Shouldn't your mum be here?'

'Oh, we'll do it again when she gets in from work.' She began to sing 'Happy Birthday to You' and I joined in and Mansell cocked his head and stared at the candle. At the end Sylvie said, 'Blow out the candle!' and he looked at it. She blew it out for him and his lower lip trembled. So she did it again. And again. After the fifth time he was laughing.

'OK, my darling,' she said to him, 'that's enough.' She switched the light back on and handed me an unopened packet of paper strips. 'This is your pile. Let's see what you can do.'

For five minutes we sat in silence, licking and sticking, creating decorations. The electric fire hummed and Mansell grizzled for the candle till Sylvie gave him a rusk.

'How are Rat, Trap and . . . Danny ?' she said casually, licking the end of a red strip.

'I don't see them very much these days,' I said. 'Sandra said the police are after Danny.'

Sylvie looked at me thoughtfully.

'But she said we're in the clear.' It was a relief to talk about it.

'I think you'd know by now if you weren't. What did her parents say?'

'They never knew about the parcels, and they never found out about the elopement – not officially. But they whisked her away on holiday straight after she got back. I think Danny's disappeared, but Sandra's not saying anything.'

Sylvie tilted her head to one side. 'And you're not asking her?'

'I'm not seeing her,' I said. I felt suddenly lonely.

'But you're very busy at school with all your clubs and things.'

'Yes.'

She smiled. 'You really are moving on up, aren't you?'

'What do you mean?' I said suspiciously.

'Nothing – it's just, your world is obviously changing. All your groups and activities, things at school. You're moving off the estate. And that's good.'

'Is it? You told me to do it.'

'Did I?'

'It was your idea. You said.'

'What did I say?'

She knew very well what she'd said. 'You said I should relish school. You said I should make the most of it. So I joined the drama club, I started doing my homework. And now I'm in the school pantomime. The pantomime!'

'But that's good, isn't it? Your face is telling me it's not good.'

'Because you're saying I'm moving on up.' I wasn't ready to go. 'Do I have to move off the estate?'

'Well, not just yet, obviously. Wait till you finish school. Then you can live anywhere. Anywhere in the world.'

'But the world is so huge.'

'That's the point. The estate is so small.'

'You came back to the estate.'

'I don't think that was something I really chose to do. It happened to me.'

'You mean, Mansell. Mansell happened to you. And if he hadn't, you wouldn't be here at all, telling me what to do, saying I should live in France. Well, that's hardly fair to . . . to Mansell! Or me!' I knew my face was red.

Sylvie looked at me with her head on one side. 'I'll tell you what we need.'

'What?' I said.

'We all need a slice of the birthday boy's cake, and you and I need a cup of tea to wash it down.'

I burst into tears.

'And I can tell you,' she went on as if nothing embarrassing was happening, 'that it's a very good cake. Mum made it, courtesy of Betty Crocker, because it's nice to have a cake around the house.' She sat down beside me. 'Linda, you are on the verge of something wonderful. I can feel it. You have your whole life ahead of you. I only say the things I say because . . . because I care what happens to you. Look at me, I've made so many foolish mistakes. I did things, I made choices – and now I'm here, terrified that I shall lose my son. I went for the easy option. I hung out with . . . the wrong people, I danced, I laughed.'

'Dancing and laughing are nice things to do.'

'I know, of course,' she clucked. 'But, if you have a glass of lager and then another, laughing and dancing take you somewhere else. To the back of the dance hall, for a kiss and a cuddle and then . . . Anyone can dance and laugh. You – you can go places. You are a very special person.'

'Am I?'

'Well, perhaps not right at the moment with those red eyes, but yes, yes you are. Don't get caught up like I did. I got as far as Paris, and now I'm passing the baton to you.'

'Really?'

'Yes!' She bounced up. 'And now for cake. And then you need to listen to one of the most beautiful voices in the world – Nina Simone.'

I felt empty and tired and scraped dry. I wanted to lie down on the settee and go to sleep.

Sylvie came in with a tray. She put the tray on the sideboard and went over to the record player. 'Listen to this.'

I found a hanky, creased, at the bottom of my bag and I blew my nose. I scrubbed at my face as syrupy violins filled the room, then a tinkling piano, and a woman with a deep, creamy voice began singing, 'I put a spell on you'.

Her voice rose, rich and powerful, and I wanted to cry all over again.

'Angel food!'

Sylvie handed me a slice of cake. It was delicious. Not like Mum's Viota sponges, which were only nice if you ate them while they were still warm, before they went cold and hard and dry. This was soft and creamy. The word 'moist' came into my mind.

I drank my tea. Surrounded by the tea, the cake and the music, I felt like an invalid who was being looked after. Like an invalid who was feeling better. Silently Sylvie passed me my unfinished paper chain. 'Do you want the blue?' she said.

'No.' I was trying to work out my own sophisticated colour scheme for the living room.

'So tell me about your rehearsals. What is this play?' Sylvie said.

I told her about the drama group, my proposed double act with Charlotte, the current lack of a proper script, the ad-libbing and the exciting prospect of a group called Styx, made up of grammar school boys, actually playing during the performance.

Sylvie licked the end of the yellow strip of paper in her hand. 'I'd really like to come.' She ruffled the paper strips left on the floor. 'What goes with yellow?' I looked at her and she said, 'No, honestly. It sounds so wonderful, and you are obviously enjoying it very much. I would love to see you in action.'

'All right,' I said.

'Will you get me a ticket?'

'They're not on sale yet.'

'Can you get me two?'

I looked at her.

'I might take Mum.'

We hung the chains round the room with drawing pins. Mansell watched us with serious eyes, giving an occasional small, rasping cough. Sylvie found two old candlesticks – the type you carried up to bed like Wee Willie Winkie – and put them on the sideboard, with candles from under the stairs. She struck a match and the two candles flickered and shimmered. She turned on the standard lamp in the corner of the room and then switched off the overhead light. The room looked pretty and mysterious and celebratory and Christmassy. The paper chains dipped and swayed on the walls and we sang 'Happy Birthday to You' again. Mansell clapped his hands.

Sylvie stroked his head and murmured, 'You're my little ball and paper chain, aren't you, sweetheart?' and wiped his nose with her hanky.

That night I rang Sandra. She was in. 'Doing anything?' I said. 'Fancy a bag of chips?'

'See you at the chip shop in five minutes,' she said.

I hadn't seen her for weeks. She was wearing a new coat, black and white dogtooth check, but apart from that she looked the same. I was wearing my duffel coat, so I knew I looked the same. It was so good to see her. We bought two bags of chips, covered them in salt and vinegar and carried them back to her house. We sat on her front wall, eating them.

'Heard anything from Danny?' I said.

She made a sort of hissing noise. 'I haven't heard a word.' She picked out a large chip. 'So I suppose you could say they've got the result they wanted.' She jerked her head towards the house.

'Do you miss him?' I said.

'I don't know. After all that in London, I never want to see him again. But if he walked up the road right now, I don't know. I do miss him. I miss his ring.' She touched the chain at her neck. 'He took that back the first night, said he was going to make it smaller. And I miss his letters.'

Anger rose in me. 'Sandra.' I stopped myself. I didn't want to argue.

'But what's the point?' she went on. 'I don't know where he is, though I know where he should be – in the nick. Running off with my ring and all my money. Him and that Trevor. It was all about the parcel. Danny kept asking me about it, "Where's the parcel?" "What have you done with it?" "Keep it safe." Nothing about "Ooh, nice nightie".'

'I blame Trevor,' I said.

Sandra smiled. 'You're probably right. Danny said Trevor's record is three miles longer than his. But it wasn't Trevor who left me. It was Danny. If we'd been married I could have divorced him for desertion.' She screwed up the newspaper and scrunched it into a ball. 'So, I've decided what I'm going to do for the rest of my life.'

'What?'

'Forget him. Do something completely different,' she said.

I looked at her. Perhaps this was the moment. She would pass her scooter test. We could swoop away from Chelmsford together, get those jobs in hotels. I really could leave the estate. 'Oh Sandra,' I said. Tears were pricking my eyes. 'I think that's a fab idea.'

A few days later I was walking home from school. It was dark going home from school now, but I liked it like that, the lamp posts alight and glowing and the air so cold you could see your breath.

We'd just had a rehearsal for the pantomime. Sylvie was right. I was enjoying it all, being part of a group that was working together, making suggestions, being asked for my opinion. And I'd had a history essay returned with an A+ mark and the comment 'Excellent work!' from Miss Beasley. Perhaps I didn't hate school as much as I thought. I was half-dancing along the road, singing 'Out of Sight', doing James Brown's moves, when the green-and-white Corsair went past, slowed down and then stopped.

'Cooky's everywhere,' I thought.

As I got closer, the window on the passenger side slid down and Sandra stuck her head out. She grinned at me.

'Why aren't you at work?' I said.

'Why aren't you at school?'

'School's finished.'

'So's work.'

'What do you mean?'

'It's home time.'

'No it isn't.'

'It is for me. Cooky and I have just been to Southend.'

A rush of emotions burst from my stomach up into my throat. It was Cooky. She'd been to Southend, with Cooky, in his car, when she should have been at work, and she hadn't told me about it, let alone taken me with her. But mostly I felt disappointed. This was her doing something completely different. Cooky.

'Shut up,' Sandra said, as if I'd spoken out loud. 'You wouldn't have come, you wouldn't have liked it and we never got there anyway, because the car broke down. We only got as far as Canvey Island. But we're going to see Mark Shelley and the Deans at the YMCA tonight. Do you want to come?' She leaned out of the car window, bent round and opened the back door. 'Get in.' She was half in and half out of the window. 'This is like *Cool for Cats*,' she said, and began singing, 'Last Train to San Fernando' and doing the hand jive. If she missed this one, she'd never get another one. Slowly she tipped out of the window, slipping towards the pavement. She started yelling and I grabbed her arms, shouting because she was heavier than she looked. We were laughing.

When I climbed into the back of the car, Sandra said, 'What are you doing, coming home so late?'

'We've had a pantomime rehearsal.'

'I told you,' she said to Cooky. 'She's not just a school-girl, she's an actress. We'll come, won't we, Cooky?'

Cooky said, 'Yeah, if you like.'

Sandra turned up the radio. It was Brenda Lee singing 'Sweet Nothin's'. Sandra and I used to sing that when we were ten or eleven, sitting on their front doorstep as the sun went down and the street lights came on, scaring each other with stories of bats flying into our hair and worms coming out of the grass.

'What station's this?' I said.

'It's Radio Caroline,' Cooky said.

'Radio London's better,' I said.

'Don't start that,' Sandra said. 'Have a crisp.' She handed a packet over to me and said to Cooky, 'Don't worry, you can share mine.' She was happy, and it was nice sitting in the car, eating crisps, listening to the radio, thinking about nothing. I stopped minding about Sandra and Cooky and their trip to Southend. Perhaps I'd go to the YMCA with them. I liked Mark Shelley and the Deans; they were Chelmsford's best group.

'Wake up, England,' Sandra said. 'You can get out of the car now.' We were at the shops.

I got out while Sandra said goodbye to Cooky, which involved a lot of stopping and starting of the car and her getting out and in again and then banging on his window and laughing.

We walked up to her gate. 'So?' I said.

'I'll try anything once,' she said, and laughed. 'He wants to buy me an eternity ring.'

'He doesn't!' She hardly knew him.

Her face drooped. 'What alternatives have I got?'

'I don't know. You could get a new job. We could go to London. Or Manchester?' I said wildly. 'You're bound to pass your test.' Her scooter driving test was the next week. 'Once you've got your licence, you can do anything. We could go anywhere.'

'I've cancelled it,' she said. 'What's the point, if I'm courting? And courting someone who can drive. Legally.'

This was awful. 'But is Cooky exciting?' I said. 'Does he make you laugh?'

'He's a good kisser,' she said. 'That was a surprise. And he's got good genes.'

'Jeans or genes?'

'His mum's got nice hair and all her own teeth.'

'Oh, well, that's good.'

She looked at me. 'I told you. I've got to look elsewhere. I'll have to settle down sometime.'

'So should I start saving up for another torch?'

'No.'

'You mean you might not actually get married?'

'I mean I don't want another torch.'

'Aren't you meant to give back the presents when an engagement's broken?'

'You can't have it back. It's the only thing I've got left of Danny.' She gave a small hiccup, like a sob.

'Tell me two good things about Cooky,' I said, to stop her thinking.

'He hasn't got a criminal record. My mum and dad should be pleased.'

Perhaps he was the right one for her.

'You coming to see Mark Shelley?'

'No,' I said, with regret, shifting my school bag from arm to arm. 'I've got too much homework.' It was too late. We were heading in different directions. We both knew it.

CHAPTER 28

Rehearsals

THE PRODUCTION WAS COMING TOGETHER. A beautiful girl called Gwynedd who was in the upper sixth was Cinderella. There were no Ugly Sisters, just the Beverley Sisters, who were played by Miss Soames, Miss Harmon and Miss Laybourne, the youngest members of staff. Charlotte and I were the comic relief. We were Pete and Dud, from *Not Only ... But Also*. I was Dudley Moore, the short one. Charlotte, who was taller, was Peter Cook.

We were now having rehearsals almost every night, except for the mistresses, who had private rehearsals with Rosemary in the lunch hour.

Rosemary said that although she had the final say, Charlotte and I could write our own script. Charlotte was in the lower sixth and had been in the drama group for years, so Rosemary trusted her. Charlotte and I had started slipping away from rehearsals and walking down to Snows, sitting at the back of the café, trying out lines and laughing. Sometimes, if we really made ourselves laugh and the session went well, we'd put on 'Dancing in the Street' by Martha and the Vandellas, which was Charlotte's favourite, or 'Hi-Heel Sneakers', which was mine, even though the small silver jukebox which sat on the counter was really quiet.

One day, three weeks from the first performance, we were laughing hard over a new idea for the ballroom scene, something to do with pouring tea into Cinders' discarded shoe, which we knew would never make it into the final version. Charlotte was searching for a sixpenny piece so she could put on our two favourites, when Tap walked in.

I hadn't seen him for weeks. I hadn't seen anybody. These days my life was filled with the pantomime, with Quaker meetings on a Sunday, the occasional CND meeting and some homework on the side. As he stood in the doorway, looking round the room, he felt like a stranger. But he didn't look well. He looked almost scruffy.

There were no mods in the room, no one from the Orpheus except me. I was the only person. He walked over to our table. Normally this would have thrilled me, that he was coming to speak to me, just me; but now I wasn't sure.

'Watcha,' he said.

I could feel my cheeks reddening. 'Hello. Charlotte, this is . . . my friend, Tap. Tap, this is Charlotte.'

'Nice to meet you, Charlotte,' he said, twirling a chair round and swinging his leg over.

I could feel Charlotte wondering who he was, and in particular who he was to me. I hoped he wouldn't call me Lorna. There was silence.

'I'll just go and put something on the jukebox,' Charlotte said. Tap and I watched her walk over to the counter.

Tap shivered.

'Where's your coat?' I said.

'Which one? They're all down at the cop shop. They say they're evidence.'

I hesitated. 'Evidence of what?'

'Evidence that every time I get a new coat the Old Bill nicks it.' He shook his head. 'My brief reckons I'm in deep shit.'

'What does that mean?'

'Time. A long time.' He looked distant and sad.

'What's happened?'

'It was a stitch-up. The usual. The mods are always the ones that get nicked.'

'What for?'

'Nothing. It's all just fucking boring.' He was biting his finger.

I said, 'Well, that Fred Perry looks fab. Navy and cream – good colour combination.'

He looked down at his top. 'Yeah.' He gave a little smile. 'I wasn't sure at first. I got it in Carnaby Street.'

The first twanging guitar notes of 'Hi-Heel Sneakers' whispered through the room.

'So, still at school, I see. What's all this paper? Studying for exams?' He was making conversation. I wondered if he wanted something from me. If he wanted me to be something to him. I wasn't sure I wanted that now.

'It's a play – a pantomime.' I looked over at Charlotte. 'We're in it.'

'Oh yeah? Is it good? Shall I come?'

'I hope so – I mean, I hope it's good. It might be a bit tame for you.'

'Oh really?'

'And I'm going to look pretty stupid. I have to wear a plastic mac.'

'You and your macs. I'll definitely get a ticket.'

'Ha ha.'

'You don't come down the Orpheus much these days, do you?'

'No,' I said. 'No.' Did he care?

Charlotte came back to the table.

There was a pause and then Tap stood up, saying, 'Well, girls, I'm going to love you and leave you. Hope the play goes all right.' He cocked his head, listening to the music, and sang along with Donnie Elbert that we were gonna knock 'em dead. He turned the chair back to its rightful place, then he leaned down and his lips brushed my cheek. 'See ya,' he said, and walked away.

'Who was that?' Charlotte said.

'Just a lonely boy I know.'

The pantomime was two weeks away. Now Charlotte and I stayed for the rehearsals. Miss Evans brought several of her art class to watch, standing round in a huddle talking quietly to each other, making sketches on large notepads. They were 'getting a sense of the play'. They all looked a bit like Miss Evans, and somehow smelt of her intense, powdery perfume. A few days later huge vivid posters appeared in the school corridors and also, fantastically, in places in the town where people might see them. I asked Mr Wainwright if one could go up in the Milk Bar and Charlotte brazenly asked in Snows and the library, and they all said yes. I was torn between embarrassment and elation.

And Charlotte and I were good. Every time we rehearsed our scenes people sat down to watch and laughed in all the right places and even in the wrong places, when we forgot our lines and made things up. They clapped a lot.

This is what I want, I thought. Applause. Appreciation. I want to be an actress. I want to stop the show. Perhaps I'd put journalism on hold.

Now any spare time we had was spent talking about props and costumes. Our characters, Pete and Dud, both wore white mufflers and flat caps. I had my dad's black plastic mac. Charlotte needed a beige raincoat. She would ask her uncle. Cinderella was making a glorious ballgown for herself out of net curtains. The Fairy Godmother wanted glitter-encrusted shoes and had asked Finch's for a pair she could decorate. Prince Charming needed transport.

'I can sort that out,' I said.

I walked up our road. Ray was outside his house, lying on the pavement doing something to his scooter. The beam of a big torch was trained on the engine. I was still in my school uniform but he wouldn't notice in the dark, if he was even bothered.

'Watcha Ray,' I said.

'Watcha,' he said. He stopped for a moment and grinned at me, then frowned slightly and shook his head. He carried on working, picking up screwdrivers and nuts and bolts.

'Ray,' I said.

'Yep,' he said briskly. He was studying something greasy in his hand. 'Pass me that spanner, will you?' he said.

I picked up something metal and hoped it was the right thing.

'Thanks.'

'Ray?'

'Yeah.'

'Would you say your scooter is precious to you?'

He swivelled round and looked at me. 'Is that a trick question?'

'Maybe. Does your scooter actually work?'

'Not in its present condition, but usually, yes.'

'Would you ever part with your scooter?'

'Do you want to buy it?'

'No. It's just . . .'

'What?'

'I'm in the school play – pantomime, and we need a scooter. I wondered if we could borrow yours.'

He sat up straight. 'Well, for one thing, I'm not sure you can come up to me three months since I last saw you and ask me a favour.'

'Is it three months? I've been busy. I've been . . . at school. You didn't come that night we were going to the pictures.'

'I know when I'm not wanted.'

'You . . .!' I stopped. I was going to say; *You are wanted.* Which he was. But I wasn't sure whether it was him I wanted or the scooter. Now. 'You . . .'

'And for another thing . . .' He slid down to the engine again. 'I've been busy myself, at night school. I didn't know you were in a play. Can anyone come?'

I screwed up my face. 'Do you really want to come?'

'Why not? And lastly, if you really want the scooter, when, where and how much are you going to give me?'

'You'd have to make the generous gesture for nothing. I might get you a free ticket.'

'Oh, I'll need a bit more than that. Tell you what, I'll come into Wainwright's and you can give me that free coffee you're always talking about, how's that?'

'It won't be free, I'll have to pay for it.'

'That's the point.'

'You drive a hard bargain. But all right.'

I wondered if it was too high a price when he came into the Milk Bar the next Saturday. I gave him his coffee and put sixpence from my own pocket into the till. Ray said, 'Thanks. Here.' He gave me a record. I looked at him. 'Early Christmas present,' he said.

'We haven't got a record player.'

'You could come and play it round ours.'

'Oh, don't give me this,' I said as I took it out of the Dace's bag. It was 'River Deep and Mountain High'.

'Don't you like it?' he said.

'Yes, but . . . Why have you given me this?'

'I like it.'

'But the words.'

'What's wrong with them? They say a lot.'

'I know. That's what I mean. You can't say things like that.'

'It's just a song.'

'Oh, Ray.'

'You're funny,' he said. 'Keep it anyway. Or give it to Val.' He winked at her. 'Giving it back to me won't make it any less true. Keep it, or I'll tell everyone how cute you look in your school beret.'

'Shut up,' I said, but I took the record over to the espresso machine and left it on Elsie's shelf till I went home.

CHAPTER 29

The Pantomime

It was the day of the pantomime. It was after lunch, and we were in the changing rooms preparing for the final dress rehearsal. The changing rooms, between the assembly hall and the dining room on one side and the gym on the other, were normally where classes of girls climbed in and out of divided skirts and Aertex shirts for gym or hockey. Now they had become dressing rooms. And it wasn't just a different name. The lighting people had put in some extra bulbs above the mirrors so we could see properly to apply our make-up and legitimately gaze at our bright, sparkling reflections.

Cinderella stood in the doorway and said, 'Who's that boy who looks like James Dean, out in the car park?' Heads turned. One or two people stood up. 'I was thinking I might ask him to take me for a ride,' she murmured.

Almost everyone left the room and rushed to the window of the dining hall. I followed slowly behind. I had a feeling I knew who it was. 'Oh, he's luscious,' said Jane, the Prince's Best Friend. 'Do you think he's coming to the show? Do you think he'll see us?'

'Yes,' I said. 'He's coming.' It was Ray on his scooter, wearing his white t-shirt and blue jeans, swerving round the teachers' cars, looking for somewhere to park.

'What night's he coming?' Jane said.

'Friday.' The last night.

We performed the dress rehearsal in front of the first- and second-years. We did it all: the make-up, the costumes, the rock group from the grammar school. It was almost successful. Even though half of the scenery wasn't finished, the first-years laughed and clapped all the way through – when the pumpkin was still on stage as the carriage appeared, and when Cinders' missing slipper fitted a Beverley Sister perfectly and then wouldn't come off. When Charlotte and I came on, the second-years cheered in a mock-bored kind of way, but clapped, too, and laughed at our best lines.

Now, three hours later, it was the real thing, the first night, open to the general public. Audience members were already trickling into the school hall. Two of my aunties were coming.

I was sitting in the changing rooms, trying to quell my nerves. The sound of Mr Wallis, the caretaker, dragging chairs into the back of the hall, drifted into the room. The assistant stage manager, a very organised girl from the fourth year, with a clipboard and some first-year helpers, walked back and forth to the hall carrying piles of boxes, programmes, props. People swept by, muttering their lines: 'What comes after "Monks are going to matins on their Vespas"?' and checking their cues: 'I say, "I'm going on the bus", and you say, "I'm riding on cloud nine".' Cinderella was sitting, shaking under pieces of left-behind sports kit hanging on hooks.

Charlotte and I weren't on until a third of the way through. The little ones from the first form who played Mice and Fairies sat with us and asked for help with their shoes and their hair and waited for us to make jokes as we did our make-up. The Panstik had been brought in by Miss Evans, who had a friend in the business. We didn't really need Panstik, but I liked the ritual of smearing it on, feeling the thick greasiness on my cheeks, watching my face change. I loved it all: the make-up, the costumes, the tension, the knot of fear in my stomach. I drew a creamy stripe of orange down my nose.

Rosemary called the cast together. 'You're all completely marvellous, and it's going to be a great show,' she said. 'The hall's just over half-full at the moment, and a lot more are expected. The audience have paid good money to attend this evening, and we are going to give them the show of their lives!'

One of the second-years said weakly, 'Hooray!'

'And try not to corpse.' She turned to Charlotte and me. 'There is nothing worse than a comedy duo laughing at their own jokes.'

Charlotte and I looked at each other. I'd be lucky if I could remember my lines, let alone laugh at them.

The lights in the hall dimmed into darkness. People in the audience settled into their seats, a few rustled their programmes, someone gave a last cough and gradually silence fell. Charlotte and I crept into the wings to watch. The curtains opened to reveal the brilliantly lit stage, with the dazzling images of a kitchen with a castle in the distance, that the art department had finished half an hour before. There was a spatter of applause from the auditorium. The Beverley Sisters sat round the table in the middle of the stage, exchanging comments about their clothes, their hair and whether they needed a husband or if they should pursue their careers.

'Why aren't they laughing?' I hissed to Charlotte. This scene had received a roar of applause and laughter in the dress rehearsal.

'They're listening,' she whispered, draping an arm round my shoulder. 'These are the school jokes. The adults are trying to understand the story.'

'It's *Cinderella*! How much do they need to understand?'

Then there was a cheer as the handsome prince, Rosemary, looking cool in a parka and a crown, puttered onto the stage on Ray's Lambretta, the maroon panels smooth and glowing as if Ray had polished them for days.

In Scene Four, Charlotte and I shuffled onto the stage, in front of the closed curtains, me in Dad's black plastic mac that came down almost to my ankles and Charlotte in the beige raincoat her uncle had finally donated. There was a ripple of laughter and then silence. 'We should never have done it,' I thought. 'Peter Cook and Dudley Moore are too big to impersonate.' We moved over to the small round table where we would sit and ruminate about the world and Cinderella, over cups of tea. Perhaps the audience didn't even know who we were meant to be. I should never have joined the Drama Society. I could have been sitting in the Orpheus staring at a cup of cold coffee. There was a titter and a chuckle I recognised as my Auntie Sheila's. She probably realised it was Dad's mac. Then silence again. We sat down.

We spoke our lines and people clapped and Auntie Sheila laughed. Almost at once, it seemed, the curtains behind us opened and the group stepped forward and started to play. Our first scene was over. The time had flown.

At the end of the performance Charlotte and I joined the rest of the cast to take a bow. The applause went on. We came off stage and stared at each other. 'We did it!' Charlotte whispered.

One of the first-year Fairies came past. 'You were really good,' she said, shyly.

'Thanks, Cherry,' I said. 'So were you.'

It was the last day of term.

I didn't care how many people came to the last night, as long as they laughed loudly. But the place was full. Everyone had come; they'd brought their friends, it was standing room only. Charlotte and I peered through the curtains. Sandra was walking in, in her brown leather, looking around to see if she knew anyone. I heard Sylvie's voice, calling Sandra to join her where she was sitting in the second row. Beside Kenny! Cray, in some new glasses and a fancy dress she had knitted herself, strolled in with other girls from our form and walked to the back row. 'That's my fan club,' I said to Charlotte. 'I'm expecting them to say they didn't enjoy it.'

'Ah, you mean critics,' Charlotte murmured. 'We love them, we hate them. Oh, look.' She pointed out her mum and dad, her mum walking very erect and holding a pair of gloves. Then Val and Noelle from the Milk Bar came in, followed by Mrs Grenville from the Quakers with Jeremy, one of her boisterous sons. And just as the lights were going down, Ray ambled into the hall with his complimentary ticket.

Apart from my classmates, everyone I knew was sitting near the front. I could hear Sylvie's laugh, warm and gurgling. It was infectious. When Sylvie laughed, people joined in and laughter rippled across the whole hall, as if everyone had just realised what the joke was.

Then it was time for our entrance and, as we wandered onto the stage under the bright, hot lights, I forgot they were there.

When we took our final bow Charlotte and I grinned at each other. Rosemary, in her parka and glittering crown, pushed us forward and a huge cheer filled the room. We held hands and bowed. Then Cherry came forward, careful and self-conscious, and gave a bouquet of chrysanthemums to Rosemary for being an excellent director.

As the curtains closed Rosemary said we had made her proud, we had been great and a pleasure to work with and if she could do it all again she probably wouldn't. We all clapped and then we left the stage.

In the changing room for the last time, we slathered on cold cream to wipe off the Panstik. The smell of grease-paint and fresh sweat and Miss Evans' perfume was every-where. People were laughing and hugging each other and talking about near disasters: when the Prince's Lambretta had failed to stop at Cinders' feet and she had to jump out of the way, and the moment the curtains opened to reveal the grammar school boys standing around chatting because they had forgotten they were in the scene, and Charlotte and I had to step in. 'You were great!' Rosemary shouted from the showers. 'Thank goodness you knew the words to "Poison Ivy"!'

'I didn't,' I said. 'I made them up.'

I was taking off my baggy trousers when there was a knock on the door of the changing room. A small Gnome, still in her green tunic, answered it. 'It's for you, Dud,' she called.

I went to the door. It was Ray, coming backstage to find his scooter. He grinned at me. 'You were good,' he said, 'but you should have gone on like that. You'd have got even more applause.' I was wearing Dad's long white shirt, that stopped just above my knees, and a pair of big socks that were wrinkled round my ankles.

'Ha ha,' I said. It was good to see him. I leaned against the door. 'Thanks for coming. I think I heard you laughing.'

'You were funny,' he said.

I wanted him to keep talking. 'I can't invite you in, there are people changing.'

'It's OK,' he said. 'I'm just being a Stage Door Johnny, and I think this is the nearest you've got to a stage door.' He said he'd enjoyed the play and he thought the scooter had performed very well. 'It sounded really smooth. I was quite proud.'

'It did look very clean,' I said.

'I don't suppose you want a ride home?'

I gestured to all the people in the changing room. 'I can't,' I said reluctantly. 'It's the last night. We're all saying good-bye. And I'm meeting Sandra,' I added. I wanted to be everywhere. I touched the side of his face as Rosemary came up, thanking him for the scooter. They went off together to find it, talking about engines and CCs.

'Was that someone offering a lift home?' Cinderella said innocently, with a pretty smile. 'I think I've missed the last bus.'

'He's going the other way,' I said, although I didn't know where she lived.

I pulled on my ski pants and Fred Perry and stuffed my costume into my duffel bag. Charlotte came over. 'Come and meet the parents,' she said, 'or I'll never hear the end of it.'

We called goodnight to everyone. I slung my bag over my shoulder and we walked out of the changing rooms.

The hall was still quite full. Mice and Fairies were jumping up and down with their mums and dads. Buttons and the Prince's Best Friend were talking to some beatniks in the corner. The group were packing up their instruments and swearing because someone had broken something. Charlotte introduced me to her mum and dad.

Her dad said, 'Ah, we've heard a lot about you, Dud.' He was trying to do Pete's cockney accent in his posh voice. Charlotte rolled her eyes. 'Oh, Dad.' They offered me a lift home but I said no. Charlotte hugged me. 'We were good, weren't we? Let's make sure we're both in *Pygmalion* next term,' she said.

Cray rushed up and said, 'I only realised it was you right at the end! I knew I should have worn my old glasses.'

'Yeah, yeah.'

She slapped me on the back. 'The others thought you were great, too, though they weren't sure who Pete and Dud were. They do too much homework. You'll be off to RADA now, I suppose. If not, I'll see you next term, dahling.'

Olivia from YCND came across. 'You were great. We'll have to think about a play we can do for CND. You could be a star!'

'Of course,' I said.

Val and Noelle were leaving and I ran over to them. 'Did you enjoy it?'

'You were beautiful,' said Noelle. 'Particularly the singing.'

'It was fab,' Val said. 'Will you be strong enough to come into work tomorrow, or have you got a date with Hollywood?'

'I'm accepting no offers tonight,' I said. 'See you in the morning.'

Mrs Grenville came across, buttoning her coat. 'We enjoyed it very much. Didn't we, Jeremy?'

Jeremy frowned. 'I liked your plastic mac,' he said.

I smiled. 'See you on Sunday.'

I walked over to the side of the hall where Sandra was waiting for me. But I didn't want to go home. I wanted to stay in the half-magic that was left of the pantomime.

'I didn't know your part was going to be so big.' Sandra lowered her voice. 'I was so embarrassed. Sylvie was laughing like a hyena all the way through.'

'She did that on purpose. I was pleased about that.'

'You didn't have to sit next to her.'

A little girl who had been a Dancing Broomstick in Cinders' kitchen came up to me, still in her besom costume. 'Bye, Linda, see you next term,' she said sweetly.

'OK, Libby, have a nice Christmas.'

'Thank you. And you.' She slid away.

Ruth Danes, the Head Girl, came past. 'Well done, Linda, you were great.'

'Thanks, Ruth.' She would never normally talk to me.

Sylvie appeared. 'You were wonderful, my girl.' She paused. 'Kenny says shall we go to the Compasses for a celebratory drink?'

I didn't want to go there, either. I looked at Sandra. She frowned.

'OK, chicken,' Sylvie said. 'Enjoy your night.' She and Kenny walked off, arm in arm.

'That Kenny,' Sandra said. 'What does she see in him?'

'He's a good man,' I said carefully.

'If you say so, but imagine kissing someone with a beard.'

'No thanks.'

Sandra looked at her watch. 'Come on. If we're lucky we might get a lift.'

'At this time of night?'

'Cooky had to work late but I said if he was outside your school at half past ten he might discover the secrets of the Orient. Well, the secrets of our estate. Some of them.'

My eyes flicked down to her left hand. There was no eternity ring on her third finger.

Everyone had gone. Mr Wallis the caretaker was limping round the hall, rearranging chairs. 'I like Dudley Moore,' he said as he passed us. 'You weren't bad.'

Sandra and I walked out of the school, arm in arm, singing, 'I'd love you on a scooter if your hooter didn't make me break my heart', which was a song the Beverley Sisters sang in Act One of the pantomime. I still felt drunk with the play. People laughing and laughing. Charlotte and I harmonising to 'Poison Ivy'. A perfect day.

And now it was the start of the school holidays, it was only a week till Christmas and I had an idea that I knew where I was going. I wanted to be an actress. I would apply to drama school; perhaps I'd even try for RADA, like Cray had said. I would be famous.

As we got to the road, the lights of the Corsair flicked on. The car rolled towards us. I said I didn't want a lift, I'd walk home. 'Sure?' said Sandra.

'Yes.' I grinned.

She frowned. 'Are you all right? You've not taken a few purple hearts, have you?' she said.

'I didn't need to,' I said. 'Goodnight.'

I walked up to our house, round the side to the back door and into the kitchen. 'Better a Lambretta, than a carriage for a marriage', I sang to Judith, who was making a cup of cocoa. It was the song from the last scene.

'Well, after the pain of tonight's rendition of "Poison Ivy", I am happy to announce that I don't need to listen to your singing anymore,' she said.

'Are you leaving home?'

'No. Come into the front room.'

It was a record player, in square brown leatherette. 'Dad bought it for all of us for Christmas.'

'But we haven't got any records,' I said.

'That's what you think, but James, who is so boring in your eyes, brought round this.' It was an LP of the Supremes.

Carefully she took it out of the cover and then the inner sleeve. She turned a knob with a click, slid the record onto the turntable and gently put the needle in place. The echoing handclapping which was the start of 'Baby Love' filled the room.

'How come he's given you the Supremes?' I said. 'I thought he liked folk.'

'He says they're very good.' She held out her hand and we started jiving in a clumsy, mismatched way. We'd just decided to do the hand jive when the phone rang.

'It won't be for me. Everyone I know has gone off somewhere lovely for the holiday,' Judith said, dramatically. 'It's only me left in this dreary little town.'

'Well, don't let me hold you back,' I said. 'This dreary little town might be less dreary if you went with them.'

The phone kept ringing. I answered it.

The line crackled and I could hear the sound of people shouting and laughing, then Sylvie's voice came down the line. 'Ah, you're at home, Linda! So now I must ask you, would you like to come round to our house for a Christmas drink on Christmas Day? All the family are coming, including the Braintree crowd, so it would be rather nice if you could be there too.'

I took a breath. There were a million reasons why I would not like to go round to their house on Christmas Day, and not just because I didn't really want to be in the same room as her Uncle Peter. Christmas Day was so lovely and special. Waking up early to find a pillowcase full of presents at the foot of the bed, and then going downstairs to open our big presents, a different armchair for each of us, spilling with gifts from the aunties as well as from Mum and Dad. And then handing out the presents I'd bought and painstakingly wrapped in the gold and red cellophane paper I'd sent off for with Vim coupons. Spending the morning trying on new clothes, reading new books and writing with new pens on new stationery. Then Christmas dinner, chicken and roast potatoes and brussels sprouts, and Christmas pudding with sixpences. And Christmas *Top of the Pops* while we were eating.

'I suppose I could come in the afternoon.' There was always a lull in the afternoon till Uncle Don came up with our Christmas annuals, although this year I had asked for a copy of *Bonjour Tristesse*, in English, that Miss Harmon had mentioned in class, because *Honey*, my magazine, didn't have an annual.

'Do you think you could come in the morning? Because it is going to be quite an important day and the morning is – is the special part,' Sylvie said.

'What do you mean?'

'Come and you'll see.'

I told Mum, thinking that she'd say no, you've got to stay in and be with the family, like she did when I asked if I could go over to Sandra's on Sunday mornings. But no. 'Of course you must go,' she said. 'She's had a very tough year.'

'So have I,' I said to Judith. 'Nobody's coming to see me.'

'That's probably because there is no one who wants to come.'

CHAPTER 30

Christmas Day

MRS WESTON, WITH A RED, cooking face, wearing one of her pink work overalls, let me in. She walked into the kitchen and, alone, I stepped into the living room. It was hot and crowded and full of cigarette smoke. Kenny was there, sitting on one of the hard kitchen chairs, his banjo propped up against his leg. I'd forgotten about the banjo. Sylvie's Auntie Rita and Uncle Peter, in a check shirt with all its buttons, sat smoking in the armchairs. Her nan and Uncle Tommy, from Braintree, were on the settee. Sylvie, in her old brown cardigan and black skirt, stood by the sideboard, with Mansell squirming in her arms.

Everyone stopped talking as I came into the room. 'At last!' Peter said. 'Now perhaps we can get on with the show. Ooh, fancy shoes. Have you just come out of *Emergency Ward 10*?'

'It's called fashion,' I said. I was wearing my new Christmas outfit, grey skirt and white broderie anglaise blouse, with my moccasins. 'Mod fashion.'

'Thank God for rockers, then, that's all I can say. At least with a winkle-picker you can poke someone's eye out. Moccasins!'

'Leave her alone,' Rita said.

I perched on the arm of the settee, feeling showy and new and out of place.

Sylvie passed Mansell to me. 'All right, chicken?' she said. I nodded.

'I'm so pleased you're here.' She put on a yellow frilly apron and brought a plate of mince pies from the kitchen and handed them round. Every time she passed Kenny, she touched his hair or plucked the sleeve of his jumper. Once she trailed her fingers across the strings of the banjo, and a small plinky-plonk sound followed her round the room.

The mince pies were dry and had a strange aftertaste, and the coffee was very pale and tasted like hot water. Peter had a small bottle of something that he was pouring surreptitiously into his cup.

I felt homesick, even though I was just down the road and I was only staying for half an hour before I went home for my dinner.

Peter suddenly said, 'Let's have a cracker!' It wasn't how we did it at home. We didn't have crackers till teatime. But it was something to concentrate on.

Sylvie's nan said, 'Where's my bag? They're in my bag.'

'It's behind you, Nan,' Sylvie said. She brought round the box of crackers, stroking Kenny's cheek as he selected his. We pulled the crackers and everyone put on a paper crown and marvelled at their tiny plastic gift, then rifled through the crepe paper and the inner cardboard roll to find the joke.

Her nan read aloud, 'Why do bees hum?'

Kenny said, 'Pardon?'

'Because they don't know the words!' Sylvie said. 'We had that one last year.'

Peter stood up, put his lighted cigarette behind his ear and coughed loudly. 'What do you call a man with only one ball?'

'You didn't get that out of the cracker!' Rita slapped his arm and pulled at him to sit down.

Sylvie tapped the side of her cup with a spoon and said, 'He-hem. Can we have a little hush? We have an announcement to make.' She looked at Kenny and a sickly smile came over his face, and a weird sort of expression came over hers. 'Go on, Kenny.' She nudged him.

'We . . . Sylvie and I . . . we . . .'

'What?' Peter called. 'What's going on?' He turned to Rita. 'She's not having another one, is she?' Rita shook her head sharply.

Kenny looked at Sylvie.

'Come on, mate. Then we can all go down the pub.' Peter looked at me and winked.

'You're not going down the pub,' Rita said.

'Well ...' Kenny coughed. Sylvie stroked his arm encouragingly. 'Today we're ... we're getting engaged today, and we'd like to invite you all to our wedding.'

There was silence in the room.

'Oh dear.' Rita wiped her hand across her face. 'Well, I suppose it'll keep that Bob at bay.' Her voice echoed round the room.

There was a pause, then, 'Let's have a party!' bellowed Peter. 'Let's drink to the happy couple.'

'I have to go,' I said. I didn't want to have to say no to Peter when he offered me a drink, as he surely would, and then we'd get into an argument about goody-goodies and probably my mum would come into it. I wanted to go home. I wanted to be anywhere but here.

Sylvie walked me to the front door. 'Oh, Linda, don't look sad. I'm sorry Peter was so raucous.'

'It's not Peter,' I said. 'It's ... it's your announcement.'

'Oh,' she said. 'Oh. But won't you smile, just a little bit, and wish me luck?'

I ducked my head away from her hand as she stretched to stroke my hair. 'When did you decide to get engaged?'

'The night of your pantomime.' *I should have gone for that drink*, I thought.

'And you and I had had that very helpful conversation about what one wants from life.'

417

'Did we? Wasn't that my life we were talking about? I mean . . .'

She smiled dreamily. 'And it was very nice to meet up with him again on the Aldermaston march.'

The Aldermaston! That was months ago. All this time, Kenny could have been dealing with her and all her problems. I needn't have worried. I could have been doing other things, spending more time with Sandra; I could have been concentrating on my schoolwork. Well, perhaps I had been doing a bit of homework, but I wouldn't have been worried about Sylvie. She was always at the back of my mind: where was she? how was she feeling? was she safe? I had wasted my time.

As if I'd spoken aloud, she said, 'But he could never have looked after me like you do, Linda, chicken.'

I pulled open the front door.

'Oh, don't go like this,' she said mournfully. 'I'll tell you something special. Just you.'

I thought she was going to say she wanted me to be a bridesmaid. That might, just might have made it all right.

'You will be the first person to know the date of the wedding.'

'Oh, great.' I stepped petulantly onto the porch. Then I swivelled round. 'If you love Bob, why aren't you marrying him?'

'Oh, Linda,' she said. 'We've talked about this.'

'But how can you marry Kenny? He's so – so –'

'He's serious, yes, but he thinks about things and he has a nice, quiet sense of humour.'

'He must have, to wear those clothes.'

She smiled, sadly. 'And if I . . . if I have a husband, I'll be Mrs Stable, the perfect mother. Mrs Sane and Serious.'

'And Mrs Sadd,' I said.

She shook her head. 'He asked me, Linda. Nobody else asked me.' She gazed at me with that strange expression again.

I had left Sylvie's earlier than I'd expected, so I walked round to Sandra's. We had already exchanged gifts, on Christmas Eve. I had given her some earrings and she had given me a silver bangle. Now I told her about Sylvie's engagement.

'What did you say?' Sandra said.

'What could I say?'

'Am I invited to the wedding?' she said.

'I hope so. I'm not going on my own.'

'You had a visitor,' Judith said, as I walked through the front door. She was swaying up and down the hall with her new guitar, pretending to be a walking troubadour who knew three chords.

'Who?'

'He left you this.'

Judith handed me a smooth, pale blue envelope. I didn't recognise the handwriting. 'Perhaps it's an early Valentine's card,' I said, hopefully, ripping open the envelope. Small pieces floated out.

'That looks like confetti,' Judith said.

It was an invitation, on thick white card embossed with silver. 'That was quick,' I said. 'Sylvie's getting married.'

'Bully for her.'

'I bet Kenny brought it. She must have been feeling guilty.'

Judith strummed a chord.

I peered at the ornate silver writing. 'Blimey! I'm not surprised it was hand-delivered.' Judith looked up. 'The wedding's in three weeks!'

CHAPTER 31

Tap

Two days after christmas, Dad was in the front room listening to an LP of the Red Army Choir he'd bought himself as a Christmas present; Judith was in the bedroom, playing her guitar; Mum and Auntie Sheila, who was staying with us for a few days, were in the living room watching telly, eating the sweets that were left over from a selection box; and I was in the kitchen, cooking. I was making a cheap, egg-free pudding because eggs were expensive. Apple crumble didn't have eggs.

The mixture was just turning into crumbs between my fingers when the phone rang. 'Telephone!' I shouted. 'Phone!' The phone kept ringing.

I walked into the hall, wiping my hands on the apron I was wearing. It made me feel like a different person, like someone sensible. I picked up the receiver.

And yet still my heart thudded when a voice said, 'Is that Linda?' I had dreamed of Tap's phone calls so often I knew who it was. And he had said my name. Now. When it almost didn't matter.

'Yes,' I said.

'At least you're in,' he said.

'Mmm. Yes, I am.' His tone implied I was last on the list. I wondered who else he'd rung.

'How you getting on?' he said uneasily.

'Fine,' I said. 'I'm just doing some cooking. How did you get my number?'

'Phone directory.'

'Really?' He knew my name and my surname? Now?

There was a pause. 'You coming to the trial of the century?'

'Which trial do you mean?'

There was silence.

'Your trial! When is it?'

'Tomorrow.'

'Well, I'm not at work this week,' I said. 'I'll try and come.'

There was a pause. 'How's the Mini?' I said.

'History. I'm about to get myself a new car. American. It's a Corvette. Powder blue. Pretty flash. I'm getting it tonight.'

'Tonight? It's a bit late, isn't it?'

'What? It ain't nine o'clock yet. Yeah, tonight's the night.'

'Will it be expensive?'

'Depends what you mean, expensive.'

I didn't know what I meant. 'So at last you're getting your American car.'

'What you talking about?' he said suspiciously.

'You were going to get one from the base, weren't you? A Chevy?'

'Blimey, you've got a good memory. Nah, that fell through.' There was silence.

'So . . . so this one,' I said. 'Has it got those big wings?'

'Yup.'

'I can see you driving round town in that.'

He laughed. 'Yeah?'

'I can see you with the windows down,' I said, 'your elbow on the window, good music coming out.'

'Not the Beatles,' we said together.

'Driving down London Road, giving them all a wave.'

'Or two fingers. Yeah.' There was a pause. 'And then?'

He wanted me to keep the conversation going. 'Then if you wanted to show people what the car could do, you could . . . take it on the bypass.'

'Yeah!'

'And it would be the Animals on the wireless, singing "It's My Life".'

'Yeah, man,' he said in his put-on American accent, 'that'd be great. Then where?'

'Well . . .' I couldn't think. 'You could drive it to court. You could park it outside, run up the steps, slam open the doors of the courtroom and tell them, "You can't put me away, I've got a car that needs a lot of attention".'

'It ain't funny.'

'I know. I know.' I'd spoiled it. 'I'm sorry.'

There was a silence and then a sort of gulp. I wondered if he was crying. He coughed. 'So anyway, I'm getting it. The car. From this Yank.'

'I bet it'll really suit you.'

'It will.'

'I bet.'

'Yeah.' He sounded so sad. 'Fuck off!' he shouted.

'What?'

'Not you, someone wants to use the phone. Will you come, then? Tomorrow morning. Ten thirty.'

'Yes,' I said.

From the front room the voices of the Red Army Choir rose to a crescendo of powerful harmony and now I felt a sob in my throat. They didn't sing about religion, they sang about work and struggle, they sang together with enormous emotion and control, first whispering in a sort of chant and then bursting out into a glorious celebration of victory and justice. At that moment the music reflected my own feelings. I would go to court alone; I would support Tap in his hour of need. I would be there and he would know it, and he would turn and see me and be uplifted by my presence.

Grey clouds hung low in the sky and cars had their headlights on as they swished by in the rain. I ran up the steps of the Shire Hall. I scanned the list of cases. There was Tap's name, R v Tappling, 10.30 in Court Two, but beside it there was a note in blue pencil, 'Adjourned till 2'.

Four hours! I decided I'd go to the library for a while, and then I'd go to the Orpheus.

As I came out of the Shire Hall, Mick Flynn was walking past the Saracen's Head pub with his mate Jeff. As they came towards me Jeff said, 'Watcha, Linda.' He looked as if he was on his way to work, in white overalls and big boots that were streaked with rain and dust. 'You didn't come for the trial?' Mick said.

'Yes, he rang me last night.'

Mick sighed. 'It's not happening.'

'I know. It's been adjourned till two o'clock.'

'It won't be happening today.'

'What do you mean?'

Jeff said, 'I've got to get off to work. All right, Mick?'

'Yeah, I'll be all right. I've got Linda with me now.'

Jeff ambled down New Street.

'So what's happened?' I said.

Mick lifted his head. 'He nicked a car from some Yank.'

'Nicked it?'

'There was a chase.'

'But he was buying it, last night.'

'Well, he didn't buy it. And then there was an accident.'

'No!'

'Not him,' Mick said. 'He crashed the car, the car turned over and he knocked this lady down. Then he got arrested. Half past eleven last night.'

I stared at him.

'Was it an American car?'

'Yeah, apparently,' Mick said.

'Is he all right?'

Mick almost drawled, 'He broke his leg.'

I took a breath. An image of a crash flashed into my head, the crack of a bone. I couldn't understand his expression, he looked so serious.

'The lady he knocked over didn't make it,' Mick said. 'It was a pensioner. She'd just got off the bus. He knocked her flying.' Mick almost spat, as if he was reliving his own stupid crash. 'She's dead.'

I looked at Mick, but I wasn't seeing him; I was seeing Tap in his new powder-blue car, his American dream come true, cruising down the highway, murmuring in an American accent, flicking cigarette ash out of the window, listening to the radio, tapping out the rhythm of a song on the steering wheel. And then what? Catching sight of the police in the rear-view mirror, and speeding up? Did he skid? Did he see what was happening?

'Where is he?' I said. 'I ought to go and –'

'He's in hospital, under arrest.'

'How do you know?'

'His mum rang me. No one can see him.'

I didn't want to be out here in the rain. I wanted the safe darkness of the Orpheus. I wanted Blond Don to dance round the corner. I wanted someone to shout out, 'Hey Brenda, give us two coffees.' I wanted a good, loud record on the jukebox, the trumpet blast of 'Harlem Shuffle', to drown out the clamour of questions in my head.

'Let's go up to Snows,' Mick said. 'I'll buy you a glass of milk.'

'All right.' I felt such an idiot. I thought I was going to save Tap, but he was nothing to do with me; he had a whole other world. Sandra was courting strong. New young mods were parking their scooters in the street outside the Orpheus and Mick Flynn was going to Snows. Even Sylvie was getting married. Everything was changing. I had no choice; I was going to have to find another life for myself. I felt something like relief. It was time to move on. I was free to move on.

I left Mick in Snows and caught the 52 to the bottom of Sperry Drive. As I approached the shops, I crossed over into the Crescent. Sylvie answered the door. She looked at me questioningly, and it felt awkward, remembering how we parted on Christmas Day, and I hadn't replied to the wedding invitation. But then she smiled at me and my face crumpled.

'Linda, lovely, what's happened?' she said.

'Tap's killed someone,' I blurted out.

'Oh my Lord come in.' She put her finger to her lips. 'Mansell's having his nap.' We crept into the kitchen.

As she made tea I told her about Tap and the car, the police chase and the accident. She poured out two cups and sat down. She asked me how I felt. I said, 'I feel really sad, as if he's the one who's died.' It was comforting to talk about him with her. I told her about the Fred Perry, about the phone call where we'd discussed the powder-blue American car and how he'd put on his American accent. 'But now I feel almost relieved,' I said. 'I don't have to worry about him anymore. Is that terrible of me?'

'Not at all,' she said. 'I think it's quite appropriate. And you've been very good to him. He was lucky to have you as a friend.'

I looked at her, being so kind and thoughtful. I said, 'And Kenny's lucky to have you.'

'That's a nice thing to say.' She took a mouthful of tea. 'I'm going to marry him.' She hesitated. 'I think I rather want to.'

'Are you sure you don't want Bob?'

'You don't give up, do you?' she said. 'I'm sure there's a job where persistence will be an admirable trait. But don't let Kenny hear you. He worries. About Bob.' She shook her head then briskly stood up and said, 'I think I can hear our boy. Let's go and find him.'

We were in Sandra's bedroom, sitting on her bed. It was New Year's Eve, but neither of us wanted to go out.

I told her about Tap, and she was shocked and sympathetic but said in her view I was better off without him. She had brought up her mum's catalogue and was flipping the pages to find the ring section.

'Ooh, not wedding rings,' she said, and quickly turned the page. 'No thanks. Wonder what sort of wedding ring Sylvie's going to have. A curtain ring, probably. Or a Polo, the mint with a hole. She'll say, "It's white gold, you know".'

'She doesn't talk like that,' I said.

Sandra had also been invited to Sylvie's wedding because she was my friend. 'And because I babysat before you did,' Sandra reminded me. Mr and Mrs Brady had been invited because Mrs Brady worked with Mrs Weston.

I gazed at the glossy page of rings. 'She says Kenny's a good man,' I repeated. 'And she needs security.'

Sandra snorted. 'Has he still got that beard?'

'Yes.'

'It's a lot to pay for security.' She put her finger on the picture of an eternity ring she liked. 'What do you think about this one?'

It was marcasite. I didn't like marcasite. I'd thought she didn't either. 'Mmm, not bad,' I said. It was nice to be with Sandra again, laughing and gossiping like the old days. I was pleased she was coming to the wedding. Things were changing, but perhaps some things could stay the same.

CHAPTER 32

Resolutions

ON THE FIRST SATURDAY OF THE New Year I was at work in the Milk Bar. Sandra and Cooky were in London, choosing an eternity ring. She'd decided against the catalogue versions.

It was a bit like déjà vu, being in the Milk Bar, worrying about rings and Sandra going to London, but it was different. Cooky wasn't going to abandon her.

Ray came in and sat on a stool at the end of the counter. He smiled at me.

'Mmm,' murmured Val, over my shoulder. 'Lucky old Linda. Remember what I said. If you don't want him, I'm standing right behind you.'

'Careful,' I said, 'I might tread on your toes.'

I picked up some cups that needed to go in the sink and walked towards him.

'I heard about Tap,' he said. 'How are you?'

'I'm OK.' I looked at him. 'Just don't say I told you so.'
He shrugged, but at least he'd asked. 'What do you want?
To drink?'

'Horlicks, please.' He was drumming his fingers on the
counter.

'Really?'

He nodded. As I measured the powder into the flask he
said, 'Any good New Year's Resolutions?'

'Yes,' I said. I wanted to say, this year my resolution is to
do more acting. I could become a star, go to Hollywood. It
sounded mad, even to me. I couldn't say it. 'My resolution
is . . . not to make Horlicks this year.'

'Really?' he said. 'That's not fair.'

'I'm saving people from the taste,' I said. 'And the
lumps. Don't worry, I'm already making yours.' I hooked
the flask onto the whisking machine. He was still tapping
out a rhythm. I turned to him. 'Are you all right?' There
had to be a reason he'd come in. 'What's your New Year's
Resolution?'

'To get going.' He was smiling. 'I've got an interview for
a place in college.'

I stared at him. That wasn't what I'd expected. 'You're
leaving the garage? You kept that under your hat. What
subject?'

'Engineering. I mean, I do it already in the garage, but I
want to take it further. You know, making sure the scooter

didn't disgrace itself for your pantomime, knowing I'd put it together, understanding how it all worked. It made me think. I had a good time.'

'Nothing to do with me, I suppose.'

'Of course, that was part of it. You both sounded so beautiful on stage.'

'I thought you wanted to do art.'

'In my spare time, maybe. I've got to earn a living. Keep you in the style you'll be accustomed to.' I shook my head. 'But it is artistic. Smooth, logical, perfect. And if I can build a scooter engine, I can build other things, trains, aeroplanes, rockets. It just came to me. That's what I want to do – engineering.'

'Like me and acting. That's what I want to do.' There, I'd said it. Out loud. I looked round. The world hadn't ended.

'That's a resolution! Go on the stage. You'll be great,' he said. 'The *Newsman Herald* thought you were good. They even mentioned your name.'

'Did they?'

'Yes. Sounds like you're definitely on the way to fame and fortune.'

He'd seen me act, so perhaps he knew what he was talking about. 'You'll be good, too.' The scooter had been perfect on stage. 'Where is it, this college? When's the interview?'

'Next week. It's in London.'

'London?'

'Yup, if I get in, I'll move up there in February. It's a sort of apprenticeship. I'll do day release in some of the big firms up there. Might even work on that new supersonic plane everyone's talking about.'

'And you can join the union,' I said. I put his Horlicks in front of him and took his money. 'Well, good luck.' I didn't know what else to say. I didn't want him to go.

Val came up behind me as I was spooning beans onto a plate for another customer. 'So how's lover boy?'

'He's going to engineering college.'

'Mmm, good-looking and good with his hands. A perfect combination.'

'He hasn't started yet.'

'Well, he's been a good-looker for a long time. Give him my number.'

'No!'

'You'd better ask him out quick, then.'

I laughed. I put down the spoon and turned back to Ray, just as he pulled open the door and disappeared into Tindal Street.

CHAPTER 33

Sylvie's Wedding

SANDRA HAD AN ALICE BAND with little lilac flowers and a square of net that she had bought in London for her elopement. It was not exactly a wedding veil, but it was something a quiet bride would have worn. She wanted to wear it at Sylvie's wedding.

'She's going to wear a bride's headdress,' I complained to Sylvie. We were in her living room, considering her three pairs of shoes. Mansell was pulling himself up on the arms of the chair. 'And she's not the bride. You are.'

'But I'm a bride who doesn't really care about the veil,' she said.

'She'll almost be a bridesmaid.'

'I don't think so. She's really only going to sit behind me. As will you. You'll both be . . . what shall we say? Unofficial Assistants. Hooray!' Mansell had staggered from the chair to the settee.

'Except I shan't have a veil.'

'Linda!' Sylvie said. 'Surely you don't believe in all that nonsense. I'm disappointed in you.'

'I know,' I said. 'But still.'

'And you've been such a help to me behind the scenes over the last few days. Helping with my wedding shopping, the lovely flowers. And then opening the replies to the invitations.' There were hardly any flowers to organise, and almost no replies. 'So you get the ultimate role of looking after Mansell. I really wouldn't trust him to anyone else.'

'Lin!' Mansell shouted and threw himself at my legs.

'But I'm wearing a black dress!' I said. I'd used all my newly saved-up money to buy it. It was silky pleated Tricel with a white collar. 'What if he's sick on it?'

'He won't be, but there you are, Linda, you couldn't really wear a veil with a black dress. That would send out the wrong message at a wedding, I think.' She looked at me. 'Although it's a wonderfully individual colour to wear, of course, and only you, Linda, in my current circle of friends, would have considered such an original outfit.'

'I wouldn't have bought a black dress if I'd thought it would mess up my chances of being a proper bridesmaid,' I sighed.

The day began in Wanda's Hairdressers, Sandra and I sitting side by side under the hot heavy metal hoods, our hair in large rollers. As our cheeks reddened and a slight smell of scorching drifted through the air, we painted our fingernails with pink pearlised nail varnish, read magazines and shouted new fashion at each other. Every now and again Sandra looked at her new eternity ring, holding her hand out, moving it slightly so the crystal chips caught the light.

'Right, you're done.' Wanda pulled back Sandra's hairdryer and took her over to the mirrors. I watched Sandra's reflection as Wanda took out the rollers and began brushing her hair, pulling it back from her face, expertly twisting it into a shower of curls. Then she sprayed it with lacquer till it was hard. 'There you are!' she said.

'Don't forget this.' From her bag Sandra pulled out the alice band. Expertly, Wanda clipped it into place. The alice band looked really nice, but Sandra's eyes were gazing at something far away.

It was my turn, and I slipped into the big cream leatherette bucket seat. Wanda unravelled the rollers from my hair. 'It's thick, isn't it?' she said.

She looked anxious as I described my outfit to her. 'So you don't want it pulled back?'

'Not really.'

'You don't want curls?'

'No.'

Doubtfully she said, 'Well, I suppose I can backcomb it.' She turned to the woman she worked with. 'I don't know what else to do with someone who's going to wear a red beret to a wedding,' she murmured.

We returned to Sandra's house to get ready, moving carefully, holding our heads stiffly. In her bedroom I slithered into my dress. 'Now who's the rocker?' said Sandra. We looked into her dressing-table mirror. My hair was huge.

'Do this up for us,' Sandra said. She was reaching behind her back, grasping for the zip of the lilac satin going-away dress she would have worn if she'd married Danny and had a reception and then left the reception to go on honeymoon. 'I'll never get another chance to wear it,' she said. 'I can't wear it for Cooky, can I?'

With the alice band of net and flowers, and the lilac of the dress, she looked strange and new and shinily lovely. 'Danny missed a trick,' I said.

'Don't say that. I can't start crying yet, we haven't even got to the wedding.'

There was a sharp knock at the front door. It was my mum. We clattered out to the car, opening umbrellas against the drizzle. Mrs Brady sat in the front with Mum. We were going to pick up Mrs Weston and Mansell. Sandra's dad was going in the car with Sylvie, as he was giving her away, there being no Mr Weston.

'Didn't her uncle want to do it?' Mum said.

Mrs Brady looked at Mum and said, 'Drink,' in a low tone that was audible to all of us, even with the windscreen wipers knocking back and forth in the rain.

It was the first time I'd been to a register office wedding. It felt strange, like sitting in my dad's office – yellow walls, green lino, hard chairs. Perhaps it was better to get married in church.

There was an almost embarrassed feeling in the room. Hardly anyone was there, even though Mrs Weston worked in the shop and knew practically everyone on our estate. Kenny sat at the front wearing a brown corduroy jacket and brown tie, tapping his foot nervously. A short bearded man who looked so like him it had to be his brother sat next to him. I was sitting with Mansell on my lap and Sandra next to me, behind two empty chairs. Sylvie's mum, nervously playing with a pair of white gloves, sat with the uncles and aunt and nan. My mum and Mrs Brady sat together. Further back were a few people I assumed were from Kenny's side, and that was it. Even Sylvie's friend, Janet, had written to say she couldn't come because she was working away.

There was a bustle at the back of the room and Sylvie and Mr Brady walked in. Sylvie was wearing a two-piece suit which was just too big for her, and the black slingbacks we'd decided on together. Her hair was backcombed into a defiantly high beehive with a black hat pinned onto the side. In her hands she clutched a small posy of rust-coloured chrysanthemums. Mrs Brady murmured, 'A black hat!' and glanced at me, as if I'd given Sylvie the idea that black was a wedding colour.

Sylvie turned and handed the flowers to Sandra and the ceremony began. Mrs Weston remained perfectly still throughout and so did Mansell, watching his mum with big serious eyes. Sandra stared straight ahead, holding the chrysanthemums. I was the one who wanted to cry. I was thinking over the last year, meeting Sylvie and Mansell, and all that had happened: the gas, the tears, Bob and the great love story. I thought about Tap, sitting in his cell with his broken leg. I thought about Ray moving to London. Then I thought about the fun of the pantomime and the inspiration of the CND group and how much I was enjoying French this year, and I thought about what Sylvie had said, that I was going to move on. And I would.

When the registrar said, 'If any man present knows any just cause why these two should not be joined together, let him speak now . . .' there was a hush, as if we were all holding our breath, and I had an image of Bob turning up at the back of the room and shouting something terrible and wonderful. Sylvie turned, as if she wanted him to be there too. She gave a gasp and I thought she'd seen him, but she was laughing. She waved her fingers at Mansell but then she seemed to have trouble with the expression on her face. The registrar gave a little cough and Sylvie turned back and he started speaking again, more quickly now, as if he knew what the risks were, and Kenny put the ring on

Sylvie's finger and they signed the register, and they were married.

Sandra and I ran outside with Mansell, struggling with our umbrellas, and threw confetti over everyone as they were leaving. Mr Brady took some photos, herding people together, shouting at them to smile. He took a photo of Sylvie and Kenny alone together, side by side, hardly touching, hardly smiling, and then we had to get out of the way for the next wedding.

The reception was in a room at the Golden Fleece. We hunched against the rain, crossing the road, past the posh toilets, round into Duke Street and through the double doors into the foyer. People shivered and shook their umbrellas, then climbed the stairs to the large function room, where two lonely round tables had been set up. Mum wasn't coming to the reception; she said she had a meeting. I wondered if she'd nipped up to the room earlier and seen the plates of ham salad already wilting on the paper tablecloths.

There were handwritten place cards by every plate, making sure everyone sat where they should. 'She obviously thought there might be trouble,' Sandra murmured. On one table sat Sylvie, Kenny with Mrs Weston, Mr and Mrs Brady and Kenny's relatives. Sandra and I were sitting with Sylvie's family. Sylvie had told us to be extra nice to her Uncle Peter because he was still annoyed she hadn't asked him to give her away. Mansell sat in a high chair between the two tables with a plate of mashed potato in front of him.

Sandra said, 'I like what he's having.'

The room was quiet as two unsmiling girls circled the tables, pouring tea from large aluminium teapots. Sylvie's Uncle Peter looked round the room. 'Is this all they could afford?' he said loudly.

'Hush!' said Rita.

'If I'd known it was going to be this small we could have had it in our front room.' He looked at his cup of tea.

'And spent the rest on a decent drink,' Sylvie's Uncle Tommy said.

'And where's the music?' Peter said. 'No bloody music? Who has a wedding reception like this? I'll tell you. Someone who's . . .' He put his finger to his head and twisted it, making a stupid face.

'She wanted a quiet wedding,' I said hotly.

'Oh yes? This ain't a quiet wedding, love, it's a lively funeral. Or are you and your friend offering to do some dancing for us later on? I bet you two can shake it about a bit.'

He had salad cream on his tie.

'A black dress is a funny thing for a wedding, isn't it?' he said. 'But you know what they say about red hats . . .'

'Leave her alone!' Rita said, and slapped his arm.

'Red hat and no knickers!' He roared with laughter. I tried to stop my hand touching my hat to check it was still on straight.

Peter sat back in his seat and slid his thumbs under his braces. 'Anyway, I heard you're a bit of a radical, Linda, like Silly Sylvia there.' He snorted. 'Ban the bomb and all that, eh? Are you going to do a sit-down protest for us? Oh, look at her face – you could stop a bomb with that.'

Tommy laughed.

'Wouldn't need the four-minute warning if we had Linda around,' Peter said.

Tommy roared.

'Who pulled your chain?' Sandra said.

'Now, now,' Peter said. 'You know your trouble, missy, always the bridesmaid, never the bride.'

Sandra and I frowned at each other. I could see her rubbing her eternity ring.

'We are not bridesmaids,' I said stiffly. 'We are unofficial assistants.'

'Bridesmaids,' he said.

When we got to the toasts Mr Brady thanked everyone for coming, and spoke about Sylvie being a catch for any man. Peter shouted, 'If you say so, mate.' Mr Brady asked us to raise our glasses in a toast, but there were only the cups of tea. I stood up and pulled Sandra to her feet and then other people slowly followed and the words, 'The bride' rippled unevenly round the room. As we sat down, Kenny rose, tugging a piece of paper from his pocket. His hand was trembling so much he almost dropped it. Peter groaned. 'Two of a kind,' he whispered loudly. 'God help the children.' I looked into my cup and felt Sandra nudge me under the table with her foot. Everyone else on our table laughed.

Kenny stammered through his speech. He thanked everyone for coming. 'Anything for a free meal,' Peter called, staggering to his feet. Kenny thanked Mrs Weston and Sylvie. 'No, thank *you*,' Peter shouted, halfway out of the room. He was going down to the bar. Kenny finished with a long joke about a bride and groom on their wedding night, that ended with boiled eggs. We'd all heard it before on the *Billy Cotton Band Show*, but everyone laughed and clapped politely. Peter appeared through the door with two bottles of beer which he raised, as Mr Brady asked us to stand to toast the happy couple. Then the tables were cleared and moved to the side. People sat round the walls of the room, while one of the sulky waitresses circulated with a tray of coffee.

In fact there was music – Kenny had organised a record player. 'Oh, very modern,' Peter murmured as Kenny lugged it into the room. 'I suppose we should be pleased it's not him playing a zither.' Kenny's brother was in charge and had a small stack of records. He flicked through them nervously then dropped a record onto the turntable. It was the Bachelors singing 'Charmaine'. Everyone except Peter was looking over at Kenny and Sylvie, smiling and nodding, dipping their heads towards the empty centre of the room. And I, too, wanted Kenny and Sylvie to step onto the dance floor, to swirl and swoop about the room, smiling at each other, being in love and happy, but the music played and Kenny and Sylvie sat still, talking.

'I wonder why you're keeping us all waiting,' Peter bellowed, almost in time with the record. Kenny looked up, his face pale, and suddenly he rushed towards the door to the toilets.

'Perhaps he's realised he shouldn't have married her,' Sandra murmured. 'Or it was the ham salad.'

The floor stayed empty.

Kenny came back into the room, walking slowly across the floor to where Sylvie and Mrs Weston sat. Sylvie stood up, but Kenny flopped into a chair, his head in his hands. Sylvie looked at him. Absently she slid her right foot out of her high-heeled shoe and rubbed it along the back of her leg.

For a moment it seemed there wouldn't be any dancing at all, but then Mr Brady walked over and asked Kenny's mum if he could have the pleasure. They did a funny kind of waltz and then Peter and Tommy joined in, doing the twist, holding the beer from downstairs, exaggeratedly moving their hips from side to side. It was so embarrassing that almost everyone rose from their seats and started dancing so they didn't have to look at them. Mrs Weston danced with Mansell. Sandra and I danced together, our mod jive. It was nice to dance with her again, even if it was to the Bachelors. Peter called out, 'Put some backbone into it, girls!' Sandra stuck her fingers up at him, but down low, so her mum didn't see.

When the record ended, Sandra's mum called her over.

'Oh for God's sake,' Sandra said. But it wasn't about the V-sign. Kenny had disappeared again. Mr Brady had looked in the toilets and he wasn't there, and Sandra had to go and find him because she was the bridesmaid.

'Unofficial assistant,' I said.

'I bet he's having a fag in the car park,' Sandra said as she walked down the stairs. I stood near the door, by a table full of empty cups.

Peter twisted his way across the room. 'Put on some Lonnie Donegan,' he shouted to Kenny's brother. He waved his Mackeson bottle towards the cups on the table. 'Cheer up, mate,' he said to me. 'Help yourself to a nice cup of tea. Let's all raise a cup to the happy corpses.'

'We've had the toasts,' I said. 'And anyway, you've got a beer.'

'That's not all I've got, Linda.' He smirked at me, swivelling his hips suggestively as if the thought of 'Putting

On the Style' had put ideas into his head. 'Come on, girl, here's your chance.' He tipped his head towards the dance floor.

'What?' Was he asking me to dance?

He shrugged his shoulders and kissed the air towards me. 'What do you mean, "what"? You're the one with the red hat.'

I stared at him.

'Oh,' he whispered exaggeratedly. 'Don't you know? Haven't they told you yet? Here, look, come outside and I'll teach you about the birds and the bees.'

Where was Sandra when I needed her? She probably wasn't even looking for Kenny anymore. She'd probably walked out into the car park and found Cooky and gone for a drive.

The record changed. It was 'Blue Velvet'. Peter started singing, 'She wore a . . . re-e-e-e-ed hat and no knickers.'

'I'm going to the toilet,' I said, and walked out of the room, pulling off my beret. The sound of Peter's laughter faded as I stomped down the stairs and stepped into the dark space beside the public bar where they kept beer barrels and boxes of crisps. It was quiet and empty and I leaned against the wall and looked at my reflection in the peach-tinted mirror opposite.

'Having a good time?' The voice came from the far corner under the stairs. I peered into the gloom and made out shiny black shoes and beige cotton twill trousers.

I stared at him.

'The girl with the pram,' he said. His voice was smooth and American.

'The man in the street,' I said.

A small smile crossed his lips. 'You're not pushing the pram today.' It was almost a question.

I was about to reply that there was no need because Mansell didn't go in a pram anymore, he had a pushchair now, and anyway he was asleep upstairs on his nan's lap, but I realised the possible consequences of that. I shook my head.

'So what are you doing down here on your own?'

I would have told him about Peter and my hat, but I didn't want anyone else laughing. 'Getting some crisps,' I said.

'And where's the beautiful bride?'

Was that sarcastic, or did he really think she was beautiful? 'She's having her wedding reception,' I said carefully. I was worried that he might get angry.

'A reception?' He looked puzzled.

'You know, a meal, the party after the wedding.'

'A breakfast.'

At half past twelve? 'Yeah,' I said, 'that's right. You can have breakfast any time you like in Chelmsford.'

'Well, I guess if you have a wedding, you need a breakfast.'

'I wish it had been breakfast,' I said. 'We might have got bacon and eggs instead of ham salad, and people wouldn't have drunk beer.' From upstairs there was the sound of someone singing the wrong words to Diane. 'And we wouldn't have had the Bachelors.'

He grinned at me. 'Bachelors always drink beer at weddings.' He came and stood beside me. He pulled out a strange, soft packet of cigarettes, offering me one which I regretfully refused. He shook one out for himself then bent his head over his lighter. He turned his face upward, exhaling a plume of smoke, his profile outlined against the wall. His dark hair was brushed back from his forehead, his nose was straight, his mouth soft and full, and in a burst of comprehension I knew the whole story, how she met him and saw how beautiful and exotic he was, how she wanted him more than anything in the world, to be with him, play poker with him and then to . . . to make love with him. And I knew she really shouldn't have married trembling, nervous Kenny; she shouldn't be looking anxious and silent, she should be happy, she should have married Bob.

'Her mom OK?' he said, picking a piece of tobacco from his lip.

'Yeah.'

We stood in silence in the damp hallway, then the voice of Del Shannon came sobbing down the stairs. At last, a good record.

449

I said, 'Del Shannon!'

'Yeah, right! You're the Del Shannon fan.' He smiled. 'You know, I saw him once.' He looked at the embers on the tip of his cigarette.

'At a concert?'

'No, in the street. In Jersey. He'd come to do a show, but I was just coming out of . . . Woolworth's, I think, and he was there.'

'How did you know it was him?'

He looked at me as if I'd said, 'Do you know what Elvis Presley looks like?'

'I said, "Hi Del, how's it going?" And he smiled, and I think he thought I wanted his autograph, but I didn't, I just wanted him to know some people thought of him as a regular guy. I gave him a wave and I got in my car.' Bob looked at me as if to see whether I was impressed.

Woolworth's made it a stupid story, but not going to the concert and not stopping for his autograph was cool, so I smiled.

'Do you want to dance?' he said. 'To the music of our favourite entertainer.' I put my hat on a pile of boxes and he put his cigarette in his mouth. He took my hand and we did a slow jive, him squinting from his cigarette smoke and me trying not to grin as he pushed me round and pulled me towards him. Del Shannon was singing 'Hats Off To Larry', breaking her heart, saying they must part. It seemed wrong for a wedding day. But lots of things were wrong on this wedding day, and not just me wearing a red beret. Bob being here was certainly not right, not now, not at this stage. And I was dancing with him. Perhaps it was just that kind of day. I felt a curl of pleasure that he'd remembered who I was. For a split second of a moment I wondered if he might have come to the reception looking for me.

But then, reflected in the peach-tinted mirror, I saw Sylvie walk down the stairs in her loose cream suit, heading for the ladies' toilets.

I thought I should do something. I should protect her from Bob. She was married now; he had no hope. I dropped his hand and stood in front of him, trying to hide him, hoping he merged into the dark wood of the staircase even though he was almost a foot taller than me. But Sylvie seemed to have a sense of him, his presence, his warmth, because as she walked towards us her eyes flickered onto his face. Her expression didn't change. Had she been expecting him? Was that why Kenny was so upset? She gently shook her head, and then she barged into me, so I bumped into Bob, and she kept moving, pushing, walking forward, so that he and I stumbled backwards till all three of us ended up crouched in the gloomy shadows under the stairs, tipping against beer barrels and crates of Mackeson bottles. Pressed up against Bob I could feel the hard muscles of his chest under the cool, freshly ironed cotton of his shirt.

Then she moved me aside and, in a strangled whisper said, 'What are you doing here?'

'Were you really gonna do it, get married without telling me?'

'It's nothing to do with you.'

'You do have my son there.'

'What do you care? Really. We never see you.'

'I thought that was the deal. You could have told me about . . . about this. I found out from the woman in the bakery.'

'Did you want an invitation? Would you have come to the ceremony?' She said the word 'ceremony' as if she had no regard for it, as if we really had all been sitting in my dad's office for half an hour.

'I was outside your house at ten thirty this morning.'

'We'd gone by then.' The sentence ended in a sob. 'I didn't know where you were. I haven't seen you for months.' That wasn't what she'd said to me.

'I wasn't that hard to find. You found the base easy enough when you wanted to.'

She slapped his face. He put his hand to his cheek and looked at her.

They seemed to have forgotten I was there. I made a move to go back up to the reception, but Sylvie grabbed my arm. 'Linda, chicken, stay. You have to stay. You're my alibi. Please. Keep watch.'

There were so many dangerous possibilities. We were near the door that led to the car park, near the bottled beer that I suspected was Peter's source of alcohol and near the ladies' toilets. Any of the guests could come down at any time, looking for something, and find us all. I didn't want to be an alibi.

Sylvie and Bob sank down onto two beer barrels, staring into each other's eyes. Bob was breathing heavily. He bent towards her. They were almost close enough to kiss.

I snatched my beret from the pile of crisp boxes and threw it in the air, trying to fill up the lobby, to hide her costume and high heels and his long legs in the American trousers.

I heard Sylvie say, 'Why are you here?' It came out like a sigh.

'I couldn't just let you do it.'

'Well, you're – you're late. Why weren't you at the registry office?'

'Yeah, you should have come to the registry office,' I said, but they turned and stared at me.

'So that's it, is it?' He sounded angry and there was a line of sweat on his top lip.

'What could I do?' I hoped Sylvie was not going to cry. Her eyeliner would run, she'd wipe it off, then she would look pale and washed out and everyone would know something had happened.

'I thought you said he was weak,' Bob said.

'He is,' I said.

They turned towards me.

'He wouldn't dance with you,' I gabbled, 'and then he just charged off.'

'He's tired,' Sylvie murmured.

'But it's your wedding day,' I said.

'Sylvia!' It was Uncle Peter at the top of the stairs, shouting. 'Someone needs to cut the bloody cake.' He peered across the banister. 'Sylvia?'

'She's got something on her skirt,' I said primly, to his reflection in the mirror. 'I'm just cleaning it off.'

'Want a hand?' He laughed.

I pulled my hanky from my sleeve. I waved it at the mirror. 'It's beer,' I said. 'Someone spilled beer over her. Was it you?'

He stepped back guiltily. 'Anyway, what are they doing back there? Tell them they should wait till they get to the honeymoon suite.' He belched, and the smell of beer and vomit floated down the stairs. I moved towards the bottom step, waving my arms as if he was a sheep or a chicken that had strayed from its pen.

He was staring at me. 'What's happened to your hair? What's happened to your hat?' Then he sang, 'She wore a re-e-e-ed hat and . . .' His voice swooped and faded as he lurched back into the upstairs room.

Sylvie and Bob were standing with their backs as close to the wall as they could get. 'You'd better do something quick,' I said, pushing my beret onto my head, 'because if you don't, they'll – they'll . . . do something.' And whatever it was, it wouldn't be good.

'What can I do?' Sylvie whispered.

'You better spill some beer on your skirt,' I said.

'I don't mean that, chicken. Anyway, aren't you meant to be cleaning it off?'

'But there aren't any marks or anything.' Sandra should be here, helping me sort this out. We should be doing this together, removing stains, creating stains.

'No one's going to care about that,' Sylvie said. Absently she brushed her skirt.

Bob put his hand to her face and twisted it towards him. 'You've got two choices,' he said. He was almost talking into her mouth.

'I know that!' she sighed, but then her voice dropped even lower. 'My darling, I don't know what to do,' she whispered. 'Do this!' Bob said, and as the sound of voices singing 'Why are We Waiting?' floated down the stairs, he leaned forward and put his mouth on hers. She shook her head, but he kept kissing her and slowly she slid her arms round his neck. I stared into the mirror at their reflection, willing everyone to stay upstairs.

Sylvie pulled back, but her arms were still round his neck. 'What now?' she said. She sounded tired, almost drunk.

Bob slid his hands down her body. Sylvie shuddered. His arms were about her waist. 'You're coming with me,' he murmured.

She was silent.

'You want to stay with him?'

'No, yes, oh, I don't know,' she whispered.

'What?' He leaned towards her again, tenderly, as if she were a frightened animal. 'I can't hear you,' he said.

'I don't know!' she shouted, sobbing into his face.

'What don't you know?' It was Kenny, walking in through the front door, into the lobby, his face pater still, his eyes glittering. Uncle Peter reappeared at the top of the stairs. He was with Tommy. 'Sylvia?' Peter shouted.

'What don't you know?' Kenny repeated, staring at us all.

For a moment no one said anything. So I said, 'She doesn't know what Bob's doing here.'

'I know what he's doing here!' Kenny said loudly, his voice high. 'He's ruining my wedding day. He's sticking his – his damn warmongering Yankee nose in where it's not wanted. Get out!'

Bob stood where he was. He seemed almost relaxed.

Kenny looked at Sylvie. 'Sylvie,' he whispered imploringly. Sylvie's eyelids fluttered.

Kenny turned to Bob. 'I said get out.'

'I heard what you said. I'm not going anywhere. Not unless she comes with me.'

With a loud noise that was a sort of shriek, Kenny lunged towards Bob, but Bob stepped backwards, just as Peter half-fell down the stairs and grabbed at Kenny's arms. The force of Peter's movement pulled both of them to the ground into a puddle of beer from Peter's bottle. Tommy slid on top of them.

Bob looked at Sylvie, then down at Kenny struggling to get out from under Peter and Tommy. 'Is that what you want?' he said.

'He's – he's confused,' she said, shaking her head.

Mrs Weston appeared on the landing and looked at us all. A spasm of anxiety distorted her face, but she took a deep breath as if she realised the situation had gone beyond the power she might exert as the mother of the bride. 'Sylvie,' she begged, 'they're ready to cut the cake.'

Sylvie stared at Bob.

Peter and Tommy pulled Kenny to his feet. His tie was askew and one side of his shirt untucked. 'Smarten up now, Kenny,' Mrs Weston said with a half-laugh. 'Mr Brady's waiting to take the photographs. Sylvie.'

Sylvie turned. She looked at me and breathed, 'Thank you, Linda. You've been wonderful. But Mansell and I couldn't live with such turbulence.' And with a straight back she moved through the lobby and up the stairs. Kenny hurried to catch up with her.

At the top of the stairs she glanced over her shoulder for a second. Then she disappeared through the doorway. There was the sound of cheering.

Bob and I were left in the lobby. I turned to him and as I watched, tears welled in his eyes and ran down his face.

I pushed my hanky into his palm. It was my favourite, the hanky Sylvie had given me for my birthday, the two deep red roses in the corner like bloodstains in the soft white cotton. 'Keep it,' I said.

He looked at his hand. The handkerchief fluttered to the ground.

I bent down to pick it up, casually, as if I hadn't meant to give it to him.

He sniffed. 'I've got a Caddy outside,' he said. 'Belongs to a guy on the base. Do you want to go for a ride?'

I did, I did, even if I was second best and even though he was American. I shook my head. 'I'd better go back,' I said, tucking the handkerchief up my sleeve. 'I've got to . . . you know.'

He looked at me but I knew he wasn't seeing me. He shrugged his shoulders, put his hands in his pockets and silently he walked out of the door.

I stood in the corridor. The words of 'For He's a Jolly Good Fellow' drifted down the stairs.

'Hello!' It was Ray, walking out of the public bar. 'Look at you, all dolled up. Where's the wedding?'

I pointed. 'Up there. What are you doing here?'

'Having a farewell beer with my boss. You look like you could do with a drink.'

'Do I? I'm supposed to be a sort of bridesmaid. With Sandra. It's not going all that well.'

'Sandra can cope on her own for a few minutes, can't she? Come and have a drink.' He gazed at me. 'That's a lot of backcombing,' he said. 'Are you swopping sides?'

'No. I'm like you, I'm moving on.'

He smiled. 'You know, London's not that far from Chelmsford. You could come up and I could show you the sights.'

'I was just thinking that myself,' I said. I linked my arm through his and we walked into the saloon.

Acknowledgements

My thanks go to the following:

To all the people who over the years have read chapters and given me their feedback and support and in particular John Petherbridge, sadly missed tutor at City Lit. To Christine Wallace for being such a good and loyal friend. To Christine Wilkinson for her support and her eye for style. And to Roy Kelly, a poet who helped me out at the drop of a hat.

Again, to all the mods in Chelmsford who made life in the Sixties so exciting and so much fun, particularly Mick Flynn, whose character cried out to be in the book.

I also want to thank my agent Annette Green and everyone at Bonnier Zaffre who all worked to make The Saturday Girls possible, including Eli Dryden, Sarah Bauer, Jenny Page and Francine Brody and, in particular, Tara Loder, for all their work and support.

And as ever my greatest thanks to Caroline Spry, for her love, confidence and encouragement, without which, none of this would be possible.

·MEMORY LANE·

Welcome to the world of *Elizabeth Woodcraft*

Keep reading for more from Elizabeth Woodcraft, to discover a recipe to create your own sixties classic and to find out more about what is coming next . . .

We'd also like to introduce you to MEMORY LANE, our special community for the very best of saga writing from authors you know and love and new ones we simply can't wait for you to meet. Read on and join our club!

·MEMORY LANE·

www.MemoryLane.club

Dear Reader

The Saturday Girls is a book about the sixties and I've been writing it, on and off, for about thirty years. At first I wrote it simply because we had such a good time in the sixties – the music, the clothes, the coffee bars. But then I realised that there weren't many novels about mods and even fewer about mod girls and I wanted to write a book that would tell their story. I kept a diary throughout those years, full of embarrassing entries, as you can imagine, but also with some comments about the outside world. I also kept scrapbooks – mainly pictures of the Beatles and Del Shannon, but a few postcards and clippings from the *Essex Chronicle* about the groups who were coming to the Corn Exchange. All of that helped me recreate the atmosphere.

I had to put the book in context. We were still close to the Second World War, and its effect continued to be felt. Rationing had only just ended. My mum still thought of eggs as luxuries. It was only in 1963 that National Service – the call up for all young men – finally ended. But people were earning a bit more money, the Welfare State was giving us all free medical and dental treatment. The country was recovering. That was the backdrop for the book.

I wanted to recreate the excitement of going to Southend or Romford or even Oxford Street, to Martin Ford or C&A, to buy mod clothes. The boys were buying parkas and the scooters to go with them, but girls were buying straight skirts, that we wore below the knee, and twin-sets in deep mod colours – bottle green, navy blue or maroon. For some of the more well-off mods, fashions came and went quite quickly, but people like me and my friend Christine had to save up for weeks, and then buy clothes that were going to last. And that's something I've tried to show in the book.

We had to be very careful about what we bought. There was no Instagram in those days, no computers, no mobile phones to give us up to the minute information. We had to rely on television and newspapers. Our family got a television in the late fifties and at first we only had BBC (yes, one single channel). We got ITV just in time to watch *Ready Steady Go!* the mods' programme that was on at 6.30 on Friday evenings. And it was *Ready Steady Go!* that gave us all our ideas on fashion, shapes, styles and haircuts, as well as showing us the new dance steps.

Looking back through my diaries of those days, remembering each individual song, each joke, each film, there is so much more to say about those early sixties years. Which is why I'm really pleased to be able to tell you that there is another book on the way.

I hope you will enjoy reading it as much as I enjoy writing about that exciting period in British history.

Best wishes

Elizabeth

Angel Food Cake Recipe

A little taste of heaven – much tastier
than Viota sponges

125g self-raising flour
300g caster sugar
1 teaspoon vanilla extract
12 medium, free-range egg whites
1 teaspoon cream of tartar
½ teaspoon salt
1 tablespoon fresh lemon juice
Icing sugar to decorate

1. Heat the oven to 180°c (160°C fan oven) or gas mark 4.
   Grease a 25cm angle cake tin.

2. Sift the flour with 150g of the caster sugar and save for
   later.

3. Either by hand, or using a mixer, whisk the egg whites
   until frothy.

4. Add the cream of tartar, lemon juice, vanilla extract
   and ½ teaspoon of salt then continue beating until the
   mixture forms peaks. Then, whisk in the rest of the
   sugar slowly until the mixture is shiny and firm.

5. One spoon at a time, slowly fold the sugar and flour into the egg mixture, taking care not to lose the air.

6. Pour the cake mixture into the cake tin and bake for around 40 minutes or until a skewer comes out clean. Turn out the cake and sprinkle with the icing sugar. You can also add fruit or jam to serve.

7. Enjoy!

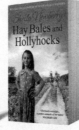